A Vow to Keep

Lana Williams

.

Cover and book design by
Hot DAMN DESIGNS
www.hotdamndesigns.com

Dedication:

⟐ ⟐ ⟐

To Brad, the love of my life. Thank you for always asking, are you done yet?

To my sons, Brandon and Jordan. Thank you for always believing in me!

PROLOGUE

England, 1245

"My lady, I beg of you. Let us turn back. There is an unnatural feel about this place."

Lady Alyna of Montvue darted a glance at Charles, her loyal servant, then looked around uneasily. She felt apprehensive as well, but wasn't certain if the cause was their surroundings, their destination or perhaps fear that her father would discover their whereabouts.

The forest, thick with undergrowth, crowded the narrow path they followed. A low-lying fog laced through the trees and added dampness to the cold winter's day. The bare, dark branches of tall oaks stretched high overhead, their gnarled fingers providing a sinister canopy. The horses seemed to share her servant's nervousness, their ears twitching at every small sound.

"Aye, my lady," her maid, Enid, agreed. "For once Charles has the truth of it. I've had a bad feeling since you received that message and it grows by the moment. Are you certain you don't want to return home?"

Her two servants were right. This place had a strange feel. But it would take more than that to make her turn back. Already she'd risked her father's wrath to come here, not to mention venturing outside the protection of their small manor and village.

They'd ridden for miles now with no sight of Broughton, the village they sought. Quelling her doubts, Alyna pulled her woolen cloak tightly about her and sat up straight. "We're nearly there. My business with the healer will not take long."

Mistress Myranda, reputed to be a healer gifted with second sight, had sent a message that Alyna could not ignore. Myranda had something that belonged to Alyna's mother who'd died when Alyna was in her tenth year. The message had instructed Alyna to come midday of the full moon to collect it. Anything that belonged to her mother was worth the risk.

The path widened at the top of a small rise. Relief filled Alyna at the sight of the village nestled in the clearing below. Livestock grazed in the tofts. Smoke added to the fog and laid a ghostly quality to the mist surrounding the thatched-roof cottages. One stood far apart from the others.

"There!" Alyna pointed. "That is the place we seek."

A woman appeared in the doorway. She stepped out with a slow, awkward gait and stood with a hand on her lower back, looking up at them. Both nervous and curious, Alyna urged her steed down the ridge.

Behind her, Charles grumbled, as he had most of the journey. Enid muttered a response, her words too low to reach Alyna, but her tone clear enough. For once, Alyna found their bickering to be of comfort. She was grateful they'd insisted on accompanying her.

As they neared the cottage, she realized Mistress Myranda was heavy with child. Very heavy with child. Some said her second sight was a gift, and others called it a curse. To Alyna, she appeared to be just a woman, and an attractive one at that. Her dark hair was thick and neatly plaited and framed a face with even features and troubled blue eyes.

Before Alyna could utter a greeting, the woman grimaced in pain. Alyna slid off the horse. "Mistress Myranda?"

"The babe is coming!" She grabbed Alyna's offered hand and squeezed until at last the pain passed. "I'm so very glad you're here."

Concerned, Alyna put her arm around the healer's shoulders. "Let us get you out of the cold. Is there someone who can help you? My servant can fetch her."

"Nay. I need no one but you."

Taken aback at both her words and the conviction with which she said them, Alyna sent a worried glance at Enid. "Once you're settled inside, you can tell me how I can help."

"I'll care for the horses, my lady," Charles said, his brow creased with concern. "Let me know if you have need of me."

Alyna nodded. Before going more than a step into the cottage, Myranda gasped and bent over in pain. Uneasy with the frequency of the contractions, Alyna supported her until the pain passed, then guided her the rest of the way inside.

The pleasant fragrance of dried herbs wrapped around her. A small fire on a raised stone hearth warmed the interior. In the flickering light, Alyna could see a narrow straw bed tucked against one wall. She and Enid settled Myranda on it and made her as comfortable as possible. Enid examined what Myranda had readied for the birthing.

"How long have you had the pains?" Alyna asked.

"Some time now, my lady. The babe will come soon. But 'tis most urgent that I speak with you."

"I, too, look forward to talking with you and seeing

what you have for me. But first, we have a babe to deliver." She hoped her tone didn't reflect her concern. Though she'd assisted in several births, those had been with a midwife or an experienced mother present. The thought of delivering a babe with only Enid to help was daunting. "Enid and I have some experience, but surely there's someone we should send for."

"Nay, my lady." The woman shifted as though still uncomfortable. "I fear I was not honest in my message to you."

Something about the look on Myranda's face made Alyna's worry increase threefold. "What do you mean?"

"In my visions, I have seen the outcome of this day. And I have seen you. Many times, I have seen you. Trouble comes your way, my lady. I will not be there to help you." Myranda sucked in her breath as another contraction seized her. Several moments passed before the pain eased.

"What sort of trouble?" Alyna asked as Enid bathed Myranda's face with a cool cloth.

"Your father is involved with those who will bring him harm. And he will make arrangements that bode ill for you." Myranda clasped Alyna's hand, her vivid blue eyes boring into Alyna's. "You must not follow through with his plans."

"I don't understand," Alyna said, confused by her words.

"I have two gifts to aid you." She motioned Enid to a nearby table where a book lay. When Enid brought it, Myranda placed Alyna's hand on it. "This journal was your mother's. She entrusted it to me to give to you when the time was right."

Touched, Alyna traced her hand over the smooth, brown leather book cover carved with the image of a howling wolf. Alyna opened it, and her heart soared as she recognized her mother's handwriting. Enid had mentioned that Alyna's mother and Myranda had sometimes shared methods of uses and preparation of herbs. "I remember this. Mother wrote notes in it."

"Aye. She gave it to me when she felt her time was at end." She laid her hand on Alyna's. "I'm sorry I couldn't save her."

Her mother had fallen ill and despite her attempts to treat herself, had died within days. Alyna studied Myranda more closely as a hazy memory struck her. "You were there that day. The day she died."

Myranda nodded. "I've missed her, but I know my loss paled compared to yours." She looked back at the book. "My own notes are in there along with your mother's. It will aid you in the days to come. Study it so you'll be ready to assist those who need you."

Overwhelmed, Alyna set the book aside. She had little knowledge of healing but looked forward to reading her mother's words. Now more than ever she wished she knew more. "Myranda, is there a remedy we can make to ease your pain?"

The healer moaned as pain gripped her. "Nay. It matters not, my lady. I will not see the end of this day."

Alyna's stomach dropped. "Please do not speak so. You and your babe will be fine." She shared a frightened glance with Enid. Surely Myranda's statement came from nothing more than the fear most birthing women experienced.

Myranda's eyes glazed with pain. Her words came between pants. "You were meant to assist in the birth of my child. He – is your second gift. You must raise him and care for him."

Alyna froze, stunned at her words. "But, Myranda–"

"Nay. I know this. He'll help you. He'll have the sight as well."

"My lady, surely you know you can't do this," Enid whispered in Alyna's ear. "Your father would never allow it."

Alyna nodded in acknowledgement. Her father barely tolerated her. Never would he allow her to raise an orphan, especially if the mother was reputed by some to be a witch. There had to be an alternative. "Who is the babe's sire?"

That brought a weak smile to Myranda's face. "Do you wish to know if I have lain with the devil as others believe?"

"Nay. I don't believe that. Wouldn't you like me to let the man know he has a son or daughter to care for?"

"This child is a strong, healthy boy, my lady. As for his father, he was a good man. Handsome and strong. But he was killed in battle months ago. The day he was struck down, I knew he would not return to us. My heart broke, for I realized our son would never know either of us." Myranda cried out as another contraction ripped through her.

A lump stuck in Alyna's throat. She could think of no response to the words Myranda had spoken with such sincerity. While it might be pleasant to know what life held, to foresee one's own demise was not something Alyna wished to experience.

Myranda clutched Alyna's arm, her grip noticeably weaker, her voice a mere whisper. "You must listen, for I have much to tell you and little time. When the trouble comes, go north. There you will find your answers."

Alyna had no chance to ponder Myranda's advice as the woman's pains increased. Terror was a hard, hot ball in Alyna's stomach, but things progressed so quickly, she didn't have time to panic. Before long, Myranda began to push. Enid moved aside her gown to check her progress. To Alyna's surprise, they could see the baby's head. "The babe has dark hair just like you," Alyna whispered in awe.

"And like you, my lady." Myranda spoke between pains. "You must raise him. You've been chosen to be the mother of my child. I know I ask much—but he'll have powers as I do. Aid him with his gift. He'll help you find the one—with a crystal the color of the sky."

"Myranda, please," Alyna begged her. "Save your strength for the baby. Soon you'll be able to hold him." She closed her eyes briefly to say a prayer that it would be so.

Myranda appeared to take Alyna's words to heart. She rested when she could and pushed when the pains came. Time ceased to exist as they all focused on the birth.

"Push, Myranda," Alyna urged her. "You've almost done it."

With a cry, Myranda bore down again and brought the baby into the world.

"A boy, Myranda, just as you said!" Alyna laid the wet, crying babe on Myranda's stomach with shaking hands.

"Oh, my." Myranda's tears flowed down her cheeks. She touched his head, his hands, his legs and toes, as though she needed to see and feel all of him. She cuddled him tightly and looked at Alyna, her eyes full of pride and tears, her voice quivering. "Isn't he perfect? How beautiful he is!"

"He is indeed." Alyna wiped away her own tears.

Enid completed the birthing while Alyna cleaned the infant and swaddled him in a cloth. Alyna gave him back to Myranda, relieved beyond words that mother and babe had survived.

The exhausted healer held her son with great care. She pulled out a blue blanket from beside her on the bed. "I made this for him," she told Alyna as she placed it around him. With gentle fingers, Myranda lifted his tiny hand free of the blanket and held it against her cheek. Her tears flowed as she cuddled him. "Always remember, I love you." Then, she kissed him on the forehead and gave him to Alyna, simply saying, "His name is Nicholas."

"'Tis a fine name for him," Alyna said as she admired the beautiful baby. She ran a finger down his velvety cheek. His complexion held none of the ruddiness some newborns bore. Cloudy blue eyes looked up at her with innocence and trust and grabbed her heart. Surely all Myranda had said would not come to pass now. Everything seemed fine. She grasped Myranda's hand. "What can I do to help you regain your strength?"

Myranda merely shook her head, her tears falling. "The one with the crystal...will be your guardian knight. But you will have much to overcome before...true happiness can be yours. Always know you're stronger than you think." Her voice faded on the last words.

Panic skittered down Alyna's spine.

And then it started. Blood. So much blood. It flowed from Myranda and soaked the linens, changing the bedding to crimson. The sickening metallic odor scented the air.

"Oh, dear God." Alyna looked at Enid. "What do we do?"

"I know not, my lady." The maid checked Myranda. "I don't think the afterbirth came properly. We need more cloths."

Alyna refused to sit and watch life drain from the new mother. "Myranda, tell me how to help you," she begged as a panicked Enid attempted to staunch the flow of blood. Myranda seemed oblivious to their fear.

"Your knight may seem unwilling...but he'll help you. Nicholas will give you a sign. Let no one stop you," she whispered in an ever weakening voice.

"Myranda, please," Alyna begged as tears streamed down her face. "Tell me what to do!" She gripped Myranda's hand tightly, trying to lend her some of her own vigor. "Your son needs you."

Myranda's eyes closed, then opened suddenly to capture Alyna's. "Please, love my Nicholas." She squeezed Alyna's hand and closed her eyes, her face tranquil for the first time since Alyna's arrival. Her hand slid from Alyna's.

Numb, Alyna stared at the healer, unable to believe she was gone. But death was unmistakable. Alyna murmured a prayer, then rose with the quiet babe in her arms, unable to make out his face through her tears.

There was no way she could raise this baby as her own. Yet what else could she do with him?

"Mayhap there's someone in the village who'd take him," Alyna murmured.

"The babe of a witch?" The doubt in Enid's tone made Alyna realize how impossible that would be. "They think his father's the devil!"

"You know that's not true, Enid," Alyna admonished. "Look at this baby. He's perfect."

With slow, careful movements, she drew him closer and kissed his satin smooth cheek. She inhaled, breathing in his scent. Myranda had entrusted her with this child's life. She had to find a way to keep him safe.

Her father be damned. Somehow, she'd do as Myranda had asked.

A warm glow filled her heart at the precious gift

she'd been given. "You're mine from this day forward, Nicholas," she whispered. "I will love you always."

Enid gasped in dismay. "My lady, what about your father?"

The question only deepened Alyna's determination. In the past hour, the course of her life had changed forever. She would not fail. Resolve filled her as never before.

Alyna stared into those blue eyes and made her vow once again. "Nicholas, I will love you and keep you safe. Always."

CHAPTER ONE

"One large leaf of feverfew can be
eaten to ward off a headache."
Lady Catherine's Herbal Journal

Spring, Four Years Later

Sir Royce de Bremont's stomach grumbled as he watched the comings and goings at Montvue from his well-hidden spot in the trees near the manor gate. The time for the evening meal had passed and darkness would soon fall, but he made no attempt to ease his hunger. The pieces of dried bread and cheese in his pouch had already served for two meals and had held little appeal even then.

After fortnights of planning, revenge was almost within reach. That knowledge was all the sustenance he needed.

As he'd been advised, the manor was not well guarded. Two men-at-arms stood at the gate discussing something with great enthusiasm, if their slaps on each other's backs were any indication. They were the only soldiers in sight. Though the manor was relatively small, Royce thought the lack of guards reeked of laziness. To keep the things he had, a man had to hold on with both hands. And sometimes even that wasn't enough.

A woman emerged from the manor gate and caught Royce's attention. She wore a fine cloak, her veil fluttered in the light breeze, and she carried a basket over her arm. From her bearing and attire, she appeared to be a lady. No maid accompanied her, but a small boy walked by her side, dragging a stick behind him. After a few words with the soldiers, she bent down to speak with the boy then turned and pointed.

Royce's breath halted when her finger aimed directly at him. How could she have spotted him?

He released the breath in a whoosh when she kissed the boy's cheek and left him standing guard with the men-at-arms, his stick raised and ready. She hastened down the path that skirted the forest and led to the small village nearby, taking her directly past him.

Royce remained concealed behind the thick trees as she hurried by. The brief description he'd been given left him little doubt that she was indeed the one he'd come for but had not prepared him for her loveliness. Her white veil framed an elegant face blessed with alabaster skin. Her full lips were a deep red that drew a man's eye and his thoughts toward more pleasurable pursuits. High cheekbones and dark brows emphasized large, amber-colored eyes, a color familiar to him.

He stilled as she glanced at the trees where he hid. Her brow creased and her steps slowed as if she could feel his gaze. She perused the area more closely then continued on her way.

Royce could see why his uncle, Lord Tegmont, was said to covet this woman. By the look of her father's holding, her dowry would be small, but the lady herself was a prize for certain. It would give him great pleasure to snatch her from his uncle's grasp and prevent their marriage. The thought of his uncle's rage made Royce smile. If halting the wedding disappointed the lady, so be it. Her feelings were not his concern.

He needed to move farther from the guards before he took action so followed her at a distance, curious to see where she went in such a rush. Surely, she'd return home before nightfall, and that meant he wouldn't need to find a way into the manor to fetch his quarry after all, though he'd come prepared for a fight. This would be much easier than he'd hoped.

⚜ ⚜ ⚜

Alyna glanced over her shoulder as she hurried toward Sarah's cottage, unsure what caused her unease. She'd walked this path many times before and never had a worry. Nicholas was safely occupied on guard duty and out of Enid's way. The maid had enough to do with the packing.

Most likely her nervousness of what lay ahead this evening caused her concern. She needed to complete this one last errand and then all would be ready for their escape.

"Lady Alyna," called Sarah, the miller's wife, from the distant door of her cottage, waving madly as though Alyna might not see her. "Good evening to you."

Rather than holler across half the meadow, Alyna merely returned the wave until she drew closer. "And to you, Sarah. Beatrice told me your stomach is ailing you."

The sturdy woman sighed as she laid a hand on her middle. "Indeed, my lady. I hated to bother you, but I've been miserable all the day."

"I'm pleased to help." A sliver of guilt shot through

Alyna. Who would help Sarah and the other villagers the next time they felt unwell?

"We're blessed to have you," Sarah insisted as she led the way into her small cottage. "Why, you're as skilled with those herbs as your sainted mother."

Alyna smiled, pleased by the compliment. She'd spent many pleasurable hours studying her mother's herbal journal in the past four years, preparing remedies, and experimenting with poultices. She was proud of how many people she'd helped. There was much wisdom in the journal, and not all of it pertained to herbs.

Myranda had added entries on the best use of various remedies as well, making the book all the more precious. Someday, Alyna would add comments of her own to pass on to another healer.

She looked around the sparsely furnished miller's home, realizing she might never again see Sarah or this cottage. A narrow trestle table and two benches were near the door. A bed with a small wooden trunk at the end of it stood against the back wall. Small, narrow slits in the walls allowed in the remaining daylight.

A pang of regret shot through her. She would miss many of the people here, including Sarah. The past few days, she'd caught herself looking at the oddest things—the bench in her room, the cook, the herb garden—all with the realization that she'd never see that person or thing again. That both excited and frightened her. But the people most important to her would be with her.

"We will miss you sorely."

Alarmed, Alyna looked up from the basket she'd set on the table. How could Sarah have possibly found out they were leaving?

The woman frowned, obviously confused by

Alyna's expression. "When you marry Lord Tegmont."

Relief made her knees weak. "Oh, aye, of course."

With luck, Charles, Enid, Nicholas, and she would be gone come morning and not so that she could become Lord Tegmont's fourth wife. Certainly not when the third one was freshly buried. She shivered at the thought.

Though she feared her grandfather remained out of the country as he hadn't responded to her message, she'd determined to set out for his holding anyway. She had nowhere else to go and time was slipping away, stealing her options. "It will be a new experience to be away from home."

Alyna mixed the dried peppermint with hot water. "Let this steep then sip it slowly. I'll leave you with some in case your stomach pains you again."

She bid Sarah goodbye, anxious to get back to the manor before darkness fell completely. Nicholas hadn't wanted her to leave and the sooner she got back, the sooner she could calm his restlessness and help Enid finish packing.

She stepped out of the cottage and realized dusk had arrived quicker than she'd expected. She pulled her cloak tighter to guard against the cool, spring air and walked briskly up the path in the fading light.

The thought of leaving home and all that was familiar frightened her, but her father left her no choice. The betrothal he'd arranged to Lord Tegmont was unacceptable. Surely the marriage was the plan of which Myranda had warned her. That aside, her father had told her she'd have to leave Nicholas behind when she married Tegmont.

Nothing on this earth would part her from her son. Each day, she gave thanks for the love and joy he brought her.

Her relationship with Nicholas was the one area

she defied her father though she did her best to hide it for fear he'd send Nicholas away. The times he'd noticed her attachment to the boy had resulted in heated arguments, but Alyna refused to change how she treated Nicholas. Her father had been livid when he'd first heard Nicholas call her mama, but Alyna had held her ground. Still the awful possibilities of what her father might do to Nicholas if she wasn't constantly on guard made her desperate with fear. Myranda had given her a precious gift and Alyna would do anything to keep her son safe.

Marriage and a family of her own had always been a dream of hers, but she knew few men would marry a woman such as she. She had only a small dowry and was nothing much to look upon, as her father often told her. Her long, dark hair held no curl. Her eyes were a strange amber color that might've looked better upon a cat. Her figure was too slim.

And she'd come to realize no man would want to raise another man's child as his own.

Some time ago, Alyna had reconciled herself to the idea of never marrying. After all, she had her own family in Nicholas, Charles, and Enid. What more did she need?

She'd been convinced her father wouldn't allow her to leave as he relied on her to manage Montvue. She was an only child, and her father treated her more as servant than daughter. Never before had he brought up the subject of marriage. Not until Tegmont. The thought of the lord made her shudder with unease.

The last time she'd seen Lord Tegmont had been at a banquet held at Montvue over a year ago when his third wife had still been alive.

He was a distinguished looking man, tall with a long, narrow face framed by black hair with eyes that matched. Eyes that unsettled her with their unwavering regard despite sitting beside his wife. She'd seemed a timid thing and had remained at his side most of the evening. Alyna had been uncomfortable in his presence and done her best to avoid him, but had often felt the weight of his gaze on her.

Much to her dismay, he'd cornered her on her way to the kitchen. She could still feel him leaning over her, his hands caressing her shoulders through the thinness of her gown.

"Lady Alyna," he'd whispered. "What a beautiful woman you've become." He'd stood so close to her that his breath brushed her neck as he spoke. Something in his dark eyes had seemed unbalanced, evil even.

She eased back, but he followed. "Thank you, my lord. If you'll excuse me, I've an errand in the kitchen I must see to."

"A lady as lovely as you has no place in the kitchen. You should be waited upon hand and foot." He drew a finger slowly along her collarbone just above the neck of her gown.

Stunned by his forwardness, Alyna backed up again only to be blocked by the wall. "My lord, I believe your wife needs you." She'd slipped away when he'd looked back into the hall where he'd left his wife.

She'd come away from the brief encounter aware she'd had a narrow escape. Now she would make her escape for good, and her father would have to pay someone to run the manor in her place.

While prepared to do her duty as a lady and marry, she couldn't bear the thought of spending the rest of her life with someone who made the hair on the back of her neck rise.

Rumors told of Tegmont's involvement with a group of barons unhappy with King Henry III. What they plotted and planned was anyone's guess, but now her father had become embroiled with them. Alyna knew his involvement had been a catalyst for him arranging her marriage to Tegmont.

Tegmont's timid third wife had died not long ago, God rest her soul. Some whispered that her death had not been an accident, nor had the deaths of the wives before her. None of them had given him an heir. The thought of him touching her made Alyna shudder with horror.

She neared the place where the path edged the forest. The budding trees looked quite cheerful in the day, but now, their dark branches loomed over her. The dense undergrowth and dim light made the path difficult to see.

Her heart pounded and her breath quickened. What was there about this spot today that caused her such disquiet? Shaking her head at her overactive senses, she walked faster but kept a careful eye on her surroundings as she hurried along.

A shadow moved on her right and fear tore through her. The shape shifted again until it took the form of broad shoulders. Before she could scream, a hand covered her mouth and an arm caught her around the waist.

"I wish you no harm, my lady," a deep voice whispered in her ear.

Alyna responded by driving her elbow into the man's stomach. Her elbow struck chain mail and vibrated with pain. She stomped on his foot, but received only a grunt in response. She slammed her basket into the man's face. Her captor loosened his grip, and she ran.

Hope of escape filled her as she raced toward the manor gate. She made it two steps, then five. The edge of the clearing was just ahead, where the guards would be able to see her.

The man's body slammed into hers. She hit the ground with a force that left her breathless. Immobile and disoriented, she lay on her side, trying to make sense of what had happened. Her attacker's hard form lay partly under her, as if he'd twisted to take the brunt of the fall.

He eased to the side and leaned over her, his hand again covering her mouth. She could make out the slash of his brows, the strength of his jaw, and the scrape left by her basket on his cheek. He was a handsome man and wore a knight's attire. What could he possibly want with her?

"I need you to come with me, my lady." The deep timbre of his voice echoed through her.

Her stomach knotted with panic. She struggled against his firm grip and tried to pry his hand off her mouth. Her basket was gone, so she groped for a rock or stick to strike him with.

"Hold," he demanded.

But Alyna had no intention of complying. She continued her search for something to aid her when he grabbed her hands with his and held tight. "Your grandfather sent me."

Alyna stilled, trying to determine if she'd heard him right. She tugged at his hand on her mouth and this time, he allowed her to ease it off. "What?"

"Lord Blackwell sent me." The knight watched her closely, his distrust of her obvious.

"I don't believe you." Alyna's maternal grandfather had been out of England for years. To her knowledge, he'd left soon after her mother's death and hadn't returned since. He spent his time in Brittany and Poitou on the king's business. She'd sent an urgent message to her grandfather's holding regarding her betrothal with the dim hope that he'd returned to

England, but had received no answer.

Alyna refused to allow her hopes to build from a few words spoken by the knight. "I don't believe you." She repeated her words with more force.

"I realize you're anxious to marry Lord Tegmont, but your grandfather would like to speak with you first."

His sarcastic tone confused her, as did his words. Had her grandfather received her message after all? "Why did he not come himself?"

"That was not possible."

Alyna studied the knight closely. "Who are you that you do my grandfather's bidding? Why did you not announce your presence at Montvue if you represent Blackwell?"

The knight smiled but no humor was evident. Alyna's stomach tightened in response. "Surely you realize your father would not welcome a delay of your wedding while you disappear to discuss the matter with your grandfather."

Alyna had to admit the knight had the truth of the matter. "Who are you?"

"Sir Royce de Bremont."

His name was not familiar to her. "Why should I believe any of what you've told me?"

The knight leaned closer. Alyna caught his scent, a clean, earthy fragrance combined with the tang of sweat. His eyes were the same color of slate blue reflected in the darkening sky above him. A nasty scar marked the corner of his eye. "I give you my word as a knight that I speak the truth."

Something about him made her want to believe him, but she wasn't so naïve as to think she could trust a stranger.

"You have your grandfather's eyes."

Alyna stared at the knight, her doubts melting

away. Few people knew that. Apparently, he spoke the truth.

He continued to gaze at her, as though he could convince her by his stare alone. Never before had she been the sole focus of a man such as he. And never had she felt a man's weight upon her. Warmth spread along the length of her body at every point they touched. Heat suffused her face. She was grateful for the dusk to hide her blush.

Uncomfortable with these strange, new feelings as well as the knight's stare, she berated him. "You could think of no better way to tell me this than to frighten me half to death?"

A flash of movement caught Alyna's attention out of the corner of her eye. To her amazement, Nicholas rammed the knight's shoulder with his stick.

"What the hell?" The knight rolled off of her and jumped to his feet, his hand on the hilt of his sword.

"Nicholas!" Alyna cried out.

Nicholas looked at Alyna as though to make certain she was all right before he looked back at the knight. His little face held a fierce expression, and he kept the stick pointed at the knight. "Don't hurt Mama!"

Alyna scrambled to her feet and put herself in front of Nicholas. "Don't you dare draw that sword!"

The knight dropped his hand, shaking his head. His confused gaze took in the pair of them before lighting on Alyna. "You have a son?"

Alyna reached for Nicholas. The little boy needed no urging and jumped into her arms to bury his face in her neck, holding her tight. "Aye."

The man shook his head as he paced before them. "I was not told you had a child."

Alyna ignored him as she kissed Nicholas's head, her arms trembling as she held him tight. "What a brave boy you are, Nicholas. How did you get here?"

The boy shrugged in response and cuddled closer. "You needed me."

The knight shook his head once again. "Who else should I be on guard against?" He glanced warily at the bushes and trees nearby.

The expression on his face nearly made Alyna smile. She could hardly believe that Nicholas had managed to escape the guards and find her, let alone strike the knight with the stick. He might only be just past four years, but he was an amazing little boy.

The knight offered her his hand. "Let us go."

"I need to fetch my servants and our things." Alyna took his hand and rose with Nicholas on her hip. Her grandfather had obviously returned home and gotten her message even though he'd chosen an unorthodox way of responding. The accompaniment of a knight would make their journey far easier. This was more than she'd hoped for. "We'll be ready shortly."

The knight kept her hand in his. "Nay, my lady. We leave now."

Alyna pulled her hand away. "Nay. We do not. It will only take a few minutes to gather everything."

"I have enough for all of us. A little one such as he can't eat much." The knight bent over until he was eye to eye with Nicholas. "I mean your mother no harm, so no more sticks. Understood?"

Nicholas stared at the man for a long moment. He lifted his hand and touched the knight's cheek, his expression solemn. "You won't hurt Mama?"

The knight startled at Nicholas's touch. "Nay. But both of you must come with me. Now."

Nicholas dropped his hand and looked at Alyna. He nodded, as though giving his permission.

"After I fetch my servants and our things," Alyna

repeated.

"You can send for them later if you wish."

Scared, Alyna pulled Nicholas closer, unsure what to do. Unsure she had any choice in the matter. "Where is my grandfather?"

"He awaits you at his holding, Northe Castle. I will take you to him." Sir Royce grasped her elbow. "We must leave now, my lady. After you've spoken with Blackwell, you can send for the others."

Fear pulsed through Alyna. Just when she thought her problems were solved, he refused to cooperate. "I will not accompany you unless my servants come with me. I must have some sort of escort. Surely my grandfather would agree with that."

⸙ ⸙ ⸙

Royce stared at the determined lady, uncertain how to proceed.

Her chin rose a notch in response.

Nothing she could say would allow her out of his sight. Too much was at stake if she deceived him. He would not risk it. He already had more than he could handle with her and the boy. If he had to tie them up and stuff them in a bag, they were coming with him now.

However, it would be much easier if he could convince her to come with him willingly. He summoned what he hoped to be a smile full of charm and reassurance but it felt stiff on his face. "I fear we must go to your grandfather's with all haste. There's no time to summon anyone else. He feels this matter is urgent and needs to be resolved at once. There is more at stake than you might know."

She frowned. "Now you sound like my father." She shook her head, her frustration obvious. "I assure you

I'm most anxious to hear what my grandfather has to say. It will take no more than a few moments to gather Charles and Enid and meet you here."

"If your father or someone else sees you leaving, what will you do?"

She looked at him as though considering his comment. "It'd be easier if we left after everyone has retired for the night."

Royce nodded as if she had just agreed with his point. "My horse is nearby. The sooner we arrive at Northe Castle, the quicker you can send for the others if that is what you desire. After speaking with your grandfather."

"A bit longer will make no difference. If I'm delayed for any reason, I'll send someone to advise you when to expect me." With the boy still on her hip, she took a step in the direction of Montvue.

Royce gritted his teeth. Somehow, he'd known this wouldn't be easy. Nothing involving women ever was. He held her elbow to stop her, then plucked the child from her arms. He lifted the boy onto his shoulders, well out of the lady's reach. The boy giggled in delight. "My horse is this way, my lady."

CHAPTER TWO

"Celery seeds are effective in sweetening the
blood but should not be harvested the first year."
Lady Catherine's Herbal Journal

Alyna stared in horror at the knight's retreating form, hoping he spoke in jest.

Nicholas looked back at her. "Come on, Mama," he demanded.

"Wait!" She hurried after the pair, her heart pounding with fear. "Sir Royce, please wait!"

Though she knew the knight heard her, he didn't slow his pace. His long strides covered more ground than she could match. "Nicholas!"

Nicholas merely beckoned her to hurry.

How dare the man use her son against her! Outrage gave her speed, and she quickly caught up with them. She grasped the knight's arm, but still he ignored her. "I insist you stop at once."

"I've told you we must go now."

"If you refuse to listen to me, then I have no other choice." She screamed loud and long.

Royce halted immediately. His gray eyes burned into hers, cutting her scream short. "If you persist in that noise, I will have no choice but to render you silent."

Alyna thought for a moment, but couldn't think of

a way he could silence her that wouldn't hurt.

"Mama?" Nicholas said. He held a finger alongside his nose mostly missing his lips. "Shhh."

Alyna stared at her son, wondering whose side he was on. "I want Charles and Enid to come with us."

Nicholas nodded. "They'll come soon."

While she pondered his odd comment, Royce continued walking. Alyna's head pounded with frustration and fear. She had no choice. If help hadn't arrived by now, it wasn't coming.

"Oh!" Nicholas gasped in delight as they came to the knight's horse. "Mama, look!"

A huge gray destrier with a mane as black as night stood before them. The horse nuzzled his master's hand, but merely snorted in Alyna's direction. Though she looked around, no other horses were nearby. They were going to ride this beast all the way to her grandfather's?

The knight settled Nicholas on the horse and made certain he held tightly onto the horse's mane, then turned and offered Alyna his hand, but she made no attempt to take it. She looked up at him, his features barely visible in the darkness of the cool spring night. "Please, let me fetch my servants. They'll worry so if we don't return."

For a moment, her hopes rose that he understood. "Your wish is not mine to grant, my lady. We must get to your grandfather's with all speed. Others depend upon us."

"I already have people depending on me, and they are waiting for me at Montvue."

"I'm sorry to part you from your servants," he said, his tone dripping with sarcasm as he took her arm to pull her closer to the horse. "Perhaps you can make do with me to care for you and the boy for a few days."

She held her ground and wrenched her arm from

his grip. "They will be punished if my father finds me absent. Punished until they tell him where I am."

"They don't know where you are, so they will be safe enough."

"You obviously don't know my father."

"I cannot delay, my lady. Your grandfather's orders were most clear. We must leave now."

Nicholas looked down at her from his tall perch and smiled. "Let us go."

Despair filled Alyna. She guessed it would take at least two days to reach her grandfather's. And another two days or more to send some sort of message to Charles and Enid. In the meantime, they would be worried sick with no idea to where she and Nicholas had disappeared. She could only guess at her father's reaction to her absence, and what he might do to the two servants most loyal to her.

The knight placed his hands on her waist, prepared to lift her onto the horse. He paused for a moment and looked down at her, his gaze holding hers. "All will be well."

Alyna wished she could believe him. "I don't see how." She hated to upset Nicholas by fighting the knight further. In reality, there was nothing more she could do.

Still Sir Royce looked at her, his hands warm on her waist. For a heartbeat, he stared at her mouth, and unfamiliar warmth curled through her.

He bent closer, and her breath caught in her throat. Suddenly she was in the air and then sitting on the horse behind Nicholas, confused by the moment and the knight.

He mounted behind her. As she settled her skirts, her chin brushed her veil which had caught in her cloak. Casually, she pulled the veil free and it fluttered to the ground. If anyone happened to find her basket along the path and her veil here, perhaps they'd realize she hadn't left of her own free will. She wasn't sure what good it would do, but she had to try something.

The horse set off at a brisk pace, much to Nicholas's delight. He was thrilled with the ride and seemed to think she should be as well. She couldn't help but smile at his pleasure but still held him tightly.

Darkness had fallen in full and with it came a chill that made Alyna wish for a heavier cloak. She pulled her thin wrap around Nicholas, though he seemed oblivious to the cold.

How the knight could tell where they were going was a mystery to her. The moon was not quite half full, and the darkness made the forest unwelcoming. Lords and villeins alike were tucked inside on a dark night such as this, the better to keep ill-meaning spirits away.

She kept her back ramrod straight, as far from the knight as possible, anger stiffening her posture. The man had complicated things beyond measure. She'd had a solid plan of escape and now the situation was completely out of her control, a feeling she did not appreciate.

The swaying of the horse soon put Nicholas to sleep, his weight heavy in her arms. Her own weariness tugged at her and as time passed, she caught herself leaning back against the solid form behind her, fatigue overcoming her resolve. Annoyed, she sat up straight again and pondered what might be happening at Montvue.

By now, Enid would've told Charles she hadn't returned from Sarah's. Charles would look for her. He'd speak with Sarah. Would he find her basket? Not in the dark. Mayhap he'd find it and her veil come morning. Then what?

Somehow, she couldn't think past that. She had no idea what Charles and Enid would do or how her father would react to her disappearance. If she'd left with them as planned, her father would've known why she was gone for she'd made her unhappiness of her betrothal quite evident. She remembered well the day he'd summoned her to inform her of the upcoming marriage.

She'd stood before him at the high table as a servant would, braced for a reprimand. His countenance was stern, as always. He looked every one of his fifty years, the lines on his face a testament to the displeasure he wore like a cloak. His blond hair was streaked with white, and bushy eyebrows a shade darker than his hair loomed over his cold blue eyes. "Mayhap you're not so worthless after all. I've finally made a match for you. I found someone who'll look beyond your appearance and take you to wife."

Alyna had been filled with trepidation. As far as she knew, her father had met with no one, save Lord Tegmont. That meeting had simply been regarding the narrow forested border their holdings shared, hadn't it?

"Lord Tegmont has offered for you."

Alyna's stomach turned. "What? But his wife died less than a fortnight ago."

An expression flashed across his face that she didn't understand. "All the more reason for him to marry again."

"Father, are you certain a match with him is wise?"

He rubbed a hand over his face as though weary. "Aye. This is a complicated arrangement." Something in his voice sounded less than convincing, but he waved a hand at her in dismissal.

She gathered her courage in one deep breath. "Truth be told, I do not feel Lord Tegmont and I would suit."

"Your feelings do not matter. You're no longer needed here."

His words struck her heart. She'd tried so hard for so many years for him to need her, to want her, to love her. But each attempt he had thrust aside. He simply didn't care for her. This match proved it. "I beg you to reconsider."

He laughed, but it was not a pleasant sound. "Reconsider? That is not possible." He shook his head, his gaze focused on some point over her shoulder. "Sometimes the desires of a few must be set aside for a greater cause."

"What 'greater cause' would that be?"

Her father's gaze pierced her. Never before had she questioned him. Now she had little to lose. After a long pause, he simply sighed. "You and I will both be forever bound to Tegmont."

"But, Father—"

"And don't think you'll take that bastard with you either. Tegmont doesn't need some other man's child hanging on your skirts while he tries to fill your belly with his own." He emphasized his order by pointing his finger at her, a habit of his she'd grown to detest.

She'd tried to discuss the matter with him several times after that, but to no avail. Nor had he explained his words. Now, all the plans she'd made to flee had changed. But she would not lose hope.

As they rode into the night, she realized events could be much worse. She could be on her way to marry Lord Tegmont. She said a prayer of thanks and reminded herself to count her blessings.

◈—◈—◈

Royce felt Alyna's form sag against him yet again. This time, she stayed in place, her body at last giving up the fight to remain awake. He put his arms around her and the boy, readjusting her position slightly to one more safe and comfortable. Her hair was soft and smooth and smelled of some sort of flower. He sniffed again, but couldn't determine what the fragrance was.

Her pleas for her servants had nearly undone him. If she'd begged him one more time, he might've relented and allowed her to return to Montvue. Logically, he'd known he couldn't risk it. If she'd gone back into the manor, she might not have found it as easy as she thought to escape with her servants. Then he'd have had to go in after her. No, it had definitely not been worth the risk.

But logic aside, he'd felt...otherwise. Something about her pulled at him. She was a strong, beautiful woman. Resourceful, too, he thought, as he touched his cheek where her basket had left its mark. Her son was as well. They'd given him more of a fight than he'd bargained for. He'd been astonished to learn she had a son, and he'd be willing to bet Lord Blackwell would feel the same. That must mean she'd been married before, but what had happened to her husband?

Someday, she'd thank him for taking her with him. Aye, he thought. She'd be grateful to him. Though she might not realize it yet, he and her grandfather had just saved her from a miserable life. Perhaps even death, for it was said by some that his uncle had murdered his first three wives for failing to produce an heir.

He regretted having to use Alyna to aid him to fulfill his vow of vengeance. But now she'd be free to find some other lord to marry, one that would make her happy for he knew Tegmont would not. He wondered if she cared for his uncle. They'd surely met on more than one occasion because of the proximity of their estates. His uncle was said to be pleasant to look upon and had aged well. The thought of any sort of affection between this beautiful lady and his traitorous uncle made his stomach turn. Hopefully, the match was not one of love, at least not on her part.

As for his uncle, the more he desired Lady Alyna, the more pain he'd feel when he discovered she was no longer his. That put a smile on Royce's face.

❦—❦—❦

Alyna shifted restlessly, trying to find a more comfortable position on the horse. Nicholas's form had listed to one side and caused her arm to go numb. She wriggled again, but realized it was no use. The knight who'd taken her was not a comfortable pillow. The surcoat covering his chain mail gave no protection from the metal links. She thought about straightening, but Royce's form, mail-clad as it was, provided warmth and support she was grateful for. By the look of the moon, several hours had passed. Her stomach growled. Or was that his?

"We will stop for a rest soon, my lady." His voice was deep and rumbled through his chest.

Alyna nodded. The farther they traveled, the sooner they'd get to her grandfather's. She closed her eyes and sighed, her heart heavy.

She would not complain, though she longed to. She was stiff, both from the cold and her position on the horse. She was thirsty, but didn't want to ask for a drink. She was hungry, as she hadn't yet had supper.

She smoothed Nicholas's hair, wondering how he'd come to be in the woods with her. Had he sensed she was in trouble? Perhaps he was showing signs of second sight as Mistress Myranda had promised. He'd said some odd things of late, but she'd put it down to the imagination of a child.

The near miss of having to leave Nicholas behind made her ill. And that was exactly the reason she could not marry Lord Tegmont. She would never consider a life without Nicholas. It wouldn't be worth living. She needed him as much as he needed her.

The moon seemed brighter than before and now she could tell the horse followed a narrow path. The destrier showed no sign of tiring, even with the burden of three on its back, nor did the knight who guided it. Did a knight such as Royce name his horse? She shook her head at her fanciful thoughts.

"What is it?" Royce asked.

"Nothing of import." She shifted again and heard him grunt in response. "My apologies. Did I hurt you?"

"Nay."

His voice sounded very odd. She sighed and wiggled her numb bottom. She felt a strange combination of restlessness and tiredness. It was going to be a long night. "How long have you known my grandfather?" Alyna asked.

"Several years."

She waited, but he said nothing more. It appeared as though she'd have to drag every last word from him. "How did you meet him?"

"At a jousting match." He paused, then added, "In Normandy."

She'd known her grandfather had left England soon after her mother's death at the king's bidding. Royce and her grandfather had both traveled far beyond England's shores. She could only imagine the different places and people they'd seen.

There had been many times over the years when

she'd wished her grandfather would return to England and come to take her away, at least for a time. Though she didn't know him well, her mother had told her stories of him. He sounded so very different from her own father.

Her feelings for her father were complicated. At times she resented that he'd lived when her mother had died. Then guilt would take over, and she was certain God would punish her for her wicked thoughts. Other times, she thought that if she could be a better daughter and work harder, he would love her.

"It seems as if all this would have been much simpler if Grandfather had come to Montvue. Why didn't he?"

"We did not think your father would take kindly to a visit from him."

Alyna had to admit that was true. Her father's relationship with her grandfather had ended poorly upon her mother's death. "In my message to him, I suggested I'd meet him at a place of his choosing."

"He did not receive a message from you."

Alyna turned her head to look at Sir Royce, careful not to jostle Nicholas. "What do you mean?"

He frowned. "He did not receive any message from you."

She studied the knight's expression, unsure why he would say such a thing. "Of course he received it. My messenger confirmed he presented it to someone at the keep."

"Nay, my lady. We would've been given the message."

"But then how did you know to come? How did Grandfather learn of my betrothal?"

"Lord Blackwell learned of it when he returned to England. He decided it best to speak with you, and the only way to do so was to have you come to Northe

Castle for a visit."

A visit, Alyna thought as she turned back around. Was that how her grandfather intended to explain her absence to her father? If she had any voice in the matter, she would not be returning to Montvue.

She wondered what her grandfather would say to her. There must be something about the betrothal that had caused him to send Sir Royce to fetch her if it hadn't been her message. Perhaps he'd be able to explain her father's words about her marriage being part of a "greater cause". Or should she even mention her father's strange comments? Could she trust her grandfather?

"He's a good man, your grandfather."

Alyna smiled, comforted. Mayhap the knight wasn't much for conversation, but he'd said the right thing this time.

CHAPTER THREE

*"Mugwort is said to protect against bad visions,
but in truth, I have seen no evidence of this."*
Lady Catherine's Herbal Journal

Alyna opened her eyes and saw a stretch of pale blue sky between tall evergreens. A squirrel chattered above them as if annoyed by their presence. She looked around, confused as to why she'd woken up outside.

Then she remembered.

The frost-covered ground had seeped into her bones despite the pallet of furs Sir Royce had provided. The tip of her nose tingled from the cold. A glance to her side showed the knight slept an arm's length away. Nicholas lay sound asleep between them covered with a fur, his warm form tucked against hers. A touch on his soft hair reassured her.

She barely remembered stopping for a rest. She'd been exhausted and not much help in getting Nicholas off the horse and settled for the night. Sir Royce had taken good care of them. The thought made her warm inside. Her captor was very considerate now that he had her where he wanted her.

The trees were too thick to allow her to see the sun, but a closer look at the delicate blue of the sky indicated it was early morning. She stretched and nearly groaned at her sore muscles. How could sitting on a horse cause every part of her body to hurt so? She glared at the steed where it stood nearby, but the large gray beast paid her no mind.

She had no idea where they were or which way was home. Nothing looked familiar. She prayed that Charles and Enid weren't suffering at the hands of her father. With luck, she'd be able to send a message to them on the morrow.

Frustrated, she frowned at the man who'd foiled her plans and caused her this worry. His eyes remained closed, so she took the opportunity to study him. He lay on his side facing her on the hard ground, still in his chain mail, his head cradled on his bent arm. He was close enough that she could reach out and touch him if she wanted.

If she dared.

Her midsection did a long, slow roll at the temptation. Now that she could see him clearly in the light of day, she realized how attractive he was. He exuded strength and power even while he slept. His sandy brown hair was streaked from the sun and brushed the top of the mail that covered his broad shoulders. A scrape marred his cheek. She and Nicholas had certainly not made his task easy.

A few scars marked his face, but they did not detract from his appeal. His nose was straight, his brows a strong slash above his eyes, his expression serious even in sleep. Long, dark lashes, which many women would give an arm for, emphasized eyes the color of a gray winter sky.

Eyes that were open!

Heat filled her cheeks but she managed to hold his gaze. "Good day to you," she whispered, surprised she could speak.

His slow perusal of her face did nothing to lessen

that heat, especially when it lingered on her mouth. She licked her suddenly dry lips and swallowed. After what seemed an eternity, he caught her gaze again. "Sleep well?"

"That brief respite couldn't even be called a nap."

He got to his feet with a natural grace, showing none of the stiffness that plagued her. He stepped around Nicholas, leaned down, and offered his hand.

She pushed aside the fur and placed her hand in his, surprised at the heat of his palm. With little effort, he pulled her to her feet, and she brushed against him. Breathless and embarrassed, she dropped her gaze and tried to pull her hand from his, but he didn't release it, leaving her no choice but to look up at him.

Those incredible gray eyes were warm and released a storm of butterflies in her stomach. The raw scrape on his face caught her attention. Without thinking, she reached up and touched it. "I'm sorry for this. Does it pain you?"

"Nay." He smiled. "Luck was with me that you didn't carry a larger basket."

She returned his smile. "Indeed. I'm wicked with a bucket as well. And as you discovered, Nicholas is quite good with a stick."

His deep chuckle set her to trembling. What was it about this knight that stirred her so? Never before had she felt this aware of a man. But never before had she experienced this sort of turmoil. She'd been awake most of the night and was exhausted. Mayhap all these new feelings were simply a reaction to the situation and not the man. Somehow, the thought disappointed her.

"What is it?"

Embarrassed at how easily he read her thoughts, she shook her head. "Nothing."

He reached out a finger and touched the spot between her brows. "Something worries you, my lady, else you wouldn't wear this frown." He cupped her chin and raised it so she had no choice but to meet his gaze again. "As I told you before, all will be well."

Startled by the odd feelings his light touch evoked, Alyna stiffened, uncertain how to react. How easy it would be to lean on this man, to use some of the strength and confidence he exuded. His gray eyes softened and pulled at her. The scent she'd caught earlier filled her senses, a clean, masculine smell that held the outdoors and something uniquely his. She inhaled the appealing scent and her mind cleared of all but him.

He laid a hand along her cheek, his callused thumb moving back and forth, creating sensations she'd never felt before. As though to seal his promise, he lifted her hand to his lips and held it there for a moment, the heat of his mouth burning her skin. The warmth in those gray orbs kindled into a low-banked fire. Heat curled through her, lifting her worries. She could only wonder at what it would feel like to have those firm lips pressed to hers.

"We must go soon," he advised her, then released her and moved to his horse.

Alyna stood immobile, stiff with surprise. Her hand tingled; her body was suffused with heat from the inside out. A glance at Nicholas assured her that he still slept. She shook her head, berating herself for forgetting for even a moment that this man had abducted her and forced her to leave behind so much of what she held dear. She couldn't afford to trust him.

Royce turned around with chunks of bread and cheese in one hand and a skin filled with something to drink in the other. "I fear I can offer you but simple fare to break your fast."

She put a hand on her stomach, not certain food would agree with the variety of emotions fluttering inside her. "That will more than suffice."

Royce readied his steed, so Alyna woke Nicholas and coaxed him into eating a few bites with her. He was excited to ride the horse again. Alyna wished she could drum up some enthusiasm for the ride, but her sore legs demanded otherwise.

In less time than she'd hoped, she was back on the huge gray horse, her thighs aching in protest. She reminded herself that the quicker they got to her grandfather's, the better.

Nicholas pointed to all the things that caught his eye from his new height atop the tall destrier. Though young, he was very intelligent and observant. To her knowledge, few children his age could carry on a conversation as he did.

Enid often laughed at the things Alyna attempted to teach Nicholas. She said he wouldn't grasp the art of candlemaking or remember the proper spices to add to stuffed wood pigeons. But Alyna was determined to show him all she knew, which included everything involved in properly running a household. Nicholas was her son in every possible way, regardless of her father's disapproval. She was an obedient daughter in all other areas, but she refused his demand to abandon Nicholas.

As she'd watched Nicholas grow and learn, she often thought of Myranda and was saddened to think of all the woman had missed. Though Alyna would never admit to it, she also thought of Myranda's prediction that he'd have special powers. He hadn't wanted her to go visit Sarah, which made her wonder if he'd somehow known what was going to happen. And he'd left the gate and found her in the woods. The last few months he'd said and done surprising things that made her wonder.

The cool morning air soon warmed from the sun. The sky remained clear though clouds hung on the distant horizon. This was the farthest Alyna had ever been from home, but the scenery looked much like the rolling forested hills that surrounded Montvue, so did not hold her interest. She did her best to sit up straight, conscious of the knight behind her. But with a squirming four-year old in front of her, her tired body often sagged back against Royce. His mail was cool and permeated her cloak and clothing, reminding her to sit up straight again.

He placed his hands upon her waist, causing her to gasp in surprise. "I will not bite, my lady," he said as he settled her back against him, then helped to resituate Nicholas. "I'm certain you're weary and as that is my doing, the least I can do is provide something for you to lean upon."

Somehow she knew he could do much worse than bite. With a deep breath, she tried to slow her pounding heart as the sway of the horse brought her closer to him.

Nicholas turned and looked at her, his brow lowered. "Quiet, Mama."

Alyna was about to ask him what he meant when she felt Royce tense as he reined in the horse. She glanced at him to see what was wrong. He listened intently and scanned the forest ahead of them. She did the same, trying to see what had his attention for she hadn't heard anything. The path before them rose up to a small ridge. The forest on either side was thick with budding oak trees and evergreens and held only a few shadows from the midday sun. Nothing moved that she could see.

The horse snorted, its ears twitching. Royce motioned her and Nicholas to be quiet and drew his sword. Though concerned, Alyna could think of no threat this man couldn't handle.

With a gentle squeeze of his thighs, he urged the destrier forward. The horse seemed to know his master's mind and slowly walked up the path to the crest of the ridge. Just before the top, the steed jerked its head and snorted yet again. Alyna felt Royce tense further and her concern grew.

A man on a horse stepped out on the path above them. The rider appeared to be a knight even larger than the one she rode with. To her surprise, she felt Royce relax.

"Miss me, did you?" he called out.

A sharp bark of laughter dispelled the rest of Alyna's tension and increased her curiosity instead. "Miss you? Ha! The air is much fresher with you gone."

Royce shook his head as he sheathed his sword and urged the horse forward. "All is well then?"

"'Tis now."

"Lady Alyna, may I present Sir Hugh, a friend of mine, and another in the service of your grandfather."

The large knight moved forward, as comfortable on his horse as Royce was. He must've had Danish ancestors as he had the fair coloring and hair of the Danes that had invaded the coasts of England so many years ago. His face was darkened from time spent outdoors and his bright blue eyes seemed to twinkle whether he smiled or not. A heavy, double-bladed axe was tied to his saddle, its menacing appearance making her wary.

"Sir Hugh," she greeted him.

"My lady." He bowed as best he could while mounted on a horse. "We've looked forward to your visit." His gaze wandered curiously to Nicholas. "And who do we have here?"

"This is my son, Nicholas." She put her hand on his shoulder. "Say hello to Sir Hugh."

"Good day, Sir Hugh." Nicholas tipped forward in his own version of a bow.

The large knight chuckled. "Good day to you, Nicholas." He turned his horse to ride beside them. "You're closer to home than I'd thought you'd be, Royce."

Alyna turned back to look pointedly at Royce, her resentment at his unnecessary haste bubbling. "I believe a bit more time to fetch my servants wouldn't have been out of order after all."

Hugh raised a brow as he glanced at Royce. "Aye, well, Royce's orders were to bring you to Northe Castle with all haste. He tends to take commands literally." The big man gave her a broad smile that echoed his cheerful blue eyes. "We're happy you're with us. Your grandfather is most anxious to visit with you."

"I look forward to seeing him as well." Again, Alyna wondered what her grandfather had to say to her. How would he react when she told him she had no intention of returning to Montvue? She knew it was much to ask of a man she hardly knew even if he was her grandfather, but she had no choice. She would not marry Tegmont.

"The men await us up ahead. Kenneth is preparing a meal."

"Kenneth? How many accompanied you?" Royce asked.

"You didn't think I'd come all this way alone, did you?" Hugh looked astounded at the thought. "You never know who might be hiding in the forests waiting to accost an honest man." He winked at Alyna. "Besides, I knew you'd need a hearty meal to improve your sour mood."

Royce merely grunted in response. Alyna looked

back to see a small smile on his face. "I must warn you, my lady, Hugh tends to think everyone's mood is a direct result of the amount of food in their stomach. He'll ply you with sustenance at every turn."

"At the moment, I'd be happy to accept his offer. The meal you provided was less than palatable."

Royce leaned over to whisper in Alyna's ear. "God's truth, I, too, look forward to Kenneth's meal, but I refuse to confess that to Hugh. I'll never hear the end of it."

Alyna had to force herself to concentrate on Royce's words. His breath stirred her hair and sent shivers down her back. She smiled, hoping he didn't expect her to respond intelligently when he was so near.

Hugh led the way over the ridge, down the hill, and into a clearing below. A small group of men were gathered around a cooking fire and turned as one to watch their arrival.

It occurred to Alyna that she'd never been surrounded by this many men afore. Certainly not when she was the only female in sight. Uncertain as to what was expected of her, she gave them a small smile.

Hugh put her at ease with his introduction. "Our noble leader has rescued a lady, lads. Mind your tongues as we don't want to offend her. And this other one is Sir Nicholas. Keep an eye on him because though he's small, his sword arm is strong and steady."

Nicholas beamed with pride as the men laughed in response. Hugh introduced each of them. They all seemed friendly enough and ranged in ages from one who was younger than Alyna to one with gray hair and lines upon his face.

Matthew, the youngest, blushed when he was

introduced. He glanced at her for but a moment and mumbled a greeting. His shyness somehow eased her own.

Another, Sir Edward, unsettled her with his intense regard.

Royce noted the men's interest in Lady Alyna and tamped down his ire. A beautiful woman like her in their midst was a rare occurrence. Of course they stared. He dismounted and lifted her off the horse, keeping his hands about her waist to steady her. "Sore, my lady?"

"Sore doesn't quite describe the feeling in my legs. Or rather the lack of."

"If you can bear it, the best thing to do is to walk to ease the stiffness."

She nodded but seemed unconvinced. He released her to lower Nicholas to the ground. As quickly as possible, Royce moved away from the pair before he did something he'd regret. His time would be better spent on his plan of vengeance. That plan might involve Lady Alyna, and he could not afford to have any sort of feelings for the lady or her son.

"Well?"

Royce turned to find Hugh behind him, an expectant look on his face. "Well, what?" Royce asked as he gathered his horse's reins and led it toward the small creek.

"How does it feel to hold a lady beyond compare in your arms?" He matched his stride to Royce's.

Royce wondered what Hugh would say if he told him of the path of his desirous thoughts. He prudently decided not to. Nor would he tell him of the jolt he felt each time he touched her. He was not an impulsive man, but something about the lady made him wish he was.

Hugh was more brother than friend and one of the

few who knew of Royce's vow. He'd met Hugh when they were both newly knighted. They'd found they worked well together; their strengths and weaknesses complemented each other. Though Hugh was the elder, 'twas Royce who was the leader. He arranged to sell their services for a high premium for short periods of time as they traveled. They'd slowly built their reputation and could now name their price.

The years they'd spent in Normandy had been fruitful in many ways. He'd accumulated nearly enough wealth to rebuild what his uncle had used and destroyed from his family's holding. But more importantly, he'd met Lord Blackwell. In him, Royce had found both an employer and a friend.

With the help of Blackwell and Hugh, he'd already put his plans for vengeance into motion. Soon his uncle would feel some of the pain Royce had felt ever since that night long ago when his uncle had betrayed his entire family.

In addition to that, he and Blackwell had gained valuable information regarding the group of barons that Tegmont was involved with who were disgruntled with King Henry.

Henry III had inherited the crown at the tender age of nine. The monarchy had been in the capable hands of regents, including William the Marshall, God rest his soul, until Henry reached five and twenty. During that time, all had been well. But after that, Henry had infuriated many barons by granting favors and appointments to foreigners rather than to the English nobility. Just over a score ago, a baronial revolt had erupted. Although Henry had restored order, he continued to surround himself with French nobility, including relatives of his wife, Eleanor of Provence and his own Poitevin half brothers, and therefore, the unrest continued.

While Royce could understand the unhappiness of the English barons with their king, England could not afford to be torn apart by civil war. That would make the country vulnerable to its enemies.

"What happened to your cheek?" Hugh stood beside Royce as his horse drank its fill from the small stream. He peered closer yet. "That's a nasty scratch."

Royce looked at him to determine if he was being deliberately obtuse. "The lady is more resourceful than she looks."

"Really?" From Hugh's tone, he apparently found the idea fascinating and continued to examine the mark with great interest.

"Do you mind?"

"Humph." Hugh pursed his lips. "Didn't she want to accompany you? Do you think she desires the match with Tegmont? Surely she wants to know what her grandfather has to say."

"Aye, she seems eager to meet with him, but she wanted to return to the manor to fetch her servants. Apparently she fears for their safety as her father might take his anger out on them when he realizes she's disappeared. I had a difficult time convincing her to come with me." Royce tethered his horse nearby. "As for whether or not she wants the match, I cannot say. She has not advised me of that. She did tell me she sent a message to Northe Castle."

"There was no message."

"She insists there was. One more mystery for us to solve." Royce sniffed the air in appreciation. Whatever Kenneth had cooking in that pot smelled marvelous. "Have there been any more raids?"

"Nay. It has been quiet since you left. Too quiet. 'Tis why I took some of the men and came looking for you."

Royce smiled. "Your concern for me is touching."

"It wasn't your ugly face I worried about, although now I can see I should've worried." He eyed Royce's face yet again then sobered. "It wouldn't do for us to allow harm to come to the lady."

"Nay." Against his will and certainly against his better judgment, Royce's gaze found Lady Alyna.

She walked with more ease than before, her stiffness only slightly evident now. Nicholas trotted by her side, then stopped to pick up a stick. The pair made their way over to where Kenneth stood by the fire. Alyna spoke to him, and the cook beamed with pride. He wasted no time dishing up what looked like stew into a wooden bowl. He placed a chunk of bread on top of it and handed it to her with a smile bright enough to light the darkest cave. Then he gave a smaller portion to Nicholas, squatting down to look the boy in the eye.

Royce knew if he wasn't more careful, the lady would have him grinning like an idiot and jumping to do her bidding as well. He shook his head at his fanciful thoughts.

"We'd best get our meal afore Kenneth forgets to save some for us," Hugh said. He scowled at Kenneth as though the man had already committed the sin.

❈ ❈ ❈

Royce had to admit he did feel much better with a full stomach. But he didn't say it aloud. Of late, he'd found it more and more difficult to endure time spent away from the comforts of a warm bed and a good meal. Truth be told, he was weary of fighting, weary of traveling, and weary of waiting. He was more than ready to lay claim to what was his by right and would soon be by might.

Before long, they were back on the horses.

Uneasiness filled him, but he was uncertain as to why. The sooner they arrived at Northe Castle, and he placed Lady Alyna safely into Lord Blackwell's hands, the happier he'd be. The lady was a distraction he did not need.

He pushed the group as hard as he dared. Guilt shot through him as Alyna sighed and shifted restlessly yet again. The boy had ridden with them a short while, then had agreed to ride with Hugh. It hadn't taken long for the child to fall asleep in Hugh's arms.

Royce knew Alyna was tired and sore. And he also knew that if he slowed the pace or better yet, stopped for the night, it would be much easier on her, but something drove him on.

Hugh looked at him more than once with a question in his eyes, but had refrained from voicing his opinion.

Just before dusk, Royce called a halt at the edge of a clearing underneath a gnarled oak, pleased with their progress. They would easily arrive at Northe Castle by midday on the morrow. Hugh, with the help of Nicholas, directed the men to set up camp, leaving Royce to assist Alyna.

He slid off his horse, aware of how he must smell, a combination of sweat and horse. He brushed aside his sudden self-consciousness and reached for Alyna.

She shook her head.

Royce paused, puzzled. "You don't wish to dismount, my lady?"

"I don't think I can," she said, her expression doubtful. "I've tried to shift my legs, but they won't budge."

Angry with himself for pushing her so hard, he put his hands upon her waist. "I'll move slowly and won't let you go until you tell me to."

"Promise?"

A surge of possessiveness shot through Royce, taking him by surprise. He'd never thought he desired to hear such a request from a woman's lips. It was unfortunate she didn't mean it the way he wished. He held her gaze, those familiar amber eyes reminding him of his duty to her grandfather. He nodded, not trusting himself to speak.

Embarrassed, Alyna lowered her gaze. Why had she asked such a thing? He must think her an idiot. She put her hands on his shoulders, and he eased her off the horse. Sharp pains shot through her legs and hips. She gritted her teeth until the hurt eased. Royce watched her expression closely, so she tried to hide her anguish as best she could.

"Better?"

She nodded, not certain she could yet speak. Unfortunately, he took her agreement as permission to set her on her feet. She sucked in her breath at the pain, certain someone jabbed red-hot pokers into her thighs.

Royce immediately lifted her so she didn't bear all of her weight. Then slowly, he released her. "How is that?"

"Good. My thanks, sir." Now, if she could just get him to go away until she had a chance to try to actually move her legs, she'd be much happier. No need to embarrass herself any further. "I'll walk around a bit to ease the stiffness."

His gray eyes still intent on her face, he moved to her side and kept one hand about her waist, prepared to accompany her.

"I'll be fine if you've other things that require your attention." She gave him a smile and a wave of her hand to encourage him to be on his way. To prove her steadiness, she took a small step and found the pain had already eased. A few more steps and his arm no longer supported her. That was both a relief and a disappointment.

She closed her eyes, annoyed with herself. This handsome knight had caused her such fright and worry, yet somehow she admired him, liked him even. In truth, she was starting to depend on him. While he'd shown her nothing but kindness since they'd left Montvue, she needed to remember what he was capable of—he'd pushed aside her wishes and put his own first when he'd taken her from home. He was a stranger and his kindness to her and Nicholas was no reason to trust him.

Anger bubbled forth and she looked over her shoulder at him to find him watching her, an odd expression on his face.

Unable to stop herself, she said, "You may think you know what's best for others, but the day will come when someone will insist their way is right and you'll be powerless to stop them."

She turned away to look for Nicholas, pleased that for once she'd spoken her mind.

CHAPTER FOUR

*"A draught made of mullein can aid ox suffering
from coughs. The difficulty lies in getting
the stubborn creatures to take it."
Lady Catherine's Herbal Journal*

Lord Tegmont drank deeply of the cool amber ale, the finest he'd ever tasted and far different than the rot served at his own table.

His arse was cradled by a chair, the cushion embroidered with gold thread, nothing like the hard pine bench at his keep.

Ornate tapestries draped the walls of the great hall along with a fine display of weaponry that told all who entered of Lord Stanwick's wealth. Even the servants' clothing was nicer than the ragged ones his wore.

Wealth changed everything for a man—every moment of a lord's day and night. If this meeting went well, soon he'd experience that for himself.

"Henry's got to go and soon," Lord Stanwick demanded as he slammed his cup to the table, splashing the ale.

Tegmont hid a smile as he set his cup down with care, not wanting to waste it. Already it seemed the lords here were in agreement and willing to do more than simply talk about it.

"He wastes the taxes we pay on his damned Poitevin relatives," Lord Cummins said.

"England needs his attention and his money," Tegmont added. "If he'd award some of the barons on his own shores who deserve it, our country would be all the stronger."

"But how do we get rid of Henry?" Cummings asked, always the practical one. "A war is the last thing England needs."

"True," Lord Markett agreed, the most cautious of the group. "The last revolt was far from successful."

The momentum of the conversation died. Silence reigned as the four men at the table eyed each other warily.

Tegmont waited, his nerves stretched taut, but no one stepped forward with a plan. He didn't want to be the instigator in case things went awry yet it seemed he had no choice.

"Mayhap those barons loyal to Henry could be convinced to change their mind," Tegmont suggested, as though the idea had just come to him.

"How?" Cummins asked, his bushy brows drawn together.

"If trouble should befall them, they'd see things differently," Tegmont said, hoping his comment would provide one of the other lords with an idea.

"Speak plainly, Tegmont," Stanwick insisted. "What do you mean?"

Realizing subtly was getting him nowhere, Tegmont leaned forward and lowered his voice. "We eliminate them, one by one, starting with Pimbroke."

Markett shifted in his chair, obviously uncomfortable at the idea.

Stanwick slammed his fist on the table. "Brilliant. When they realize Henry cannot protect them, they'll see things our way."

"Are you volunteering for this task?" Cummins asked.

"Nay." Tegmont paused as though considering the question further. "I know of some mercenaries who have aided me in the past. They might be willing to help us, for the right price of course." He drew a slow breath to savor this moment. Years of plotting for power and wealth were at last coming to fruition.

Soon the details were confirmed and the lords prepared to depart.

"Tegmont, I offer you both my condolences and my congratulations," Stanwick said.

"Aye," Cummins added. "You've lost a wife but quickly found a replacement for her and a young one at that."

Lust speared through Tegmont at the mention of Alyna. He could hardly remember what his other wives looked like. "Hopefully my new bride will ease my grief."

Markett slapped him on the back. "You run through wives quicker than most men run through horses."

Tegmont gritted his teeth. Was it his fault that none of his wives had given him a son? Obviously not. They'd left him no choice but to replace them. He'd taken Larkspur with the intent to build a strong family with many sons. At times he worried his actions had cursed him for he had yet to sire even one heir. But he knew marriage to Alyna would be different.

Everything in his life was changing for the better.

❦ ❦ ❦

Lady Alyna's words haunted Royce as they settled the camp for the night. She had the truth of it. He'd manipulated her to suit his plans. Though he realized he'd frightened her and caused her worry over her servants, he did think he knew best. He couldn't risk the possibility of her father discovering her departure. Nor could he risk taking it slow on the journey. Speed was of the essence.

Alyna would be much surprised to find that he'd already been subjected to one more powerful than he. His uncle. In one horrible night many years ago, everything he'd held dear had been taken away. He promised himself it would never happen again. But he soon learned the desires of a young boy counted for nothing. He'd been at the mercy of those who thought they knew best what his path in life should be.

Now, he was master of his own destiny. Mayhap he'd forgotten the frustration and resentment that being powerless could generate. He'd need Lady Alyna's assistance in the days ahead, and she was unlikely to provide that if she was angry with him.

Again he wondered at the depth of Alyna's affection for Tegmont. Was part of her frustration and anger due to worry over her marriage being delayed? Though tempted to simply ask if she cared for his uncle, she had no reason to trust him with an honest answer. Besides, it was none of his affair. That subject was for her grandfather to broach with her.

Getting it off his mind was another matter. An image of Alyna in his uncle's embrace filled his head.

He had little stomach for the evening meal.

Annoyed with himself, he focused on his duties and posted two guards to keep watch and set two more to relieve them halfway through the night. Then he looked for Alyna. Hugh had made a bed of sorts for her, and she sat upon it near the fire. Nicholas lay asleep tucked beside her. The fire highlighted her cheekbones and revealed the shadows under her eyes.

She was obviously exhausted. But what struck him more than anything else was the sadness that etched her features.

She glanced up at him as he sat beside her, but said nothing. He was almost disappointed. His respect for her had increased another notch when she'd spoken her mind to him earlier.

"We should reach Northe Castle by midday on the morrow," he told her.

She nodded, but remained quiet.

Uncomfortable with her silence, he searched his mind for something to say. "How old is the boy?"

She turned her head and studied him, as though trying to determine if he asked the question out of genuine interest or if he was making conversation. "Just past four years."

Royce pondered her answer. He'd been around few children, but he would've thought Nicholas much older than that. How old had she been when she'd become a mother? And who was the child's father?

Before he could satisfy his curiosity, she lay down snuggled next to her son and pulled the fur covers over both of them, clearly finished with their brief conversation.

⚜—⚜—⚜

Alyna awoke to a strange tremor shaking her body. She rolled over to find Royce quivering, obviously gripped in the throes of a nightmare.

"Royce?" She rose on an elbow and put her hand on his shoulder. "Royce?"

He opened his eyes and looked at her. Or rather, through her. His large body shuddered. He gripped the hilt of his sword and for a hair's breadth, she thought he meant to use it on her. Darkness hid his expression, but she knew it took him a few moments to orient himself.

"Are you well?" Though he hadn't moved, she felt as though he'd stepped back from her and gone to a place she couldn't follow. She withdrew her hand, uncomfortable with the contact. "Is all well?"

He sat up and looked around the camp. "I'm fine. 'Twas nothing but a dream."

A dream? She'd wager her last coin that it was more like a nightmare, and a terrible one at that. "Aye. A dream."

She patted his shoulder, unsure what caused her to want to comfort him. A quick glance at Nicholas ensured that he still slept. The dim glow from the coals of the campfire revealed the forms of the other men and none stirred.

"Rest, my lady," Royce said as he rose. "I'm going to check on the guards."

Alyna watched him walk away, concern for him heavy on her mind. She could only imagine what type of nightmare would have the power to disturb a man like Royce. The thought of such a vision caused her to shudder, and she burrowed under her covers to keep watch for his return.

⚜ ⚜ ⚜

Royce moved away from Alyna, grateful for the darkness and the cool night air. One hid the emotions he could not cover and the other helped calm them.

He could just make out Hugh in the dim light. His friend rose up on an elbow, but Royce motioned for him to remain where he was. Royce walked the perimeter of the camp, noting all was in order even as his mind processed the nightmare.

It had been some time since he'd last had it.

Visions of his parents' deaths had filled his nights for a long time after they'd died. They eased as time passed. Of late, he only dreamed of it when he was upset or extremely fatigued.

The question was, what had brought it on this night? To his knowledge, he was neither upset nor especially tired.

Mayhap it was a reminder. A reminder for him to concentrate on what was truly important.

Vengeance.

He fingered the amulet held by a leather thong around his neck tucked in his tunic. The coolness of the blue stone helped to calm him and keep him focused on his goal. His uncle would pay for his greed and jealousy. The people who lived under Tegmont's rule would soon be free from his tyranny.

It had taken Royce many years to understand what would make a man turn against his own brother, his own flesh and blood. Royce had seen traces of that trait in other men, men who thought they were entitled to take what didn't belong to them. Somehow, earning it for themselves never entered their minds.

Honor was nothing but an empty term Tegmont used at his convenience. Not something he felt in his soul. Not something that guided every decision he made. Not something he lived every day.

For Royce, it gave his life purpose. And he would use honor when he fulfilled his vow and at last made his uncle pay.

❦ ❦ ❦

Alyna next awoke to the sound of Nicholas crying. She bolted upright, heart pounding, scanning the camp to locate him.

Royce sat on the ground and held her son gently in

his arms. Even as she watched, Nicholas's tears subsided. The two of them examined Nicholas's skinned knee with great interest. Something Royce said made Nicholas giggle in response.

Warmth pooled in the region of Alyna's heart. The strong knight had a gentle side.

Royce spoke again, and Nicholas clapped his hands in delight, a huge smile on his face. Hugh joined the pair as Royce produced a small stick.

Alyna looked closer. It wasn't a stick, but a skillfully whittled dagger. Touched, Alyna stared at Royce, amazed at his thoughtfulness. Nicholas's minor injury was forgotten as he held the wooden knife high to show Hugh.

Hugh took the knife and examined it closely before handing it back to her son with a solemn nod of approval.

Nicholas turned to look at her. "Mama!" he cried. He walked carefully toward her, holding his new prize before him. "Look," he said, as he proudly presented it for her inspection, the scrape on his knee long forgotten.

Alyna made certain the tip of it was dull enough for her young son to play with, then returned it to Nicholas. "Did you thank Sir Royce?"

Nicholas nodded, gave her a quick peck on her cheek, before going back to the men.

She smiled at Royce, touched by his consideration. The look he gave her in return set off more butterflies in her stomach. Alyna turned away before she made a fool of herself. Hadn't she just told herself not let his considerate behavior fool her?

Stretching to ease her stiff muscles, she grimaced at the thought of riding a horse yet again not to mention wearing the same clothes a third day, but it couldn't be helped. Her gown had been donned for its serviceable brown material rather than for attractiveness. With a sigh, she thought of the saffron gown she'd packed in her bag to wear when she met her grandfather. The bag that was still at Montvue with Enid. Her hair and everything else on her body felt filthy from the dust of the road, and she longed for some hot, steaming water.

Her gaze sought the powerful knight across the clearing. What had filled his dreams that disturbed him so? Whatever it was, it had shaken him. No sign of that remained now. He appeared at ease and back to the confident man she was beginning to know.

"Good day, my lady." Hugh greeted her. His blue eyes sparkled with an inner mirth that made her smile. "How do you fare this fine day?"

"I'm well, thank you, Sir Hugh. And you?"

"Very well. Might I interest you in something to ease your hunger?" He offered her his elbow.

"Indeed." She walked with Hugh to where Kenneth stood near the fire. "I'm certain Sir Royce is anxious to be on his way. I'll eat quickly so we can leave anon."

She had just finished her solitary meal when shouts drew her attention. A man galloped into camp and stopped before Royce. The others gathered around, including Hugh and Kenneth, and listened as the soldier spoke. He gestured broadly with his hands and pointed in the distance.

Royce questioned him, then called out orders as he and Hugh strode toward the horses. They wasted no time mounting. Three other men followed suit. Nicholas ran to Alyna where she stood near the fire. Alyna kept her gaze on Royce, alarmed at the thought of him leaving.

He glanced her way, looking every inch the fierce knight once again. His huge steed seemed to bear down on her, and it took all her courage to stand her ground as it drew closer. She pushed Nicholas behind her, then released the breath she'd been holding when the horse halted beside her.

"One of my men found the trail of some troublesome thieves who've caused your grandfather much strife. I'm taking a few men to see if we can eliminate this problem." As though his thoughts were already on his destination, he glanced away. His horse stomped its feet, as ready as its master to be off. Royce's gaze returned to her. "I regret the timing of this, but they've burned cottages and stolen livestock and must be stopped."

"I understand. I wouldn't want to be the reason you missed the opportunity to disband them."

"I don't plan to disband them, my lady. I plan to kill them."

Uneasy at the thought of him leaving to face such danger, she put her hand on his leg and looked up at him. "When will you be back? Shouldn't you take more men?"

"Nay. There's a chance this is a trap, and I would take no risk with your safety. As to when I'll return, I cannot say. We may not catch up with you before you reach Northe Castle." He leaned over and placed his callused palm along her cheek. "I wish you well, my lady."

She caught her breath at his touch, her gaze locked with his. His warm, gray eyes held her with an intensity that promised something more. His thumb moved against her cheek, and it was all she could do not to lean into the warmth of his hand.

"Sir Edward will see you safely delivered to Lord Blackwell. Call upon him should you need anything." With a brief nod, he withdrew his hand and galloped off, Hugh by his side, his men falling in behind him.

Nicholas reached for her hand and, together, they watched them depart. She was less than pleased with Royce's decision to put Sir Edward in charge. Why had he left her with him of all people? She scowled at Royce's departing back.

She hadn't realized how comforting Royce's presence was until he was gone. Somehow, despite their differences, she trusted him.

But Sir Edward was another matter entirely. Worst of all, she had no horse of her own, so she'd be riding with him.

Conscious of Sir Edward's gaze upon her, she did her best to keep her expression neutral. Nothing would be gained by letting him know of her dislike. "When are we leaving, Sir Edward?" she called out to the handsome knight.

"We await your command, my lady." He bowed low as he spoke, but to Alyna, it was nothing more than a courtly gesture with no sincerity behind it. His dark, nearly black eyes remained cold and the smirk on his face offered her no solace.

She tried to shake off her unease. 'Twould not pay to become dependent upon Royce. His presence or absence should matter not. She thought instead on what the remainder of the day would bring. "Let us leave at once then."

Soon the remaining men mounted and their journey resumed. Nicholas rode with Matthew, the youngest of the knights. He'd refused to ride with Edward, much to Alyna's surprise. It didn't seem like he'd been around Edward enough to form a dislike of him.

Alyna insisted on riding behind Edward so as not to have him breathing down her neck. Whatever the knight had eaten to break his fast caused him to have foul breath, and she had no desire to smell it any more than she had to. The other advantage to her position was that she didn't feel obligated to make conversation with him.

Unfortunately, he didn't feel the same way. "Your grandfather is an important man, Lady Alyna. These past years spent in Normandy and Poitou have given him much wealth and prestige. He's developed a reputation for training knights along with Sir Royce. They now have to turn men away, so many seek to join their ranks. Why, I myself, have spent nearly three seasons with Lord Blackwell."

"Were you raised in France?"

"Nay. My uncle raised me for a time, then sent me off to squire for his overlord. From there, I demanded to be sent to Lord Blackwell."

Alyna frowned, unable to bear the thought of sending Nicholas off at eight years to begin training as a knight. Surely most mothers protested this custom, but luckily 'twould be some years yet before she needed to consider it.

Sir Edward's arrogant manner seemed to be in keeping with his looks. Cold and sharp. His efforts to impress her were for naught. While she wasn't able to put her distrust of him aside completely, she did her best to ignore it long enough to find out more of her grandfather.

"How long have you been in England?"

"Hardly more than a fortnight. 'Tis good to be home. I don't know why we couldn't have returned sooner."

Alyna had no reply so didn't offer one.

"If I were in charge, many things would be different." The underlying bitterness to his tone was unmistakable. He glanced over his shoulder at her. "Your grandfather and Royce mean well, I suppose, but good intentions do not produce results."

Uncomfortable with his comments, she changed the topic of conversation. "I'm sure you've seen many interesting places in your travels."

He needed no further prompting and launched into a story of a place she'd never heard of, involving people she didn't know. Alyna was grateful he enjoyed speaking of himself and his life, as he required little if any response from her.

Perhaps sooner than she was prepared for, her grandfather's castle came into view.

"Quite an impressive sight, wouldn't you agree?" asked Sir Edward.

It was indeed. The castle perched high on a steep incline and could be seen for miles. The gloom of the day seemed not to have reached it, for it alone reflected sunlight.

The castle was much larger than Alyna had imagined. The gate was flanked by two massive, round towers. The thick walls splayed at the base. Built of wood and stone, the large square keep was a full three stories in height with round turrets at either end. Creneled walls surrounded the battlements. The majority of the village resided within the stone wall, but additional cottages sat just outside as well.

Northe Castle was obviously thriving, despite its lord's absence.

A memory struck Alyna. *When the trouble comes, go north. Answers will be there.* Could this be the "north" that Myranda had referred to when she had told Alyna to go north?

Her gaze caught on a glint at Sir Edward's hip. As she looked closer, she could see the pommel of Sir Edward's sword held a pale blue crystal the size of her thumb in its center. *A crystal the color of the sky.*

A quiver ran down Alyna's spine.

CHAPTER FIVE

"Barberry is excellent for sore throats;
be certain to administer in small doses."
Lady Catherine's Herbal Journal

Could fate be so cruel as to thrust a knight she had taken an immediate dislike to as the one chosen to help her?

She sincerely hoped not.

Alyna glanced again at the knight's sword, noting the sparkle of the stone in its pommel and sighed. A crystal the color of the sky, Myranda had said. At the time, that had seemed fairly straightforward. But the sky could be so many different shades, dependent upon the weather, the time of day, the season even. Was that pale blue the color she'd meant?

Perhaps most knights had such a stone in their sword. As unobtrusively as possible, she studied the swords of the other knights. Only one was close enough for her to see clearly and it carried a swirled metal design, but no crystal.

She closed her eyes and prayed Sir Edward was not the knight who would be 'reluctant to help her'. Nor did she want him to be eager to help her, she quickly clarified in case God was listening. After a deep breath, she opened her eyes to see the massive gate of Northe Castle ahead. The horses' hooves clattered on the cobblestoned entrance in rhythm with her heart.

It was hard not to be intimidated by massiveness of the place. Alyna had never visited a castle so large, so impressive. Nicholas stared all around him, his mouth agape, eyes wide. As the portcullis lowered behind them, she bit her lip, wondering what this meeting would bring.

The guards called greetings to the men who accompanied her, their camaraderie obvious. The village appeared prosperous; cottages stood in an orderly fashion and in good repair. Most villeins went about their business, but some paused to stare at their small party.

Heat suffused her cheeks. Self-conscious of her disheveled, dusty appearance, it was all she could do not to raise a hand to check her hair and adjust her gown. She knew even on a good day, her features would not impress anyone, but she had always prided herself on being neat and tidy. On this day, she'd been stripped of even that. Frustration and anger filled her. Her grandfather had no idea what he'd done by sending Royce to fetch her with such haste.

She took a deep breath to cool her ire. Greeting her grandfather with anger would gain her nothing, and she had every intention of getting what she wanted from him: a safe home in which to raise Nicholas.

They rode to the back of the bailey where she could see the keep. As she watched, a tall, white-haired man came out of the large wooden doors and down the stairs. Her memory had served her well though the last time they'd met had been coated with grief.

He held himself erect and confident, as befitting his title of lord. He was fit for a man of his age; his broad shoulders filled out his dark blue tunic.

For a few moments, Alyna had the advantage of being blocked from her grandfather's view by Sir Edward, but before she could fully prepare, they'd stopped at the foot of the stairs.

Matthew dismounted and lifted Nicholas down, then came to help her. Sir Edward glared at Matthew, a snarl on his lips. Matthew's face flushed, but he remained where he was. "Might I offer assistance, my lady?"

She smiled. "Why, certainly, Sir Matthew." She put her hands on his shoulders and, to her surprise, he lifted her with ease from the horse. The young man was stronger than he looked.

He flashed her a shy smile, his face still red. "My pleasure."

Sir Edward dismounted, narrowly missing Matthew's toes when he jumped to the ground. "Lady Alyna?" Edward offered her one elbow while his other landed in Matthew's stomach.

The younger knight grunted in response.

"Step back, you dolt," Edward commanded.

Alyna ignored Edward's elbow and gestured for Nicholas to come to her. Grasping his small hand in hers, she approached her grandfather. She had no need of assistance from a man as boorish as Sir Edward. The rude knight deserved the same treatment he'd given Matthew.

Before she could utter a greeting, Sir Edward said, "Lord Blackwell, I'm pleased to deliver your granddaughter, Lady Alyna, to you."

Annoyed, Alyna glared at the knight. Was she some sort of bundle he'd carted about?

"Alyna." Lord Blackwell took her hand before she could offer it, smiling as his gaze took in her face. "I'm pleased you're here. For so long, I've looked forward to seeing you again."

Lines etched his mouth and creased his forehead, but his eyes had not changed at all. Their amber depths studied her even as she studied him. Heat rose in her face at his close scrutiny. "I, too, have waited a long time to visit with you."

As though he remembered the reason for their last meeting when her mother had died, a shadow crossed his face, then passed as quickly as it had come. "You've grown into a lovely young woman."

Disbelief and pleasure fought within her at his words. She pushed aside the feelings to concentrate on what was more important. "I'm anxious to hear what you have to tell me. Sir Royce insisted speed was of the essence. We left Montvue rather abruptly."

Her grandfather surveyed the group of men. "Where is Royce?"

"My lord, I would speak to you about Royce's absence," Edward said.

Lord Blackwell raised a brow. "Aye?"

"In private, if it pleases you."

The older man frowned. "It does not please me. I have no intention of leaving my granddaughter when she's just arrived. What is it?"

Edward glanced at Alyna as though he wished she'd honor his desire for privacy. She refused to accommodate him. She tilted her head to the side and did her best to act as though she didn't understand the look he'd given her.

His mouth tightened with displeasure. He turned again to her grandfather, leaned toward him, and lowered his voice. "I'm sorry to advise you of this, my lord, but Royce left Lady Alyna this morning to chase after some thieves supposedly nearby."

Alyna was shocked. His tone suggested he disapproved of Royce's departure and the reason for it.

He was obviously trying to cast a shadow over Royce in her grandfather's eyes. But why?

Her grandfather seemed unaffected by Edward's words. "If they are the ones who have been troubling us, then I would be most pleased if Royce destroyed the lot of them."

"But, my lord, leaving Lady Alyna went against your orders. Sir Royce was to personally accompany your granddaughter to Northe Castle, was he not?"

"Edward, I'm certain Royce's decision to leave Alyna was well planned, just as all his other actions. Should I doubt your ability to watch over my granddaughter in Royce's absence for so short a journey?"

"Nay, my lord," sputtered the knight. "Of course not."

Lord Blackwell turned back to Alyna. At last he noticed Nicholas, who peeked at him from behind her. "Whom do we have here?"

Alyna drew a deep breath, not sure what reaction she would receive at her announcement. "This is my son, Nicholas."

"Your son?" He looked with disbelief at Alyna then back at Nicholas. "But how...I mean when?"

"Nicholas is just past four years." Alyna held Nicholas's hand firmly in hers.

Lord Blackwell shook his head, still bewildered at the news. "It seems I've missed more than I thought." He looked again at Nicholas and squatted down. "How do you do, Nicholas?"

Nicholas stepped forward and stared for a long moment. He bowed to Lord Blackwell, much to Blackwell's delight. "Well. Thank you."

"We have much to discuss," her grandfather said, with a pointed look at Alyna.

She nodded, but held her tongue, not offering any

explanation for her son.

Lord Blackwell rose and tucked Alyna's hand in the crook of his elbow. "I'll wager you have your hands full with this lad. Come, let us go inside and see you settled. You must be famished."

They walked up the steps to the forebuilding that protected the entrance to the keep. Inside the massive, carved doors, the great hall spread out to the right with a stone staircase rising to an upper level on the left. Trenchers of food had been set on the long, oak tables in the hall, awaiting their pleasure.

The great hall was enormous, impressive but for the cobwebs and dust coating the entire space. Soot marred the display of weaponry that hung above the huge stone hearth dominating the room. Alyna could easily step inside the large hearth along with most of the other occupants of the room and still have space left to fill.

Two tapestries graced the wall opposite the hearth, their pattern dinged by soot and grime. The meager furnishings in the hall were in a similar condition as was the floor. It looked as though only the pack of dogs sprawled in one corner had cleaned it in recent memory.

Alyna couldn't help but wonder if the kitchen looked anything like the hall.

Her grandfather seemed to read her thoughts. "The keep has not yet been set to rights since our return from Poitou, so please forgive the disorder. The steward I left in charge had more interest in the grounds of the castle than in the keep and disappeared before our return." He shook his head as though puzzled. "Let us ease our hunger while we visit."

Alyna removed her cloak and laid it on the bench beside her. Only she, her grandfather, and Nicholas sat at the head table, but others sat at the tables nearby. The hall was less than half full much to her surprise.

"I trust Royce treated you well?"

She looked at him, trying to determine what he meant and how she should respond. Did she tell him Royce had scared her half to death and then seized her when she tried to escape? Just thinking of the incident brought heat to her cheeks. Then again, she'd hit him with her basket hard enough to leave a mark. Perhaps they were even. "Royce surprised me and was...most insistent that I accompany him with all haste."

She could feel her grandfather studying her expression, so she kept her gaze on the food before her until she could think of some way to change the subject. "I'm eager to hear what you have to say, especially of my betrothal."

Her grandfather looked away. "This is a difficult and complicated situation and I would speak with you in private."

Alyna nodded, disappointed that she'd have to wait. "As you wish."

"Tell me how you've fared these past years. Is your father well?"

"Aye, he is...fine." She could think of nothing more to say about her father that would be both truthful and pleasant, so she moved on. "Montvue has done well. Our harvests have been plentiful, and the villeins healthy."

Lord Blackwell glanced at Nicholas, then looked back at her and lowered his voice. "Alyna, is the child Tegmont's?" His eyes were so big that it might have been comical had he discussed any other subject.

"Nay, Tegmont is not his father." The mere idea of it made her shudder. She gave a quick prayer requesting forgiveness for her lies as an omission of the truth was no less than a lie. "His father died before he was born."

"I see." He stared at Nicholas and rubbed his chin as he absorbed her explanation.

"He's a delightful boy and a true joy to me. I think you'll enjoy getting to know him."

He turned and looked at her, as though still trying to understand how all this could've happened in his absence. "Indeed. I'm pleased to have the chance."

"Might I send for my servants, Charles and Enid? I was not able to tell them I was leaving when Royce came for me. I'm certain they've been terribly worried about my absence."

"Aye. We'll send a message at once." He took her hand in his. "I know I've lost touch with you, but it is my intention to rectify that, if you'll let me."

Touched and pleased, Alyna gave his hand a squeeze. "I would like that, too, Grandfather."

As the meal progressed, he left her little time to observe, so intent was he on learning more of her life. He treated her with warmth and kindness, just as she remembered. He kept Nicholas entertained as well. The boy's laughter warmed Alyna's heart.

All of her grandfather's attention was not enough to distract her from the meal. While the serving dishes appeared clean and the meal edible, the pheasant lacked much in flavor and the sweetmeats were hardly that. Alyna thought longingly of her well-stocked spices and bountiful herb garden at Montvue. Perhaps at a later date her grandfather would allow her to give some advice to the cook.

After their appetites were satisfied, her grandfather refilled their cups and continued their conversation. The hall had been cleared and grown quiet before at last he rose from the table. "Let me show you to your solar. I'm sure you're in need of rest."

Alyna nodded and rose before lifting a sleepy Nicholas into her arms. She was certain her grandfather would explain everything to her once they reached the privacy of her chamber.

He gestured toward the stairs and followed them up to the second floor where he opened a door to reveal a room generous in size with two narrow windows. A large tester bed dominated the room, draped with red woolen curtains coated in dust. Cobwebs clung to the corners. Time and effort would be needed to set the room to rights. Nicholas wiggled to be let down and hurried to the window.

"Oh, dear," her grandfather said as he looked around with dismay. "I thought Florence was going to see to the room. I'm sorry, Alyna. I'll send someone up to get it cleaned before you settle in."

"Thank you." Relieved, Alyna moved to where Nicholas peeked out the windows. One overlooked the main inner yard and the other the herb garden, or at least what used to be the herb garden. In the distance, she heard the ringing of the blacksmith's hammer.

She wondered how long ago the steward her grandfather had mentioned had left. Who was Florence and why hadn't she seen to the cleaning of the keep?

"I'll send a maid." He turned to leave, much to Alyna's dismay.

"Grandfather, I was hoping we could speak of the reason for my being here."

"We will. Very soon." He placed a hand on the door. "You and Nicholas need a chance to recover from your journey."

"What I most desire is an explanation," she argued as her frustration spilled over at last. "I was taken from my home against my will by a knight I'd never met before. I don't even have any clothing except what

I'm wearing. I would appreciate some sort of account for all of this."

Lord Blackwell turned back from the door to face her. "Alyna, I know you don't know me well, nor do you have any reason to trust me. But I would assure you that I have your best interests at heart."

She waited, but he said nothing more. "Your words mean much, but I would still like to know why you brought me here."

He moved toward the window where Nicholas stood. Blackwell smiled down at him and tousled his hair before addressing Alyna. "I'm not certain of the depth of your affection, if any, for Lord Tegmont."

He turned to her and paused as though waiting for her to confirm or deny, but as he said, she did not know him well, and until she knew what this was about, she would keep her own counsel.

With a sigh, he looked out the window again. "Nor do I know why your father chose to make such an arrangement, but your marriage to Lord Tegmont would be most unwise, in my opinion."

Alyna waited, but again he remained silent. While she agreed with his assessment and had no desire to marry Tegmont, she still felt she deserved more of an explanation than that. "Unwise? In what way?"

Lord Blackwell pursued his lips as though he'd tasted a sour apple. "It would be a poor match for a variety of reasons." He nodded as though he thought that should be sufficient.

Alyna gathered her patience. "It would be most helpful if you could tell me more."

"Aye, well, I'm sure it would. As I said before, this matter is quite complicated. Let us address it once you're settled and rested from your journey." He laid his hand on her shoulder. "I truly am pleased to have you here. I hope you'll consider staying for a time, at least until all this is sorted out. It might take time to do so. I can tell you that much."

Alyna could tell his words were spoken with sincerity and that pleased her. Not knowing the real reason for his objection to her betrothal made her uneasy, but he was obviously not going to tell her now. Did it matter when she objected to it as well?

"So, I'm a great grandfather now, eh?" He shook his head and smiled at the thought.

Alyna ruthlessly squelched her feelings of guilt as she smiled in return. Mayhap one day soon she would explain the full circumstances of Nicholas's birth, but that day would have to wait until she knew her grandfather better.

Besides, he was withholding information from her as to why he didn't want her to marry Lord Tegmont. Surely turnabout was fair play.

A knock sounded at the door.

"Enter," her grandfather commanded.

Matthew stood at the door, his face flushed, as it always seemed to be when Alyna saw him. "My lord, my lady." He looked at each of them uneasily.

Alyna's breath caught in her throat. Something was wrong.

"My lord, I beg your pardon, but there are some people at the gate, and they insist upon speaking with you about Lady Alyna."

CHAPTER SIX

"Sage can calm those in a fit of temper
but add a bit of rose to further please their spirit."
Lady Catherine's Herbal Journal

Alyna paced her chamber, alternately peeking out the door to listen for sounds of her grandfather and looking out the narrow window at the yard below.

Neither provided her any satisfaction.

Who could possibly be at the gate asking about her? No one knew she was here.

Was it her father? He might've guessed where she was though she thought it unlikely. She knew his search for her wouldn't be driven by concern but anger that she'd interrupted his plans.

She sighed in frustration. Why hadn't she heard anything by now? Unable to remain where she'd been instructed she gestured for Nicholas to follow her and descended the stairs only to find the great hall empty.

She looked with impatience at the door of the keep but her grandfather had specifically told her to wait inside. Perhaps he, too, thought her father might be here and wanted to keep her hidden from view.

"What should we do, Nicholas?"

The boy looked up at her and shrugged before returning his attention to his wooden knife. What else had she expected?

Just when she thought she could bear the suspense no longer, she heard commotion outside. Her lip between her teeth, she hurried to the door of the keep. Surely no harm could come if she took a quick look. She eased the heavy door open a crack to peek out.

Her heart rejoiced!

Charles and Enid rode toward the keep with her grandfather walking alongside them.

Alyna hurried down the stairs with Nicholas beside her. "Enid! Charles!"

They reached the group and Nicholas flew into Enid's arms with a squeal of delight. The maid laughed as she steadied them both and squeezed him as hard as he squeezed her.

"We found you!" Nicholas declared.

"Aye, that you did, you clever boy." Enid shifted Nicholas as he reached for Charles.

"How did you know where to look for us?" Alyna asked as she hugged them both, pleased beyond words to see them safely arrived.

Charles shook his head, his relief obvious. "In truth, we didn't come here looking for you, but for help. When you didn't return to Montvue at dusk, I went to see Sarah and found your basket. I knew something was wrong." Charles's gaze found Enid's. "We didn't know what could've happened to you."

"The only thing we could think to do was come here. We rode through the night." Enid laid a hand on Alyna's arm. "We hoped that perhaps Lord Blackwell had returned and would help us find you."

"Father doesn't know where I am, then?" Alyna asked.

"Not that we know of, but we left soon after night fell." Enid's pale face and slumped shoulders told of their exhausting journey. She held Charles's gaze, making Alyna wonder what had occurred between the pair along the way.

"We rode a very long while. Did you?" Nicholas asked as he slung his arm around Charles's neck.

The tired servant sank to the steps as though holding the boy was too much. "Indeed. That was far too long on horseback."

Alyna lifted Nicholas from his lap. "Charles and Enid are even more tired than we are. We'll need to help them get some food and then get settled so they can rest."

"Come rest, Enid." Nicholas took Enid's hand and led her to sit beside Charles.

"These two are very dear to me," she explained to her grandfather. "They're the ones I wanted to send a message to."

"Alyna and Nicholas have been worried about you," Blackwell told them.

"How did you come to be here, my lady?" Charles seemed very puzzled, his face drawn with exhaustion. The journey had obviously been hard on him as well. Dust grayed his tunic to the same shade as his thinning hair.

Lord Blackwell cleared his throat. "I wanted to speak with Alyna and, as I didn't think her father would consent to that, I sent Sir Royce to bring her here. I'll leave Alyna to help see you settled." With a nod, he crossed the bailey.

Enid leaned close to Alyna. "You look tired, my lady."

Alyna nodded. "As do you. The past few days have been challenging." She tapped Nicholas on his nose. "And you, Nicholas? Are you tired, too?"

He giggled and shook his head.

"I was afraid of that. You never want to rest when we do. Why is that?"

The boy giggled again as they made their way slowly up the steps, as happy as Alyna to have their little family together again.

❖-❖-❖

The next morning, Alyna stood in her chamber with Enid and Nicholas, attempting to reassure the maid. "Truly, Enid. It looks worse than it is. A thorough cleaning will set it to rights in no time."

Enid sighed and looked about the room yet again. "If the solar your grandfather gave you looks like this, what must the rest of the keep look like?"

Alyna hid her smile. She'd had the same thought. Despite her grandfather's promise, neither Florence nor a maid had appeared to clean the room the previous day. She and Enid had been too tired to do more than shake out the linens enough to sleep on them. Unfortunately, a good night's sleep hadn't improved the appearance of the room at all. "Grandfather did say he'd send a maid up to assist us."

Enid gave another heavy sigh. "He's a man, so I'm guessing he's already forgotten about that promise. I'll go below stairs and see if there's a maid or two or ten to help us."

Alyna shared a look with Nicholas as Enid shut the door behind her. "How about you and I go outside and explore for a bit while Enid finds some help for us?"

He nodded emphatically and darted to the door.

Alyna chuckled. "Wait for me."

He grabbed her hand, pulled her out the door and down the stairs. He kept going until they stood at the front door of the keep. Try as he might, he couldn't budge the heavy wooden doors. That was a good thing,

she decided, as he wouldn't be able to go outside
without someone knowing.

She guided him around the side of the keep to
where the herb garden was, curious to see what state
it was in. If she was going to try to improve the meals
here, she'd need all the herbs she could get.

Nicholas fought imaginary foes with the wooden
dagger Royce had given him while she poked through
the herbs. Much like her solar, the garden would need
some work, but quite a few of the plants were
salvageable. There was even some parsley growing
that could be used for cooking. If her grandfather
didn't mind, perhaps she could get Charles to help her
with it soon. She knelt down to more closely examine
some green sprouts pushing their way out of the
ground, hoping to determine what they were.

"What do you think you're doing?"

Alyna bolted upright at the stern tone to see a
lady dressed in fine clothes.

"Who are you?" the lady asked rudely.

Some might describe the mature woman as
attractive but for the scowl upon her face. Her eyes
were a deep blue and her golden locks were artfully
arranged and covered with a fine net. She'd surely
seen many more years than Alyna, and those years
had not treated her kindly. The biggest mar on her
looks was her expression, which held a bitterness that
Alyna doubted could be erased by a smile, if she ever
chose to do so.

Embarrassment flooded Alyna. Though she'd
washed with a basin of water the previous evening,
there hadn't yet been time for a proper bath, nor had
there been any point in thoroughly cleaning before
scouring her chamber.

At this moment, she felt every tiny speck of dirt
from the journey from head to toe. She drew herself up

and took a firm grip on her emotions. Without looking down, she held out her hand for Nicholas. His warm little hand gripped hers tightly, and she took great comfort in it. "I am Lady Alyna, Lord Blackwell's granddaughter."

A startled expression passed over the woman's face before she masked it. She looked Alyna up and down. "And what is it you think you're doing?"

Alyna straightened further as ire filled her. She had done nothing wrong and, until she knew who this woman was, owed her no explanation. "Who are you?"

"I am Lady Florence." She raised her chin in the air as she announced her name and waited for Alyna's reaction.

Only Alyna's good manners stopped her from an inappropriate response. Instead, she continued to look at the woman, wondering what reaction she'd hoped for.

With an impatient sigh, Lady Florence crossed her arms in front of her. "I am your grandmother's younger sister."

Taken aback, Alyna could only stare at her. She didn't remember her mother mentioning an aunt of any sort. Nor could she see any real family resemblance, and there was the age difference to consider. "I wasn't aware my grandmother had a younger sister."

Lady Florence huffed, apparently annoyed she had to provide any further explanation. "We shared the same father, but different mothers."

"I see." Alyna realized this was the person her grandfather had mentioned when he'd shown her to her dirty chamber. That made her resent Florence even more. "How...nice to meet you."

She ignored Alyna's words and moved nearer, trampling the budding plants Alyna had been examining. "From now on, you will check with me before you wander about the grounds."

"Pardon me?"

"I'm surprised Lord Blackwell didn't tell you, but I am acting as steward until he's able to find a suitable replacement." She plucked a piece of lint from her sleeve, then raised her nose into the air again. "In order to properly act upon my duties, I must be kept informed of all things at all times. I have complete authority here."

"I'll be certain to keep that in mind." Alyna's face heated with ire, but she held her tongue. For now.

"See that you do." She glanced down at Nicholas. "And see that you keep that child under control. My duties are difficult enough without the added problems a child brings."

Nicholas squeezed her hand. Alyna bent down and picked him up. "My son will not present problems for anyone. I am the person responsible for his well-being. Not you."

Lady Florence sniffed. "There's no need to take that tone with me."

It was all Alyna could do not to give the discourteous woman the berating she deserved. She decided it best if she spoke with her grandfather about Lady Florence's position here before she said anything more. While it might have been fun to discover a long lost relative as she had so few, this wasn't how she'd envisioned it. After looking at only a few rooms in the keep, she knew that Florence was not fulfilling her duties as steward. That much was obvious. "Perhaps your time would be better spent seeing to your duties rather than touring the grounds."

Florence gaped like a fish gasping for breath. "How dare you! I'll discuss this with Lord Blackwell at the first opportunity." Head held high, she departed.

Alyna released the breath she wasn't aware she'd been holding. She hated confrontations of any sort. At least she'd held her own with the unfriendly woman.

Nicholas tapped her hand. "Mama, she's not nice."

"Nay, she certainly is not." She looked at him. "And I think it would be wise if we avoided her as much as possible."

Nicholas's expression grew thoughtful, then he solemnly nodded as he stared at where Florence had gone out of sight.

At times like this, Alyna would give anything to know what her son was thinking. She couldn't help but wonder if Florence had left her chamber filthy in an attempt to make her feel unwelcome. Surely she was reading more into the woman's actions than warranted.

"Come. Let us give Enid a hand. There is much to be done."

❊──❊──❊

"Ah, my lady, there you are," Enid exclaimed as Alyna and Nicholas entered the chamber.

Two other maids paused in their cleaning to curtsy. Alyna greeted them and looked about the chamber. They'd already improved its appearance. The bedding had been changed and the bed curtains removed. "You've worked wonders. What can I do to help?"

"Not a thing. Beatrice and Mary are all the help I need."

The maids beamed at Enid's praise.

"Come this way, my lady." Enid pulled Alyna into an adjoining chamber where a large tub of steaming water sat along with a change of clothing.

Alyna sighed with pleasure. Just the sight of the

steaming tub was enough to make her feel better. "Are you certain I can't help clean first?"

"Indeed I am. Take your time. Nicholas and I will sweep the floor in the other room. Won't we, Nicholas?"

"Aye!" he exclaimed.

Alyna shared an amused look with Enid. "Any chore that involves something that resembles a sword is fine by him."

"I'd best supervise so the dirt goes out of the solar and not back in," Enid said as she followed Nicholas out of the room and closed the door behind her.

Since Enid seemed to have things well in hand, Alyna gave into the temptation of the water. The pleasure of the bath melted away the memory of the uncomfortable scene with Lady Florence. She'd speak with her grandfather about Lady Florence's role at Northe Castle as soon as she saw him. The lady did him no favors by acting as steward. She would also like to know if the woman was truly her grandmother's sister.

Nicholas's laughter from the next room made her smile and curbed the temptation to dawdle in the warm water. A sniff of the pot of plain, harsh soap made her long for some of the herbal soap she made herself. That would be near the top of her list of things to be done.

She scrubbed every part of her body twice over, then washed her hair twice for good measure. That done, she stood and rinsed from head to toe with the bucket of clean water Enid had set aside.

Luckily for Alyna, Enid had brought the bag Alyna had packed in preparation for their departure from Montvue. The maid had set out one of her better gowns in a rich blue. In no time, she was dressed in clean garments. The matching slippers had seen better days, but would be covered by her gown, so shouldn't matter. The bath had washed away the fatigue along with the dust from the journey, and Alyna felt renewed.

Nicholas was next in the tub and only Alyna's promise to take him outside after his bath kept him from splashing in the water for the remainder of the day.

Before long, Alyna was outside, watching Nicholas play. She kept a wary eye out for Lady Florence, but luck was with her and the woman did not make an appearance.

The afternoon spring sunshine warmed Alyna as she sat on the grass and leaned against the stone wall of the keep. She closed her eyes and tipped her head back to let the sun bathe her, a rare pleasure.

For just this one moment, she would let peace and happiness fill her heart. She would be grateful that God had brought her little family back together and that she had avoided marriage to Lord Tegmont, at least for the present. And she'd been reunited with her grandfather. It appeared as though he cared for her, and that she might be able to stay here for a time.

She heaved a sigh and opened her eyes. The reality of her situation was not as pleasant, for in truth, little had been resolved. Her grandfather had yet to explain why he'd sent for her, or why he thought her marriage to Tegmont was unwise. If nothing else, at least she knew her distrust of Tegmont was correct. How would her betrothed react when he discovered she was gone? What would he do to her father for breaking the marriage contract?

At last she allowed the worry she held surface— had her grandfather snatched her to use as a pawn in some game? Did he intend to marry her off to someone else? If he chose to, there was little she could do, other than escape again.

She reminded herself not to worry over things that had not yet come to pass. Instead, she'd enjoy this moment.

As she watched Nicholas play, she said a prayer of gratitude to Myranda. Nicholas was such a joy to her. He was fascinated with the wooden knife Royce had given him, both as a weapon and a tool to dig in the dirt.

What would the healer say now about the future for her and Nicholas? Were the predictions she'd foretold yet to come or had she managed to avoid them because of the choices she'd made? Had she already overcome all she needed to in order to find happiness? Alyna rubbed her arms to erase the goose bumps that appeared along with her doubt.

Visions of Royce filled her mind for the hundredth time since his departure. Somehow his absence made her restless. She shook her head. She was concerned for his safety. That was all. She didn't miss him; she barely knew the man. Yet while he'd been near, he'd managed to wrap her in a comforting blanket of protection, something she hadn't known she was missing until he'd given it to her. Just a feeling of well-being. That was all.

By now, she knew she'd imagined the breathless attraction she'd felt. That had been nervousness at the change her life was taking. Nothing more.

Nicholas saved her from her own thoughts as he stood before her, feet braced wide apart. One hand rested on his hip while the other held his dagger in a fierce grip. From the determined expression on his face, she knew he was prepared to do battle with any foe foolish enough to get in his way.

Alyna couldn't help but chuckle. The number of times he made her smile each day was countless and so precious. He dashed off, attacking some imaginary enemy.

"Nicholas, don't run with that," she called after him.

A distant call from the main gate announced someone's arrival, and Nicholas paused to listen. Without warning, he flew as fast as his small legs could carry him toward the entrance.

"Nicholas, hold," she demanded. When he didn't obey, she ran after him, heart pounding at the vision of him trampled when the visitors entered through the portcullis.

❈ ❈ ❈

"Do you feel as though we were led by the nose upon a merry chase?" Hugh asked Royce as they neared the portcullis.

"That I do. Odd how they always seem to be one step ahead of us." Royce considered the matter as they neared the entrance to Northe Castle.

"Trouble is brewing. Of that, there is no doubt."

"Aye. But what is it they want? And who are they?"

"Patience and persistence will no doubt bring you those answers as they have in the past. Those two qualities have become your strengths."

Royce could only hope they'd hold him in good stead not only with this challenge but with his next, the most important one he'd ever face—vengeance at last.

But this puzzle had to be solved first. He owed that much and more to Lord Blackwell.

He'd feared he was being led away from Alyna soon after they'd left her. It would ease his mind to see her for himself. He was concerned for her safety. That was all.

And that was surely the reason she'd been on his mind so much since he'd left her in Sir Edward's care. He'd chosen Sir Edward deliberately, knowing the knight would do his best to convince Lady Alyna of Royce's unworthiness. Royce well knew Edward considered himself superior.

Once he'd confirmed Alyna's safety, Royce planned on staying as far away from her as possible. Then the inappropriate desire he had for her would end. It had to. He did not need the distraction and complication an attraction for Lord Blackwell's granddaughter could cause.

Royce led his men through the portcullis then reined his horse to the side while they passed into the outer bailey. He removed his helm and tossed it to his squire, who waited nearby.

As soon as the men were inside the curtain wall, he'd head for the stables. He wanted to see his tired destrier groomed and fed before seeking his own food and rest.

His thoughts elsewhere, Royce directed his horse toward the stables behind the others. The small child was underfoot before Royce saw him. His heart in his throat, Royce jerked the reins back, using his knees to urge his horse away from the boy. He feared for one brief moment that the tired horse would not respond.

Nicholas stopped, unafraid. His blue eyes looked up with absolute trust at Royce. The horse reared as Alyna snatched the boy into her arms and backed away. Royce had the large animal back under control within moments, but not so his temper.

He dismounted and stalked around the front of the horse to confront the woman who haunted his thoughts, day and night. "What do you think you're doing? I nearly trampled him!"

Alyna stiffened and clutched the boy tighter. "And you, sir, should be better able to control that great beast of yours." Her amber eyes flashed, making it clear she did not appreciate his reprimand.

Royce moved closer, intent on flaying her further when the little boy held out his hand. Taken aback, Royce stared at the small hand for a moment before grasping it in his own rough and callused one.

Nicholas smiled up at him, his bright blue eyes compelling Royce to hold his gaze. The boy placed his other hand on Royce's cheek before looking at Alyna. "He's good, Mama."

Royce looked at Alyna, puzzled by the comment, still holding his warm little hand. "What does he mean?"

Alyna's face flushed. "I have no idea."

But Royce was certain she knew more than she admitted.

Before he could question her, Nicholas patted his cheek, drawing his attention again. The boy's dark hair resembled Alyna's, but that was where their similarities ended. Royce would've sworn an old soul resided within him. The boy seemed to examine something deep inside Royce and find it pleasing. Royce couldn't help but smile. "Nicholas, you gave me a scare."

He grinned, and his eyes looked again like those of a little boy. "I wanted to see you."

Royce squeezed the boy's hand, and a warm sensation swelled within him. It erased a good deal of the fear and anger the near disaster had caused. Alyna's pale face reminded him of the danger the boy had been in. "You must be more careful around my horse, Nicholas. One stomp of his hoof would break you in half."

"Nay," the boy denied with an earnest expression.

"A different horse will hurt me."

Startled, Royce looked to Alyna for explanation. Based on her alarmed expression, he didn't think she understood either. "What other horse?"

"A big, black one," Nicholas answered.

"Indeed? Well, you'd best take care around black horses, then." Royce glanced at Alyna and decided it best to change the subject. "And you, my lady, how do you fare?"

Alyna lowered her gaze. "I am well, thank you. Was your mission successful?"

"Unfortunately not." She looked quite different than the travel worn lady he'd left behind. She was even more beautiful than he'd remembered. "Were you able to send a message for your servants?"

"There was no need. They arrived yesterday, much to my relief."

"That worked out rather neatly, didn't it?" Too neatly, he thought but pushed the notion aside. Unable to resist touching her at last, he tucked a strand of her hair behind her ear, lingering there for just a moment. Just long enough for his finger to slide along the delicate alabaster skin of her jaw. Long enough for him to realize he hadn't imagined the desire touching her produced. He dropped his hand, amazed he'd so quickly forgotten his intention to stay away from her.

More troubled than he cared to admit, he muttered an oath under his breath. He gave Nicholas a pat on the shoulder, nodded to the lady, and walked away before he did something he'd regret.

His squire had led his horse to the stable, so Royce followed. Glancing around the grounds, he caught sight of Lord Blackwell, watching from the steps near the keep. Not certain how much of his encounter with Alyna his lord had seen, Royce could only guess that

Lord Blackwell had no desire to see a landless knight with tenuous prospects pay court to his granddaughter.

Again he pledged to stay away from the lady. No good could come of it. Not only did he owe much to Lord Blackwell, he didn't need any diversions from his plans to avenge the murder of his mother and father.

"Sir Royce," Lord Blackwell called out. "I would speak with you. Anon."

Royce drew a deep breath, glanced over his shoulder to where Lady Alyna still stood watching him, and moved to answer his lord's summons, stamping out the tug of desire that still lingered.

CHAPTER SEVEN

"Rosemary can be used in an amulet to ward off evil or ill humors, but it does not appear to work on everyone."
Lady Catherine's Herbal Journal

"You seem quite friendly with my granddaughter, Royce."

"My lord, I would explain. I have no intention of—that is to say, I would not be worthy of—" Royce shut his mouth before he said something that either insulted Lord Blackwell or put more weight on the situation than merited. "She is special, my lord."

"Indeed, she is." Blackwell stood with hands clasped behind his back, his head tilted to the side, as though he found Royce's bungled explanation of great interest. The amber eyes that looked so much like Alyna's seemed to wait patiently while Royce sorted out what he wanted to say.

Royce sighed and changed the subject entirely. "I fear we were not successful in catching the thieves."

The older man gave Royce a considering look. "I'm certain you caused them some worry and grief?"

Royce allowed himself a small smile, relieved Lord Blackwell was willing to discuss a different matter. "Indeed. Next time they will not be so lucky."

"We will hope there won't be a next time." He

gestured for Royce to follow him and led the way into the keep. "Perhaps you've scared them off permanently."

Royce pondered the idea then shook his head. "I think not. This is not the first time they've attacked us. Their persistence tells me we have something they want, and they'll come back time and again until they get it. I just haven't discovered what it is."

"There is the possibility they're connected in some way to the other situation we're pursuing."

"The thought crossed my mind as well." Royce kept his voice low. "Did Lady Alyna mention to you the message she sent here before I went to fetch her?"

"Nay. We didn't receive a message from her."

"That's what I told her. I don't know what could've come of it." He held open the door for his lord. Edward stood on the other side as though on the verge of leaving.

"My lord, Sir Royce," Edward greeted them as they entered the keep. His gaze lingered on Royce. "I see you've come back empty-handed, eh?" He laughed. "They outsmarted *you*, Royce?"

Royce turned to look at Lord Blackwell, wondering if his lord was thinking the same thing he was. More than once, the thieves had information that could've only come from within the walls of the keep. Someone privy to their whereabouts and their plans had to be sharing details. Could Edward be that someone?

Lord Blackwell looked at him blankly for a moment, then a dawning awareness spread over his expression, and he raised a brow in question.

Royce shrugged in response. He turned to Edward, wishing he could place his fist in the younger man's face rather than respond to his comment. "We weren't able to catch them."

Edward laughed again.

Royce found it to be a most annoying sound.

"I thought you would have the situation well in hand by now." Edward's smirk loosened the tight hold Royce held on his temper.

As Royce opened his mouth to respond to the insult, Lord Blackwell spoke.

"I fail to see what amuses you about the situation, Edward. Perhaps you'd like to give us your opinion on how best to proceed."

Clearly taken aback at the request, Edward's eyes opened wide. "Well, my lord, I would certainly be willing to give my advice." There was a long moment of silence as the wheels seemed to turn in Edward's mind. "Mayhap at the evening meal I could share some of my thoughts on the matter."

"That would be most generous of you, Edward. I look forward to it." Lord Blackwell nodded in dismissal at the younger knight. "Until then."

Edward bowed and left the keep, clearly disgruntled that his barbs at Royce had been redirected.

Royce smiled at his departing back. "Will he be suddenly ill prior to the meal?"

Lord Blackwell chuckled and placed his hand on Royce's shoulder. "Would you care to place a small wager on it?"

※─※─※

Alyna watched Royce follow her grandfather into the keep, noting his impossibly broad shoulders, how his light brown hair was streaked by the sun.

And drew a deep breath to slow her pounding heart.

She rubbed the underside of her chin on Nicholas's soft hair in an effort to erase the sensation Royce had caused with the briefest touch.

Sir Edward came out of the keep, and she realized how very different the two men made her feel. Why was it that Royce drew her, whereas both Lord Tegmont and Edward repelled her? All three men were handsome and strong. Each cut a fine figure and was powerful in his own way. But there, the similarities ended.

She knew not what attracted her to Royce, only that her heart beat quicker when he was near. She was drawn to him in a way she'd never before experienced.

Sir Edward's attempts to undermine Royce upon their arrival played through her mind. Should she tell Royce what the knight had said? Would Royce believe her? Obviously, he had some confidence in Sir Edward or he wouldn't have left her in his care for the remainder of her journey.

Well, 'twas not for her to judge if Royce believed her or not. She'd tell him at the first opportunity and let him decide for himself what he believed. If that presented her with a chance to speak alone with him, it was merely an added benefit.

Nicholas wiggled in her arms. "Let's go play, Mama."

"Certainly not. You scared me when you ran off. You need to listen better."

"Mama." There was a distinct whine in her son's voice. "The black horse will hurt me," Nicholas told her with a solemn face, his lower lip protruding, his blue eyes more serious than they should've been.

"When? What black horse?"

"Not yet, Mama."

"When will this horse hurt you?"

A shrug was her only answer. Uncertainty filled her as she thought about his words. "You stay far away from all of the horses. Do you understand? And you're remaining inside until you can remember to come when I call."

Alyna made it to her chamber without encountering Royce or her grandfather.

Enid shared Alyna's fright when told of the near miss. She lifted Nicholas into her arms. "Do you have any idea of the danger you were in?"

Amused that Nicholas had to endure two scoldings, Alyna couldn't help but smile, which earned her a stern look as well.

"This is no laughing matter, my lady. He could have been killed and I'd thank you to remember that."

Sometimes, Enid acted more like her mother than her maid. Removing the smile, she reassured the older woman. "Nay, Enid, 'tis nothing to laugh at." She turned to Nicholas with a more solemn expression and pointed her finger at him. "You need to heed my call the next time."

He shook his finger back at her, his blue eyes sparkling with mischief, but he agreed. "Aye, Mama."

Alyna stopped, disgusted with herself. How often had her father jabbed his finger at her? She instructed Enid to keep Nicholas in the chamber until it was time for the evening meal then left the pair to seek her grandfather.

Lady Florence stood at the top of the stairs with her back to Alyna. Somehow, Alyna couldn't think of the woman as an aunt. Alyna hesitated, hoping she would proceed down the steps so a confrontation could be avoided, but Florence remained there, immobile. Curiosity drew Alyna closer. As she neared Florence, she could hear the murmur of voices coming from below.

Lady Florence was eavesdropping.

Amazed at her audacity, Alyna donned an

innocent expression. "Is something wrong, Lady Florence?"

So startled, the woman nearly lost her footing. Alyna reached out and grabbed her arm to prevent her from tumbling down the stairs. "I'm sorry. I didn't mean to frighten you."

Gasping, Florence jerked her arm out of Alyna's hand. "Why you–you had no right to skulk up on me like that!" The intensity of the snarl on Florence's face surprised Alyna.

"Why are you standing here?"

"I owe you no explanation." With a huff, Florence flicked her skirts and moved to the door of another chamber beyond Alyna's.

Good riddance Alyna thought. Curious as to whom Florence had listened to, Alyna continued down the stairs.

Her grandfather and Royce stood near the entrance of the keep, discussing the progress of the men's training. Why Florence would find that of interest, she couldn't imagine.

Royce halted in mid-sentence when he caught sight of her on the stairs, his gaze following her as she descended. She forced herself to concentrate on the stairs so she didn't trip. He was an intense man, and when that intensity was focused on her, it was all she could do to remember to breathe.

Lord Blackwell turned to see what held Royce's attention. "Good day to you, Alyna."

"And to you, Grandfather." She felt a flush rise up her cheeks as Royce continued to watch her, those inscrutable gray eyes pale and clear.

"Royce and I were discussing some training. Have a cup of ale with me, Royce. Alyna, will you join us?"

Before Alyna could respond, Royce cleared his throat and at last pulled his gaze from her. "My lord, I had best go check on the men. We will talk more this evening."

"Until then," Lord Blackwell agreed. "I'm anxious to see who will win our wager."

Royce smiled. "As am I." He bowed to both of them, his eyes lingering on Alyna in a way that set her stomach fluttering before he turned and left.

Lord Blackwell turned to Alyna. "How do you fare, Alyna? Do you have everything you need?"

She drew a deep breath to slow her racing heart. Surely there would be a better opportunity to speak with Royce about Edward. With luck, it would be after she found her tongue. "Aye. My thanks, Grandfather. My chamber is very comfortable."

"You mean now that it's clean?"

Alyna paused, uncertain what her response should be. She had no wish to insult him.

He chuckled. "You can be honest with me, Alyna. In all things, you can be honest."

Emboldened by his comment, she asked what was uppermost in her mind. "I had the...opportunity to meet Lady Florence earlier."

Her grandfather's eyes narrowed. "Oh?"

"Aye. She says she is Grandmother's younger sister."

Lord Blackwell placed her arm on his and guided her into the hall. "Your great grandfather sired her late in life with his second wife," he replied, his voice low. "Your grandmother left to marry me before Florence was born."

"Why is she here?"

"She was here when we returned from France. I don't think she has anywhere else to go. She has no husband and no other relatives, at least none that I'm aware of." He looked at Alyna, as though to gauge his words. "Florence is a rather difficult person. The few

A VOW TO KEEP

A VOW TO KEEP
101

times your grandmother and I saw her while she was growing up, 'twas always the same. She seems to feel entitled to the things she does not have yet unable to appreciate the things she does."

A warm feeling filled Alyna at the realization that he trusted her enough to share this information. "I have to say I have yet to see her smile. She doesn't seem to be a happy person."

"True."

"She mentioned that she's acting as steward temporarily until you find someone more suitable for the position," Alyna continued, determined to guide the direction of the conversation.

Lord Blackwell sat down at the head table. He poured them each a cup of ale from a pitcher and handed one to Alyna. "I fear Florence overstepped her bounds when she came here. The steward I left in charge wanted nothing to do with her, so he left." He shook his head. "I can't convince him to come back, at least not as long as Florence is here, and I can't very well ask her to leave without a reason."

"Perhaps I could be of service in some way."

He raised a brow in question, his interest obviously caught. "What did you have in mind?"

Alyna took a sip of the ale, partly to quench her thirst, and partly to gain courage. Somehow, she felt the duration of her stay hung on these next few moments. If there was anything she could do for her grandfather, any way to prove her worthiness of his affection, this was it. "I have some experience in the duties of steward. Perhaps I could lend a hand in those areas where Lady Florence is..." Alyna bit her tongue. Incompetent was such a strong word. "Where assistance is needed."

"Nay. That won't be necessary."

Stunned at his refusal when Florence seemed to

do so little, Alyna couldn't help but feel he rejected her right along with her offer of help. "As you wish."

He covered her hand with his. "I did not bring you here to put you to work."

Relief filled Alyna. Many times over the past few years she had feared the only reason her father kept her with him was for just that purpose. "I would be happy to help." Somehow she had to convince him to let her do something to prove her worth. "Truly."

"Well." He rubbed his finger above his lip. "I suppose it wouldn't cause any harm for you to provide assistance where you see fit."

"I thought I might have a few words with the cook and see what can be done there first."

He squeezed her hand, his amber eyes warm with what she hoped was affection. "I look forward to enjoying the results of your efforts."

Determined to make improvements on the meal that evening, Alyna took her leave and went directly to the kitchen. She hated to admit it, but she wanted to impress Royce as desperately as she wanted to impress her grandfather. She shook her head, annoyed with herself. Had the worry over her future caused her to latch on to the first solid and dependable person she'd met?

She pushed aside the uncomfortable thought and entered the kitchen. A young boy stood near the hearth turning the spit of roasting hens. He returned her smile with a shy one of his own, his face reddened with the effort. She introduced herself to the cook, and after a few minutes of conversation, found out the woman had known Alyna's mother well.

Preparations had already begun for meat tiles and stuffed pheasant. Before long, Alyna had charmed her into trying a few new seasonings. With only a small selection of dried herbs to choose from, Alyna suggested using thyme and rosemary on the dishes and discussed other possibilities as well.

The tantalizing aroma of freshly baked bread scented the air. Alyna took the cook's young helper to cut some of the parsley she'd spotted in the garden earlier. They returned with enough to season the vegetables to be served that night.

With a promise to visit again on the morrow, Alyna moved into the great hall, still empty except for a few servants setting up the long trestle tables and benches for the evening meal. A few words had some of the maids clearing the old rushes from the floor and going in search of fresh ones. She had the other servants line up the tables at an angle to the head table so all who dined there could see her grandfather. Clean tablecloths were found. A more thorough cleaning of the hall would have to wait until the next day. She and Enid had their work cut out for them.

Alyna returned to her chamber to make herself presentable but found the room empty. Her kirtle was dirty from her activities so she searched inside the chest Enid and Charles had brought. Her thoughts drifted back to the scare with Nicholas. The incident would give her nightmares for weeks. Thank goodness Royce had been able to control his mount and avoid trampling her son.

What had Nicholas meant when he spoke of a black horse hurting him? Was it merely something from a child's overactive imagination or an event he knew of because of his second sight?

She longed to have someone to discuss his budding gift with, for what else could it be? Someone who understood and could help make sense of the things Nicholas said or did. There was no point in discussing it with Enid. The maid refused to believe in Myranda's abilities, let alone a young boy just past four years of age having that kind of gift.

The chest revealed little that caught her fancy. The garments all held the familiar scent of lavender, but nothing there could compete with what Florence had worn earlier in the day. She wondered what Royce thought of Lady Florence.

Just thinking of him made her catch her breath. Lord, but he was handsome. Not just his face was pleasant to look upon. Her cheeks warmed at the thought of his broad shoulders and narrow hips. Something about him stirred her in a way she hadn't known she was capable of feeling.

She shed her gown but kept on her linen shift as she pondered her meager choices.

Enid entered the room. "There you are, my lady. I'd wondered where you'd gone. I've left Nicholas with Charles for a time with stern instructions to keep an eye on him." She watched Alyna sort through the chest. "What is it you hope to find in there?"

Somewhat embarrassed at being caught in her indecision, Alyna merely shrugged. "There is another lady here—my great-aunt. She dresses quite nicely, and, by way of comparison, I didn't want to look as though I'm better suited to scrub the floor."

Enid smiled and shook her head. "Should you be dressed in sack cloth, you wouldn't look like that." She reached into the chest. "How about the plum-colored bliaut, my lady? We could use the cream riband to lace it."

A short time later, Alyna pushed her feet into her soft leather shoes, and smoothed her hands down her gown, pleased with her appearance. The gown clung tightly to her slim figure and the color was quite complimentary. Enid placed a circlet with a sheer veil over her hair. Alyna felt better, knowing she looked her best.

"You look lovely, my lady."

"Why, thank you, Enid. Will you be sitting by Charles this eve?"

The maid gave her a suspicious glare. "Why do you ask?"

"I'm just surprised how well the two of you traveled together without shredding each other to pieces," she said, delighted when Enid's cheeks flushed. "You haven't said an unkind thing about Charles since you arrived."

"Well, of late, he seems to have found some intelligent and rather interesting things to say." Enid took a thorough survey of Alyna, then pinched her cheeks to give them some color, adjusted her gown one last time, and turned her toward the door. "Be off with you."

Alyna entered the hall with resolve. Somehow, before the night was over, she would find a way to speak with Royce and tell him of Edward's comments. She would remain calm and not act like the simpleton she always felt like when he was near.

Her breath caught in her throat when she saw him. She'd never seen him without his mail—and she had to say he looked even more dangerous without it. Amazingly, his shoulders and chest looked no narrower covered by the burgundy tunic he wore than they had when covered with mail. The deep color set off the steel gray of his eyes and the light streaks in his hair.

The only thing marring his appearance was the hand of Lady Florence, which rested possessively on his arm. Unless Alyna was mistaken, the older woman flirted with Royce. Lord Blackwell sat on Royce's other side, sipping from a cup as he looked about the hall.

Just as Alyna had feared, Florence had outdone herself with her attire. She favored the color gold this time, though Alyna wasn't certain why as it didn't flatter her fair coloring. There was gold in her hair net and matching circlet, her bliaut, and gold trim on her shoes. She tipped her head back and laughed at something Royce said, as though he was the cleverest person she'd ever set eyes upon.

As for Royce, he gave her the barest of nods when she moved past him. Florence spared her a glance, but only to look with disdain at Alyna's gown. Uncomfortable, Alyna moved toward the opposite side of her grandfather and hoped for a warmer welcome.

He greeted her with a sparkle in his eyes as he rose to take her hand. "You look lovely, my dear. That color suits you."

"Thank you, Grandfather." She shared a smile with him. The more time she spent in his company, the more her affection for him grew. Her mother had been very lucky to have a father such as he.

As they exchanged pleasantries, servants made their way into the hall with trenchers of food. They spread the trenchers among the tables, each dish containing enough food for two and some, four, people. There were herbed vegetables, miniature pastries filled with cod liver, broth with bacon and sops, and meat tile. The latter was prepared as Alyna had instructed, consisting of simmered pieces of chicken served in a spiced sauce of almonds, toasted bread, and garnished with more almonds. Wine flowed freely.

Hugh sat at one of the lower tables and sent her a grin and a wink, brightening her mood. Edward wasn't present, but she caught sight of Matthew and gave him a smile that he returned with a shy one of his own.

Her grandfather spoke with her between his conversations with Royce, but Royce spoke only to him or to Florence, never to Alyna. The rest of his attention was absorbed by the food placed before him. What had changed from earlier when they had spoken? Had she caused him some offense? She told herself it mattered not, but the evening carried a shadow because of his odd behavior.

Still, the meal was different than the ones at home. At Montvue, her time was spent aiding the servants. Her father never discussed anything with her. He merely barked out orders for her to do his bidding. But here, she enjoyed chatting with her grandfather who seemed truly interested in her opinion on a variety of topics.

"Alyna, the taste of the meat tiles is remarkable," Blackwell commented. "Even these vegetables are...I can't quite think of the word."

"Flavorful?" Royce suggested.

"Aye, that might be it," Blackwell said with a smile. "Do I have you to thank for that?"

Behind him, Florence's eyes narrowed as she looked at Alyna accusingly.

"I'm sorry you decided not to take my wager, Royce," Blackwell said.

Royce's slow smile caused heat to pool deep within Alyna, making her forget Florence sat at the same table.

"I have learned to avoid losing coins to you, my lord, for you only seem willing to bet on a sure thing."

Blackwell laughed in response. "True enough. Well, he has only delayed his pain, not eliminated it."

"I look forward to the morrow. Surely, he'll have thought of a clever response by then."

Though Alyna made little sense of the conversation, she enjoyed listening to their light-hearted banter. Their mutual respect and affection for each other was obvious.

The highlight of the meal was the stuffed

pheasant, displayed on a large platter with the tail feathers back in place. Everyone praised the meal, including Royce. She couldn't resist going into the kitchen to share the compliments with the cook and her helpers.

Upon her return, she directed some of the servants to gather the remaining food from the table and replace the wine with a spiced one that went well with the dates and almonds drizzled with honey that served to end the meal.

Florence had a strange way of acting as steward. Alyna had yet to see her direct a servant or lift a finger of her own to help. Of course, she had yet to see the woman take her eyes off of Royce despite their age difference.

Thoughts of retiring to her chamber crossed Alyna's mind, for she was tired. However, she wanted–nay, needed–to speak to Royce of Sir Edward. Heaving a sigh, she resigned herself to wait until Royce took his leave so that she could follow him and speak with him privately.

At last, Royce bid her grandfather good night and left the hall. Alyna made her excuses and followed as quickly as she dared and stepped outside, hoping he hadn't gotten far.

Cool, crisp air laced with the scent of spring greeted her. Dusk had fallen and, after the brightly lit hall, made it difficult to see the way down the steps of the keep.

She'd only walked a short distance across the bailey when a hand grasped her elbow and pulled her into the shadows. Certain it was Royce, she permitted the odd behavior as what she wanted to tell him required privacy.

"Good evening, my lady," a voice whispered in her ear.

She gasped in dismay, for she knew instantly the man was not Royce.

CHAPTER EIGHT

"A decoction of beetroot in the nostrils
is effective to stay noise in the ears."
Lady Catherine's Herbal Journal

"Sir Edward, release me at once!" Alyna demanded.

"There's no need for alarm. I hoped to speak with you and here you are." He pulled her close as he spoke, his hands grasping her waist. "I'm grateful you feel the same way."

"I assure you I don't. Now release me." Fear skittered through her. His hands were impossibly strong and his breath reeked of wine.

"I've been thinking about you, Alyna. You please me. Has anyone told you how beautiful you are?"

"Sir Edward," she said as she tugged again at his hands, "I must be on my way."

"Stay, my lady. You won't regret it."

"Is all well, Lady Alyna?" Royce asked from behind Edward.

Edward spun around, a bit too quickly it seemed, for he staggered with the effort. "Royce? What are you doing here?"

Alyna released the breath she'd been holding, relief and gratitude filling her at Royce's timely arrival.

"You were missed at the evening meal, Edward," Royce said.

The drunken knight seemed to ponder the comment before responding. "I fear I was indisposed."

"So it would seem." Royce looked again at Alyna. "May I escort you back to the keep, my lady?"

She took his offered hand, grateful to be out of Sir Edward's reach. "Thank you. Good eve to you, Sir Edward."

The wobbling knight bowed low. "Until we meet again, my lady." For a moment, it appeared as though he couldn't stand upright. At last he rose then turned to fade into the darkness.

"My apologies if I was...interrupting," Royce said, his tone questioning.

Surely he didn't think she had welcomed Edward's advances. "In truth, I followed you outside with the hopes of speaking with you." She shook her head at the irony of the situation. "Of Sir Edward's behavior, if you can believe that."

Royce's eyes narrowed. "Did he accost you on your journey here? Why didn't you tell your grandfather?"

"Nay, it was nothing like that." Alyna couldn't resist looking back over her shoulder to make sure Edward hadn't returned. "Could we move farther away? I'd prefer our conversation to remain between us."

Obviously the lady didn't realize what thoughts that suggestion put in his mind, Royce reflected as heat stirred deep within him. The anger that had engulfed him when he'd seen Edward's hands on Alyna left him angry and unsettled. How angry could he be with Edward when he had thoughts of holding her himself?

"This way." He gestured toward a path that led away from the keep. He took her arm, telling himself he did so only because he wanted to assist her over the uneven ground, not because of the urge to touch her again.

He picked a secluded area and turned her so she faced the moonlight. Edward was right on one count—she was beautiful. Tonight she looked especially so. The deep color of her attire suited her. The thin veil covering her long hair only made his desire to run his fingers through her dark tresses all the stronger. Her bliaut had drawn his eyes to her curves as she'd moved about the hall, making certain all was well with the meal. The few times she'd passed by, he'd caught the same scent that had captured him when she'd ridden before him on his horse.

Though he'd done his best to avoid her at the evening meal, countless times, he'd had to tear his gaze away from her lithe form. He could only hope Lord Blackwell had not noticed the attention he'd paid to his granddaughter. Royce hadn't been able to keep his distance since he'd met her. Then again, thank God he hadn't or the night might have ended much differently. His anger resurfaced at the thought.

He forced himself to release her arm and waited for her to explain.

"I'm certain what I'm about to tell you means nothing, but I thought it best for you to know, so you could decide for yourself." She paused and looked around as though to make certain they were still alone.

"What is it?" Royce asked, puzzled.

"Upon our arrival, Sir Edward made suggestions to my grandfather that you were wrong in pursuing the thieves and implied your men were in disagreement with your departure, including him."

Not surprised, Royce considered what she'd said. Everything was a competition with Edward; he couldn't seem to help but do all in his power to win. Although Edward's past actions had proven him a trustworthy knight, his words were not always so. When he added this information to the suspicions he'd shared with Lord Blackwell, Edward's loyalty became increasingly questionable.

What struck him more than Edward's attempt to undermine him was Alyna's trust. Royce had known Edward would do his best to turn Alyna from him. In fact, he'd almost hoped Edward would succeed. It would've made Royce's wish to stay away from her easier. Many ladies succumbed to Edward's dark good looks and the charm he portrayed when it suited him, but apparently not Alyna.

She had much to be concerned with in her own life, yet she took time to speak to him of this. In all honesty, he was touched.

"I'll add my thanks to you for the improved taste of the meal this eve." Royce changed the subject with a compliment as he thought about the information she'd provided. The women he'd known were easily distracted and responded to compliments like fish to water.

She looked confused by his comment. "Why, thank you. I'm pleased you found it to your liking, but what of Sir Edward? What will you do? Should I say something of this to my grandfather?"

So much for his attempt at distraction, thought Royce. He tried another. "Are you happy here, Alyna?"

Silent, she stared up at him, obviously confused by his question.

He couldn't blame her, as he didn't know where it had come from. All he knew was that her eyes held a sadness that pulled at him.

"I've only just gotten here, but so far, I'm content. Why do you ask?"

Royce merely raised a brow while those amber eyes seemed to look right through him to his very soul as though weighing him to see if he deserved an honest answer. At last Alyna looked away, and he released the breath he hadn't realized he'd held.

"There have been many changes in my life of late," she said softly. "I have yet to determine where my future lies, so until then, I find I am no more than content. I'm not certain why I'm here or what my purpose is."

"Purpose? Why do you need a purpose?"

She opened her mouth to speak, then shut it. She turned her head, and a lock of hair fell free of her veil to lie against her cheek.

A wave of yearning filled him, and he gritted his teeth. He would not touch it. He already knew her hair carried the same fragrance that followed her everywhere, that it was as soft as fine silk. Her lips moved, and he focused on her words in a poor attempt to rein in his lust.

"I would prefer to provide some sort of assistance to my grandfather while I am here."

"Lord Blackwell expects nothing from you."

A smile turned the amber golden. "So it seems. That is something I'll have to adjust to, but I would like to help, to earn my place here. Grandfather and I still have much to discuss. He has yet to answer my questions."

Royce shook his head, frustrated that Blackwell had not told her more. He could only hope she didn't ask him instead. Eyes like hers would make it difficult to resist sharing all he knew. And if she smiled at him again, he'd say anything she wanted to hear.

"I'm sure he will soon," Royce offered.

More than anything, he wanted to comfort her, to lift the sadness and uncertainty from her face. Again, the strand of hair at her cheek teased him, and he could resist the urge no longer. With a slow movement, he gently eased the lock behind her ear. The moonlight emphasized the elegant lines of her face, hollowing her cheeks and lighting her eyes. She looked up at him with such a sweet, earnest expression.

What was a man to do but...

Kiss her.

Slowly. Passionately. Waiting for her to withdraw and demand he stop. But no protest left her lips, only a soft moan that heightened his desire. He kept the kiss light, not wanting to frighten her away, needing more than anything for her to stay right where she was, in his arms.

The longer he held her, and the longer he kissed her, the more he realized it was not enough. He ached for her touch, to feel her softness against him. He pulled her closer and molded her body to his.

As though she read his thoughts, her arms reached up to his shoulders, their warmth burning through his tunic. She deepened the kiss and tentatively twined her fingers into his hair. Shivers of longing rolled down his spine.

Never had a woman affected him like this. But never had a woman been so wrong for him. A landless knight set on vengeance was a terrible match for a lady. Royce knew this could go no further, not here, not ever. He had to let her go.

In just a moment.

After he had one more taste of her. He would hold her a bit longer, because this would be the last time he did. The memory of this kiss would have to sustain him in the lonely nights to come for he feared he'd never feel like this again.

Her soft whimper was nearly his undoing, nearly

more than he could take. Releasing her mouth, he leaned his forehead against hers and took a deep breath to rein in the desire pulsing through him.

Hell's teeth. What was he doing? This woman was his lord's granddaughter. Why the thought didn't force him to release her with great haste was beyond him. It mattered not that she was already a mother, a woman experienced in the ways of the world. She was not his to take and never would be.

With great effort, he set her away from him. "My apologies, my lady. That was a mistake."

"Excuse me?" Her confusion overrode the desire lingering in her eyes.

Royce felt his resolve weaken and took a step back to shore his defenses. "That was an error."

Alyna stiffened, obviously affronted at his words, just as he'd intended. "What do you mean?"

He turned away. Another moment of looking at her, and he'd draw her back into his arms.

"If you don't find me attractive, then why did you kiss me?"

Surprised, Royce spun back toward her. Not find her attractive? How could she think that? His need for her strained his chausses. But a closer look at her vulnerable expression confirmed the beautiful Lady Alyna didn't realize how desirable she was.

"Nay, it's not that. It's..."

"It's what?" Her hurt expression gave him pause.

Even as he opened his mouth to tell her the truth, he knew what he must do. "My lady, I fear you misunderstood."

"Indeed?" Those eyes drilled into his, her brow raised in question, her tone cool enough to chill wine. "What is it I have wrong, sir? When you avoided me all through the evening meal or when you kissed me and seemed to thoroughly enjoy it?"

Instead of being pleased by her cold tone, he felt only remorse. He'd never meant to add to her unhappiness. Perhaps this method was not going to work after all. The idea of her thinking so little of him did not please him.

Nay, it did not please him at all.

But it was for the best. Nothing would be gained from his desire for her. Better to sever it now, before it progressed any further. He took her elbow with a firm hand and guided her up the steps to the keep door.

"You have my word it will not happen again."

"Forgive me if I don't anxiously wait to learn to which 'it' you refer." She jerked her elbow away from him and stormed into the keep.

The heavy wooden door didn't slam shut, but he knew it had closed firmly in more ways than one. With a heavy sigh, he turned and walked away, wishing he could leave behind the disastrous results of the evening.

He did not go to his bed, which he'd longed for earlier in the day. He knew sleep was beyond him.

His only hope for some rest was a long, cold swim in the small lake outside the curtain wall. A temporary solution to a problem that seemed unlikely to go away on the morrow.

CHAPTER NINE

*"The root of cowslip can rid stubborn coughs.
Unfortunately, it doesn't stop other stubborn
behaviors."*
Lady Catherine's Herbal Journal

Alyna studied the dingy tapestries that hung high on the wall of the great hall. Soot and grime coated the battle scenes depicted; at least, she thought they were battle scenes.

The haziness of the pattern matched her emotions this morning. Obscure and unclear. How could a simple conversation about the questionable behavior of Sir Edward have escalated into a passionate kiss that had ended in disaster? It had been passionate, hadn't it? There was no question it had ended in disaster. Then again, it had been her first real kiss. She had no experience on which to judge.

She'd hoped her thinking would clear after a good night's sleep, but sleep had eluded her. Though remembering Royce's rejection of her still hurt, when she focused on that kiss...

With a sigh, she let the passion swirl through her once again. Royce was a man like no other. She counted herself lucky to have shared her first kiss with him. She couldn't imagine it with anyone else.

Remembering the feel of his mouth on hers

brought a flush to her face—and other areas of her body she wasn't sure she was comfortable with. In truth, that kiss had been glorious. For those few moments, she'd felt like the most beautiful and desirable woman in the country. He'd held her like she was some sort of treasure at first, a delicate object to be treated with care. But then, oh then, it had changed. He'd pulled her against his hard body and held her like he'd never let her go.

She'd felt...she couldn't even describe how she'd felt. It had been wonderful and had certainly erased the memory of a drunken Edward's advances as well as Lord Tegmont touching her.

Her pleasure faded as she wondered yet again what she'd done to make Royce set her aside. Was something wrong with her, some fault deep inside her that didn't allow her to please a man?

"Frowning at them won't remove a bit of that dust, my lady."

Alyna sighed and turned to Enid. "Aye. The condition of the hall is a shame. 'Tis the heart of the keep. It should declare the glory of the castle for all to see."

"Well, if I know you, it won't look like this for long."

She smiled. That was just the sort of practical comment she needed to hear. "I'd like to see the look on Lady Florence's face when she realizes what we're about."

Enid laughed in response.

Alyna knew Enid had seen how upset she'd been when she'd entered her chamber the night before. She also seemed to understand Alyna hadn't been ready to speak of it.

"If she was doing what she was supposed to, then we wouldn't be forced to do what we're about to," Enid advised her.

Alyna chuckled, just as she knew the older woman meant her to. "The frightening part about your statement is that I understood it." She looked up at the tapestries again and at the weaponry draped with cobwebs. "Grandfather said he'd welcome our help. Are Beatrice and Mary available?"

Alyna remained where she was as Enid hurried off to find the maids and ask Charles to help. An undertaking of this sort was just what Alyna needed today. Something to work on that she could control. Besides, it would keep her well away from Royce. She wasn't ready to beard that dragon. Florence seemed to pale in comparison.

Before long, Enid returned with Beatrice and Mary as well as rags and a bucket of steaming water. As Alyna explained what needed to be done, the two maids looked at her with doubt-filled expressions.

"Charles is on his way with a ladder," Enid added in an attempt to reassure them.

"'Tisn't that," Beatrice said. She glanced around the hall and lowered her voice. "Lady Florence told us no one was to touch the hall without her permission."

"That's right," Mary added. "We wanted to clean it weeks ago, and she wouldn't even let us change the rushes before his lordship's return."

Alyna shared a look with Enid. Why would Florence order such a thing? What could she gain by not performing the duties she'd volunteered for? Obviously, Florence felt no need to prove her worth by excelling at her responsibilities.

Florence's actions mattered not. There was no logical reason to delay cleaning the hall, and Alyna refused to ask Florence's permission to do anything.

"All will be well. I take full responsibility. If Lady Florence questions you about this, send her to me."

The maids warmed to the task with Alyna's words.

Charles arrived, carrying a ladder with Nicholas trailing behind, his hand on the ladder too. "Good morn to you, Lady Alyna."

"And to you, Charles." Alyna smiled when he winked at Enid, who in turn blushed like a young maid. The journey to Northe Castle might have been difficult for them both, but they'd bonded in a way she would've never guessed possible.

"We men are here to aid you, aren't we, Nicholas?" Charles said as he leaned the ladder against the wall.

The boy nodded, his expression solemn. He mimicked Charles stance and stood with hands on hips as Charles greeted Beatrice and Mary. The maids giggled like young girls until Enid glared them into silence. A wise man, Charles said nothing and proceeded with the task. He climbed the ladder toward the first tapestry with Nicholas right behind him.

"Oh, no, you don't, young man." Alyna snatched Nicholas off the rungs just before he climbed out of her reach.

"Nay, Mama!" His bottom lip quivered and his big blue eyes filled with tears. "We are men!"

Well used to his tactics, Alyna shook her head. "That is very convincing, don't you think, Enid?"

"Indeed. An especially good performance, Nicholas."

"What do you think of this one?" Alyna asked. Then she tickled him until he laughed so hard he could barely catch his breath.

"I prefer that one." Enid tickled him as well, and Nicholas was happily occupied until the tapestries and weapons were lowered down to the maids.

Mary recruited more servants, and they hauled everything outside for a thorough cleaning. Beatrice saw to the scrubbing of the stones above the hearth and Alyna pitched in where she saw a need.

The battle scenes in the tapestries were clearly visible now as they lay drying in the sun, their colors vibrant and true.

If only the same were true of how she felt about Royce. Even more confusing was the question of how he felt about her.

❖—❖—❖

Royce watched the men training in the bailey, the sound of metal clanging in the crisp morning air. Edward rode his black destrier through the portcullis and Royce gestured for him to draw near.

With obvious reluctance, Edward guided his mount to where Royce stood. "Greetings, Royce. A fine day, is it not?"

Royce looked up at the knight, anger taking a strong hold on him. "Have you recovered from your foul behavior of last night?"

"Aye, that I have." He nodded to emphasize his point.

"Stay away from Lady Alyna, Edward."

The younger knight's eyes narrowed at Royce's demand. "I answer only to Blackwell, Royce. With whom I spend time is none of your concern."

"It is when you behave like an oaf. Stay away from her." Royce clamped down on his anger. Emotions of any sort would not serve him well. "I expect you to join the training. Now."

Without bothering to answer, Edward rode his horse toward the stables.

Royce found Edward's actions disturbing, especially when added to the information Alyna had shared. He'd keep a closer watch on the surly knight.

"What excuse does he have?" Hugh asked, as he approached Royce, his axe strapped to his side.

"None that bears merit."

"I think we need to keep an eye on the man."

"Indeed, we will. I'm not the only one who thinks he's acting strangely, eh?"

Hugh scoffed. "Edward has always acted strangely, but lately, his behavior has moved to suspicious. Either he has a wench distracting him, or he's up to something."

The mention of a woman made Royce grit his teeth. If Edward failed to heed his warning to stay away from Alyna, there would be hell to pay. Never mind that he was demanding Edward behave the way Royce seemed unable to.

If he relived his kiss with her once more, he was certain he'd...he didn't know what he'd do, but it wouldn't be good. He'd never thought to encounter a woman who aroused him so. The mere thought of her distracted him completely from whatever task he was supposed to be doing. Her beauty took his breath away, but it was more than that. Much more. He was at a loss to explain it.

He'd thought about it all night, certain if he discovered why she affected him the way she did, he'd be able to remove that reason by whatever means necessary. But he could find nothing at which to take aim, nothing upon which to strike a blow.

The look of hurt on her face when he'd put her aside had pierced his soul as surely as an arrow. To know that he'd added to the sadness she wore like a cloak was nearly more than he could stand.

Even this morning, as he'd watched the sun rise after a long, sleepless night, he'd thought of telling her the truth. There was nothing wrong with her. She was...well, she was perfect. It was him. The fault lay with him.

However, the very act of telling her would remove the barrier he'd erected. He was certain she'd keep her distance from him after last night. Lord knew he didn't seem to have the strength to do it, but now he could rely on her to stay away.

He had no time for lust. All his energies needed to be focused on resolving the issue of the thieves who besieged Northe Castle and on vengeance. Nothing else.

"And you, Royce? Are you preoccupied by a woman?"

Royce looked at Hugh in attempt to discern his meaning. Surely no one had witnessed the kiss he'd shared with Alyna.

Hugh elbowed him in the side, a sly smile on his face. "I saw the way you watched Lady Alyna at supper. She is lovely, isn't she?" He looked back at the sparring men. His voice softened as he continued. "It's as if she has no idea how beautiful she is. There's something about the way she moves, with a grace that only a true lady has."

Royce caught himself nodding in agreement. He looked more closely at Hugh and could see a glint of humor in the man's expression. His friend had led him down a path to a neatly laid snare he'd nearly stepped into. Two could play at this game. "I didn't really notice Alyna last eve. But you know who captured my interest?"

He paused just long enough to make certain he had Hugh's full attention. "Lady Florence. Did you note her attire?" Royce shook his head as though still in awe. "A mature woman like she, who knows her own mind, would surely know how to please a man."

Hugh stared at him in utter disbelief.

With as much innocence as he could muster, Royce

asked, "What?"

Hugh shook his head. "You, my friend, are a sick, depraved soul." The large man heaved a sigh. "We need to have a long talk, you and I." He stalked away, his hand gripping the head of his axe, still shaking his head.

Royce allowed himself a smile. He'd definitely won that round. He sensed a presence behind him and turned. Alyna's son stood a few feet away and stared up at him, a perplexed look upon his face.

Royce glanced around but didn't see the lad's mother anywhere. Relieved, he drew near and squatted down to the boy's level. "Nicholas, what are you doing out here?"

The boy just continued to look at him.

"Does your mother know where you are?"

Solemn, Nicholas shook his head.

"Then shouldn't you go inside and find her? She'll be worried about you."

The boy just looked at him, those blue eyes examining him with a scrutiny that most adults didn't use. "Do you have any rocks?"

Puzzled, Royce looked at the ground around him, but saw none. "You're searching for rocks?"

"A special rock."

Royce had spent very little time with children, but he knew Nicholas was no ordinary child. He enjoyed spending time with the boy. Yet he knew the longer Nicholas remained with him, the more likely Alyna would come in search of him.

"If I promise to look for rocks, will you go inside to your mother?"

The little boy pondered his suggestion for a moment before nodding in agreement. He walked slowly toward the steps of the keep, but paused and looked back at Royce.

As sure as he breathed, Royce knew Nicholas would remind him of his promise. Royce nodded to reassure him, and Nicholas smiled. The boy trotted up the steps, slipping inside the heavy door as someone came out.

Royce smiled to himself as he walked back toward the men, scanning the ground for an interesting rock.

⚜ ⚜ ⚜

Alyna dug in the warm damp earth, happy with her progress in the few days since her arrival. Her grandfather had been pleased with her efforts in the great hall. The memory of his reaction made her smile. His eyes had lit with pleasure at the vivid tapestries, and he'd explained that her grandmother had woven them. His appreciation for her small accomplishments was so different from how her father reacted, always making her feel as though what she did was never enough. Her grandfather's kind words and attentiveness, along with the way he treated her as an equal, had increased her confidence in the short time she'd been here.

Now if only she could convince him to explain why he'd brought her here. She was beginning to suspect more was going on than what she'd first thought. He'd told her there was no hurry to discuss details, that he was simply enjoying her company. While she appreciated his sentiment, the time was nearing when they needed to have an honest discussion on all fronts.

Thanks to Charles, the herb garden was taking shape. He'd widened it and turned the soil where he could without disturbing the few plants that grew. After the mid-day meal, she'd put on her oldest kirtle and intended to make the most of the remainder of the afternoon.

The sky was cloudless, a blue so deep, so bright, that her eyes hurt to look at it. The air was beginning to lose the underlying chill winter had left. Alyna took a moment to enjoy the beauty of the day before focusing on the work before her.

She cleared out the weeds and found more salvageable herbs than she'd hoped for. Rosemary, sage, and parsley she transplanted to one side of the garden for use as seasonings for the kitchens. She'd met with the cook again to discuss what was needed for meals. The suggestions she'd made for preparation and seasoning of many dishes had been well received and before long, they'd have more herbs to use.

The ground she now worked would be planted with herbs used for healing and other needs around the castle. Lavender and tansy would be needed to spread on the straw mattresses. They'd need marjoram to use in healing salves for the injuries that were a matter of daily life. The small plot would eventually have to be widened. She had a collection of seeds Enid had brought from Montvue along with some basic supplies and her mother's journal.

That book was very helpful, as her mother's interest and knowledge had ranged far and wide. She'd studied and experimented with herbs for the most effective methods to help others. Alyna only hoped she would one day become as talented at healing as her mother had been.

She heard the side door of the keep open and looked up from her work, hoping Nicholas had come to visit her.

Florence.

They'd had several unpleasant encounters over the last few days and Alyna expected nothing less from this one. The woman was always picking a fight.

"Well, well. What do we have here?" Florence

asked, a condescending smile upon her lips. "The lady of the manor doing a little gardening? How quaint. I see you even donned your peasant attire for the task."

"What do you want, Florence?" She continued to weed, not bothering to look at her or stand to address her with courtesy.

"Why, I want for nothing, Alyna. Haven't you yet observed that?"

Alyna's snort may have been unladylike, but she truly didn't care.

Her face tight with anger, Florence said, "Do you think to enter Lord Blackwell's good graces by cleaning his keep?"

Alyna stopped weeding. Was it so wrong to want her grandfather to need her?

Florence continued on, apparently aware she'd hit a nerve. "Servants are for cleaning. Ladies are for beauty and pleasure, but I can see why you try to compensate for your lack of talent in those areas by trying to excel as a steward. Besides, I specifically told you to consult me if you needed any of the servants."

Anger drove her upright despite her fear that Florence spoke the truth. "I do not answer to you, Florence. If you don't care for what I do, discuss it with my grandfather."

"Don't think I won't." She took a step closer. "How I pity you. Perhaps someday a man will come along who's willing to offer for someone with your questionable looks. Of course, with that boy hanging on your skirts, 'tis not likely, is it?"

As Florence spoke, she carelessly trampled the patch of herbs Alyna had so diligently tended. Her comments had the same effect on Alyna's emotions as on the tender plants. Alyna was not about to let Florence know that. Her father had often told her she was no beauty. She didn't need to be reminded of it.

And what harm could come from endearing herself to her grandfather with a little hard work? From being helpful and contributing to where she presently lived?

"Beauty will fade with time, Florence. Surely someone of your own maturity is already noting that fact. Perhaps you should've accepted an offer some time ago before the affects of time were so evident." Alyna warmed to the topic. "Oh, but perhaps you didn't receive any offers. That would certainly explain your presence in my grandfather's home. Now get off those plants."

From Florence's gasp of outrage, Alyna was certain her aim had hit its mark.

With a huff, Florence flounced back into the keep. While Alyna was ashamed of her own behavior, she refused to dwell on it. She hoped Florence had learned she was not an easy target. 'Twas a shame she had no cowslip flowers to calm Florence. It seemed the woman was always in an overexcited state. Alyna bent down to repair the damaged plants as best she could, trying her best to put the unpleasant encounter out of her mind.

⁕⁓⁕⁓⁕

Royce knocked on the chamber door, reluctant to disturb Lord Blackwell so late at night, but the news he'd received left him no choice. "My lord?" he called out softly, "'tis Royce."

After a brief pause, Blackwell answered, "Enter."

Royce heard the concern in his lord's voice. Someone at the door in the middle of the night was never a good thing. He entered the room, closing the door behind him. A lone candle provided meager light and revealed Blackwell as he sat up in the large bed, his brow furrowed with concern. "I'm sorry to disturb you, my lord, but a messenger has arrived."

"What news does he have?"

"Not good I'm afraid. An attempt has been made on Lord Pimbroke's life."

Blackwell closed his eyes. Royce well knew that hearing his liege lord's life was in danger was disturbing. "He yet lives?"

"Aye, but it sounds like it was a near miss. The messenger awaits you in the great hall."

Blackwell threw back the covers and stood. "We can't take any chances. If Pimbroke is killed, our cause could be lost."

"True, but this could be a trap, an attempt to force us to reveal ourselves."

"We will proceed with caution, but action must be taken. I'll leave at once," said Blackwell as he drew on a tunic and chausses.

"My lord, I would ask that you let me go in your place. The danger is too high. We can't risk losing you."

Lord Blackwell put his hand on Royce's shoulder. "I appreciate your concern, but 'tis I who must speak with Pimbroke. He is my liege lord and while this information will be difficult to believe coming from me, coming from you..." He shook his head.

"It would sound implausible." Yet Royce was loathe to have Blackwell make a hurried trek in the middle of the night when danger was so near. "Mayhap if I took your seal? Surely he'd believe me then."

"Nay, Royce. It's time for me to tell him what we know, or at the very least, suspect. I must gain his trust in this matter. If I fail to do so, not only will Tegmont keep Larkspur, but others will be in danger as well."

Royce was reluctant to agree, but saw Blackwell's

logic.

"Let's hear what other details the messenger can provide. The more we know, the stronger our position," Blackwell said.

Once again, Royce was grateful he'd found Blackwell. Without his support, Royce would be in no position to challenge his uncle.

CHAPTER TEN

*"Waybread applied to the skin
promotes healing of sores and wounds."*
Lady Catherine's Herbal Journal

Alyna sat near the window of her chamber, her eyes focused on the needlework she attempted to complete, her mind focused on anything but.

A gentle breeze from the open window filled the chamber with fresh spring air and drew her gaze away from her work. If she leaned forward a bit, she could see the men-at-arms and knights who trained outside, their swords and shields flashing in the afternoon sun. The yard rang with the sound of metal striking metal and the men grunting with their efforts, some shouting encouragement, and others shouting reprimands.

With a heavy sigh, Alyna turned back to her needlework. The gray thread had tangled and knotted as surely as her thoughts. She studied the dark strands, certain she should've chosen a different color. This one reminded her too much of Royce's eyes, the blue-gray of storm clouds.

Royce wasn't the only reason for her confused thoughts. She'd awakened that morning determined to speak with her grandfather regarding the questions that had burned in her mind since Royce had taken her. She'd ventured into the hall early, but none of the servants had seen him since the night before. At last she'd found one who had told her that he'd left before daybreak and wouldn't return for several days.

Alyna was disappointed and hurt that he'd said nothing to her of a trip last night when they'd conversed during supper. She'd nearly made an excuse to be absent from the meal as she grew tired of listening to Florence's subtle digs. The improvements Alyna had made annoyed the woman to no end as had Blackwell's approval of the changes.

However, Alyna had no intention of allowing Florence to gain any advantage over her, especially with her grandfather. Their relationship was too new, and Alyna knew it couldn't bear the weight of disapproval. She needed more time to prove her worth to him.

She hadn't felt prepared to face Royce either, but decided she wasn't willing to hide like a mouse in a corner. Though she'd thought long and hard about how she should act with Royce, she'd come up with nothing clever, other than acting as though the kiss they'd shared had affected her little. Ha! That would be no easy task. Just thinking of the kiss now brought a blush to her cheeks.

All the worry and nervousness had been for naught, as neither of the two people who complicated her life had bothered to come for the evening meal.

So worried had she been about their imminent arrival, she hadn't even attempted to broach her questions with her grandfather. Now she berated herself for the wasted opportunity.

"Mama?" Concern laced her son's voice, interrupting her thoughts.

"What's wrong, Nicholas?" One look at his expression told her it was something serious.

He crossed the room from where he'd been playing with some wooden blocks that Charles had made for him and took her hand. "We need to go out," he said.

Unsure what bothered him, she smoothed a hand over his soft, dark hair and cupped his cheek. "Let me work a bit longer, and then we'll go outside and find Charles. How does that sound?"

"Nay, Mama. We need to go out now." He pulled her hand, trying his best to get her to move.

Something was bothering him and until she found out what it was, she decided it best to humor him. She set aside her needlework and stood, glancing out the window as she did so.

She could see and hear Hugh, his size alone enough to make him obvious. She also recognized Matthew and Edward, who parried back and forth, one thrusting, the other blocking, then their roles reversed. They paused and Matthew removed his helm to wipe his brow. He glanced up and caught sight of her. With flourish, he bowed deep at the waist and sent her a grin. She smiled and waved in return.

Edward looked up as well to see what held Matthew's attention. He bowed his head and smiled. She acknowledged his greeting with a nod, but didn't return his smile. He was another person she'd been avoiding at all costs. Perhaps it had just been the drink that had made him so bold, but she had no desire to find out.

She recognized some of the other men but saw no sign of Royce. Had he left with her grandfather?

"Mama, please," Nicholas pleaded.

"Show me what's wrong, darling," she told him, his hand firmly in hers.

A shout from below stole her attention yet again. Nicholas dropped her hand and ran to look out the window, stretching up on his toes. Alyna lifted him and held him tight as she leaned out the window casement to offer them both a better view.

The men gathered around someone lying on the ground. Her heart in her throat, she searched the crowd of men, but even at this distance, she knew Royce was still not among them. Surely the injured man couldn't be him.

"Oh, dear," she muttered.

"Hurry, Mama."

"Aye, we must hurry." She set Nicholas down and fetched her bag with herbs and remedies for common injuries that Enid had brought from Montvue.

As she and Nicholas hurried down the stairs, she could only hope her limited knowledge would aid the injured man.

Enid stood with one foot on the stairs as though on her way to fetch Alyna. "There's been a terrible accident, my lady," she said as she plucked Nicholas off the bottom step.

Alyna pushed through the small group gathered in the great hall and caught sight of a soldier lying prone on top of one of the long, oak tables.

Her breath caught when she at last saw who it was. Matthew lay pale and still upon the table. How could this be? She had just seen him with that shy grin of his moments before. Blood coated the mail on his shoulder and as she neared, she could see more blood pooled near it. The links of mail had been split open. She could only wonder at the force of the blow that could penetrate the protection of the metal rings and cause so much damage.

"Remove his mail as carefully as possible," she directed one of the knights who stood nearby. "Enid, fetch some cloths and water."

Hugh stood near Matthew, worry etched upon his somber face, his blue eyes dark with concern.

"What happened?" she asked.

The big man helped ease the mail from the unconscious young knight, no easy task when a knight was awake and well, let alone when he lay motionless. One of the men on Matthew's other side assisted him. "He was engaged in swordplay when something went amiss, my lady. I wasn't watching them when it happened and from what I can garner, no one else seemed to be either."

Alyna waited impatiently as the two men completed their difficult task. Matthew remained unconscious. She felt the weight of a stare and looked up to see Edward's gaze upon her from the back of the group. Had it been his sword that had struck this terrible blow? Even as the question formed in her mind, Edward looked away, his face blank of expression.

At the moment, discovering the guilty party was not her concern. She hovered beside Hugh, helping when she could. At last the mail was off, and she realized the wound was even worse than she'd thought.

Blood soaked Matthew's aketon, staining the padded garment a bright crimson. She instructed Hugh to cut the side of it, taking care not to jostle his shoulder as its odd angle spoke of a broken bone. Her stomach turned at the sight of the bleeding wound, her concern for Matthew mounting. He remained unconscious, his color pale, his skin clammy to the touch.

Enid handed her cloths and a basin of water, but as fast as she wiped away the blood, more took its place. Small links of steel and bits of thread were embedded in the wound. She dipped the linen in water and wrung it over the wound, washing away some of the pieces, but until the bleeding slowed, she couldn't see well enough to remove them all.

She looked for Edward, certain he was to blame, her anger at the extent of Matthew's injuries guiding her gaze. But the knight was no longer in her line of vision.

Alyna feared this task was beyond her modest skills. Panic clawed at her as blood soaked the cloth she pressed against the injury. The last time she'd seen this much blood had been when Myranda had died. She well knew that if the wound festered, it could lead to death.

A deep breath did little to ease her fear that they would lose Matthew, but she focused on what needed to be done next. She folded clean strips of linen into thick pads and placed them over the wound. Hugh shifted Matthew so she could bind them in place, and she discovered the weapon had plunged through. "Oh, dear."

"I was afraid of that," Hugh said as he looked at the wound on his back.

"How bad is it, my lady?" Royce asked from beside her.

Relief washed through her at the sight of him. "The sword penetrated his shoulder. He's losing a lot of blood. The front bone of his shoulder is broken."

Royce shook his head, his concern obvious. "Tell me how to help."

His steady regard gave her the confidence she needed. "We need to get the bleeding stopped so the wound can be cleaned. Pieces of mail and cloth are in there and the injury won't heal properly until they're removed."

He nodded in understanding.

"We should move him to where he'll be more comfortable," she suggested.

"I'll see to that. What else?" he asked.

She blew out a breath to release the tension that gripped her. This wasn't something she had to deal with alone; Royce was by her side. The thought steadied her, allowing her to think more clearly. "I need some supplies to prepare a remedy for the pain. Is there a healer in the village we could send for? Someone who would have the herbs I need?"

Royce's gaze left her face and rested on the still form of Matthew. "Mayhap we should send for Gunnell."

Hugh looked startled at the suggestion. "Gunnell? Surely not." Turning toward Alyna, he asked, "Is there not more you can do for him, my lady?"

Confused by their comments, Alyna sorted through her bag, though she knew exactly what it contained. She had marjoram to keep the swelling down, but no white willow to use if he developed a fever and very little of anything for his pain. "The few things I have won't be enough." She looked at Royce. "Is there a problem with the healer? If you feel she'll do more harm than good, I'll try my best, but I at least need supplies from her."

"Gunnell will have the herbs you need," Royce said. "Hugh, go get her. Tell her she must come, that Lady Alyna needs her assistance."

"But, Royce—" Hugh began.

"We can't risk losing Matthew. Now go and be quick."

Hugh left with no further argument, but his expression told his thoughts well enough.

"What is the problem with her?" Alyna asked.

"She is a good healer, but there is some talk that she is..." Royce hesitated. "That is to say, she's not quite..." He rubbed his chin with a finger. "Well, some say she's crazed."

"Crazed?" Alyna repeated in amazement. "How

so?"

"You'll understand after you meet her." Royce gave a small shrug. "Shall we move him to a chamber?"

"Aye." As best she could, she pushed aside the concern that Royce's comment raised.

With the help of a few of the men, they moved Matthew to a small solar as gently as possible. The room was reserved for guests who stayed the night. A single narrow window allowed bright sunshine to stream in.

Alyna sent everyone out of the room except for Royce and a maid, who helped remove Matthew's boots and his remaining clothing. Alyna adjusted his pillow and pulled a blanket over his still form. The bandage would need to be changed soon, but hopefully the healer would arrive by then.

The maid left to fetch some hot water and a few other things to use in preparation of a poultice Alyna wanted to make, assuming Gunnell had the herbs she needed. She checked her bag one last time to see if she'd overlooked anything.

Then there was nothing to do but wait for Gunnell. Time crawled by as Alyna and Royce waited, both staring at the unconscious Matthew.

Alyna's gaze slid to Royce, wondering what his thoughts were. He was without his mail again today; his simple cream overtunic showed the breadth of his shoulders and emphasized his sun-darkened skin. She couldn't help her attraction to him, no matter that he didn't feel that way about her.

She'd been so angry when he'd called their kiss a mistake. Angry and disappointed. How could she have thought for even a moment that a man like Royce might find her attractive? She had no attributes to hold his attention, and she would do well to remember that.

The squeeze on her heart hurt, but how much worse would it feel if she grew to care for him? And, oh, she knew she could. She must guard her heart or risk losing it forever.

Now was not the time to dwell on the matter. Matthew's life was more important than any feelings she might have for Royce. With that thought firmly in mind, she asked, "Should I trust Gunnell?"

Before he could answer, a quiet knock sounded at the door.

"Here she be," Hugh announced from the doorway, his hand holding the healer's arm, disapproval written on his face.

The woman looked normal, much to Alyna's relief. She appeared to be a little older than Alyna, but perhaps that was only due to a hard life. A wimple hid her hair, and her stout form was clothed in a plain brown woolen tunic. She carried a wooden box tucked under her arm. It reassured Alyna to think the woman had come prepared. "Thank you for coming, Gunnell."

The woman tugged her elbow away from Hugh's grasp, gave a quick curtsy to Alyna and Royce, then went to Matthew's bedside. She briefly touched his head, then his chest, and finally the wrapped wound. In a calm and steady voice, she announced, "He will live, but he has a battle before him."

Surprised at her quick prognosis, given without examining the injured knight, Alyna sent a puzzled look at Royce. One corner of his mouth lifted, something vaguely resembling a smile. Hugh, on the other hand, looked horrified.

Alyna realized neither man would offer any help in interpreting the healer's pronouncement. "Gunnell, what do you mean by this?"

A blush rose up the woman's cheeks, and she stammered a response. "I–I believe he will survive this wound, my lady, nothing more." Obviously uncomfortable, she set her chest on the bed, opened it, and took out several small pouches.

The maid had all the things Alyna had requested as well as more linen strips to bind the wound.

Alyna removed the blood-soaked bandages, relieved to see the bleeding had slowed. With Gunnell's competent assistance, Alyna slowly removed bits of mail and linen from the injury, relieved Matthew was unconscious rather than moaning in pain as she poked and prodded.

Gunnell handed her a small pot. "Oil."

Alyna nodded in understanding, and then dabbed a light coating of it on the area surrounding Matthew's wound.

"What purpose does that serve?" Hugh asked.

"It keeps the herbs from sticking," Alyna answered. With Gunnell's supplies, she made a healing poultice of thyme, mustard, hot water, wine and milk then applied it. She wrapped his shoulder in linen strips to hold the poultice in place.

"Well done, my lady. You have a fine touch," Gunnell commented, her gaze steady on Alyna's.

"Thank you," Alyna said. It was nice to have another healer's approval. "The broken bone should heal as it appears to be in alignment."

"Aye. Lucky for him that we don't have to set it. I'll leave this with you for his pain," Gunnell said and handed another small clay pot to Alyna. "You'll need to add some wine to it and get him to drink it."

"Excellent. Do you have something for a fever as well?"

At last, Gunnell prepared to leave. Without warning, she grasped Alyna's hand for a brief moment and stared hard into her eyes. As Alyna watched, the healer's pupils dilated. In a quiet tone, she told Alyna,

"Your destiny has not yet changed." She squeezed Alyna's hand before releasing it, almost as though she knew this was not what Alyna had wanted to hear. "I would like to meet the boy."

Mouth agape, Alyna stood frozen in shock.

The healer tucked her box under her arm and turned toward the door. "I'll return later to check on the knight."

With a worried glance at Alyna, Hugh followed Gunnell.

Stunned at the healer's words, Alyna put a hand to her stomach to ease the sinking sensation there. What could Gunnell have meant? How had she known about Nicholas?

Royce came up behind her and placed his hands on her arms. "What did she say to upset you so?"

Well aware of how closely he watched her, she did her best to regain her composure. "Nothing. 'Twas nothing."

"'Nothing' would not have you this upset." He turned her to face him, his hands still holding her.

She shook her head and attempted a small smile. Though she knew she should step back, she remained where she was. His concern comforted her. Heat from his warm hands spread up her body to her cheeks, and she bowed her head to hide the flush he could surely see.

But he did not allow it. He lifted her chin with a gentle finger. "Alyna, tell me what she said," he demanded.

She swallowed, determined not to make a fool of herself by throwing her arms around his neck and holding tight. She would not lean upon him. She couldn't. He was not for her. "She told me my destiny had not changed, and she'd like to meet the boy."

His brow furrowed. "Do you know what she

meant?"

"Aye, I think I do."

He rubbed her arms lightly. "Do not put too much credence in the things she says."

"Why?"

Royce shrugged. "None of us really understand Gunnell."

Alyna bit her lip. If he thought Gunnell was crazed, what would he think of Nicholas as his second sight emerged? Though he'd shown only minor evidence of his ability, she knew it was only a matter of time. Nothing was more important to her than protecting Nicholas, including her feelings for this handsome knight. The day would come when someone called Nicholas crazed. The thought itself was nearly more than she could bear, but what if that person were Royce?

CHAPTER ELEVEN

*"Bites from rabid dogs can be treated
with wild rose, but I wonder if
effectiveness improves with a full moon."*
Lady Catherine's Herbal Journal

Matthew stirred, moaning as he moved.

Royce glanced at the knight and then back at Alyna. Why did she seem suddenly distant? What had he said that closed her off from him?

Matthew moaned again, and Alyna pulled away from Royce to see to the injured man.

"This conversation is not finished, my lady." Somehow, Royce felt he'd disappointed her, but he had no idea how. Frustrated, he joined her as Matthew's eyelids fluttered open. His gaze rested first upon Royce, then upon Alyna. Royce recognized the glaze over his eyes, for he had seen it many times and had felt it for himself. Pain.

"How do you fare, Matthew?" Alyna asked as she touched his forehead.

As always, Alyna brought a smile to the young knight's face. Royce wondered if Alyna realized Matthew was half in love with her.

"I'm a bit–sore, my lady." His gaze locked on Royce. "What happened?"

"We're hoping you can tell us," Royce answered.

Alyna's look berated Royce better than any words could have. "Matthew, just rest now. You can tell us later what happened. Suffice it to say you were injured during training."

The younger man's eyes fluttered closed, making Royce wonder if he had lost consciousness again. He grasped Matthew's hand and squeezed gently, hoping to give him some of his own strength.

Matthew opened his eyes again. This time his gaze settled on Royce. "How bad...is it?"

Royce glanced at Alyna. He knew she'd prefer he make light of the matter. "You will survive to fight another day," he said in a tone that brooked no argument. "The sword went through your shoulder and broke a bone."

"Did you send for a priest?"

"No need. As I said, you'll be fine."

He shifted, wincing with pain. "Gunnell?"

"Aye."

"And?" At Royce's hesitation, the younger man prodded him, his gaze worried. "I must...know. Tell me."

Reluctant to repeat anything the woman said, Royce answered all the same. "She said you will live." No need to worry him with talk of a battle to fight.

"Truly?"

"Ask Lady Alyna if I speak the truth."

Alyna nodded and a small smile graced Matthew's lips, easing the pinched expression on his pale face.

"We have something to give you for your pain, Matthew," she said as she prepared the remedy Gunnell had left.

Together, Royce and Alyna lifted Matthew so he could drink.

At the first sip, he grimaced. "Oh, 'tis nasty."

Alyna shared an amused look with Royce. "I know,

but 'twill ease the pain in your shoulder. Drink it down quickly," she encouraged him.

Just as Royce knew he would've done, Matthew took one look at Alyna and drank the whole cup of potion without further complaint, though he couldn't hide a scowl after he swallowed the last of it. Before long, his eyes grew heavy, and soon he rested peacefully.

Royce sat on the edge of Matthew's bed, once again wondering how this had happened. He knew Edward had been Matthew's sparring partner, but Royce couldn't believe Edward would deliberately hurt one of the men. What purpose would it serve? Royce had no doubt that Hugh would find out the circumstances, even if he had to beat it out of Edward.

"He has a long night ahead of him," Alyna murmured. She still held the empty cup, her worried gaze on Matthew.

"Aye," he answered, "but Gunnell said he would pull through, and we must have faith in that."

Alyna looked surprised at his words.

He shrugged. "Sometimes she speaks the truth. I hope that it is true with Matthew. Will you explain what she said to you?"

Alyna's gaze rested on him for a moment, her expression somber. "'Tis a long story and best saved for another day."

She moved to the small table and tidied the various pots and pouches Gunnell had left. Her movements were efficient and graceful and riveted his attention. He couldn't help but wonder what those clever hands would feel like on him. With a sigh at his wayward thoughts, he closed his eyes in an attempt to get her out of his head. Why had he thought staying away from her would change anything?

"Royce, do you know when my grandfather will

return?"

Royce opened his eyes but kept his gaze on Matthew, pretending his thoughts were centered on the young man lying in the bed rather than on the lady beside him. As though his mind hadn't been tangled with visions of her since he'd met her.

He'd expected her to ask about Lord Blackwell's departure. Although Blackwell had known he'd eventually make this journey, neither he nor Royce had realized it would be quite so soon.

Lord Blackwell thought the best way to improve Royce's chance of regaining Larkspur was to convince his liege lord, Lord Pimbroke, of their cause. While they had little proof that Tegmont murdered Royce's parents, they did have a few pieces of information that pointed to Tegmont's involvement with a group of barons said to be disloyal to the king. That alone should be enough to gain Lord Pimbroke's aid.

Yet all that would be for naught if Pimbroke was murdered before Blackwell got to him.

"A few days is all," he said at last, hoping his answer would come to pass.

Alyna studied him, her gaze narrowing, making him wonder if he'd sounded as uncertain as he felt.

Blackwell had been waiting for Lord Pimbroke to return from a tour of his holdings, a trip that took months. But the threat to Pimbroke's life changed everything. It was too easy for someone to arrange an accident or a robbery for a traveling lord. Pimbroke's loyalty to the king was well known which made him an obvious target. The information the messenger had brought might be true, simply a rumor, or even a way to lure Lord Blackwell away from the fortifications of Northe Castle. Yet Blackwell had had no choice but to respond.

He and Blackwell had briefly discussed what to

tell Alyna and had agreed it was best if she knew as little as possible about Tegmont's involvement with the barons until they were able to confirm their suspicions and finalize a plan.

But what to tell Alyna now? While she deserved answers, he had few to offer her, and Lord Blackwell should be the one to give them. His gaze still on Matthew, Royce added with what he hoped was a casual tone, "His business shouldn't take long."

"And what business would that be?"

He berated himself for not holding his tongue, for she latched onto the comment like a hound with a juicy bone.

Royce looked up at her, yet found he'd made another tactical error. How could a man look into those eyes and not confess all? She seemed confused and hurt by her grandfather's abrupt departure. "He didn't mention to what it pertained."

She stared hard at him, and he steeled himself to keep his mouth shut. "Where did he go? How many men did he take with him?"

Royce nearly squirmed. "I'm not certain."

Disbelief crossed her face. "You don't know how many men he took?"

Another mistake. Would this interrogation never end? "I believe it was six or seven."

"Indeed." Now she paced before him, all but ignoring the injured knight she'd treated so tenderly moments before. "What direction did they ride?"

He stared at her, incredulous at her question. "What possible difference does that make?"

She colored slightly, but held her ground. "Did he ride to Montvue?"

"Why would he do that? I just brought you from there." Royce started to enjoy himself, curious to see how her mind worked and where she thought her grandfather had gone.

She lifted a shoulder. "I thought perhaps he needed to speak with my father about...things."

"What things would that be?" He well knew but was curious to see how she'd explain it.

She turned away, obviously exasperated by his questions. "My broken betrothal, of course. Do you think Lord Tegmont will accept my disappearance without question? That he'll take no retribution against my father?" She began to pace again. "If you know Lord Tegmont, then you know he will make someone pay."

Alyna had obviously been thinking about the matter for some time. She did not speak of how she felt about her broken betrothal, only of how it affected her father. Just as Royce opened his mouth to ask, Matthew stirred.

Immediately, Alyna was at his side, her hand on his forehead. "He's cool yet, but I'd be surprised if a fever doesn't take hold before morning."

She wet a cloth in the basin of water nearby and wiped Matthew's face, and he soon settled down again.

Royce reminded himself it mattered little how she felt about not marrying Tegmont. It did not concern him. The sooner he could get her out of the chamber, the better. He didn't want to answer anymore of her questions. "I'll stay with him for a bit. Then I'll have one of the maids sit with him."

Alyna opened her mouth to protest, but Royce placed a finger against her lips before she could speak. Her eyes locked with his and drew him nearer. "Matthew will get worse before he gets better. You'll need your strength in the days to come." Unable to resist, he lifted his finger and touched the softness of her cheek. "Go and get something to eat, my lady."

Those amber eyes remained on his, but when she

released her breath, the soft sound drew his gaze to
her parted lips. He traced their outline with a gentle
finger. Her mouth was perfectly shaped, not too
narrow nor too wide. All thought and reason drained
from his mind. He cupped her cheek and lowered his
mouth to hers. The sweetness proved irresistible, and
he deepened the kiss to better taste her.

She froze and for a moment, he thought she'd pull
away. Then her soft tongue responded, and desire for
her burned through him. He reached for her waist to
draw her closer, but somehow his hands arrived at her
elbows.

She drew back to look up at him. "I believe the last
time we kissed, you called it a mistake. I would not
want you to regret it yet again, Sir Royce."

The color on her cheeks belied the formality of her
words and the coolness of her tone. "I bid you good
day." She glanced one last time at Matthew and left
the room.

He watched her depart, unsettled by the finality of
her farewell. Heaving a sigh of frustration, he sat in
the chair beside Matthew's bed. With a wince of
discomfort, he leaned back to adjust his chausses.

What was he going to do about that woman? Why
couldn't he simply leave her be? Where was his famed
determination when she was near? Somehow, that
quality worked against him when he was with her.

Matthew groaned, bringing Royce's thoughts back
to the task at hand. He'd seen men slain before and
dealt with the consequences, but Matthew held a
special place in his life. He was a kind, good-hearted
lad and didn't deserve to be in this situation.

Royce closed his eyes and rubbed his hands over
his face, tired from the events of the day. He sensed a
presence and caught his breath, wondering if Alyna
had returned. But Nicholas stood before him, his blue

eyes alight with a smile.

"Slipped away from your mother again, did you?" Royce asked.

The little boy grinned in response, and Royce couldn't help but smile.

"Do you have the rock?" Nicholas asked, a hopeful expression on his face.

"I have something you might like." Royce dug in the pouch tied to his belt, glad he'd taken the time to find the shiny, multi-colored stone. He handed it to the boy, certain he'd be pleased. "What do you think of this one?"

His dark head bent, Nicholas examined the stone from all angles. With a solemn face, he looked up at Royce and shook his head.

Disappointed, Royce asked, "Not the one you were looking for?"

Again, the boy shook his head. Then, with the quick change of moods that only children master, he grinned. "May I keep it?"

Royce chuckled, his own mood lightened by the boy's. "Aye. You keep it, and I'll look some more."

With a wave and a grin, the boy was gone, leaving Royce with a lingering smile and determination to continue searching for just the right rock.

❖ ❖ ❖

Alyna rose before dawn, surprised one of the maids hadn't fetched her during the night. Anxious to check on Matthew, she washed and dressed, moving quietly to avoid waking Nicholas and Enid.

In the dim light of the room, she could just make out Nicholas's sleeping form. He lay on his stomach on a mat on the floor, his legs tucked under him, his bottom high in the air. She knew the blue blanket that

Myranda had made for him would be tucked underneath him. She didn't think he could sleep without it.

Unable to resist the sweet picture he made, she knelt down beside him and ran her hand over his soft hair. At moments like this, she wanted to stop time. He was so precious just as he was; she didn't want anything to change. God had obviously known what he was doing when he created this little boy, and she was so blessed to have him in her life.

She leaned down and kissed his cheek, breathing in his little-boy scent. He slept deeply and didn't stir. Hopefully, he'd rest awhile longer. It was a rare occasion when he took a nap of late, so the longer he slept the better his mood.

Enid stirred, but Alyna gestured for her to remain where she was and pointed at Nicholas. The maid nodded, and Alyna was pleased when she snuggled back down under the bedding. Although the older woman wouldn't admit it, she tired more easily than she used to, and some extra rest would do her good as well.

Alyna closed the door behind her and went below stairs to check on Matthew. In his chamber, she could hear the soft snores of the servant left to watch over him. She cracked open the narrow window shutter to let in the dim light of the predawn sky so she could get a better look at him.

"Oh, my lady," Alice whispered, covering a yawn with her hand. "Good morning to you."

"And to you, Alice. How does Matthew fare?"

"He slept through most of the night, though he seems to be getting more and more restless." Alice rose and stood beside his bed, her voice low. "He doesn't care for the potion Gunnell left for him. It's a bit of a battle to get him to take it."

Alyna sat on the bed beside the pale knight and laid her hand on his forehead. He seemed warm to the touch, but not overly so. "Aye, but it certainly eases his pain when he does. Why don't you get some rest, Alice? I'll keep an eye on him."

Morning had risen in full when a knock sounded at the door.

Florence entered the room, concern etched on her features. "Alyna, I came to see how poor Matthew fares."

For some reason, Alyna wondered if she'd practiced that look to make certain it held the right degree of worry. She brushed the thought aside, determined to be pleasant. "How kind of you. 'Twas a terrible accident."

"An accident of the worst sort," Florence agreed. She approached Matthew's bedside with caution, as though she feared she might catch what he had. "How is he?"

With a sigh, Alyna laid her hand on his cheek. "The worst is yet to come, I fear."

"Oh, dear."

Alyna looked again at Florence, curious as to why she was really here. She still couldn't view the woman as her aunt. Though Alyna had no experience with relatives, she was certain Florence hadn't acted like an aunt thus far. She waited for the woman to berate her again for using the servants without her permission, ready to defend herself and put the blame squarely back on Florence.

Florence clasped her hands and continued to study Matthew as though she'd never seen a wounded man before.

Alyna glanced back at Matthew to make sure he wasn't performing some amazing feat to warrant Florence's attention, but the knight hadn't moved.

Alyna let the silence draw out, too concerned for Matthew to risk riling Florence and cause a scene that might disturb his rest.

At last, Florence cleared her throat. "Alyna, my dear, I fear you and I have gotten off to a rather difficult start. If you felt the need to assist me in the duties of steward, you had only to ask. There was no need for you to approach Lord Blackwell. He is far too busy for household matters."

"Then I would think it even more important that you fulfill your duties. If I see something that needs to be done, I'll make certain it gets done."

Florence's eyes narrowed at her response. "Before Lord Blackwell left yesterday morning, he suggested I speak with you to clarify how we might...work together from now on."

A wave of hurt filled Alyna. "Grandfather spoke with you before he left?"

Florence smiled kindly at Alyna. "Well, of course, my dear. He wouldn't have left without letting me know his plans."

Alyna rose and moved to the small table beside Matthew's bed. She tidied the already neat pots and pouches that held herbs while she gathered her poise. Florence's words struck to her deepest fear–her grandfather didn't find her worthy enough to bother with. Why would her grandfather have let Florence know of his departure and not her? Perhaps he wasn't as different from her father as she'd thought.

"Why don't you oversee what you want, and I'll do the rest," Alyna suggested with an effort at civility.

"You obviously have your hands full helping Matthew recover, so I'll continue with my duties. Lord Blackwell does so appreciate my help." Florence paused for a moment. "Do you truly think Matthew will recover? I heard his injury was quite severe and I have to wonder if your limited knowledge will be sufficient."

Alyna turned to face Florence, outraged she would say such a thing, especially when Matthew might hear. "While his wound is indeed serious, he will recover. The healer from the village is assisting him as well."

Having Florence question her healing skills when she already felt so vulnerable put another chink in the fragile confidence she'd gained since she'd arrived here, but she was determined not to let Florence see that.

Florence offered a condescending smile. "Of course, he will. I'm certain you'll do your best. I'll see to the keep while you're occupied with Matthew and...Nicholas."

Alyna gritted her teeth. The woman acted as though she could barely remember her son's name. And what had Florence ever done to 'see to the keep'?

Before she could utter a word, Florence continued. "If you need assistance, perhaps need me to stay with Matthew for a time, I would be happy to do so. Of course, I'll need to know in advance so I can arrange my duties to accommodate an additional task."

Alyna sighed. Every word the woman uttered irritated her.

Florence stepped closer to Alyna, took her hand, and smiled warmly. "I'm so glad we had this chance to clear the air. I know we're going to get along well. Lord Blackwell will be pleased to hear we're working together."

Without saying a word, Alyna pulled her hand from Florence's grasp. She had no intention of working with Florence in any capacity. There were several people at Northe Castle that she did not care for, and Florence was one of them. Yet if the woman had her grandfather's trust, Alyna worried she'd somehow convince him to send her and Nicholas away. Did she risk too much by not befriending Florence?

The door pushed open and saved her from a response.

"Mama?" Nicholas's sleepy voice beckoned her.

"Come here, darling." She picked him up and he burrowed his head in her shoulder, his body still warm and pliant with sleep. She held him tightly and turned back to Florence. "I'm sure your many duties are pressing, so I'll let you return to them."

Florence glanced at Nicholas as though he was an oddity of some sort and paused at the door. "Please let me know if you need my assistance with Matthew." She smiled again and pulled the door shut behind her.

Alyna snuggled Nicholas's neck. "What are you doing up so early?"

"I don't like that lady," he answered, his voice barely audible.

Alyna could tell from his even breathing that he was nearly asleep once again. "I don't like her either. But I'm not sure what we can do about it."

Nicholas adjusted his position, placing an arm around her neck and snuggled in tighter. "I'll know soon."

CHAPTER TWELVE

"White willow is excellent for fever."
Lady Catherine's Herbal Journal

Lord Tegmont strode into the hall at Montvue, pleased at the trepidation on Lord Garyle's face as he rose to greet him.

"Surely you're not surprised to see me," Tegmont said as he removed his gloves and tossed them on the table. Alyna's father had proven useful on occasion but recent events made Tegmont question his loyalty.

"I'm always pleased to see you," Garyle said nervously, sidestepping the question.

Tegmont let the lie slide past. "I heard a rumor you lost something that belongs to me." Anger pulsed through him, stealing what little patience he had. "When did you plan on telling me?"

"I assume you speak of Alyna?" Garyle sank to the bench at the table and reached for his drink.

With one sweep of his hand, Tegmont sent the cup bouncing across the table and leaned forward within a hair's breadth of Garyle's face. "Do not try me. Where is she?"

The old lord shook his head. "I do not know. We've searched the area but found no trace of her."

"Did she leave on her own accord?"

"Mayhap. 'Tis difficult to say."

"Explain yourself or you'll be feeling the prick of my sword deep in your gullet."

Garyle swallowed hard. "Two of my servants are also missing, the two most loyal to her. And that damned boy."

"What boy?"

"'Tis no concern of yours. I would've made her leave him behind when she married you."

"You had better find her and soon, else I will take Montvue from your sorry hands and leave you with nothing. Do you hear me?"

Garyle nodded, the fear on his face convincing Tegmont he understood. Blast the man for his incompetence. Tegmont did not need this complication, not with all his other plans moving forward.

For a brief moment, he wondered what had caused her to leave. But as quickly as the question formed, it fled, for the answer didn't matter.

Alyna would be his. She'd end the curse that had befallen him and all his carefully laid plans would come to fruition.

⚜⚜⚜

Late that night, Alyna dozed in the chair beside Matthew's bed, her dreams mixing in strange combinations with his moans. She woke with a start when his hand rattled the basin on the small wooden table beside the bed, her mother's herbal remedy book still on her lap.

Matthew continued to stir restlessly, tossing and turning in his own bout with the night but didn't wake. She put down the book and stretched to relieve the crick in her neck.

Gunnell had checked on him earlier in the

evening, but had left soon after to tend to her two children. Alyna had assured her that she'd send for her if Matthew's condition worsened.

She rose and touched his hand, then his cheek. Heat radiated from his body. She wet a cloth and wiped his face and neck, then rinsed the cloth again and laid it across his forehead.

From his restless movements, she knew it was time to try to get him to drink something for both his pain and fever. The healer had made it look easy when she'd trickled it into his mouth earlier.

After mixing the dried herbs with warm water and wine, Alyna placed the small wooden cup on the table and sat on the edge of the bed. She lifted Matthew's head and cradled him against her and tilted his head back.

Matthew's eyes opened, glazed with fever. "Ah, Lady Alyna." His words slurred, whether from the fever or the medicine he'd taken earlier, she didn't know. "How very beautiful you are, my lady."

Alyna was surprised at his words, but even more surprised when he nuzzled his cheek against her breasts. He sighed as though content and closed his eyes.

Certain he knew not what he spoke or did, she ignored his foolish behavior. "Matthew? Matthew, I need your assistance."

The young man smiled up at her, eyes still closed. "For you, I would do anything, my lady." Alyna felt his body relax against her.

Concerned he wouldn't remain awake long enough to drink the potion, Alyna reached for the cup. "Matthew," she called, and shook him gently. "Drink this. It will help you feel better."

Obediently, he took a small sip, only to grimace at the taste. "Nay, my lady. I do not care for it." He looked up at her with a dazed but worshipful expression. "But I do care for you."

With a strength that belied his weakened condition, he pulled her head down with his good arm and placed a kiss upon her lips. Shocked, Alyna tried to pull back, but with one hand pinned under him and the other holding the medicine, she had no choice but to endure the pressure of his mouth on hers until she worked herself free.

Matthew's grip loosened, and she was able to straighten to move out of the knight's range. She shook her head, then looked up to find Royce standing at the foot of the bed watching her.

His eyes narrowed with suspicion. "You seem to have a habit of kissing men, my lady."

Embarrassed and annoyed, Alyna glared at Royce. "Quite the opposite, sir. They have a *bad* habit of kissing me." She waited a moment, but Royce continued to watch her. "Are you going to just stand there or are you going to help me?" She now understood why some women chose not to marry. It took a saint to put up with a man's foolish ways.

He lifted a brow but complied with her request. "What is it you're doing? Some new method of healing?"

With a huff at his lack of wits, Alyna spoke in the slow and even tone she sometimes used with Nicholas. "I am trying to get him to drink this medicine. He doesn't find it to his liking."

Royce lifted the vessel from her hand and passed it under his nose. From his expression, 'twas obvious he didn't find it to his liking either. "What is this concoction? Is it supposed to help him or put him out of his misery?"

By this time, the injured knight had fallen back asleep and looked quite comfortable nestled against

Alyna. Frustrated with both of them, she held out her hand for the cup. "If you're not willing to help, simply say so."

Against his better judgment, Royce moved closer and knelt down with the potion in hand. Remnants of the jealousy he'd felt seeing Matthew kiss her plagued him though he knew it had been harmless. The dark smudges under her eyes, evidence of her long bedside vigil, softened his ire. He shifted his focus to Matthew rather than the beautiful lady beside him. Or at least tried to.

A change of view did little to distract his attention from her. The fragrance that followed her everywhere drifted up to wrap its beckoning scent around him. Matthew snuggled against her breasts, looking as content as a newborn babe. Her smooth alabaster skin swelled at the neckline of her bliaut, hinting at the curves that lay beneath.

Damn the woman.

And damn Matthew for enjoying the very place he desired to be.

This task would best be done quickly so he could leave. He lifted the younger man's head to allow Alyna to free her arm, but froze when he realized the back of his own hand now lay against her breast. Desire surged through him, and he clenched his teeth to repress it. He eased his hand to a safer location, then opened Matthew's mouth, noting the unnatural heat of him. His condition was obviously worsening, just as they'd expected.

Alyna appeared to be as anxious as he to finish the deed and nearly choked Matthew in her haste to give him his medicine. After several attempts, they got him to swallow the majority of the potion.

Royce stood and backed away before he did something he'd regret. He wasn't sure what had awakened him in the middle of the night and prompted him to check on Matthew, but he wished he hadn't given into the urge. He'd known she'd be here. Before he'd entered the room, he'd told himself that he only wanted to check on Matthew's condition, that it mattered not if Alyna was the one who tended him.

Now, as he looked at her, he admitted the truth to himself. Any chance to be in her presence drew him like a moth to a flame.

Yet this couldn't be. He had to stop. Why couldn't he accept that? Instead, he tortured himself by seeking her company at every turn.

Hell's teeth. What was he to do about it?

For now, the answer was a simple one. He'd remove her from his presence as quickly as possible. "If you'd like to get some rest, I'll remain with Matthew."

"Oh, truly?" Alyna appeared tempted by his offer, but looked at him with doubt. "Well, I suppose it will be all right. Gunnell should be here soon after dawn to check on him, but let me know if you need something before that. Are you quite sure?"

"Aye."

She gave him a tired smile, her face pale. She rubbed a shoulder with one hand and arched her back.

He kept his hands fisted at his sides, determined to resist the urge to help ease her stiffness.

She adjusted Matthew's covers one last time, then glanced at Royce as she walked out the door. "My thanks, Royce."

Royce couldn't ignore the ache in his chest her departure caused. What was she doing to him?

⚜ ⚜ ⚜

Exhausted, Alyna went upstairs to her chamber,

her steps slower on each stair. She couldn't help but remember the sleepless nights when Nicholas had been a babe. Thank goodness she'd had Enid to aid her.

Her chamber was empty, but as dawn had arrived, she assumed Nicholas had awoken hungry, and Enid had taken him to the kitchen to find something to break their fast. Too tired to worry much over their absence, she moved directly toward the bed, taking time only to remove her slippers. She settled her head on the pillow and drew the covers over her.

As she snuggled down into the comfort of the bed, a familiar scent caught her attention. Royce. She opened her eyes, only to realize the scent came from her gown. The fresh aroma curled deep within her and filled her with a now familiar longing. Her attraction to the knight continued to deepen, despite her attempts to halt it.

The man annoyed her and fascinated her, all at the same time. He acted as though he was attracted to her one moment, then ignored her the next. He kissed her as though she was special to him, but kept his distance at other times.

What was she to do with such a man?

One long look from those gray eyes was enough to make her toes curl. He brought out feelings of which she hadn't known she was capable. The whole business was maddening.

She must've dozed off, for a knock at the door startled her awake. Hoping it wasn't a servant sent to inform her Matthew had worsened, she rose and went to the door, conscious of her bare feet.

The strange woman curtsied, a servant by the look of her clothes. "Beg your pardon, my lady. Lady Florence requests your presence in the hall."

A wave of irritation filled Alyna. What could the

woman possibly want? "I've been up all night with Matthew. I'm certain whatever she needs can wait until later."

"I'm sorry, my lady, but she asked me to tell you that it is of the utmost importance." The maid didn't look apologetic in the least.

"What is your name?"

"My name, my lady?"

"Aye, your name. I don't believe I've seen you before."

"I'm new here."

Alyna waited for an answer but none seemed forthcoming. The maid reminded her of a muted version of Florence with her narrow face, thin lips and displeased expression as though unhappy with the errand she'd been sent upon.

At last, she seemed to realize Alyna waited for a response. "Oh, I am called Hilde, my lady."

If Alyna didn't know better, she would've thought the maid was being deliberately obtuse. Her exhaustion must be getting the better of her. She yawned and looked longingly at the bed. More sleep would have to wait. For some reason, she suspected Florence was up to no good, and she had best find out what it was as quickly as possible.

She put on her slippers and moved to the door where Hilde waited. "Let us see what Florence wants."

Her face void of expression, the maid gestured for Alyna to go first.

"You lead the way, Hilde." For some reason, she didn't want the maid behind her.

"As you wish, my lady."

Hilde made her way to the great hall with Alyna a short distance behind. Alyna realized she must've slept longer than she thought for morning had come in full.

As she entered the hall, she noticed Beatrice and Mary, the two servants who had assisted in cleaning the hall. They stood to one side, anxious expressions upon their faces. Alyna immediately went toward them to find out what was wrong.

"Alyna," Florence called to her from nearby.

"In a moment," she answered with a brief glance at the insufferable woman, determined to find out what was wrong with the maids first.

Beatrice gasped. "Oh, my lady! Please don't make her angrier than she already is."

"'Tis true, my lady," Mary agreed. "Lady Florence is not pleased with us." The older woman touched Alyna's arm. "I am so very sorry, my lady."

"Whatever for?" Alyna was puzzled by her apology as well as her behavior. "What's wrong?"

"Alyna." Florence's impatient tone commanded her attention. "I would speak with you anon."

Already irritable, Florence's words only angered Alyna further. "I will be with you in a moment." She turned to glare at her aunt, but the sight over the woman's head made her catch her breath. "What happened?"

One of her grandmother's beautifully woven tapestries now had a gaping hole near the center of the design. The bright colors that had been revealed by the cleaning had faded in several spots.

"We don't know, my lady." Beatrice sniffed.

"It makes no sense," Mary added, wringing her hands.

Florence moved toward Alyna, a condescending smile on her lips. "Alyna, my dear, I realize you were only trying to help, but..." As though at a loss for words, she turned and gestured toward the damaged tapestry. "It appears as though your skills lie in some area other than cleaning."

Alyna felt her cheeks flame as dismay and embarrassment washed through her. How could she have been so careless as to ruin the tapestry? Her grandfather would be so disappointed in her. She quickly thought back to the day they'd cleaned the hall but could think of nothing they'd done that would have caused any harm.

"I know you meant well, but really," Florence continued, shaking her head. "I can't allow this to happen again."

"I can assure you that nothing we did caused damage to the tapestry." Alyna didn't know what had happened, but she did know it wasn't her fault, nor was it Beatrice's or Mary's. She gave the two servants a look of reassurance. They looked rather startled at her show of support.

"Then how do you explain this?" With flourish, Florence raised her hand to gesture to the tapestry.

Alyna looked closer at Florence. If she didn't know better, she'd think the woman had somehow planned all this. Alyna glanced around the hall. A small audience was even in attendance for the event. It seemed this was the price she'd pay for not being friendlier to Florence.

Anger consumed her, and it felt so much better than the hot wave of embarrassment had. "I have no explanation for it." She took a step toward Florence. "I do know that nothing that I, nor the servants who assisted me in cleaning this hall, caused that harm."

Alyna turned to Mary and Beatrice. "Please see that the tapestry is taken down so we might examine it to determine the cause."

Florence took a step back and glanced at Hilde, who stood near her side. She looked at Alyna and scoffed. "Dear child–"

"I am not your child, and I do not wish you to refer

to me as such."

"Well, really." Florence folded her arms. "I am simply trying to fulfill my duties. I've tried to befriend you, but you rebuff me at every turn. 'Tis not my fault that you cleaned the hall with such disastrous consequences. Whatever will I tell Lord Blackwell?"

"If you had been fulfilling your duties, the hall would already have been clean, and my interference wouldn't have been needed." Alyna refused to fall prey to Florence's tactics. She would not take the blame for the damaged tapestry, nor would she allow blame to be placed on those who had aided her. "I will be the one to speak to my grandfather of this. You need not concern yourself with the matter any further."

"As steward–"

"When you act as a steward, I will give you the respect due a steward. If you truly cared for my grandfather, you would be of more assistance. As you so kindly pointed out to me, he has many other things on his mind and shouldn't have to worry about whether or not a chamber is prepared for a guest."

Florence's face turned an unbecoming shade of red. Her lips narrowed until they were all but invisible. "Is that what all this is about? You are angry because your chamber wasn't prepared for your arrival?"

"Nay. I am angry because you act as though you do my grandfather a great service and yet nothing gets done." Alyna continued despite the woman's anger. It felt good to speak her mind. "Perhaps you should rethink your position here, Florence."

Hilde took a step closer to Florence. Her gaze held Alyna's, her message loud and clear. She was on Florence's side and would aid her in any way she could.

Alyna felt a presence at her elbow and turned to

find Enid beside her, Nicholas in her arms. He reached for her and held on tight, his gaze warily on Florence.

"We've been looking for you, my lady. Nicholas insisted we find you," Enid said in a quiet voice.

Beatrice and Mary stood next to Enid, their anxious expressions replaced by a resolve Alyna found heartening.

Florence eyed them all, but her gaze landed on Alyna, hatred glaring out of her blue eyes. "You will regret this outburst, Alyna. In fact, I can guarantee you will rue the day you crossed me."

CHAPTER THIRTEEN

*"Celery seeds are effective in sweetening
the blood but should not be harvested the first year."*
Lady Catherine's Herbal Journal

Alyna hurried along the well-worn path, a basket of fresh herbs from the garden in tow. She'd left the keep later than she'd planned since Nicholas hadn't wanted her to leave him today.

But she was more than ready for some fresh air. She was beginning to feel daft from being indoors so long.

After the confrontation with Florence, the past few days had been dedicated to tending Matthew, although Alyna had managed to more closely examine the damaged tapestry. Just as she had suspected, someone had applied lye in several places, causing the destruction. The odor and appearance of the woven threads made it obvious. She'd considered showing Florence, but the woman would merely insist Alyna had done it while it was being cleaned.

The only thing Alyna could do was remain on guard against additional trouble. Beatrice and Mary had told her that Hilde was wearing a wrap of some sort on her hand. That was very interesting information indeed. If she'd handled the lye improperly, it could have very well burned her skin.

Alyna had looked for Hilde several times, but the maid was nowhere to be found. Alyna didn't trust her any more than she trusted Florence and had instructed Beatrice and Mary to keep a close eye on them both.

Matthew was well on the road to recovery and so the rest of the day was hers to do with as she pleased. She'd left instructions with Enid for his care during her absence, and Nicholas was with Charles. Today, she would do something she'd wanted to do since Matthew had been injured. She was going to visit Gunnell.

Though Alyna had been concerned with the knight's progress at times, from what little Alyna could get out of the close-mouthed healer, Gunnell had not seemed concerned. No matter how kind or friendly Alyna had been when Gunnell checked on Matthew, she remained aloof and distant.

Alyna knew why—the woman had second sight.

Mayhap Royce and the others preferred to use a different explanation for what she said and did, but Alyna knew the truth.

She was quite certain Gunnell hadn't yet come to grips with her gift. The servants' gossip said that a change had come over the woman when she'd been recovering from a sickness that had nearly taken her life three years past. As to the extent of her ability, no one would say.

As far as Alyna could tell, Gunnell knew everyone called her crazed and played upon it, using it as a way to keep people at a distance. Perhaps Gunnell even felt she truly was mad.

Whatever the matter, Alyna intended to find out. She and Gunnell needed each other. In the years since her mother's death, Alyna had felt she didn't belong in her own home, thanks to her father. The feeling of isolation, of not fitting in, of having to earn affection and respect from others continued to plague her. Perhaps helping someone else would help ease her own feelings of insecurity.

Gunnell appeared to be uncomfortable with her gift and speaking to someone about it who understood might help. If Gunnell could control her talents and understand them better, Alyna was certain she'd be happier. Perhaps she could better assist the people in the village, resolve Royce's problems with the thieves or even foretell the results of the harvest. There were endless possibilities, as well as responsibilities, that came with second sight.

Gunnell was right to guard her ability as it took little to strike superstition in the villeins. The matter had to be handled with caution.

Though it seemed selfish, Alyna hoped with all her heart Gunnell could explain what she'd meant when she'd told Alyna that her destiny had not yet changed. She'd had plenty of time to ponder Gunnell's remark during her bedside vigil with Matthew. If her destiny hadn't changed, did Myranda's predictions still hold true? Above all, Alyna wanted to know if she'd escaped marriage to Tegmont.

Everything was so unclear to her. Her grandfather might have more answers than Gunnell, but he hadn't yet returned. Royce refused to give her any information about his whereabouts other than to say he would come home soon. What choice did she have but to seek advice where she could?

The time drew nearer when she had to plan her and Nicholas's future. With each day that passed, he showed more signs of his gift. Soon, very soon, she wouldn't be able to hide it, and she'd need more than just Enid and Charles to help protect him. She would need others to guard him against those who might hurt him or use his gift for their own purpose. It would take several years for Nicholas to learn to control it, to realize when he should reveal it and how to hide it. Until then, she would stop at nothing to protect him.

She needed a safe place to raise her son with people upon whom she could depend. While her grandfather had been very kind so far, he hadn't been forthcoming with information. His relationship with Florence also left a question in her mind as to whether she could truly trust him.

Alyna could only guess at the trouble Florence would cause if she saw any suggestion of Nicholas's talent. She might try to turn her grandfather against them. While the chance of her succeeding seemed unlikely, Alyna needed to have a secondary plan in place. Her grandfather had been very tolerant of her and her son, but all that could change when he found out the truth about Nicholas.

Alyna knew Florence was right in one respect. There were few men who would be willing to marry a lady with a young son, especially if they discovered his ability, not to mention that he was not her son by birth.

That mattered not. What mattered was Nicholas. By seeking out Gunnell and her knowledge and experience, Alyna could help him. Maybe, just maybe, she could help Gunnell as well.

"Good morning, Lady Alyna."

The words startled her. So immersed was she in her thoughts, she hadn't seen or heard Sir Edward's approach.

He guided his destrier to keep pace with her, much to her displeasure. His chain mail was covered with a surcoat, and his black hair was bare to the sun.

Her good manners were an annoyance at times like this, as she felt obligated to respond to his greeting. "Hello, Sir Edward. Where is the war this fine day?"

Edward threw back his head and laughed at her question. "No war today, my lady. I have just returned from the field below the village where I checked on the preparations for our jousting practice. We're nearly ready to begin. You will come and watch."

Alyna was reminded of why she found the knight so irksome. Never did he ask, but rather just assumed others would do as he demanded. She stepped away from his big, black horse as it pranced too close for comfort. "Nay, sir. I am out visiting for a time. Then I must return to check on Matthew."

"Who are you visiting?"

Alyna continued down the path, hoping the knight would catch her hint and let her go on her way unaccompanied. "The healer, Gunnell."

"Gunnell? Why would you want to see her?" Edward guided his horse even closer. "The village would be better off if she were sent to an abbey for care. The woman's a loon."

"Nay, she is not." Alyna again moved away from the large hooves that seemed to get closer and closer to her slippered feet. "She has a great knowledge of the healing arts. You may need her assistance one day." Alyna glared up at the knight. "After all, she saved Matthew's life."

"Matthew, ha! If that boy had half a brain, he wouldn't have gotten injured in the first place. So busy was he, staring at your window, that he didn't follow the lesson I taught. He'll learn from his mistake."

Shocked, Alyna halted. "How dare you. How dare you insinuate he is at fault when it was your sword that struck him."

"Oh, now, my lady, no need for anger. 'Tis past time for him to learn to eliminate distractions, even if they are as beautiful as you." He chuckled as though he'd made an amusing joke.

Unable to hold her temper, Alyna continued, "Beware, Sir Edward. Those you injure either by your tongue or your sword may come back to haunt you."

"Are you a witch that you can cast an evil spell over me? I believe Lady Florence would agree, but not I, my lady."

"I don't need to be a witch to see your future. You will die a lonely, old man with no one to mourn your passing." Alyna knew she went too far, but could not stop herself, not after the way he spoke of Gunnell and Matthew. If there were any justice in the world, her prophecy would be fulfilled.

"I promise to come back to haunt you if your words hold true." Edward chuckled and kicked his horse into a gallop, his laughter trailing behind him.

Alyna shook her head, astounded by the knight's behavior. It appalled her to realize he took no responsibility for injuring Matthew. Would Royce do nothing about this? She would ask him about it the next time she saw him.

Pushing aside her dark thoughts, she continued on the path, greeting some of the villagers who worked nearby in the bright, spring sunshine. The sky was clear, but held the threat of evening showers on the distant horizon. She took a deep breath of the sweet air and tried to calm herself.

Gunnell stood in the doorway of her cottage, glaring. Her hands were fisted on her hips, as though to block Alyna's entrance to her home.

Alyna could understand Gunnell's reluctance to allow strangers into her small cottage, especially if she thought those strangers considered her crazed or worse yet, a witch.

"Greetings, Gunnell." Alyna wanted to avoid any

sort of confrontation, so she sent her a bright smile and sat down on a tree stump placed outside the cottage door. Certain she would get no response, she continued on. "Sir Edward is a cabbage, is he not?"

Gunnell looked astounded at Alyna's insult to the knight.

Alyna caught sight of the herb garden at the side of the cottage and went to investigate. Several plants grew there that she was unfamiliar with. "What is this?"

Gunnell followed to see what she pointed at. "Lungwort, my lady."

"And what do you use it for?"

"Chest disorders and the like."

Moving along, Alyna found another she hadn't seen before. "And this one?"

"That would be wormwood, used to rid the body of worms."

"Your knowledge is most impressive." Alyna handed her the basket she'd brought. "I thought perhaps you used all of your toft for growing healing herbs, in which case you might like to have some for cooking."

Gunnell stared at the basket Alyna had given her as though she wasn't quite sure what to do with it.

Alyna continued her tour of the garden and exclaimed over the wide variety of herbs.

Gunnell followed her and answered the questions Alyna directed her way, her expression still wary.

"Mama?"

Alyna turned to see two young children approaching Gunnell.

"I asked you two to stay inside," Gunnell scolded gently.

"We did that already." The young boy spoke for his little sister. "We're ready to do something else now."

Alyna laughed at the boy's comment, and Gunnell allowed a small smile as well.

"Very well. Come and meet Lady Alyna."

He drew his sister forward by the hand, and the two children gazed up at her with curiosity. "This is Stephen, who is six, and Catherine who is three years."

"Nearly four," the little girl added.

Alyna bent over. "I can see you are very wise for your age, Catherine."

The little girl was a miniature replica of her mother and nodded solemnly at Alyna.

Gunnell smoothed her daughter's hair. "Where are your manners?"

"Aye, my lady."

"Stephen, you appear to be a most excellent older brother. I always wished I had an older brother."

"Really?" The little boy looked at her as though he thought her statement odd. "Why?"

"Stephen," his mother reprimanded him.

"For all sorts of reasons," Alyna answered, "but mostly because I wanted someone older and smarter to play with. You two are very lucky to have each other."

"Go on now and let me speak with Lady Alyna." Gunnell gave them each a squeeze on the shoulder as they ran off to play.

"Catherine was my mother's name," Alyna told Gunnell as she watched the children run down the hill.

"Aye, my lady, I know."

"Did you know her then?"

"I was quite young when she left, but I remember her."

For some reason, that pleased Alyna. "I miss her," she admitted in a soft voice.

"Everyone thinks you're a lot like her."

"Really? In what respect?" Alyna couldn't contain her curiosity, nor her pleasure.

"Oh, some of your gestures, the way you stand with your hands folded before you, your hair. Those sorts of things." She bent over to pluck a weed. "How old were you when she died?"

Alyna didn't think Gunnell realized she was now participating in the conversation. That was a major step forward as far as Alyna was concerned.

"I was in my tenth year." Thinking back, Alyna could still remember the horrible helpless feeling of her mother's last few days. "She took ill. I didn't know how to help her."

"Sometimes there's nothing you can do."

Alyna shook her head and continued. "Enid and I did what we could, but it happened so fast. A healer came, but she couldn't help either." She chose not to mention that the healer had been Nicholas's mother.

"'Tis a horrible thing to watch someone die."

"It must be far worse to know they're going to die before you help them," Alyna said, trying to imagine how she'd feel if she were cursed or blessed, depending on one's view, with second sight.

Gunnell bolted upright, alarm in her expression. "Whatever do you mean?"

"I know you are not crazed, Gunnell."

"I don't understand what you're speaking of, my lady."

"You have a wonderful gift, and I'd like to help you with it." Alyna held her gaze.

To her surprise, Gunnell's face crumpled, and she burst into tears. "Please, I beg you. Don't tell anyone. I'll be burned as a witch for certain. My children need me."

Filled with remorse, Alyna put her arm around

the woman. "Nay, Gunnell. My apologies. I didn't mean to upset you. I swear I won't tell anyone."

Alyna guided her inside the cottage so others in the village wouldn't see her crying. She left the door ajar to help light the dim interior and led Gunnell to the bench at the table. She searched out a vessel of ale and poured some in a small cup and passed it to the distraught woman. "Really, I'm terribly sorry. I'll leave you in peace."

Still sniffing, Gunnell said, "Nay, my lady, stay. Forgive me for my behavior." She shook her head as she explained, "It's just that no one other than my husband has ever told me they don't think I'm crazed, and I'm not even certain he believed it when he said it."

That comment brought more tears. Alyna rose from the table and found a rough woven cloth on a shelf. A pitcher of water sat on a small table. She poured a bit into a basin and wet the cloth. Apparently Gunnell needed a good cry and Alyna could think of nothing else to bring her comfort.

Gunnell took the cool cloth with gratitude and held it on her face for a moment or two.

"I'm certain your husband knows you're not daft."

"Nay." Gunnell shook her head in denial. "You should see how he looks at me sometimes. I see these things, and words pass through my lips before I can halt them. I sound like I'm possessed by an evil spirit or crazed as they say."

"Oh, Gunnell." Alyna's heart went out to the woman.

"My children." Gunnell's lip quivered with the effort to contain her emotions. "The other children tease them, and I know Stephen and Catherine can't help but believe some of the things they hear. They're not blind or deaf. They see how I act and hear what I say."

"How long have you had the visions?" Alyna was certain if she had more information, she might be able to help in some way.

"Shortly after I had Catherine, I fell ill. I was sick for a fortnight and nearly died. At times I wanted to, as I was so miserable. I couldn't care for my husband, nor my children. But I knew they needed me, so I fought to live. You don't know how often I've regretted that decision."

"Surely you don't mean that," Alyna protested.

"Oh, but I do. I'm not normal anymore. I'm not the woman my husband married. And my children, my poor children." The woman continued to sob.

Alyna gave up on the cloth and just held Gunnell. Chewing on her lip, she tried desperately to think of some way to comfort her. "Remember the positive side of your gift. I'm sure you've saved many lives. After all, you saved Matthew's."

"But I didn't save his life. He would've lived without my assistance."

"I don't believe that for a moment. You can't separate what you see from how the events would unfold without your intervention."

Gunnell drew back in surprise.

Convinced she was right, Alyna grasped her shoulders and looked into her eyes. "I think God gave you this gift for a purpose. We must determine what that purpose is, and then perhaps you can find a way to control it."

Gunnell's expression was still bleak. "You don't think 'tis some tool of the devil's?"

Alyna snorted. "If so, we'll use it against him."

Gunnell's expression lightened with a cautious hope at her words.

"I would like to help you, if you'd let me," Alyna

said.

The healer shook her head, her hopeful expression warring with helplessness. "I don't see how you could, my lady. Not that I doubt you."

"Gunnell, I truly think we could do something that would aid you. You see, I once knew another like you."

To Alyna's surprise, Gunnell froze, her eyes going wide. "Nicholas's mother," she said.

"How do you know this?" Alyna shook her head at her own stupidity. "Never mind. I know the answer to that."

"Nicholas. Oh, no, Nicholas." Seeming to come out of her trance, she held Alyna's hands. "Go. Hurry. Nicholas has been hurt, and he needs you. Go now and be quick."

Alyna's stomach dropped. She didn't wait to hear more, but took off like an arrow shot from a bow. She flew out of the cottage and up the path to the keep, running as fast as her legs could carry her, praying with all her heart that her son was all right.

⚜–⚜–⚜

Royce surveyed the field they'd prepared for jousting one last time. All appeared to be in readiness. Now they needed Blackwell to return, and they could start the training. With a satisfied nod, he rode his destrier back up the hill toward the keep.

He passed several cottages, greeting the villagers working nearby. Up ahead, a girl ran as though her life depended on it. Curious as to what caused her to rush so, he urged his horse into a gallop, easily overtaking her.

By Christ, it was Alyna.

"Lady Alyna," Royce called out incredulously.

She glanced back over her shoulder but didn't

pause in her flight. The look of fear upon her face stopped his heart.

"Whatever is the matter?"

"'Tis Nicholas!"

"Come," he bid her and held out his hand.

Alyna grasped it, and he pulled her up before him. He kicked his horse into a gallop toward the keep. His stomach clenched at the thought of the boy being hurt or worse.

Within moments, they were through the portcullis and into the bailey. "Where?" Royce asked then saw him before Alyna could answer.

The boy stood just outside the entrance to the stables. He held something in his hands and examined it with great interest.

"What is it? I don't see anything wrong."

She looked at her son for a long moment, obviously puzzled. "Well, I thought..."

As she spoke, Edward rode out of the stables, his head turned back toward the interior of the building, his angry voice audible across the bailey. "I told you not to give him oats until after he's cooled down. Next time, you will listen to me, you fool."

The scene played out with painful slowness for Royce. He could see that Edward paid no attention to the path his steed took. The black horse, eager to have its head to run, jerked at the reins, stomping and snorting as it tried to gain the upper hand. Neither man nor beast saw the small form off to the side of the entrance, right in their path.

"Edward, halt!" Royce shouted.

The nervous horse sidestepped, spooked at the sight of the small boy, and reared. Edward tugged the reins in an attempt to control his horse, but still did not see Nicholas. The boy looked up, and Royce could see the fear etched on his face. The child turned to run, but it was too late.

"Get out of the way, you stupid boy," Edward bellowed as he saw Nicholas. The horse reared again and clipped Nicholas with a hoof, striking him in the middle of his back. Nicholas was knocked to the ground.

"Nicholas!" Alyna cried as she jumped off the horse.

The boy lay motionless.

Royce's heart stopped as Edward's horse reared again. He urged his horse forward, knowing he'd have better luck moving Edward's horse aside if he remained mounted. "Get back," Royce demanded, his rage nearly blinding him.

Edward realized what had happened and tried to calm his frightened steed. Royce rode between the frightened horse and Nicholas to get the beast away from the boy. He forced the horse back into the stable and turned his steed sideways to block the entrance.

"Keep back, Edward," Royce ordered, then leapt from his horse and ran to where Alyna was bent over Nicholas's still form.

"Nicholas. Nicholas." She ran her hands lightly over his body, as though unsure where she should touch him.

Royce placed a gentle hand on the boy's back and held it there, hoping to feel him breathe, praying to feel any movement.

Nothing.

With slow and careful hands, Royce rolled the boy over. He didn't want to make his injuries any worse, but needed to make certain the child breathed.

Still nothing.

Alyna's chant changed, and tears streamed down her face. "Please, oh please."

Royce lifted Nicholas and tilted the boy's head

back. A gentle rush of air came out of the boy's mouth.

Nicholas took several shallow breaths and his eyes fluttered open. "Mama?"

"Oh, my baby. Are you all right?" Alyna's tears fell even faster.

Relief coursed through Royce, leaving him weak as a babe. Passing a crying Nicholas to Alyna with great care, he rose on unsteady legs and looked for Edward. The knight stood on the other side of Royce's horse, apparently thinking it would somehow protect him from Royce's wrath.

Several stable hands had gathered at the commotion, but Royce ignored them as he rounded his horse, slapping him on the rump to send him into the stables. He wanted to give Edward far worse than a slap. In a cold, quiet voice, he asked, "What were you doing?"

"Well, I–" Edward stammered. "That is, he–"

"This is the second accident you've had, Edward," Royce interrupted. He hadn't the patience to listen to the stuttering knight. "I suggest you reconsider your desire to remain a knight with Lord Blackwell."

"Hold, Royce. You know not of what you speak. I accept no blame with either of these incidents," Edward protested.

"And therein lies the problem." Royce shook his head in disgust. "Lord Blackwell will decide the outcome of this. Now be gone from my sight before I treat you as you have others." Though Royce's voice remained quiet, his meaning couldn't have been clearer.

With his face bright red, Edward backed away, then left through the rear entrance of the stables, his horse in tow. The knight hadn't bothered to ask after Nicholas before taking his leave.

He clamped down on his temper as best he could

and turned to check on the boy.

Alyna still knelt on the ground holding her son, her hand running over his face and hair. Though still pale and crying, Nicholas's color had improved. Despite his own tears, he rested a hand alongside his mother's cheek in an attempt to comfort her, making Royce's heart squeeze.

"Where's my butterfly?" Nicholas asked, his voice catching.

"Is that what you had? The butterfly is fine. It flew away," Alyna answered.

Warmed by the love the two shared, Royce couldn't help but smile. "Let us take you inside to examine you more closely."

Alyna looked up at Royce, her fright still evident in her eyes. "Thank you, Royce."

"I did nothing, my lady."

"Nay, I could've lost my son today if it weren't for you. I can't thank you enough." Her lip quivered with the effort to hold her composure.

Uncomfortable with her gratitude, he tried to shift her attention back to Nicholas. "Does he seem all right?"

"I believe so, but I would like to do as you suggested and look him over more thoroughly."

Royce gingerly lifted Nicholas from her arms so she could rise. The boy was lucky the horse hadn't struck his head. Royce had once seen a great knight turned into a bumbling idiot after hitting his temple.

He followed Alyna into the keep and sat Nicholas on a table in the hall as gently as possible.

"Hurts, Mama," Nicholas told her as he arched his back, his breath hitching.

She removed his tunic, revealing a large mark on his back. That would look much worse tomorrow. With those graceful hands that never failed to fascinate him, she touched the boy's arms, ribs, and neck, asking with each contact whether it pained him.

Nicholas shook his head at Alyna's questions. The only place that caused him distress was his back, though he still seemed dazed from the accident, his movements slow. His gaze followed Alyna's face, and he seemed comforted by her reassuring smile.

Gunnell entered the hall. "My lady? Is he all right?"

While the two women discussed Nicholas's condition, Royce felt compelled to do some checking of his own. "Nicholas, can you put your arms out?" Royce held his arms out from his sides and the little boy mimicked him.

Nicholas soon became far more interested in studying the sword strapped to Royce's hip than cooperating with the search for injuries. "Mamma, look. Look," he called to Alyna impatiently.

"What is it?" she asked.

He pointed to the pommel of Royce's sword.

"Aye, 'tis very nice," she said as she glanced at Royce's sword, then took a second, closer look.

Royce watched her, puzzled by the expression on her face. She stared at the pommel of his sword long and hard, as though it did not meet her expectations. In fact, it seemed to disappoint her. She looked up at Royce before her gaze fell yet again to his sword. "Is that your only sword?"

"Aye. 'Twas my father's."

His father had brought the rose-colored crystal back from a crusade and had it embedded in the pommel. But Royce would never look at the sword without remembering the night he'd lifted it, still sheathed in its scabbard, from his father's lifeless form. The sword served as a reminder of his vow of vengeance. Why the sight of it would upset Alyna, he couldn't fathom.

Before he could question her, she turned back to her son. "Can you turn your head back and forth?" she asked. "Now lift your arms above your head."

Nicholas did as she directed, but gingerly.

At last, she and Gunnell appeared satisfied. No other damage was apparent except for a bad bruise forming on his back and another on his forehead where he'd struck the ground.

Gunnell left to see to her own children, so Royce helped Alyna apply a poultice the healer had prepared, teasing Nicholas into smiling in the process.

Their ministrations complete, she picked up Nicholas with care and kissed him. She pressed her cheek to his, her eyes closed, and held him for a moment.

As always, the pair drew Royce. Their love and devotion to each other was heart-warming. A man would be lucky to have a family such as this one. Alyna was a caring, wonderful mother. He was fiercely glad he'd ripped both of them from his uncle's grasp. Tegmont did not deserve a treasure such as Alyna, let alone her sweet son. Royce moved closer and touched Nicholas on the head. "You'll be sore and stiff on the morrow."

Alyna opened her eyes and looked up at him, something more than gratitude in her expression. "Royce, I..." She swallowed hard to keep back her tears.

"Nay, my lady." He took her hand in his. "There's no need for you to say anything." Warmth spread through him, making his heart lurch. His breath caught in his throat as he held her gaze. He could still see evidence of her tears. Her look of absolute panic when he'd seen her in the village had frightened him more than he cared to admit.

Something niggled at the back of his mind as he thought back to that moment until at last he realized what it was. "How is it you knew Nicholas was hurt before the horse struck him?"

CHAPTER FOURTEEN

"Mint promotes bile flow
and can relieve pain."
Lady Catherine's Herbal Journal

Alyna's stomach clenched. What should she say? How much should she tell him?

She'd promised the healer that she would tell no one, though Alyna knew Royce already had suspicions. He'd called Gunnell crazed once before. Had that been an attempt to soften Gunnell's prediction for Alyna, or did he truly believe it?

"Remember?" Nicholas asked, his head cocked to the side. "I told you a black horse would hurt me."

Royce stared at her son as if he'd suddenly grown wings.

Could this moment get any worse? Alyna drew a deep breath. Sooner or later, Royce would've remembered that Nicholas had said he'd be hurt by a black horse. She bit her lip, waiting to see what he's say. She simply couldn't bear for Royce to look at her son as though he was crazed because...

Oh, dear heavens! There could be only one explanation for the hope and fear pouring through her.

Because she loved Royce. She closed her eyes for a moment as she realized the truth. How could this have happened? And what was she to do about it?

As a tight band bound her chest, Nicholas laid his head in the crook of her neck. "'Tis all right, Mama."

The tightness eased. She opened her eyes, grateful for her son's wise words. She hugged him gently in gratitude. He was right. Nothing could be done about it. It simply was.

Royce shook his head, a puzzled expression on his face, his gray eyes as clear as the reflection of the sky on the water on a cool winter's day. Those eyes made it difficult to stay focused when he looked at her so.

When she'd seen Nicholas standing there, looking as healthy and happy as could be, she'd felt foolish. Now that both Nicholas and Gunnell's premonitions had proven true, Alyna swore never to doubt either of them again. But how could she protect them from those who didn't understand their gifts?

"Why did you think something was wrong with Nicholas before anything occurred?" Royce asked. It seemed he'd chosen to ignore Nicholas's comment, at least for the moment.

"I was visiting Gunnell this afternoon." She began, hoping wisdom would come.

"Gunnell?" From Royce's tone, Alyna realized he already knew what she was going to say.

"Aye, Gunnell." She waited, wondering if she needed to continue.

Royce folded his arms over his chest, an eyebrow raised in question. "Continue."

Alyna heaved a sigh. It seemed he would pursue this to the very end. She decided brevity and honesty would serve her best.

"She told me that Nicholas was hurt and needed me." She stole a glance at Royce, wondering how he was taking her explanation so far. As usual, his expression revealed little. "I ran out of her cottage and the rest you know."

Royce remained silent, which made her feel obligated to explain further. She caught herself just in time. "That approach may work on your squire, sir, but it does not work on me." She could play his game as well. She waited with as much patience as he, Nicholas still cradled in her arms.

"Why do I feel there is more to this story?" he asked.

"You don't seem surprised by my explanation."

Royce seemed to ponder the matter as he gently touched Nicholas's head.

Alyna's heart squeezed. This man was special in many ways, but she had to remember that despite her feelings, he was not for her. She couldn't allow herself to care so deeply for a man who spent his days training for battle. Protecting Nicholas was her first and only priority, and becoming involved with Royce wouldn't aid her in that endeavor.

Nicholas looked up at him and smiled.

Royce winked and smiled back.

Alyna looked away, surprised she still stood and hadn't melted into a puddle at Royce's feet. Must he be so kind to Nicholas? She could resist many things, but that wasn't one of them. Nicholas obviously cared for Royce, too, and that made it all the more difficult.

Royce cleared his throat. "Gunnell's ability to...foresee events is still unclear."

Alyna forgot all about puddles. "You say that after today? When she so clearly told me what would happen?"

"There have been occasions in the past when she has been unable to provide us the information we needed."

"There is a fine line between using Gunnell's gift and allowing her to give assistance when she can. I don't pretend to know where that line is, but I do know answers are not always shown to her." She couldn't blame Royce for wanting to use Gunnell's gift, not when she'd been prepared to use Gunnell to determine her own future.

"Mama?" Nicholas rubbed his cheek on her shoulder, drawing her attention back to where it should be.

"I'm going to take Nicholas to our chamber. We can speak of this later." She gave Royce one last glance and turned away.

"Lady Alyna."

Compelled by his tone, she turned to look at him.

Royce moved closer. "I know there is more to this than you are telling me and I intend to devote some time to find out what that is." His voice was soft yet deep, hypnotic even as it sent shivers down her spine.

She released the breath she'd held as she watched him go. The strong effect he had on her senses never failed to amaze her. What was it about him that sent goose bumps over her body and an ache of longing through her?

She couldn't be in love with him. They had nothing in common. His way of life would not provide the safe place she needed to raise Nicholas nor did he seem to believe some people had gifts that others did not.

"Mama?" Nicholas pulled on her hand.

"What is it, darling?"

"I'm tired."

"I'm sure you are. Let's go lay down for a bit." Alyna pushed aside her troubled thoughts and smiled at her son, grateful he hadn't been hurt worse.

"Royce is nice," he said as she carried him up the stairs. "I like him."

"Me, too," she admitted with a heavy sigh, wishing

it weren't true.

❧—❧—❧

Royce left the keep, unable to contain his smile. What a delight Alyna was. A more intelligent and beautiful lady he could not envision. Never before had he felt quite like this about a woman. He was attracted to her in a way that was difficult to describe. Lust? Certainly. But there was something else involved. More than just his body reacted when she was near. Somehow, she seemed to lift the darkness trapped deep within him since his parents' death.

Nicholas was a delight as well. There was something about the boy that was different. Royce had known few children to compare him to but knew Nicholas was unique. His smile could brighten the darkest chamber. He looked at a person and seemed to truly see what their soul held. When Royce thought of a son of his own, he was hard pressed to picture any child other than Nicholas.

Royce shook his head at his fanciful thoughts. The next thing he knew, he'd be thinking of some sort of future with them. His uncle had long ago stolen his future.

Relief that Nicholas hadn't been more seriously injured lightened his heart. Edward had made two mistakes now with disastrous consequences, and Royce would tolerate no more. Though tempted to throw the man out on his ass, nothing could be done in Lord Blackwell's absence.

But perhaps it would be wise to keep Edward close at hand so he could better watch him. Many things were unsettled at the moment, and he didn't want to add anything more to the mix. The thieves had been quiet of late, but Royce was certain someone at Northe

Castle had fed them information. Lord Blackwell would return soon, hopefully with news of Tegmont, and they would be able to better plan their strategy for the weeks ahead.

Royce scanned the bailey, the thought of finding Edward foremost on his mind. He spotted Hugh striding toward him from the garrison.

"How fares Nicholas?" Hugh asked, concern creasing his brow.

"He should be fine, no thanks to Edward."

Hugh shook his head. "That man is a waste of skin and bones. I say we dispose of him anon."

"You won't hear an argument from me. But we had best wait for Blackwell to return." Royce continued toward the stables, and Hugh matched his stride.

"Then our wait will soon be over, for he returns this eve. He sent Roger ahead to let us know."

"Do we know if his mission was successful?"

"It appears the plot was foiled, but Roger could tell me little more."

Royce nodded. Even though Roger and several others had accompanied Lord Blackwell, they did not know the true purpose of their journey.

A chill crept through Royce, washing away the warmth from his interlude with Alyna and Nicholas. "I am most anxious to hear all Lord Blackwell has discovered." Royce paused and held Hugh's gaze. "These are dangerous times, my friend. I would tell you that it would not disappoint me in the least if you prefer to step away from all this. It is not your battle to fight."

Without hesitation, Hugh said, "You couldn't leave me behind if you tried. It is far past time for your uncle to pay for his sins."

Royce couldn't agree more and knowing Hugh was

at his side brought him comfort. What made a man choose to betray his own brother? That question had kept Royce awake many nights. Tegmont had coveted everything his older brother had, including his wife. How could two brothers raised in the same household with the same parents turn out so differently?

The answer mattered not. All that mattered was making his uncle rue the day he'd betrayed his only brother. "Indeed, it is long past time for him to pay."

"What does Alyna know of the situation?"

A pang of guilt struck Royce. He pushed it aside, reassuring himself all would be well. Their secrecy regarding Royce's relationship to Tegmont and Lord Blackwell's whereabouts had been in her best interest. The less she knew, the safer she would be. "Very little at this point."

Hugh shook his head. "Do you think that wise? She is Tegmont's betrothed and part of this. She deserves the truth."

Royce heaved a sigh, for he could not shake his guilt completely. Hugh was right, but it was too late now. "The situation will be resolved soon."

"I hope so, but don't say I didn't warn you."

"If only I had a coin for each time you told me that."

"If only I had one for each time I was right," Hugh added with a smile and a slap on Royce's shoulder.

"Have you been consulting Gunnell for your predictions?"

Hugh shuddered in response. "Nay. Have you seen the look that comes upon her face just before she says something...odd? It's the strangest thing."

"Is it the look on her face that causes you angst or fear that she'll say something you'd rather not hear?" Royce was curious to hear Hugh's response.

"I put little credence in what she says, but the

whole business seems unnatural to me."

Yesterday, Royce would've agreed with him. But after today's events, he was revising his opinion of both Gunnell and Nicholas.

"How could this have happened?" Blackwell demanded. The lord had arrived after dusk, and the evening meal had been served long ago. The deserted hall allowed them some privacy as he and Royce had much to discuss.

"Difficult to understand, isn't it?" Royce gave Lord Blackwell a chance to absorb the information regarding Edward's misdeeds.

"Nicholas is all right? And Matthew as well?"

"Nicholas's injuries were minor and Matthew is on the mend. All will be well despite Edward's actions."

"What was he thinking?" Lord Blackwell kept his voice low, as did Royce.

"Therein lies the question. Was he simply not thinking and these situations were accidents or did he have ill intent?" Royce shrugged, unable to answer the question.

"What does Edward have to say for himself?"

"He says Matthew was not concentrating during training and should he make a mistake like that on the battlefield, he would be dead instead of merely injured."

"Ah, so it wasn't his fault."

Royce smiled. The older man was obviously tired from his journey, but his mind was as sharp as ever. "Indeed."

"What of the incident with Nicholas?"

"He claims he didn't see the boy and questioned why the lad was near the stables."

"Not his fault again. I believe I see a pattern here." He took a long sip from the tankard of ale before him and sighed with satisfaction. "And how fares Alyna?"

Royce shifted in his seat, remembering his encounter with her earlier that day. He cleared his throat and tried to gather his thoughts. "She seemed upset that you left so abruptly. She thought perhaps you'd gone to meet with her father."

Lord Blackwell's amber eyes narrowed as he thought over Royce's comments. "I believe the time has come to explain the situation to her."

Royce nodded. He couldn't agree more. "She did a fine job tending Matthew. I'm convinced his recovery should be attributed to her."

"She has knowledge of the healing arts then?"

"Aye. She acquired some supplies and assistance from Gunnell. They have formed a friendship of sorts."

"Alyna is much like her mother, God rest her soul." Lord Blackwell rubbed his hand over his eyes. "Any other news to report?"

"All else is well. I am most anxious to hear how your mission went." Royce inhaled slowly, tamping down the impatience that flooded him.

"Lord Pimbroke was surprised to see me, as you might expect. He demanded to know how I'd discovered the attack on his life."

"Your knowledge of it must've seemed suspicious."

"He accused me first of plotting the attack, then of spying on him."

Royce leaned forward to rest his elbows on the table. "I assume you were able to convince him otherwise."

"After a lively argument. Then I told him all we know and all we suspect. He'd heard rumors of the barons disloyal to the king, but didn't realize he would be one of their targets. He finally grasped how effective it would be to sway others from their loyalty to the king if those most steadfast were eliminated."

Royce's tension eased. If Pimbroke believed them, they might yet succeed. "He understands they'll try again?"

"He thought the notion ridiculous until a tradesman arrived to sell his wares. The man mentioned how he came upon a large group of men in the woods near the road Pimbroke normally takes between his holdings. We took some men and found the place. It appeared ten to twelve men with horses had been camped in the area, scattered through the woods on both sides of the road for two or three days."

"An ambush?" Royce asked.

Blackwell nodded. "Pimbroke was shocked to say the least. To discover evidence of a large group hiding on his land was alarming. He intends to speak to King Henry as soon as possible."

"Will that be enough to convince the king?"

Lord Blackwell pursed his lips. "Lord Pimbroke says the king already knows of the unrest among the barons and their unhappiness with his interest in his wife's family and their affairs. Yet he continues to grant favors to foreigners rather than the English nobility. With all the information combined and Pimbroke's opinion, mayhap the king will take action."

Royce pondered the situation. "I have to wonder what scared off that group of men."

"I wondered the same. It wasn't us. They'd been gone nearly half a day before we arrived."

"I'm convinced there's an informer in our midst. Hugh and I will make some discreet inquiries to determine who knew you left Northe Castle and why. Some casual conversation might provide us with results."

"Excellent idea." Blackwell leaned closer. "Royce, it will take some time for Lord Pimbroke to reach King Henry. He feels this is something about which he needs to speak to the king personally. He'll have to convince the king of the validity of our case, and then he'll need time to form a plan."

"I am well aware the situation is larger than Tegmont. Much more is at stake than my regaining Larkspur."

Lord Blackwell nodded in agreement. "Tegmont's taking of Larkspur was only part of the barons' plans. It placed one of their own into a position of power, something they've done over the years to increase their hold over the kingdom. They must be stopped soon, or it will be too late."

Royce sighed, more disappointed than he cared to admit. He might not need the king's approval to take back Larkspur, but it was certainly necessary to keep it. He had no choice. He had to wait, as Lord Blackwell suggested. Patience would still behoove him. At least, he prayed it would.

Somehow, he had the suspicion that waiting for King Henry would take far longer than he could afford.

CHAPTER FIFTEEN

"Betony can protect one from bad dreams."
Lady Catherine's Herbal Journal

The acrid smell of smoke stung Royce's nostrils and burned deep in his lungs, bringing him from a peaceful dream to the familiar but still terrifying nightmare. Dragging himself from the comfort of his warm bed, he fell to the floor where cool, clean air greeted him.

"Mother? Father?" he called out weakly. Where were they?

Still coughing from the smoke, he hurried to the door and wrenched it open, determined to find them. His heart stopped at the sight of flames crawling up the walls of the adjoining chamber but he moved onward. His eyes watered from the thick, dark smoke that blocked his vision and filled his lungs.

"Mother? Father?" he called again, louder this time. He reached the top of the stairs, certain he heard voices in the hall below. Why hadn't they come for him? Surely he would be safe if he could reach them. He slid down the rough, wooden stairs, beckoned by the sound of their voices.

His mother's scream brought him to a halt, sending tremors of fear through him. Determined to save her from whatever monster held her in its grasp, he rushed toward the hall but a body on the floor blocked his path.

His father lay in a stream of blood, eyes staring lifelessly, his hand fisted on the hilt of his sword still in its scabbard. Cold fingers of fear wound their way around Royce's heart. "Father?"

"Royce!" The sound of his mother's voice tore his gaze from the horrible sight, only to see another–his uncle gripped her tightly, a dagger at her throat. Her terrified blue eyes pleaded with Royce even more than her words as she struggled to break free. "Run, Royce!"

As he stood paralyzed by fright, his uncle turned into a hideous devil and drew the blade across her throat. The movement stopped her screams in an instant. Lifeless, her gaze released Royce as she slid to the floor.

The devil chuckled with glee and turned toward Royce, bloody knife still in hand, the fire burning all around him.

The screaming started again. A glance at his mother proved the sound did not come from her. He looked back at the devil and knew he had to find the courage to stop him. He stepped back, nearly tripping over his father's body. He grabbed the sword from his father's hand and pulled it free of the scabbard. The rose crystal in its pommel shone up at him as though to tell him he did the right thing.

The fire roared, its noise deafening, but the cold steel of his father's weapon lent him strength. He stepped forward, arms trembling, and lifted the heavy sword. The fire billowed across the timber above him, and the ceiling caved in.

At last, the screaming stopped.

⚜ ⚜ ⚜

Royce woke with a start, chest heaving as he fought to catch his breath and rid his lungs of the burning pain that lingered every time he relived that terrible night of long ago.

"Damn," he swore softly, rubbing a hand over the tightness in his chest.

As he grew older, the nightmare came less often, but always with the same effect. Terrible, wrenching pain. Pain from the loss of his parents, pain from the beam crushing his young body. And when he woke, he experienced the same feeling of loss; a grief so deep, it tore at his soul.

He didn't remember anything after the timber had fallen on him. Henry, a loyal servant, had managed to save him though his uncle had left him to die in that fire. Henry had hidden him until he'd recovered from his injuries, at least the physical ones. The emotional ones had been more difficult to overcome.

Henry had helped Royce find safe haven with an old lord who took him in as a page and then trained him as a squire. As the years passed, his skills with weaponry grew as had his determination to become a knight, one strong enough and clever enough to seek revenge and take back the holding his uncle had stolen. Thanks to both Henry and the lord who had taken him in, opportunities to improve his skills had come his way.

Soon, after years of planning, vengeance would be his. The nightmare would fade to peaceful memories of his parents. No more would he relive the night that had forever changed his life.

The dream came only when something heavy weighed on his mind. What had brought it on this night?

Knowing sleep had come to an end, he rose and

donned his chausses, moving quietly so as not to disturb the men slumbering nearby. He stepped out of the garrison into the cool night air and drew a deep breath, trying to clear the bad dream. The full moon lit the area around him and out of habit, he scanned the bailey to make certain all was well.

He caught the scent of something pleasantly familiar and sniffed the night air again. Lavender. The same fragrance Alyna carried with her. Thoughts of her drifted to him along with the scent and softened the sense of loss the dream had left behind. Quick on its heels was a flare of desire. Blast the woman for smelling of that sweet flower.

Hell's teeth, it was not just her scent, but the way she looked, the way she moved. Had she been put in his path to tempt him and prove how truly weak he was? He shook his head at his fanciful thoughts.

He'd promised himself the best thing to do was to stay far away from her, but what had he done? Sought her out with the flimsiest of excuses. Touched her. Kissed her. He could not keep his hands off her. Should she stand before him at this very moment, he'd do much more than that. He clenched his jaw at the thought.

The reason he'd had the nightmare came, and at last, he acknowledged it. Hadn't he been distracted from his carefully laid plans of revenge by Alyna? How could he consider acting on his feelings for her when he hadn't yet made good on his vow for his mother and father?

He could not.

They deserved justice and it was up to him to deliver it. His focus had to return to where it belonged—on Tegmont. He fingered the amulet he wore around his neck, the one Henry had taken from his mother's body and given to him. His father's sword and his mother's amulet were all he had left of them and served as constant reminders of his purpose.

The feelings he had for Alyna were nothing more than lust. He'd felt lust before. If he chose not to act on it, it would soon fade. While he was more taken with her than any woman he'd met, that could be changed. He was in control. And while Nicholas made him think of the day when he'd have children of his own, now was not the time for that.

If he allowed these feelings for Alyna and Nicholas to grow, he would lose the focus and edge he needed. These tender feelings would make him vulnerable. Soft. Distracted. There was no room in his heart for anything save vengeance.

He breathed deeply again and caught another scent in the night air. Smoke. Bells of alarm rang in his head. The smell came not from his nightmare, nor from the direction of the keep, but from outside the curtain wall.

He ran back inside, rousing the men as he threw on his tunic, grabbed his sword, and rushed back out to climb to the walkway atop the curtain wall.

The sight below enraged him. Moonlight revealed men on horseback tossing lighted torches onto the thatched roofs of cottages where innocent villagers slept. Without hesitation, he called his battle cry, knowing it would bring the men running. The thieves below stopped their destruction at the sound of his call.

An arrow sang near his ear, narrowly missing him. Royce jumped down from the wall and ran to the stables. He freed his horse from its stall just as the first of the men arrived with Hugh in the forefront.

"Thieves!" he shouted. "They set fire to the village!" With no further explanation, he jumped on his horse without bridle or saddle, using his knees to guide it.

He galloped through the rising portcullis, his horse's hooves echoing on the cobblestones as he rode hard toward the burning cottages. Though well aware this could be a trap set to lure him and the men from the safety of the castle, he couldn't stand by while innocent villagers were in danger.

As he neared, he saw only four of the cottages were aflame. He rode to the worst one, hoping he could help. The thieves were nowhere in sight.

A man and woman in their nightclothes emerged from the burning cottage as he neared, much to Royce's relief. They coughed and choked from the smoke. The woman fell to her knees as she turned back toward her burning home, tears streaming down her face. "Michael?"

The man joined her frantic calls, his voice gruff from the smoke. "Michael!"

Royce slid off his horse and grabbed the man's arm before he could return to the hut. "You can't go back in there."

"Our son is still inside." The man's expression was filled with fear.

"I'll find him," Royce said grimly despite the unease coiling in his stomach.

"Nay, I'll go," Hugh appeared at his side, his concern evident as he well knew of Royce's painful memories of fire.

Royce shook his head, urged on by the parents' distraught expressions. He grabbed a wet cloak one of his men held out and crossed the narrow threshold into the cottage.

The sound of the fire roared in his head, louder than a hundred galloping horses. Heat from the flames sucked the air from his lungs so he put the edge of the cloak over his mouth. The smoke was thick inside the hut, burning his eyes, and he could barely make out the sparse furnishings of the room. He bent low where the smoke was thinner and lifted the cloak from his mouth. "Michael?" he shouted.

No answer could be heard over the thunder of the fire. He looked toward the corners of the room, unsure where the boy might be. Both beds in the cottage were empty. "Michael!"

The heat was overwhelming. Each breath he took felt like he drew in the fire itself. What had started as unease in the pit of his stomach now swelled into full-blown fear, stealing his thoughts, weighting his limbs. He had to find the boy and get him out.

The room shifted and the furnishings around him seemed eerily familiar. He shook his head and tried to concentrate. This was not his home. He could not let his memory play tricks on him. Not now. A father and mother stood outside waiting for their son. He would not let them down. "Boy, can you hear me?"

An odd sound came from above, causing Royce to look up as the roof of the cottage collapsed on top of him.

※─※─※

"Mama?"

Alyna stirred and rolled over to find Nicholas standing beside her bed. "What is it, Nicholas?"

"There's trouble. Bad trouble, Mama." The serious expression on his face forced her from the warmth of her bed.

"What do you mean, my sweet? Are you ill?"

"Nay." The little boy pulled at her hand. "Let's go outside and see."

Enid rose from her pallet on the floor near the hearth. "What's the matter, my lady?"

"'Tis Nicholas. He says there's some sort of trouble."

The maid lit a candle, took one look at Nicholas's face and fetched Alyna's kirtle. "You best see what's wrong, my lady."

Alyna gave Nicholas a kiss and a hug. "I'll find out and be back as quick as I can," she reassured him. She shared a worried glance with Enid as she quickly donned her clothes. "Stay with Nicholas, and I'll send for you if I need you."

Enid nodded. "Be careful, my lady."

Nicholas reached for the maid's hand. "Hurry, Mama."

Alyna did indeed hurry. The stairs seemed dark and endless as she made her way down them as fast as she dared.

Her grandfather was in the great hall, giving orders to several servants. "Awaken the rest of the keep and send all down to the village."

"Grandfather," she greeted him, relieved at his presence, "when did you return?"

"Alyna!" He looked surprised to see her. "I arrived some time ago."

"What's happened?" she asked, noting the flurry of activity.

"There's been an attack on the village. Cottages are burning. I'm going now. Most of the men are already there."

"I'll come, too."

"Nay, my dear. 'Tis too dangerous." He strapped on his sword as he spoke.

"The villagers may need me. I have some knowledge of healing. Truly, I can help."

He hesitated, his reluctance obvious.

"Please, Grandfather. I'll be careful. Surely the attackers have been chased off by now."

"'Tis true your assistance may be needed," he relented. "Let us go."

When they arrived at the cluster of burning cottages, she could see people had formed a line to pass buckets of water toward the worst of the fires but progress was slow as the well was some distance away.

Her breath caught in her throat at the sight of a man and a woman huddled together to one side of the burning cottage, their distress obvious.

Hugh directed the men as to where to throw the water but kept a careful watch on the door.

"Is someone still in there?" she asked.

Hugh glanced at her, his expression grim. "Royce went in to get their son."

"Oh, dear God." Alyna's heart squeezed with fright, unable to imagine how terrified she'd be if Nicholas were in that inferno. Even from this distance, the fire was hot. What would it be like inside?

Tears streaked the soot on the mother's face but her expression held a desperate hope. Alyna closed her eyes and said a quick prayer for the safety of both Royce and the boy.

As she opened her eyes, the sound of breaking timbers echoed in the night. The thatched roof of the cottage collapsed.

Hugh lunged forward. "Royce!"

Lord Blackwell grabbed Hugh. "Nay, Hugh, wait!" he demanded. He looked back over his shoulder. "We need more men over here!"

"Please, dear God," Alyna prayed as she watched with horror, her heart pounding with fear.

Hugh neared the doorway. "Royce," he called out. "Royce! Answer me!" He hurried around the structure as close as the flames allowed, calling Royce's name.

"Over here," he yelled from behind the cottage.

Alyna followed the men as they ran to Hugh and threw water where directed. Here, the fire did not have as strong a hold. Using his axe, Hugh hacked into the wattle and daub wall. Smoke rolled out of the opening. More water was thrown on the walls to keep the fire at bay.

"Quickly! Get that hole bigger!" Lord Blackwell demanded.

Other men pulled at the coating to reveal the wood frame structure underneath.

Hugh leaned into the opening. "Royce!" he called out. "Royce, come this way."

"Do you see him?" Blackwell asked.

"I can't see anything. The smoke is too damn thick," Hugh answered before he hollered for his friend again. "Royce!"

Alyna knew that if Royce had survived thus far, Hugh's booming voice would lead him to safety.

As Hugh continued to call out, other men enlarged the hole. Still, they heard no response. Despair filled Alyna as the smoke billowed out and flames licked the walls nearby.

"Royce! Damn you to hell and back! Answer me!" Hugh's voice was rough with emotion; his anguish brought tears to Alyna's eyes.

"If you'd quit your bellowing you'd hear me," a gruff voice answered at last.

Alyna stretched up on her toes to get a better view over the shoulders of the men, her heart in her throat. A small hand appeared, followed by an equally small arm, then a chest. Eager hands lifted the child out of the hole. Soot covered the boy's still form. He coughed as he breathed in the cool, clean, night air. The delighted cries of his parents made Alyna's tears flow.

Hugh and her grandfather hacked away more of

the wall as Royce appeared in the makeshift entrance. Hugh pulled Royce out with brute strength. The night air had the same affect on Royce as it had on the boy, and he coughed violently.

Hugh struck him on the back several times until Royce pushed him away. "Let me catch my breath, man," he rasped.

Hands at his sides, Hugh stood immobile as though uncertain what to do now that his mission was accomplished.

"Are you all right?" Blackwell asked Royce. "We thought we lost you for a few moments."

Royce bent over, his hands on his knees, as he continued to cough. "Indeed. You weren't the only ones." He looked at Hugh. "Good thing you're persistent, my friend. I'd about given up hope of getting out of there when I heard your voice."

Hugh's worried face lightened. "You were making me angry with your lack of response."

Royce straightened and put his hand on Hugh's shoulder. "We can't have that, now can we?"

Alyna could do little but stare at Royce, her relief at his survival so huge she forgot all else. His voice was deeper than usual, no doubt a result of the smoke. His face and clothing were covered in soot, yet he'd never looked better. He'd risked his life to save the boy. How could she possibly hold back her feelings for him now?

⁂

Royce tried to calm his racing heart as he took slow breaths to clear his lungs. There had been a moment, nay, more like ten, when he'd been certain he wouldn't make it out. If it hadn't been for the knowledge that the boy would die too, not to mention

Hugh's persistence, his life might have ended this very night. He was shaken to his toes from the near miss.

Fire was not his first choice as a method of dying.

He felt someone's gaze upon him and looked up to find Alyna watching him. She stood behind some of the men, her face smeared with soot, her expression filled with relief, but with something else, too.

He looked away before he did something he might regret. She was not for him. Why could he not remember that? "Is everyone else safe?" he asked Hugh.

"Aye, everyone is accounted for."

"And what of the miscreants?"

"Gone before we arrived," Blackwell answered.

"Damn!" Royce was certain the same group of thieves that had previously created problems had caused this destruction. Their reign of terror had to be stopped.

"Grandfather? Sir Royce?"

Reluctantly, Royce looked at Alyna, who stood before him with Gunnell.

"Gunnell would speak with you."

Royce shook his head. "Now is not—"

"They wait at the forest's edge, watching. They'll be riding north on the road soon." Gunnell looked very uncomfortable, her gaze looking anywhere but at him.

Royce glanced at Blackwell, then back at the healer. He almost hated to ask, yet he had to. "How do you know this?"

"She had a vision," Alyna answered on her behalf and confirmed Royce's fear.

Hugh muttered and looked away.

"Can you tell us anything more, Gunnell?" Blackwell asked.

The healer glanced at Alyna, then said, "One will linger behind the others."

"So they set a trap for us?" Hugh pointed accusingly at Gunnell. "She helps them attack us again!"

"Nay," Alyna argued. "She forewarns us."

"Alyna is right," Royce agreed. "If I was attempting a quick escape from Northe Castle, I'd take the northern road as well. It might be dangerous to go through the forest in the dark, but it would be faster than going around."

Hugh nodded reluctantly.

"If Gunnell is right, and we have a chance to catch one of them, we need to try." Royce glanced at Blackwell to make sure the lord agreed with his plans.

Blackwell nodded.

"Hugh, stay here and see to the villagers," Royce ordered. "Make certain everyone has a place to sleep this night. Some of the men can go with me to see if we can catch them."

Hugh looked none too happy at Royce's request, but turned to follow his orders.

Blackwell caught Royce's arm before he walked away. "Be careful, Royce. It could very well be a trap."

"Aye. I'll take half of the men with me and leave the rest here in case the thieves circle around behind us."

Blackwell nodded as he put a comforting arm around Alyna.

She appeared startled at her grandfather's show of affection. "Gunnell and I will help Hugh and see if anyone is injured," she offered.

Royce and the men rode slowly into the trees with quiet stealth. He held his hand high and stopped often to listen, but only silence greeted him. He hadn't expected to find his quarry easily. If they'd left when Royce had first spotted them, they'd be far ahead, but there was always the chance Gunnell was right and they'd watched the chaos their destruction had created before taking leave.

He let his horse choose its own path among the fallen trees and thick undergrowth. They knew the area well but took their time to avoid risking injury to the horses and watched for signs of an ambush.

At last, they made it to the edge of the forest near the road. Royce halted the men while still in the cover of the trees. He eased forward, watching the shadows for any sign of movement.

The muffled echo of hoof beats could be heard in the distance. Royce glanced up and down the moonlit road, trying to determine which direction the sound came from. A flash to the north caught his eye. Moonlight reflecting off metal. Several dark shadows topped the last rise in the road and grew smaller before traveling out of sight.

Another movement in the road, not far ahead, drew his attention. A single man on horseback rode far back from the rest of the group as Gunnell had foretold.

Royce considered his options, well aware it could be some sort of trick, a snare to catch him and his men. He watched the rider for a long moment and saw the man's horse moved with an awkward gait. He smiled. They could catch that one.

Royce waved Edward forward. Pointing to the rider, he told him, "I want him alive."

Edward nodded and seemed to understand that Royce was giving him a chance to redeem himself. He rode swiftly after his quarry.

Royce and the rest of the men rode hard, hoping to catch the other men. They had the lead, but their horses would tire soon. That might be enough of an advantage.

Perhaps thinking to save himself, the single rider

rode into the trees as they neared. Edward followed. Royce could only hope the knight wouldn't let him down. The time had come to discover why these thieves pestered Northe Castle and who within its walls fed them information. Edward's behavior tonight would show his hand.

Royce pushed his mount as hard as he dared, leaving some of the men with slower horses behind. At last he topped the rise where he'd last seen the thieves and was forced to slow down. A long stretch of road was visible in the moonlight, but there was no sign of the riders.

"Damn!" When the men caught up to him, he sent some to one side of the road, and he took the other. They might find a trace of where they'd left the road.

After a few minutes of searching, Royce knew it was no use, at least not until daybreak. The thieves could be waiting for them at the edge of the trees, close enough to spit at, and he wouldn't be able to see them. Searching now was asking for trouble.

"Hell's teeth," Royce cursed.

Never had they been this close to catching them before. With luck, Edward would capture the single rider and the night wouldn't be a complete loss. The thieves had to be stopped before they caused more damage. With each attack, they grew bolder. The cottages could be rebuilt, and he knew Blackwell would replace the meager possessions the villeins might have lost, but he could not replace their lives.

He thought of the young boy he'd carried from the cottage. Each life was precious, and he was grateful they'd lost none on this night.

"Sir Royce? Should we wait here until first light?"

Recognizing the young man-at-arm's frustration, Royce nodded his agreement and assigned another, more experienced man to stay with him. Then, he gathered his disappointed men and rode toward home, watching for Edward.

He arrived back at the village to find Hugh helping with the cleanup. "Any sign of them?" Hugh asked.

"They were headed north on the road, but disappeared when we gave chase," Royce told him as he dismounted. "We'll have to wait until dawn to track them. One rode a lame horse and was well behind the others, just as Gunnell told us."

Hugh looked incredulous. "Really?"

"She is often right. She means no harm and tonight she aided our cause." Royce didn't know why he felt compelled to defend her, ignoring the image of Alyna defending her so staunchly that played through his mind.

Hugh ignored his comment. "Did you capture him?"

"I sent Edward after him. Told him I wanted him alive."

"Edward? Have you lost your wits?"

"'Tis time to test him," Royce answered as he stared at the destruction and the now homeless villagers, his heart heavy. "We shall see if he sinks or swims with this task."

CHAPTER SIXTEEN

*"Lavender used in a hot compress
can ease many ills."*
Lady Catherine's Herbal Journal

Royce had finished updating Lord Blackwell and Alyna when Edward and Hugh entered the hall, dragging a struggling man between them.

"Where shall I put him?" Edward asked, his face smeared with dirt and marked with numerous nicks and scrapes. Though his voice was calm, success lit his expression. Victory had not come easily it seemed.

"Bring him forward, Edward," Blackwell ordered.

Edward yanked the angry man into the center of the hall. Long, dirty brown hair framed a snarling face in much worse shape than Edward's. A dark brown tunic made of coarse fabric hung on the man's thin frame. His hands were bound before him. A leather strip served as a belt and emphasized the bagginess of his clothing. Even from a distance, the prisoner smelled rank. Based on his appearance, his days on the road had been long and hard.

Hugh sat and poured himself some ale as Royce turned to Blackwell to see how he'd like to proceed. Alyna grimaced as she held her hand to her nose as the prisoner's odor filled the hall. Royce couldn't help but smile at her expression.

After several long, tension-filled moments, Blackwell nodded for Royce to proceed. He rose, hoping Blackwell would send Alyna to bed. Based on the prisoner's belligerent expression, this promised to be an unpleasant conversation, and he had no desire to have Alyna witness it. He sighed as he realized she had no intention of leaving and tried his best to ignore her presence.

"Loyal companions you have, leaving you behind on a lame horse to be taken prisoner."

The man merely curled his lip at Royce's comment, his blackened teeth making the expression all the fiercer.

Royce gestured for Edward to back away. He hesitated, glancing at Blackwell before complying, setting Royce's teeth on edge.

Royce stood in front of the prisoner, arms folded, allowing his larger size to intimidate the man. Silence pervaded the hall as completely as a shout would have. The man's eyes shifted, he licked his lips nervously before at last looking up at Royce, a scowl on his face.

Still Royce said nothing as he walked around the man, examining him closely to see what he could learn by his appearance alone.

The prisoner's gauntness suggested meals had been few and far between. His stench and ragged attire spoke of fortnights on the road. Royce knew from experience that being constantly on the move filled a man's bones with exhaustion, wearing on him in every possible way.

Two servants entered the hall from the kitchen, bearing trays loaded with bread, cheese, and roasted meat. The man's lips parted as his gaze followed the trays with longing.

"Who is it you ride for?" Royce asked.

The man's gaze jerked away from the food and returned to Royce, defiance written upon his face as he held his tongue.

Royce circled him again, stopping to the side of him. "Why do you ride against Lord Blackwell?"

Still no answer. The thief's gaze roamed the hall, the furnishings, and lingered once more on the food before studying its occupants. His gaze halted on Alyna.

And remained there far too long.

Anger surged through Royce at the man's impudence, and he moved forward to block her from his sight.

The thief gave him an insolent smile. Determined to teach the man a lesson in respect, Royce seized the front of his tunic, lifting him to his toes, and shook him hard.

Wariness lit the man's face, his attention squarely on Royce. "You will treat everyone in this hall with respect. Is that clear?"

The man nodded as best he could from his precarious position.

Royce lowered him but did not yet release him. "Your name?"

The thief scowled, but said nothing.

"Answer me." He shook him again, determined to get some answers.

"Thomas," said the man at last.

"Where are you from, Thomas?"

Silence was his only answer.

"Where?" Royce tightened his hold of the man's tunic, his patience ending.

"I call no place home."

"For whom do you ride?"

Again, he held his silence. His face reddened and his breath came in rasps from Royce's hold.

Royce wanted to throttle the man but could feel Alyna watching him. Bloody hell. His hands were tied with her in the room. A quick glance at Hugh and Edward brought forward reinforcements. Hugh stood beside him, his hand on his axe, and Edward stepped forward as well, his fingers flexing on the hilt of his sword.

"Who?" Royce repeated. "Whose orders do you follow?"

Thomas took in the three of them and swallowed hard. After a long moment, he shook his head. "He kills anyone who tells. I'd rather be killed by the likes of you than him."

Something in the man's expression convinced Royce he told the truth. A different method was needed to gain information from him. One that took less effort than it would to beat an answer out of him.

Royce released him. "If we offer you sanctuary here, will you tell us what you know?"

Cautious hope made the man's eyes grow wide. "How do I know you keep your word?"

Royce cut the bindings from his hands. "Our word is our honor. We'll give you food and a bed for the night. Sleep on it. If you attempt to leave, my offer is no longer open. We'll speak again on the morrow."

Royce turned to the table to confer with Blackwell and caught Alyna's expression of relief. Apparently, she had no wish to see the prisoner beaten before her.

Edward grabbed Royce's arm. "What is it you're doing? After everything I went through to capture him, you're going to feed him and put him to bed like some wayward child?" Though Edward kept his voice low, his derision was obvious.

Royce's temper snapped. He shoved Edward back. "Do not dare question me, Edward. It is not your place. You are here to follow my orders. You've sworn your allegiance to Blackwell. Do you take back your vow?"

Edward glared at Royce but at last nodded. "Nay, *Sir* Royce," he said with contempt then glanced at Blackwell before taking his leave.

Royce motioned for Hugh to take the prisoner out. The man's wary gaze remained on Royce as he walked away.

⊰⊱⊰⊱⊰⊱

"He has nightmares of fire. They haunt him," Gunnell said, her voice low.

"Royce does?" Alyna asked with surprise. She'd visited Gunnell this morning to praise her for coming forward with what she'd seen in her vision. She knew it had taken courage for the healer to speak last eve. "He's always so confident. It doesn't seem like he'd suffer from such a malady.

"He's had them for years now," Gunnell answered.

"Yet he entered the burning cottage to save the boy." Her heart fluttered at the thought. She couldn't think of a more impressive act of bravery. "Why does he have the dreams?"

The healer paused. "I don't know. I wasn't shown that."

Something traumatic had caused the recurring nightmares, that much Alyna knew. Is that what had happened when he'd woken on the journey here? A well of sympathy stirred deep inside her. How she wished she could help him in some way. She'd learned that speaking of such matters could minimize their effect, but knowing Royce, it seemed unlikely he would tell anyone of his nightmares.

"You must be pleased you were right about the thieves. Hopefully the one they caught will provide some helpful information."

Gunnell scoffed. "I didn't foresee the fire. Royce and the little boy could've died in that cottage. Why didn't I see the fire if I saw the thieves?"

"Oh, Gunnell," Alyna said with dismay. "You can only share what you're shown. I'm pleased you found the courage to tell my grandfather and Sir Royce what you did foresee." She patted Gunnell's arm, hoping to comfort her.

Disappointment clouded the healer's brown eyes. Fine lines creased her face and Alyna wondered if the burden of her gift had aged her.

"You're not to worry," Alyna reassured her. "Before long, we'll better understand your second sight and hopefully you'll be able to help others even more."

"But I didn't help. Not really. Sir Royce would've caught the thief without me. I don't think I help anyone. I only frighten them." She covered her eyes with her hands, making Alyna realize how truly upset she was.

"That's not true. Even Royce said everything you told him proved correct."

"If I would've had the vision sooner, they could've caught the lot of them. Sir Royce and his men could've waited for the thieves before they set the fires. That poor child wouldn't have been trapped in the cottage, and Sir Royce wouldn't have had to brave his own nightmare to fetch him. I see too little too late. This is a curse. A useless curse." Gunnell's voice choked with tears.

"Do not despair. The choice is not yours in this matter." Alyna sought the right words to comfort her friend but knew not what else to say. Perhaps action would provide Gunnell with a sense of control over the situation. "There has to be a reason or even a pattern of the things you see."

"I've seen none."

"Are the visions a result of what you touch? Do they always involve people you know?"

She thought for a moment then shook her head.

"Well." Alyna tapped her chin with a finger as she pondered the matter. "We'll keep examining them until we determine the reason. There's got to be some connection that we've yet to comprehend."

Gunnell said nothing, but the hopeless expression on her face spoke of her despair.

"These things take time, Gunnell. Have patience."

The healer shifted, linking her hands together and clearing her throat. "I've told my husband of your interest in my..."

"Gift?" Alyna suggested.

"He would more likely call it a curse, but aye, my gift." Gunnell got up and with restless movements, refolded the already folded woven blankets on the bed.

"And?" Alyna prompted her.

"He thinks it wrong of me to involve you. Perhaps he's right. After all, you're a lady and 'tis unseemly that you would aid me." She wouldn't meet Alyna's gaze as she paced the small cottage.

"I understand if you do not wish my assistance, but I value your friendship, and not just because of your gift." Gunnell stopped and stared at her in surprise. "You are a caring and generous person, and a talented healer, and I admire you. The choice is yours. If my presence and my questions make you uncomfortable, simply tell me and I will be gone."

The healer held Alyna's gaze for a long moment, tears in her eyes. "I would be relieved to have your help, my lady."

"Excellent. Between the two of us, we will find something to help you." Deciding enough had been said on the subject, Alyna said, "I stopped by the burned cottages this morning. Many of the repairs will be complete within a few days except for the cottage that collapsed, but seeing the senseless destruction in the bright light of day..." She shook her head, at a loss for words. "'Tis difficult to understand what purpose the thieves had."

"I had the same thought. I must say I'm grateful ours was not burned and that it was not our son who was trapped." Her expression grew grim again as her shoulders sagged. "Don't place hope with me to solve the problem with the thieves. The visions come when they will despite my efforts or lack thereof."

"What about the things you do just before the visions? Is there a particular spot where you sit that might bring them about or perhaps a food you eat?"

Gunnell thought for a moment, but shook her head. "I don't remember anything like that, but I'll pay closer attention. As frustrating as this is, I'm glad I don't see all things all the time."

Alyna nodded as she tried to imagine what that would be like. Second sight of that sort would be a burden indeed.

Gunnell's eyes widened and her expression eased. Was she in the midst of a vision? Her gaze locked onto Alyna with an intensity that made her uncomfortable.

"What is it?" Alyna asked, wondering if something had happened to Nicholas again.

"You have...feelings for Sir Royce?"

Alyna's face heated. She opened her mouth to deny it, but decided there was no point. How could she expect Gunnell to confide in her if she didn't do the same?

"I do," she admitted with a sigh.

Gunnell gave her a small smile. "My apologies, my lady. I don't mean to pry." Her smile grew as she sat at the table again. "He is very handsome, is he not?"

Alyna laughed and squeezed Gunnell's hand. "He is indeed. I've never met another man quite like him."

She didn't know what Gunnell had seen, nor did she want to. She wouldn't mention the tingling sensation that came over her when he entered a room, or the rush of longing that filled her when he was near. He was handsome to be sure. His gray eyes caused her heart to pound, and his broad shoulders and narrow hips were perfectly formed, but there was more to her attraction than his physical appearance.

He was a man of honor.

While this was a simple quality, she'd discovered how rare it was. His concern for Nicholas when he'd been injured showed how much he cared for her son. His rescue of the village boy despite his fear of fire was heroic. Yet she realized he was capable of violence. Hadn't she seen a brief display of that in the hall last eve?

Though tempted to ask Gunnell if she had seen how Royce felt about her, she resisted. She knew he found her attractive on some level, which was new and surprising in itself.

But it seemed to her what he felt for her paled compared to how she felt about him. She had no desire to hear Gunnell confirm that. Plus she already knew nothing could come of her feelings. She needed a safe haven for Nicholas and Royce was a knight who oft encountered violence.

Never mind the hollowness that weighed her at the idea of staying away from him.

Ready to change the subject, she asked, "What have you heard on the balancing of humours of the body?"

"Only a little from another healer."

"My mother had some notes on the importance of them in her journal. She said that the four bodily humours of blood, phlegm, and yellow and black biles are made of the four elements of air, water, fire, and earth as well as four qualities, hot, cold, dry, and wet. The combination of these determine a person's temperament, whether it be sanguine, phlegmatic, choleric, or melancholic. I thought perhaps a better balance would change your visions."

Gunnell nodded. "I've tried different stones and charms, but none of them seem to have helped."

"What of an herbal remedy of some sort? My mother's journal mentioned a special herb, erbe yve, but I've never seen it."

"It's difficult to find and nearly impossible to grow in a garden. I've found it on occasion in the forest some distance from here, but it is too far for my children to walk, so I do not gather it often. Do you think it might help me?"

"According to my mother's notes, it creates a better balance in the body. Mayhap it would give you more control over your powers."

"Well, I'm not certain of it, but 'tis worth a try. The herb is said to reduce nervousness, so it might help. I would like to be able to direct my gift rather than have it direct me." Her lips quivered. "I can't continue to live like this."

Alyna placed her hand over Gunnell's in sympathy. She knew, in a different sort of way, what it was like to have no control over your life. She didn't like the feeling either.

"If you'll give me a description of the herb and directions to where you last found it, I'll gather it on the morrow."

Gunnell protested, but at last relented when Alyna refused to be swayed from her mission.

A journey into the woods sounded like a fine venture to undertake. If the herb helped Gunnell, it

might someday help Nicholas as well and that made
Alyna all the more determined to find it.

CHAPTER SEVENTEEN

"Lemon balm is said to be effective
as an elixir of youthfulness, though
poor judgment seems to follow this path."
Lady Catherine's Herbal Journal

When Alyna arrived back at the keep, Enid advised her that her grandfather and Nicholas had gone to the kitchen. While Alyna appreciated her grandfather making the effort to get to know Nicholas, she worried her son might say or do something to alarm her grandfather. She had no desire to explain his second sight, at least not until she knew if they were going to live here for a time, so she hurried to the kitchen in pursuit.

"My lady." The cook bobbed a curtsey as Alyna entered the large room that bustled with servants.

"Good day to you, Tellie. Have you seen Lord Blackwell and Nicholas?"

The cook smiled. "They were here and shared some bread." She gestured to the work table in the center of the large room covered in crumbs. "I gave them some sweetened prunes to take with them on their walk."

"Did everything seem...fine between them?" Alyna asked with a hitch of panic.

Tellie frowned, obviously confused by Alyna's

question. "Aye. They were having a grand time together."

Alyna thanked her and went outside to find them. Nicholas's gift surfaced at the oddest moments. He'd certainly made himself clear about Edward's horse hurting him. She was grateful Royce hadn't questioned her more on that. At least, not yet. She could only hope Nicholas wouldn't reveal something to her grandfather.

She searched the outer bailey and caught sight of them watching the blacksmith pound a hot orange piece of metal. Nicholas watched from high atop Lord Blackwell's shoulders. Before she could reach them, they moved on toward the portcullis, scattering chickens as they went. She didn't know where they ventured, but followed as quickly as she could, anxious to get to Nicholas before he did or said something she couldn't explain.

As she passed through the gate, she could see knights and soldiers gathered in the field below the village. With the excitement of the fires and her meeting with Gunnell, she'd nearly forgotten about the jousting practice.

At last, she was close enough to get her grandfather's attention. "Going to watch the training?" she called out.

"Good day to you, Alyna. I thought Nicholas might enjoy it." With a twinkle in his eye, he added, "At a safe distance, of course."

From his tall perch, Nicholas nodded with enthusiasm. "Let's go see the joust, Mama!"

Alyna shielded her eyes from the sun and looked up at him. "Don't you want to rest a bit, Nicholas? You need to be careful of your back."

"Nay, Mama. I want to watch them joust."

Lord Blackwell chuckled. "I'm afraid I've been

bragging a bit about the jousting practice in an effort to lure him out here with me. Come, join us, Alyna."

"Aye, Mama."

Alyna looked up again at Nicholas, wishing she could keep him safely inside where nothing could hurt him.

"Please," he added, giving her his best pitiful pleading look. "Come with us."

How could she resist such an invitation? Hopefully she'd be able to divert her grandfather's attention from anything unusual Nicholas might say. "Why, thank you, kind sirs. I'd be honored to join you."

They walked companionably for a short distance before her grandfather broke the silence. "I hear Nicholas had a scare."

"Aye. It gave me a fright as well, but he seems to be none the worse for the wear." Quite the opposite. He was obviously thrilled with the view from his new perch, and his back seemed to bother him very little.

"I'm glad."

"Things around here have been quite..." Alyna hesitated as she struggled to find the right word.

"Eventful?"

"Indeed," she agreed with a chuckle.

Her grandfather lifted Nicholas down, and he ran ahead.

The little boy spotted a stick and seemed to find it suitable as a new sword. "Look, Mama!" The joy on his face at the simple discovery made Alyna laugh.

"Very nice," she called back.

"I would like to thank you for all of your help last eve," her grandfather said.

"I'm happy to help in any way I can."

"I've noticed. Although a full day has not yet passed, the villagers whose homes were damaged have most of the possessions they lost replaced as well as plenty of food." He stopped to face her. "They've all been quite generous in their praise of you. I can't thank you enough for seeing to their needs."

Alyna felt her face flush with both embarrassment and pleasure at his words. "As I said, I'm pleased to be of use."

"You work far too hard, Alyna."

"I only do what needs to be done." She shrugged, for that was truly the way she felt.

"You're a lot like her, you know."

"Who?" Alyna searched his face. "My mother?" she asked, guessing the path of his thoughts.

"Aye," he confirmed. "At times it pains me to watch you, you remind me of her so."

Commiseration filled Alyna. She placed her hand on his arm. "I miss her, too. Every day."

He nodded in agreement and patted her hand. After a few more steps, he stopped again. "I'm not sure how close you are to your father." He paused as though waiting for her response.

Alyna sighed. "I've tried so hard for so long to please him." She lifted her hands, palms up. "I feel as though I've never been able to earn his love."

Blackwell put a hand on her shoulder. "Alyna, you shouldn't have to earn anyone's love. Love is something freely given, not a reward for hard work or good behavior."

She pondered his words, realizing the wisdom of them. "I suppose Father's lack of regard for me has changed my outlook on love."

"Catherine was not overly pleased with me for the match I made for her, but I was certain I knew what was best. Your father had a small but strong holding and what I thought was a promising future. Before you were born, he became involved with barons who rumbled of their dissatisfaction with King Henry. I tried to warn him of the danger of such an association, but he wouldn't listen. I fear that association continues to lead him to trouble."

He rubbed his chin as he looked at the distant horizon. "After I confronted him about it, he made it difficult for me to see Catherine and nearly impossible to see you. Soon after her death, I left England on business for the king. I was gone much longer than I had anticipated. After Catherine's death, I should've stayed and insisted on being part of your life, regardless of what your father wanted. I will always regret that, Alyna."

Unsure of what to say, Alyna kept her gaze on the men in the field below them. "I was lost after Mother died, but I had Charles and Enid." She turned to face him and could see the loneliness that lay just under the surface. "Whom did you have, Grandfather?"

"If I had no one, it was my own fault." He sighed heavily. "Guilt and regret. Those have been my companions these many years." After a pause, he asked, "Did she speak of me?"

"Always. I heard many stories, all spoken with love." She was relieved to be able to tell him the truth. "While I know I cannot make up for the loss of my mother, I hope I can provide you with some measure of comfort during my stay here."

"You already have, my dear," he reassured her. "You and this little ray of sunshine you brought with you." He gestured to Nicholas. "That is quite a task you've undertaken."

"What do you mean?" Unease rippled through her.

"Alyna, Nicholas may be your son in many ways, but he is not of your own flesh and blood."

She stared at him, uncertain how to respond.

"Although I've been out of the country, I have sources of information with whom I've kept in touch.

None of those ever reported you marrying or you heavy with child. After much reflection on the matter, I added up the facts and confirmed them with Charles. You are a brave woman to raise a child who isn't yours."

"I have no intention of breaking my vow to raise Nicholas." She felt it best to be clear about her plan.

"No one asked that of you." He smiled as he watched Nicholas play.

"Please do not tell anyone of this. He is mine in every way that counts." She thought of how Florence would treat Nicholas if she knew the truth and nearly shuddered.

Blackwell nodded. "I will leave the telling to you. Let me just say that by the looks of the boy, you're doing a fine job of raising him. He is a good child."

Both pride and relief filled her. "He makes it quite easy for me." She wondered how much more her grandfather knew. Had Charles told him of Nicholas's gift of second sight? She thought it unlikely, but would confirm it with Charles at the first opportunity.

"Mama! Mama!" Nicholas ran towards her, one hand behind his back.

"What is it?"

With a smile bright enough to compete with the sun, he presented her with a small purple flower.

"Why, thank you. It's beautiful," she said, as she took it from his hand and granted him a kiss.

His smile still in place, he skipped off, searching for another treasure.

"I hope you will stay here with me for a time, Alyna. You and the boy."

"I think I would like that." Alyna spun the flower between her fingers, trying to work up the courage to get answers to the questions she'd had since her arrival. "Why did you bring me here?"

"I do not want you to marry Tegmont. I knew of no other way to stop it." He shook his head. "I'm not your legal guardian and have no say in your betrothal. I ask that you be patient with me. There are plans in place that will remove Tegmont from his title. I can tell you no more. Can you wait until the time comes when I can reveal additional details?"

"I can, but I worry, Grandfather."

"Worry of what?"

"Of my father. Of what Tegmont has done or will do to him for the breaking of our marriage contract." Alyna felt better for sharing her concern.

"That crossed my mind as well," Blackwell said. "I will see what I can find out on the matter."

"It would ease my mind."

"And mine as well." He called to Nicholas then told Alyna, "Enough of this gloomy discussion. Let us see how the knights are doing at their joust. Then, we'll attempt to appease Matthew when we return. He's disappointed to be missing all the fun."

The three of them continued down the hill, stopping just above the large, green field to better view the activities below. A crowd of villagers had gathered to watch as well.

Blackwell explained the process to a rapt Nicholas. "The men are merely honing their skills today. True tournaments, called *joust a`plaisance* or jousts of peace are held only at the permission of a king's officer."

He pointed to the field below. "The men wear armor of hardened leather for better mobility, and they carry rebated lances."

At Nicholas's frown, he explained, "They have blunted heads. The knights start at opposite ends of the lists and ride toward each other with shield and lance. They'll lower their lance at the last moment to carry it under their right arm, pointing it diagonally across the neck of the horse toward their opponent." As he spoke, two knights proceeded to do just as he explained.

"By carrying the lance at an angle, the impact of the lance striking the knight is lessened. I don't want any knights injured during practice as Matthew was." A shake of his head spoke of his displeasure over the accident.

"Points are awarded based on the knights' performance. If he shatters the lance, he earns more points, as he does if he strikes the head of his opponent rather than the torso. Points are deducted for fouls or strikes against the horse or legs of the rider."

Nicholas sat in Alyna's lap and watched the knights with interest. She hoped he didn't find it too compelling. The thought of him riding toward someone who wanted to strike him with a pointed weapon that big made her ill.

The sounds of the practice easily reached them and made it all the more impressive to watch. Lances clattered against hardened leather and helmets, horses thundered across the lists, and the men grunted from the impacts. The crowd cheered at each pass. The action kept the three of them engrossed.

"Participating in real tournaments not only tests the knights' skills, but can earn them a reputation and provide them with the chance to gain riches of their own from prizes," Blackwell explained to Nicholas when there was a break in the activity.

"A knight with skill can earn great wealth. Royce has won many tournaments and shattered more than a lance or two. He's also collected ransoms from capturing other knights in battle."

"Look! Royce!" Nicholas called out.

Alyna could see Royce mounted on his destrier, his authority and confidence evident even from their distant perch.

Nicholas continued to point until she confirmed to him that she saw Royce as well. Her son had grown attached to the knight. That made two of them.

As they watched, Royce adjusted a knight's hold on his lance and then had him take a second run. This time, the knight succeeded in knocking his opponent to the ground.

"If the men can talk him into it, Royce will ride against the winner," her grandfather said.

After watching a few more knights take their turns, a winner was declared. Royce mounted his horse again, refusing his helmet from his squire.

Alyna's heart rose to her throat as she watched him ride to the opposite end of the lists and turn, prepared to joust, easily handling the long lance and heavy shield. Compared to the knights who had gone before him, he made jousting look easy and natural.

One with the horse, he leaned back and moved his lance down at the last moment to knock his opponent off his horse on the first pass. The men cheered their approval, as did the three watching from the hillside. He nodded to acknowledge their applause. Though impossible to tell at this distance, Alyna swore she could feel the weight of his gaze on her. Her heart thumped madly in response. If only–

"Mama?" Nicholas asked as he rubbed his eyes. "I'm tired."

Telling herself she was grateful for the interruption to her wayward thoughts, she advised her grandfather, "I'll take Nicholas back to the keep for a rest."

"I'll come with you," Blackwell offered.

"Nay. Stay and watch the men. I'll see you soon."

She and Nicholas walked up the hill toward the keep. The farther they walked, the slower Nicholas moved, until at last Alyna picked him up.

By the time they reached the keep, Alyna was out of breath with a dozing Nicholas in her arms. To her displeasure, Florence stood on the steps outside the door.

"Hauling that boy around again? He's always underfoot, isn't he?" With a smirk on her face, she added, "In fact, I heard he was nearly trampled the other day."

Alyna's temper flared. "What you find amusing in that is beyond me, Florence. Perhaps if you had a life of your own, you wouldn't need to find humor in other people's misfortunes."

Florence's face reddened at Alyna's insult. "The boy is just fine, isn't he? No need for you to be spiteful."

"Your comments are the spiteful ones, and I'd appreciate it if you kept them to yourself." Alyna continued into the keep and up the stairs. Why she let Florence get to her, she didn't know.

She entered her chamber, laid Nicholas in the middle of her bed, and covered him with his favorite blue blanket. After a kiss on his cheek, and then one more because he was so adorable, she went to check on Matthew, certain her grandfather was right about him being unhappy at missing the jousting practice. It was time the knight got up and about to start regaining his strength.

She knocked quietly on his door in case he slept.

"Come in," he called out in a breathless voice.

She opened the door to find Florence bracing Matthew as they attempted to walk across the floor. Guilt flooded her as she realized Florence was helping him with the very thing she should've been doing.

Florence smiled with malice. "Ah, here's Lady Alyna at last to check on you. As you can see, you're not needed here."

The terrible and oh-so-familiar feeling of uselessness spread through her. How many times had her father told her the same thing? Her grandfather might believe that love was freely given, but that wasn't what she'd found in life.

She backed up, intent on leaving the chamber and Florence's knowing smile as quickly as possible.

"Lady Alyna! Wait!" Matthew's plea brought her to a halt. Panic lit the knight's eyes. Sweat beaded his brow. His shallow breathing hitched even as a grimace of pain crossed his features, making her realize all was not well.

She was letting her insecurity get the best of her. Worse, she was letting Florence's barbs reach their target. She stepped forward. "Perhaps that's enough movement for today. You don't want to reopen your wound."

The look of relief on Matthew's face gave her confidence to meet Florence's narrowed gaze.

"Nonsense," Florence argued. "The poor boy's been left to rot in this bed for days now. 'Tis time he's up and walking."

Alyna moved to Matthew's side and gently lifted his arm around her shoulders to help support him. "For a few moments each time. Standing by the bed is enough for now."

With grim determination, Florence pulled Matthew away from Alyna toward the window, making him cry out in pain. "Oh, please. He can at least walk to the window."

Despite Alyna's support, Matthew slid to the floor, groaning. "Matthew!"

"Give me a moment, if you please," he bid her as

he sat on the floor, eyes closed. "I fear I'm weaker than I thought."

Florence placed her hands on her hips. "You're the one who complained you were missing the joust," she reminded him.

The young man glared at Florence. "Aye, but I well know the reason why. I'm still as weak as a babe."

Florence huffed. "He told me not a moment before you arrived how tired he was of being left here alone all the time."

Matthew's eyes rounded to the size of small apples. "Nay, what I said was that—"

Florence interrupted him to address Alyna. "If he says he feels well enough to step outside for the afternoon, you are not in any position to deny him."

Alyna paused to consider the intent expression on her face. What could she possibly gain by taking Matthew's side so vehemently? "Your sudden interest in Matthew has come rather late. Where were you when we needed someone to sit with him day and night?"

Florence lifted her chin, her narrow lips tightening. "I thought you had the situation in hand. Obviously, I was wrong."

Pushing aside her self-doubt, she countered, "Matthew's recovery is progressing on course. He'll return to training soon and all this will be but a distant memory." She looked down at the knight to reassure him she spoke the truth.

"Not unless he's forced to get out of that bed."

"I have to wonder what you're about, Florence. Is your purpose at this keep to cause trouble for all of its occupants?"

Florence's eyes widened in surprise, making Alyna wonder if she'd stumbled upon the woman's goal.

Alyna raised a brow. "How is Hilde's hand? I heard she injured it. I have a balm that might aid her, but haven't been able to locate her."

Florence appeared taken aback at Alyna's words. If Alyna hadn't been watching closely, she'd have missed it as Florence smoothed her expression over with a look of puzzlement. "I am not aware of any injury. You must be mistaken."

"Where is she?"

"She is seeing to some things for me."

Alyna knew she'd gain more information from Mary and Beatrice than Florence. She turned back to Matthew. "Let us get you back in bed so you can rest. You can try again soon."

"I can see my presence here is no longer needed." Florence didn't bother to offer assistance. "Good day to you, Matthew." She left the chamber with her head held high.

"Good riddance, don't you think, Matthew?" She shared a smile with the young man as she helped him up.

"I thought for a few moments that she was trying to kill me as she dragged me across the room," Matthew admitted. "Thank goodness you arrived."

"She is rather scary. I just wish I knew what she's up to." Alyna shrugged as she checked the linen bandage. "It doesn't seem to have reopened. Rest now. Perhaps you can have some fresh air on the morrow if you're feeling up to it."

Matthew sighed. "It's hard to believe I'll ever return to normal."

"Patience. Recovery comes in small steps."

Alyna made her way to the kitchen to check on the progress of the evening meal and to see if Tellie could think of something special for Matthew to help cheer his spirits. Florence's visit had certainly not done the trick.

- ⊰⊹ -⊹- ⊹⊱ -

"My lady, this seems most unwise," Charles said, shaking his head.

Alyna stifled a sigh. Though tempted to venture into the forest alone, she hadn't forgotten the attack on the village two nights past. "Charles, this is very important to me. I've no one else to ask."

"But they have no horses to spare. The men are patrolling the area in shifts to watch for trouble and every horse has been put to use." As Charles swept his arm around the stable, she realized many of the stalls were empty. "The horses remaining are for the next watch."

She bit her lip as she considered her options. The memory of the hope on Gunnell's face reminded her of the importance of this mission. "Then we'll walk there. It will take longer, but we'll be back well before nightfall if we leave now."

"Leave for where?" Royce's deep voice had Alyna spinning around to face him. He led his destrier toward them, his brown hair tousled by the wind.

Her heart fluttering from his unexpected appearance, she sought a reply but found her mind blank. She could feel Charles' gaze on her even as Royce halted before them.

"I was merely discussing a household errand with Charles." Somehow she knew Royce would be displeased with her intent and had no wish to argue with him, not when a victory seemed unlikely.

"An errand of what sort?"

She lifted her chin, determined not to be intimidated. Her purpose might sound silly to him, but she knew it was important to Gunnell and perhaps even to Nicholas at some later date. "A particular herb we're in need of grows deep in the forest. I intend to gather it today."

"I'm sorry, but I can't allow that. 'Tis too dangerous."

A glance at Charles showed her she'd receive no help from that quarter. The servant stepped back, abandoning her. "From what I understand, the thieves are unlikely to cause trouble anytime soon," she said.

"We don't know that for certain," Royce argued. "Especially when we hold one of them."

Alyna hadn't thought of that. "They don't seem like the type of men to lay siege to a castle for one of their own."

"True. Which is why I'd like you to remain inside the curtain wall where we know it's safe."

Alyna refused to give up so easily. "I need the herb. What would you suggest?"

He appeared baffled by her question. "I suggest you do not go."

"That is not possible." She stopped there, hoping he'd offer a better solution.

"Why is this herb so important?"

She bit her lip as she pondered how best to explain it. "This herb is said to help balance the humours of the body."

"And your humours are in need of balancing?"

"Nay. It's not for me."

"Ah. I should've known." He shook his head. "Who is it for?"

"Gunnell. To aid with her visions."

Those gray eyes held hers for the longest moment. "I don't pretend to understand your need to help the healer, but I must insist you remain here."

Disappointed that he didn't realize how important this was, she nodded. He didn't need to know that she nodded in acknowledgement at his words rather than agreement to do as he asked. If she left now, she could be back before anyone was the wiser.

"Alyna." His tone held a warning.

Guilt gave her pause. He couldn't possibly have read her thoughts, could he?

"You intend to go anyway," he accused her.

"I never said that."

He shook his head. "Gather your things. We leave anon."

Charles chuckled behind her, but a glare from Royce had him coughing to cover his amusement.

Alyna hid her own smile, pleased at Royce's offer in more ways than one.

CHAPTER EIGHTEEN

"'Tis said bathing in comfrey can
restore virginity, but I have my doubts."
Lady Catherine's Herbal Journal

Royce couldn't believe he was in this predicament.
Again.

Despite his best intentions to avoid her, Alyna sat
before him on his destrier, her body warm against his.
It was good that she faced away from him, that those
amber eyes weren't staring up at him, calling to him
like a siren.

She shivered and pulled her cloak tighter. The air
held a damp chill this morn, the sun tucked behind
clouds. He stifled a groan as she shifted again in the
saddle, bringing her bottom closer. A few more moves
like that, and he'd pull her to the ground and make
her his own.

"Where is this herb said to grow?" he asked,
hoping for a distraction from her sweet fragrance that
tempted him to nuzzle her neck.

"A gnarled oak marks the spot where the path
begins."

He grunted. "Do you know how many gnarled oaks
grow in these woods?"

Her gaze scanned the area as they entered the
trees. "Gunnell said if I entered the forest directly east

of the well, I'd be sure to come across it."

Royce looked back over his shoulder to verify their location. "Then we should find it soon."

His steed picked its way through the trees and shrubs while Royce watched for any sign of the thieves as well as for the gnarled oak. The patrols hadn't found any evidence of the bandits, but Royce intended to keep up the patrols until further notice.

"Perhaps that one?" Alyna suggested as she pointed to a twisted oak tree just ahead.

He guided the horse in that direction and found a path at the base of the tree began as a faint trail, but soon took on a more worn appearance.

"We're to travel on this for a time until we come to a large rock with gray streaks down its face. Then go west until we reach a meadow full of wild flowers, among which grows this herb."

"And you were to find this place based on those directions?" Royce shook his head. "I doubt we will find this meadow, but we shall try."

"That is all I ask."

"What is it about the healer that makes you want to help her so much? Or is it because of Nicholas?"

Alyna spun to face him so quickly that Royce drew the horse to a halt. "What do you mean?" she asked, panic in her eyes.

"Surely you don't think I didn't notice." He wondered if she'd tell him the truth or deny it. Did she trust him enough to reveal this secret? For reasons he couldn't explain, he desperately wanted her to.

"Notice what?" A small frown marred her brow.

"I was with you when Nicholas predicted a black horse would hurt him, remember?" He held his breath, waiting to hear what she'd say.

"I was hoping you'd forgotten that."

He resisted the urge to tell her that he never

forgot anything that happened regarding her and Nicholas. "How many other things has he foreseen?"

She bit her lip, seeming to weigh the risk of telling him the truth. "He woke me the night of the thieves' attack but only said there was trouble." She grabbed hold of his arm, squeezing tight as she looked up at him. "I don't want others to know of Nicholas's gift. Not yet at least. He's only a little boy. His path in this life will be difficult enough without everyone realizing how different he is."

"You mean how special he is." Royce lifted her hand from his so he could touch her cheek. He nearly gave voice to the protectiveness surging through him, to tell her that he'd defend them both with his very life if necessary.

Her eyes filled with tears. "Oh! I'm so glad you understand."

"So this is why you champion Gunnell so fiercely. Because of Nicholas." At last, he understood Alyna's actions of late, including her determination to make this journey into the woods.

"In part. She's a good person in an unusual situation and struggling to understand her visions. How would you feel if people called you crazed?"

"It would be a difficult burden to bear," he admitted, trying to imagine such a thing, to imagine Alyna defending Nicholas from people calling him crazed.

"You don't seem very surprised by all this."

He shrugged. "There are many things in this world that are not explainable. In my travels, I have learned not to scoff at what I do not understand."

Unable to resist, he moved his thumb along the softness of her cheek. Desire poured through him as she tilted her head as though seeking his caress. With a sigh at his weakness, he bent his head and kissed her, wishing she'd thrust him away.

Instead, she shifted in the saddle to better face him and put her arms around his shoulders. The heat of her body burned his, her breasts pressed against him, and his desire grew ever stronger.

Her mouth was sweet, unbearably soft. He resisted the urge to devour and kept it slow to better savor the taste of her. He nibbled at the corner of her mouth then indulged himself by returning to her parted lips.

Many times had he imagined her in his arms, just like this, and now that it was a reality, he wanted to explore much more than her mouth. He threaded his fingers in her dark hair, amazed at the soft strands that spilled like fine silk through his fingers.

His exploration continued to her shoulders, her neck, pressing kisses to the spot just below her ear. He moved her cloak aside to span her narrow waist, then up toward the swell of her breasts.

He told himself to stop, convinced himself he would after just another moment of this paradise. Never had a woman gone to his head like this, as though she were some exotic wine in which he'd overindulged.

"Royce?" Alyna's breathless voice slowed his progress across her jaw and behind her ear.

"Aye, my lady?" he answered, leaning his forehead against hers, not willing to break contact with her yet.

"Your horse seems to be moving."

He smiled. That he hadn't noticed proved how enamored he'd been with their kiss. Apparently, his horse had more sense than he did. "So he is. I suppose we must continue on our journey if we want to find that herb."

He placed one more kiss upon her lips, then turned her forward, keeping her in the circle of his arms as he gathered the reins again.

The path wound through the forest, at times barely visible. Royce pushed branches aside to prevent them from scratching Alyna. The farther they went, the more pleased he was that he'd accompanied her on this outing. The idea of her venturing here with Charles or even worse, alone, made him nervous.

As they traveled, they spoke, first of inconsequential things, then of more personal topics. Royce appeased his curiosity about Alyna's life and she did the same. Her positive outlook warmed him. Her humor amused him. Her combination of innocence and intelligence intrigued him.

The brush of her hair on his chin sent awareness spearing through him. She often turned to look up at him, those long lashes teasing him, her smile inviting him to join her. He reveled in the feeling of her in his arms as she leaned back against him.

It didn't take long before he realized he'd made a terrible mistake by coming with her this day.

A deep ache at what couldn't be filled him. She deserved a husband who would cherish her and protect her, not drag her into danger with a plan of vengeance. How could he possibly offer her marriage when he was no more than a landless knight? When the mission he would soon go on could easily end in his death? He had no chance for a normal life until he took back his father's holding from Tegmont and gained the land and title that were his by right.

His enjoyment of the outing dimmed as he tried his best to distance himself. Better to endure the pain now than later when he was even more taken with her or her with him. He moved his arms from around her and shifted away, kneeing his horse to speed their progress. He needed to get this errand over and done with as quickly as possible.

⁕–⁕–⁕

The sun had emerged and warmed the air by the time they came upon the rock Gunnell had described to Alyna.

"I'm certain this is the next marker. Now we head west," she told Royce.

She was relieved to know they were nearing the meadow. She'd enjoyed their conversation and their kiss, but the farther they traveled the more Royce withdrew from her. A deep sense of loss filled her at the distance he'd put between them. She could only guess that he wanted to return to his duties and she was in the way. Hopefully, they could locate the herb and return to the keep as soon as possible.

A short distance later, they arrived at a clearing and Royce reined in his horse. "Is this it?"

"I believe so. There's only one way to find out."

Royce dismounted and lifted her to the ground. When his hands remained on her waist, she looked up to find his gaze on hers, his expression unreadable. Longing coursed through Alyna and she moved closer, leaning in for his kiss.

Royce released her abruptly to loop the reins around a nearby tree. "What does this herb look like?"

Alyna released her breath, disappointed as he turned away. "Ah, Gunnell says it has pear-shaped green leaves and grows low to the ground."

"Humph."

"She insists it's quite distinctive. It might carry small yellow blossoms as well."

Without further comment, he walked toward the far side of the meadow, searching the ground as Alyna did the same on the other side. She tried her best to stay focused on the task, but the fact that he'd chosen not to kiss her and now searched as far away from her as possible had not escaped her attention.

Had she offended him in some way? Had he had a change of heart and decided he no longer cared for her? With a sigh, she reminded herself it didn't matter. Sharing kisses with him would not benefit her or Nicholas.

Why didn't that make her feel any better?

"I think I've found it," Royce called out.

"As did I," she said, realizing she'd nearly trampled the herb.

"Do I pick the whole plant?"

"If you could just pinch off a few leaves of several plants, then it should continue to grow," she instructed him. "I'll dig up the entire herb from the one I found."

The bland look he gave her suggested she asked too much of him, and she couldn't help but laugh. With a heavy sigh, he bent down and did as she requested. Alyna was pleased he had regained his good mood.

She pulled her gaze away from him and bent to gently dig around the herb with her knife and fingers. Gunnell would be pleased they'd found it. Alyna hoped it helped her.

Royce walked over with leaves piled in his hand. "Where would you like these?"

"Would you fetch the bag that Tellie packed for us, please? We'll make a place for them in there," she said, pointing to the leather bag tied behind the saddle.

He placed the deep green leaves in her lap and walked over to get it. "This seems awfully heavy for some bread and cheese."

"I think it's more than that. Tellie is always trying to get me to eat more. There's probably enough in there to feed half your men." She looked up at him, shading the sun from her eyes. "Thank you, Royce. I'm very glad you offered to accompany me."

He set down the bag and squatted beside her. "You are never to venture outside the curtain wall without a guard. Am I clear?" He asked as he tapped her nose with his finger.

Ire at his bossiness struggled with appreciation for his concern for her welfare. Appreciation took the lead, and she smiled at him. "All right. Until the situation with the thieves is resolved."

A shadow passed over his face. He said nothing but sat beside her and took out the contents of the bag, item by item. Several were wrapped in cloths, and she gestured toward one. "May I have that to wrap the herb in?" She held up the herb, root and all.

He took off the cloth to reveal a meat pie and handed her the cloth. She wrapped the herb, taking great care not to break off the stem or leaves. A glance at Royce showed him holding the meat pie as though not quite certain what to do with it. "Surely you're hungry. Why don't you just eat it?"

"I'd rather get back to the keep. The longer we stay out here, the more risk we take."

"We've seen no sign of the thieves, nor is this the side of the castle they attacked from. Taking a few minutes to eat will surely cause no harm. Besides, I'm hungry." She couldn't help but put a hand to her growling stomach.

Looking less than pleased, he gave in, taking a bite of the meat pie as he handed her one of the cloth-wrapped parcels.

Along with the meat pies were dried fruit, fresh baked bread, cheese, and a small corked jug of wine to wash it down with. "No wonder the bag was so heavy," Alyna said as she shook her head.

"How many days did the cook think you'd be gone?"

Alyna chuckled as removed her cloak and bit into a meat pie. She could think of nothing to say, and the silence between them grew long and awkward. She knew Royce was impatient to be on their way. He probably had many duties he'd yet to see to that he'd neglected in favor of escorting her. For that, she was sorry, but she was not sorry he was here with her now. Awkward or not, she enjoyed being in his company. She well knew the chance of having another secluded afternoon with him was unlikely.

Desperate to think of something clever to say, she stole another glance at him.

To find him watching her.

Heat rose in her cheeks as she held his gaze, her mouth suddenly dry.

He reached out and touched her cheek just as he had on the horse earlier.

Her heart melted. Until she realized he was merely brushing a crumb from her cheek. Embarrassed, she smiled, hoping he didn't realize the effect he had on her.

He lowered his gaze to the meat pie in his hand. Unsure of what to make of his behavior, she continued to glance at him as she nibbled a dried peach, her stomach a flurry of butterflies.

He finished eating and took another drink of wine before handing the jug to her. As he brushed off his hands, he asked, "Are you ready? We should be on our way."

Reluctance filled Alyna. Never had she shared a meal in a pretty meadow with a man, let alone one to whom she was so attracted. Would she ever again? Saddened by the thought, she looked again at Royce, wondering how she could prolong the moment.

He packed the bag with the remaining food, then folded the leaves they'd collected into one of the cloths with care. The sun glinted on his hair and turned it golden. His features, now achingly familiar to her, were relaxed. As she watched him, her heart twisted and filled with a wave of emotion so great, it swallowed her whole.

So, this is what it felt like, she thought. Half pleasure, half pain, it threatened to erupt into something she could not control. She loved this man body and soul.

She swallowed hard and tried to put the lid back on the cauldron bubbling inside her.

Royce glanced over at her. "Are you all right, Alyna?" Concern etched his features as he drew nearer.

"Royce," she began. She laid her hand on his, willing him to understand in some small way everything happening inside her. Then she did what she'd thought of doing since she'd first met him. She stretched up to gently kiss the small scar near his eye.

He jerked back. His gray eyes darkened as he stared at her for an endless moment.

Dismay filled Alyna. What had she been thinking to act so forward? She pulled her hand from his warm skin, but he captured it with his own. He held her gaze as he turned her hand in his. Then he closed his eyes and placed his lips on her palm.

And stole her breath.

He withdrew his lips only to place them again on her palm, the addition of his tongue sending a rush of sensation through her. Shock mingled with desire and rooted her in place as his searing gaze found hers. At last, he released her hand and bent his head toward her, seeming to take an eternity before his lips met hers.

Joy and desire sang through her. She returned his kiss, reveling in the freedom her love for him gave her. Her arms wound around his neck and held on tight, wishing she never had to let him go.

He eased her down onto her cloak as his gaze searched her face as though to make sure she understood. "Alyna, I desire you more than words can say but—"

Before he could say more, she put her fingers against his lips. "Nay. Let us simply enjoy this moment." She drew his head down for another kiss, her tongue giving chase to his.

His gruff grunt of approval was all the encouragement she needed. She slid her fingers through his soft hair, moving along his neck and well-muscled shoulders, glorying in the sensations singing through her.

His desire for her seemed to have no bounds. No longer did he hesitate. He nuzzled her neck, his lips finding every sensitive spot she hadn't known she had. His hands joined the sweet torture, his fingers trailing along her bare skin before gripping her waist, moving even lower to her hips.

The weight of his upper body on hers was an unexpected pleasure. He felt so good, so right. Her hands continued their discovery of him. Her fingers caught on a thin strand of leather he wore around his neck. Again she kneaded his wide shoulders and back, marveling at the muscles rippling under his tunic.

His hardness pressed against her thigh through their layers of clothing, confirming his desire for her. Though she didn't know what could come of their attraction, she knew she wanted Royce. At least for this one enchanted afternoon, she wanted him in every way possible. This was her chance to share her passion with the man she loved.

Her roaming hands seemed to free his. He caressed every inch of her. A moan rose in her throat, and she broke their kiss to give voice to it. His lips moved to her throat, kissing, licking and nipping, until she stirred restlessly beneath him. "So beautiful," he muttered.

His words fueled her desire, and she throbbed everywhere he touched. "As are you."

His deep chuckle made her smile. Then his fingers found the laces of her kirtle and pulled them free. The garment opened to his searching hand and revealed her linen shift. He eased it down her shoulders and rained kisses as he explored her.

She followed suit and found the bottom of his tunic and raised it up his chest, running her fingers over the smooth skin of his back, then to the mat of hair that covered his chest. His muscles flexed under her fingers as he moved, making her wish she could see more of what felt so fascinating. She pulled his tunic higher, and he rose to his knees to remove it.

As he dropped it to the ground, he hesitated, uncertainty evident on his face. "Alyna," he began.

"This moment is ours." She rose to her knees and pressed her lips to the scars that marked his bare chest. A pale blue stone hung on the strand of leather around his throat that she'd touched earlier and her breath caught.

A blue stone the color of the sky.

Of course. Hadn't she always known in her heart he was the knight destined to aid her?

"Royce," she said without hesitation, "let us enjoy each other for this one day." She ran her hands over his chest and pressed kisses to the broad expanse, breathing in the clean scent of him, delighted to see what she'd only felt moments before.

His breath hitched and his muscles quivered as

she touched him, reveling in his response.

"Alyna," he said her name again, this time with desire. He reached out to cup her cheek before trailing down to the sensitive skin of her neck, then lower still to linger at the curve of her breast still covered by her shift.

She held her breath as his fingers dipped lower and lower, her breasts tingling with anticipation. At last, he grazed her nipple, and she gasped with pleasure at the sensation. Desire shot through her entire body and pulsed deep within her.

He gently pushed down her shift to reveal her breasts to his heated gaze. "You are so very beautiful, even more than I had imagined."

She smiled and for once in her life, felt beautiful. His rough fingers alternated with his calloused palm to perform an intricate dance on each breast. The throbbing in her very core kept beat with his touch until she felt she would burst with pleasure.

He lowered his head and kissed her shoulder, his mouth leaving a heated trail as he moved lower. She frowned in confusion. Surely he didn't mean to–

Oh! His mouth was so hot. She arched back and tangled her fingers in his hair as he gave each breast equal amounts of attention. She ached with need. "Oh, Royce."

"Aye," he murmured. The sight of him kissing her so intimately nearly matched the pleasure of his mouth on her. When she was certain she could bear it no longer, he eased her back onto her cloak, his body partially on hers. The wiry hair of his chest against her added another layer of sensation, and she gasped and shifted against him in response.

His hand moved to her thigh, and she caught her breath. His fingers caressed her bare skin, moving ever closer to the heat of her center.

"Let me touch you, Alyna. Let me touch all of you," he murmured against her throat. He took her mouth with his as his fingers brushed against her. She moaned, amazed at how he made her feel.

More, she thought. She needed more.

As though he'd heard her, Royce gently touched her.

Her hips raised in answer.

"Aye, Alyna," he murmured as he continued his sweet torture.

But still...there had to be more. A release from the aching need that consumed her. "Royce?"

He moved away for a moment, but only to help her remove her clothing. His gaze admired all of her, his appreciation for her evident by the intense expression on his face. Then, he removed his chausses and his manhood sprung free.

Alyna gazed in wonder, the size of it giving her pause. But she had to touch him. She trailed a finger down him, surprised at the hardness under the velvety skin. Royce moaned in response, and she looked up, alarmed, only to see the pleasure her touch gave him.

"No more." Royce grasped her hand and held it against his chest. "Your touch undoes me." He kissed her fingers and took a deep breath before lying down beside her once again.

Alyna marveled in the sensation of their bare skin touching. He felt so right against her. He kissed her before lingering in the curve of her neck. Her desire for him took on a new hue, and her heart swelled with love. Delight filled her as she realized this powerful knight was also gentle and tender.

"Your skin is so soft," he murmured. "As is your hair." He ran his fingers along her hair, then over one breast, down to her stomach, and even lower.

Desire returned ten-fold when he resumed his exploration. It started in her very center and sent waves of feeling clear to her toes. But even so, when he eased between her thighs, nervousness took hold. Though she had a basic idea of what was going to happen, never had she expected to be so overwhelmed by the feelings coursing through her.

⚜ ⚜ ⚜

Royce groaned as he tried to pull back the reins of his desire again and clenched down on the feeling that threatened to end this before it fully began.

Never before had it been this way with a woman. Never had he felt his control threatened by the very sighs that passed a woman's lips. By the tilt of her head as her eyes closed in surrender. By the restless stirring of her body as he pushed her closer to the edge.

He shifted and pressed against her heat. His hands braced on either side of her to hold his weight, he eased slowly forward, surprised at the tightness of her.

Suddenly, he stopped, knowing now why. He looked into her eyes, reading the truth there.

He was her first.

He should've picked up on the signs of her innocence, but he'd been too distracted by his desire for her. Unsure of how he felt about this or what he should do, he paused.

Her expression held no doubts as she wound her arms around his neck to pull his head down for another kiss, teasing him with her tongue. All thoughts left his mind when she tilted her hips up to meet his.

As she released a moan, he took her in full. He

clenched his teeth and stopped again, this time to give her body a few moments to adjust to the feel of him.

His body shuddered with the effort, wanting nothing more than to continue. He looked down at her, trying to gauge her reaction, afraid to discover she wanted to stop after all.

After a brief frown, she moved against him, and this time it was more than he could bear. Knowing he was near the edge, he touched her intimately. Above all, he wanted to feel her tighten around him in release.

He was rewarded when he felt her first shudder. Her response was all he needed before he yielded to his own pleasure, the intensity more than he'd ever before experienced.

Several moments passed before he could think coherently. Slowly, he lifted the weight of his body onto his elbows, surprised at how weak he felt. He raised his head to look at her, not wanting to see any sign of regret on her face at the gift she'd given him.

She smiled up at him, her amber gaze warm and tender, her face flushed with the aftermath of pleasure. He leaned down to kiss her tenderly.

He shifted to her side and gathered her against him, not prepared to let her go. "All is well?"

"Oh, yes," she said, her enthusiasm making him smile.

He continued to caress her arms, her shoulder, the delicate line of her jaw. Her skin was flawless, a creamy white, soft as the petal of a flower. Her breasts were firm, overflowing the palm of his hands with their weight. He lifted up to lean on one elbow to see her beauty again. To his surprise, she gave him the same scrutiny he gave her.

When he felt his manhood stirring, he knew he needed to think of something else, but that was difficult to do with her naked in his arms. The sight of her so warm and willing was what he'd dreamed of for many nights.

His gaze came to rest on her flat stomach. "Nicholas is not your son."

It was a statement rather than a question, but Alyna answered easily. "He is my son in every way, but not by birth."

"Why?"

She sat up and pulled on her linen shift, as though uncomfortable answering his questions while bare. "I was with his mother when she gave birth to him. Myranda was a healer too, and she had second sight."

"So that is where Nicholas gets his talents." Royce nodded and waited for her to continue.

"She died giving birth to him. I vowed to raise him as my own. So I have, and so I will."

After a few moments of silence, Royce told her, "I know of vows, Alyna, and I respect yours. It is not an easy task to raise a child, especially on your own. I'm sure your father was less than pleased."

"Nay, he was not. Of course, I dared not tell him of my vow. He didn't care for it when I spent time with Nicholas, so I made sure Nicholas stayed out of sight as much possible. When Father insisted I marry Lord Tegmont and leave Nicholas behind, I prepared to flee. I couldn't leave Nicholas. If you hadn't brought me to Northe Castle, we would've come anyway. Charles, Enid, and I had been planning our departure for some time."

But Royce heard nothing further than Tegmont's name.

That alone was enough to dim the pleasure of the day. Why did his uncle hurt every person Royce cared about? Tegmont had to be stopped. At all cost, his actions had to be halted.

"Royce?"

Royce could hear the concern in Alyna's voice and did his best to push past the rage that engulfed him.

He took a deep breath and then looked at her, still sitting in her shift, the light fabric pulled taut, outlining the curves of her body. Her dark hair splayed alongside her face and down her back, a dramatic backdrop to her creamy skin still flushed with passion. Her golden eyes watched him with wariness, and he closed his eyes with regret that he could not give her what she wanted. What she deserved.

At least, not yet. Nor could he make promises that he might not be able to keep.

"We must get you back, Alyna." He gathered both her hands in his. "We have much to speak of, you and I. But there are things I must do, things I must see to before we can truly talk." He kissed each of her hands, then stood and drew her to her feet. He hoped his sudden change in mood hadn't pushed her away, but it was the best he could do for the moment.

Somehow, he had to free himself of the black, dark hole that filled his soul. The only way he knew to do that was complete his revenge. If he didn't, or couldn't, he'd have nothing to offer this beautiful lady, neither his heart, nor a home. He could only hope she would wait for him.

CHAPTER NINETEEN

"Aster is an effective love potion,
but be certain you use it wisely."
Lady Catherine's Herbal Journal

We have much to speak of, you and I.

Royce's words kept cadence with her steps as she made her way to visit Gunnell the next morning. No matter what she did, she simply couldn't get her mind off the events of yesterday and what he'd said to her again before they'd parted.

His mood had shifted dramatically after she'd told him of her vow to Nicholas. But why? Surely that had not caused him to withdraw. Yet what else could it be?

The ride home had been long. Though he'd held her and they'd conversed, she'd no longer felt that special bond of warmth. Royce had erected a wall between them she hadn't been able to breach.

Still, she didn't regret what had been the most glorious day of her life and one she would treasure always.

Oh, but what if it hadn't been for only one afternoon? What if she could have that every day of her life? The idea gave her such fragile hope that she was too frightened to believe it might be possible.

One moment, her heart would soar with optimism. He'd shown he cared for her with his tenderness and if he did care, he'd want to make plans for a future together.

And the next moment, that same optimism plunged to despair.

When she'd first met Royce, she'd been certain he wasn't the type of man she needed or wanted. Aye, he was handsome and formed in a way that made her heart pound just to look at him, but did he represent the safety she needed for Nicholas? In the years to come, or maybe it would only be months from now, Nicholas would show more signs of second sight, and when that happened, Alyna wanted to surround him with people who cared for him and could protect him.

Royce could certainly protect him, but would he care for him? Would he willingly raise another man's child as his own? She shook her head at her wistful thoughts. She wasn't so naïve as to expect Royce to offer for her because they'd spent one afternoon together.

Her breath caught in her throat, and her hand moved to her stomach. What if she carried his child?

Luckily, the last thought brought her to Gunnell's cottage, so now she'd be forced to think of something else. Before Alyna could knock, the door flew open.

Gunnell stood there with shock upon her face. "My lady, are you all right?"

Alyna felt heat stain her cheeks, wondering what Gunnell referred to. "I'm well, Gunnell. And you?"

"I'm fine, but I thought..." Gunnell stopped, a puzzled look upon her face.

"My journey into the woods was successful." Alyna chose to ignore her odd behavior and handed the healer the small basket she carried. Though confused, she had no desire to discuss her predicament with anyone at the moment. She needed to work through things herself first.

"Oh, that's wonderful."

"I found the meadow you'd described. You'll be pleased to know several plants grow in the area, so if the one I brought you doesn't grow, we can gather more."

Gunnell glanced into the basket. "Oh, my lady, I don't know what to say." She looked at Alyna with gratitude. "How can I ever thank you?"

"There's no need for thanks." Alyna leaned forward to hug the woman. "Someday, I'll need something, and I know you'll be there when I do. That's what friends are for."

"Are you certain that time isn't now?" asked Gunnell.

Alyna laughed nervously. She'd felt this way with Enid as well. The maid had looked at her so carefully after hearing Royce had accompanied her that Alyna felt she must have some sort of mark on her face telling everyone what had happened. Alyna vowed to look at her reflection more carefully the next time she had a chance.

"Never mind." Gunnell stepped back and gestured for Alyna to enter the cottage. "Please, come in."

"I can't stay long," Alyna replied.

Gunnell paused and took a deep breath. "My lady, I must tell you." She bit her lip as she hesitated, her worry evident.

Alyna's stomach tightened with trepidation.

"I had a vision." Gunnell's warm brown eyes filled with concern. "Trouble is coming, my lady. I can't see it clearly yet. I don't know when, or who, or how, but it is terrible. I fear it concerns you."

Dread seeped into Alyna, its coldness catching her breath. It seemed Myranda's prediction was holding true after all.

❧❧❧

"Royce!" Edward's call echoed in the bailey and halted Royce's progress across the green grass.

Royce had no desire to speak with Edward and didn't bother to hide his impatience at the interruption. All he wanted was to see if Hugh had received word from Blackwell as to when he would return. Royce couldn't make it through another day without asking Blackwell for his blessing to marry Alyna once he successfully took back Larkspur. Not if. When.

Edward approached with a cocky smile that immediately put Royce on guard. "I have some interesting news for you."

"What would that be?" Unless it had to do with Lord Blackwell, Royce had little interest in anything Edward had to say.

"I took the liberty of interrogating our *guest*." Edward's derision at the term was clear.

"What?" Royce stepped forward, unable to believe Edward's idiocy.

Edward lost some of his confidence. "I spoke with the thief."

"By whose authority?"

"My own. I'm the one who captured him." Edward's face reddened with indignation.

"That does not give you permission to speak with him."

"And why not? Where were you yesterday? Wasn't that when you were supposed to speak with him?"

The barb struck true; that had been his intention. However, plans were made to be changed, and Royce didn't regret the way his had been altered.

Edward continued, "You were nowhere to be found, and I decided if you weren't going to bother to

take action after I risked my life to capture him, then
by God, I would, and I did."

Edward's belligerent attitude pushed Royce's
temper up another notch, as did his suggestion that
Royce had shirked his duties. He refused to explain
himself to Edward. "You are not in any position to
make those kinds of decisions. Have you no brain in
that thick skull of yours?"

"Don't blame your incompetence on me. If you'd
done your job, I wouldn't have had to."

Royce took a deep breath in an effort to refrain
from hitting Edward. "And what results did you
obtain?"

"Needless to say, I pressed him to no avail, but
after further persuasion—"

"You forced him?" Royce could hardly believe his
ears.

"Of course! He left me no choice. What did you
expect?"

"We gave him sanctuary. I expected you to honor
that."

"You gave him sanctuary. Not I. Feed him. Clothe
him. What kind of treatment is that for a thief?"

"The kind of treatment that will allow the man to
switch loyalties without losing face." Royce shook his
head. "Put yourself in his position. He was abandoned
by the very men to whom he'd given his loyalty. For
all they knew, he'd be killed immediately or worse.
How would that make you feel? He came here with
nothing but the threadbare clothes on his back. If
someone could clothe you and put food in your
stomach, provide a safe place to live and a coin or two
in your pocket, what would you do?"

Edward stood, hands on hips, and stared across
the bailey. By the look on his face, it was apparent
that Royce's logic was starting to make sense to him.

"Edward, the last few...situations you've been involved in have caused serious harm. Your worst failing is that you lack empathy for the people around you." Royce pressed Edward while he had his full attention. "Have you even spoken to Matthew or Nicholas since they were injured?"

Edward's brow raised in surprise. Obviously, the idea hadn't crossed his mind.

"You should. Nay, you need to." There were some things that could not be taught. A man of honor knew what the right thing to do was and acted on it. "Now, tell me what you learned from the thief."

What Royce heard next was surprising indeed.

﹉﹉﹉

"He did what?"

"That's what I said." Royce had at last found Hugh, and he was as angered by Edward as Royce. The two men made their way toward the area of the garrison where the thief was staying.

"Edward should be gone by now. Enough of his idiocy."

Royce agreed but knew the decision was Blackwell's. "Edward and I had words. We'll see how he reacts to them and what Blackwell says upon his return. Has any message arrived from him?"

"Nay. Nothing." Hugh cast a long look at Royce. "Did you have words with anyone other than Edward?"

Puzzled, Royce glanced at him. "Such as?"

The older man shrugged, but the sly grin on his face was a large clue. "You and the lady were gone quite some time yesterday."

"I told you. I assisted her in gathering some herbs for the healer."

"Forgive me, but I have difficulty imagining one of the kingdom's finest knights gathering herbs. How exactly do you 'gather herbs' anyway? Or is that code for something else?" Hugh moved his brows up and down suggestively.

Royce sighed. There was no purpose in going down this path with Hugh. The man was like a dog with a bone. Normally, Royce admired this quality in his friend, but not when it was directed at him.

"Seriously, Royce, are you sure you know what you're about? Or perhaps a better question—does Lord Blackwell?"

Royce held open the door of the garrison for Hugh. "I intend to speak with Lord Blackwell as soon as he returns. Now, let us see the condition of our guest. I want to confirm what Edward told me, and then you and I need to speak with Blackwell the moment he returns."

By the look of the man's face, Edward had been rough with him. The thief rose as they entered the small chamber and looked at them with the very wariness Royce had hoped to avoid. A large red bump grazed his jaw, and one eye had already turned a distinct purple.

Royce shared a look of disgust with Hugh. The process of gaining information from the man would only be harder now that Edward had interfered with their plan.

Hugh leaned against the door of the small chamber as Royce waved the man back onto the narrow bed on which he'd been resting. "Sit."

Though slow to respond, the man obeyed with a grimace. Royce could've struck Edward for this mess. Somehow they had to convince the thief to confirm what he'd told Edward, or better yet, tell them more.

"Thomas, right?"

"So much for your promise of sanctuary." He spat on the ground. "I've got nothing to say to the likes of you."

"My apologies for Sir Edward. He was not acting on my behalf." Royce let that information sink in before he continued, "My friend and I would like to hear what you told Sir Edward."

Thomas snorted. "I'm not repeating myself."

Royce glanced at Hugh before offering, "I think we could make it worth your while."

Hugh nodded in agreement.

They now had Thomas's attention. "How?"

Royce named a price, much lower than the one he was willing to pay, but enough to keep Thomas's interest.

"Royce! Surely you can't mean to pay the man so much." Hugh played his part well as he straightened with supposed outrage. "What could he possibly have to tell us that warrants such a sum?"

"I believe he could tell us many interesting things. Couldn't you, Thomas?"

"The information I have is worth more than that pittance," Thomas assured him with a sly look. He leaned forward, elbows on his knees. "In fact, I could tell you more than I told that other man."

He'd taken the bait. Now, the thief was on the same side of negotiations as Royce, right where they wanted him.

"Come now, Royce," Hugh complained. "Let us be reasonable. Blackwell won't pay that kind of money." Hugh could've fooled a bishop with his acting ability.

Royce pondered Hugh's comment for affect, as though unsure. He let silence linger in the room.

"I could tell you some very helpful information. I could indeed," Thomas boasted and rose in his effort to convince them of his sincerity.

"Such as?" Hugh asked with enough doubt in his tone to make Thomas nervous about losing the opportunity before him.

The thief chewed his lip, obviously unsure how much to say to convince them he was worth the coin they offered and more. "I know where their camp is."

Royce hid a smile at the success of their ploy. "I believe that is what you already mentioned to Sir Edward. I'm not sure I know where it is from the description you gave him."

"I could take you there."

"That would prove useful." Royce had hoped for this. But he also had concerns that it could be a trap, perhaps set up with Edward's assistance. "What else do you know?"

"What would it be worth to you?"

Hugh spoke again. "Royce, what is the point of this? We have no way of knowing if he speaks the truth or not."

Royce nodded in agreement.

"Believe me, you will realize the truth of what I tell you. In fact, for a small additional sum, I could tell you the purpose of our raids." He glanced nervously at Royce's sword.

Excitement stole through Royce. This was more than he'd hoped for. "Well, that would definitely increase my previous offer."

In a short time, a deal was struck and coins passed hands with the remainder to be paid when Thomas finished his tale.

"So, tell us, Thomas. Why are you preying upon Lord Blackwell?"

"He is not the reason we raid these lands." The thief swallowed hard.

"Why else would you?" Hugh asked.

"The lord who pays us–" Thomas began.

"Who is this lord?" asked Royce.

"I know not, sir. This I swear. But I do know that he believes a certain knight might plan on causing him problems in the future, so he seeks to kill that knight."

A chill ran down Royce's spine. "Who is this knight?"

"We were told he's a man of your height. Brown hair, gray eyes." Thomas paused for effect, more of a storyteller than his listeners had given him credit for.

"Get on with it, man," Hugh urged as he placed a hand on the head of his axe. "Or we'll be tickling it out of you."

"No need for that." He cleared his throat nervously, keeping an eye on them both. "The knight we seek carries a sword with a rose crystal in the pommel."

Royce shared a look with Hugh, but refused to look down at his own sword.

"What is this knight's name?" demanded Hugh.

"No one was sure, but I know now."

Royce stared hard at the thief. "Speak clearly or forfeit your life."

The thief glanced nervously at Hugh before he answered Royce. "I-I'm telling you that we were paid to find a man with a sword such as yours."

"And?" Royce asked.

"We were to create enough mischief to cause this knight to give chase, and then lure him into a trap. But we couldn't get him to follow the plan. The trap has yet to succeed." The thief seemed to grow more nervous by the moment, desperate to be believed. "I tell the truth. The pay I got wasn't good enough to buy my silence, not when the bastards deserted me."

"Who paid you? Who gave you orders?" Royce asked.

"Our leader's name is Daniel. He's the one who paid us and told us where to go and what to do. But I don't know who gave him orders."

Though they questioned the thief further, the man had little more to tell. Royce paid him the remainder of the coins with the promise of more if Thomas remembered anything else of importance.

Royce walked out the door into the clean, fresh air, something he appreciated even more after being in close quarters with the thief, clean clothes or not. Apparently the man had not taken them up on an offer of a bath.

"It has to be your uncle," Hugh said as soon as he was sure they were alone in the bailey. "Why does he not attack you outright?"

"He must not be certain of my identity or that I live. Or perhaps he fears killing a knight would bring him trouble. He may know of my association with Lord Blackwell and wouldn't want to bring down his wrath by killing me. He has to know Blackwell is close to the king. All the more reason to murder me indirectly." Royce rubbed his chin as he thought it through. "He wouldn't want anything to happen that could reveal his past misdeeds. How annoying for him that I cropped up after he left me to die all those years ago."

"Murder would be a better word than misdeeds," Hugh commented. "We need to go to that camp and speak with this Daniel as quickly as possible. We'll take Thomas with us to show us the way. Daniel will confirm for us that Tegmont is behind the attacks. We'll have even more proof of your uncle's treachery. That will justify your taking Larkspur. When do we ride?"

"As soon as I speak with Blackwell."

"But he's gone. We can't take the chance the

thieves will move the camp. We must act while the information is still valid."

"Hugh," Royce began. His friend's loyalty meant more to him than he could put in words, but this plot was growing thicker by the moment. "I want you to stay here. If Tegmont knows I live, this could be a trap. For all I know, Edward somehow arranged this with the thief and Tegmont to try to kill both of us. I will not have your blood on my hands."

The annoyed look Hugh gave him nearly made him smile. "Do not be an imbecile. I will fight by your side and together, we will defeat your uncle and regain Larkspur. When do we ride?"

⚜−⚜−⚜

The mid-day meal was about to be served by the time Alyna returned to the keep. Gunnell's words of upcoming trouble worried Alyna. Unfortunately, the healer hadn't been able to tell her any further details; she only knew the trouble involved Alyna.

Did it mean Alyna had no future with Royce? Or did the problem have to do with her father or Tegmont? There was no way to know. She had to be prepared for anything.

Alyna's stomach grumbled at the scent of an appetizing aroma in the air as she made her way into the bustling hall. Thoughts of food disappeared when she saw Florence and Hilde sitting on either side of Nicholas at the high table. Those two were trouble, of that she had no doubt.

"Nicholas, where's Enid?"

"Mama!" Nicholas bailed off the bench and into her arms. "I can't find her or you."

"You've found me now." She couldn't resist picking him up so she could look into his eyes and reassure herself that he was all right.

"I'm glad," he answered, his expression calm as he smiled at her.

"Good day, Alyna," Florence said. "We were just keeping Nicholas company until you returned from...wherever it is you ran off to. Again."

Alyna stiffened. "What is that supposed to mean?"

Florence waved a hand. "You're always off roaming the countryside leaving poor Nicholas to his own devices." She gave the boy an overly sweet smile and reached out to pat his leg. "Isn't that right, Nicholas?"

Nicholas frowned at Florence then laid his head on Alyna's shoulder without answering her in a sweet show of support.

"There is no need for you to concern yourself with Nicholas, Lady Florence. He is well cared for." The idea of her son spending time with Florence made Alyna ill.

She glanced at Hilde, who hadn't bothered to rise when Alyna had arrived. Why she sat at the head table, Alyna had no idea. If she hadn't departed by the time the meal was served, Alyna would send her on her way.

The maid gave her a knowing smile, which filled Alyna with unease. "How is your hand, Hilde?" Alyna asked. "I heard you hurt it when you were cleaning."

"I had no injury, my lady." Yet she kept one hand beneath the tablecloth.

"Alyna, my dear." Her grandfather's voice greeted her.

Alyna turned in surprise. "Grandfather, I didn't know you'd returned."

"I'd wager you didn't know Sir Royce left, either." Florence rose as she spoke, her words for Alyna's ears only.

Her words caught Alyna's full attention. Hurt and disappointment flooded her. Had Royce truly left without a word to her?

Florence pressed a kiss on Blackwell's cheek. "So glad to see you returned safely, my lord." Her gaze slid to Alyna as though to measure how her news had been received.

"I'm glad to be back," her grandfather said. His words carried an odd undertone Alyna didn't understand. The long look he gave Florence made Alyna wonder if she was somehow the cause of it.

The woman's eyes narrowed as she caught Blackwell's look. The odd exchange between the two puzzled Alyna, but she was more concerned with Royce's departure.

Florence smiled sweetly at Alyna. "I was just telling Alyna that Royce might be gone for some time. At least, that's what he told me."

Alyna turned to her grandfather, Nicholas still cuddled against her. "Is that true? Sir Royce has left?"

"Aye. He had business to attend to. I'm not certain how long he'll be gone." Her grandfather squeezed Nicholas's shoulder then put his arm around Alyna. "Let us eat. I have several things to tell you about."

Disheartened, Alyna let him guide her to the table, but her thoughts remained on Royce. Surely he hadn't taken the time to tell Florence and not her, yet the facts proved otherwise.

"Mama?" Nicholas lifted his head. "I'm hungry."

Alyna smiled, trying to put aside her hurt and remember her priorities. "Then let us eat."

Her grandfather took Nicholas from her and sat him on the bench. He gestured for Alyna to sit and did the same. Alyna realized Hilde had vanished. The maid moved about like a ghost, disappearing when it suited her.

Her mind still reeled at the news of Royce's departure as trenches were placed before them. Florence kept her distance now that she'd delivered her news. Did Royce's absence have something to do with the trouble Gunnell had foreseen?

"Alyna." Her grandfather's voice pulled her back from her thoughts. He looked about to make certain no one overheard. "I fear I return from my travels with bad news."

Her worry increased tenfold. "What is it?"

"You were right. Lord Tegmont is most unhappy with your disappearance. He has threatened to take Montvue if your father doesn't fulfill the betrothal agreement."

"Oh dear." Alyna wasn't surprised by the news; it was just what she'd expected of Tegmont. What to do about it was another matter. She couldn't possibly marry Tegmont. There had to be some other solution. "What do you advise?"

"I fear little can be done." He shook his head, his voice low. "Your father shouldn't have made the match in the first place, but I suppose he had no choice. I'd wager that Tegmont threatened to declare him a traitor if your father didn't agree. Tegmont has caused nothing but trouble for years now."

Alyna glanced at Nicholas to make certain he paid no attention to their conversation. His attention was focused on the roasted venison before them. "You mean because of his involvement with the barons disloyal to King Henry?" she asked.

"It started well before that. What he did to Royce's parents is unforgivable."

"What do you mean?" Alyna's confusion increased. "What does Tegmont have to do with Royce's parents?"

Blackwell looked at her in surprise. "I thought you knew. That Royce had told you."

"Told me what?" It was all Alyna could do not to scream the words at him. What on earth was he talking about?

"Tegmont is Royce's uncle. Tegmont murdered Royce's parents and left Royce, their only child and heir, for dead in a terrible fire in the keep. All so he could take the holding for his own."

Alyna's heart stopped beating. She was certain of it. How could anyone do something so horrible? No wonder Royce had nightmares of fire. "That's terrible!"

Her grandfather tore a chunk of bread off the trencher. "Royce has planned revenge against his uncle since that day."

The coldness filling her made it impossible to breathe. Had Royce shown interest in her only in an effort to take revenge against Tegmont?

"I had been gathering information on the disloyal barons, one of whom was Tegmont, when our paths crossed. Our motivations might be different, but Royce and I share similar goals. We would do most anything to stop those barons. Needless to say, Royce has a more personal involvement, considering that Tegmont murdered his parents."

Shocked, Alyna froze, hardly able to process what her grandfather had said. She shook her head in denial. Surely everything they'd shared hadn't been a lie. It couldn't be.

Yet the idea took hold and wouldn't let go. She could think of no reason Royce had withheld all of this from her except one.

She was part of his plan of vengeance.

CHAPTER TWENTY

"Black Hellebore is oft used to kill
wolves and foxes, but it can also be
used to cure gout."
Lady Catherine's Herbal Journal

Alyna lay in bed, the darkness of the night a match for the despair in her heart. She shivered. The furs that covered her provided no warmth. The sounds of Nicholas and Enid snoring softly brought her no comfort, not this night.

Had Royce made love with her only to humiliate his uncle? Did he care for her at all?

And her grandfather–had he used her as well? Blackwell had sent Royce to fetch her from Montvue. Had their purpose been to save her from marriage to Tegmont or simply to thwart Tegmont's plans?

The voice of doubt echoing in her mind would not be silenced. Why else would Royce act as though he cared for her if not to use her in his quest for vengeance? He couldn't possibly want her for herself. How often had her father told her how ugly and worthless she was?

Doubt burned deep in her heart until her breath came in hitches.

Her mind said it wasn't so. After all, she'd been the one to make the final choice to lay with him. She couldn't fault Royce for seeking revenge, but she could fault him for using her in the process.

She hoped she'd covered her hurt at the information her grandfather had shared with her. She didn't want Lord Blackwell to know she'd fallen in love with Royce, that they'd made love. The last thing she wanted was Royce to be forced to marry her.

For a brief moment, she allowed herself to relive their times together. Royce had seemed so sincere, the memory of his tenderness pushing back her doubt.

Oh, she wished she knew how he felt. If he had some affection for her, wouldn't he have told her? But then she realized that even if he had, she couldn't compete against his lifelong goal.

Tears slid down her cheeks as sobs burned her throat. Would she have a chance to show him the kind of life they could have together? The joy they could share? The good memories they could make to help ease the pain he'd suffered all these years?

Or would his need for vengeance erase their chance at love?

⚜-⚜-⚜

The next day dawned with a dreariness that matched Alyna's mood perfectly. She lay in the warmth of her bed, reluctant to rise and get on with the day. By the stillness of the chamber, she knew Enid and Nicholas had already woken and left her to sleep.

Unfortunately, her confusion and doubt had not resolved themselves during the night. Her thoughts took up much the same path they'd been on when she'd fallen asleep. She rubbed her temples, but still her mind continued like a mill, grinding the same worries over and over.

Annoyed with the pointlessness of her thoughts, she threw back the covers and prepared to dress.

A quick peek out the window confirmed the coolness outside, and she donned warm clothing. She splashed water on her face with the hope of erasing some of the signs of her sleepless night.

To her relief, only a few servants remained in the hall breaking their fast. The bread and cheese tasted bland, but she'd had little to eat the night before, so ate as much as she could bear. The day stretched endlessly before her, and she tried to think of how best to fill it.

The herb garden would be a pleasurable way to pass the day and a productive one as well. She dusted the crumbs from her fingers and rose from the table.

"Good morning, my lady," Enid greeted her as she made her way to where Alyna stood.

"And to you as well, Enid." Alyna managed a small smile in the hope of avoiding any questions.

"Did you sleep well?" Enid asked with a frown.

Since Alyna knew perfectly well Enid knew the answer to the question, she answered as truthfully as she could. "Nay, I did not. I fear I couldn't settle. I think I'll try a different pillow tonight."

"I'll find another for you. Perhaps a bit of lavender in the stuffing will help."

"Thank you." She managed a smile. If only the solution were that simple. "Where is Nicholas?"

"He's with Charles down at the stables. I'm certain he'll return before long."

Alyna nodded. Nicholas loved horses, even Sir Edward's, though it had caused him injury. But as long as Charles was with him, Alyna wouldn't worry. "I'll be in the herb garden if you need me."

The morning passed slowly for Alyna though she spent it doing one of her favorite things. With the low, gray clouds hiding the sun, she lost track of time.

"My lady?" Enid stepped out of the small garden door. "If I'd have known you had this much to do out here, I'd have come to help you."

"I've neglected it these last few days, so the weeding took more time than I'd intended."

"You've got it as tidy as can be now. Did Nicholas get bored and move on to other things?"

Alyna looked up in surprise. "Nay. He never came to see me. I thought he was still with Charles."

Enid's cheeks reddened. "Actually, I've been with Charles, and we both thought Nicholas was with you."

Fear gripped Alyna, but she pushed it away. "I'm certain he's fine. He's never wandered away before. Let's find Charles, and we'll decide where to look for him."

Charles was in the stables and gave Enid a sly wink when they approached. His expression grew solemn when Alyna asked him about Nicholas. "He was with me for a bit this morning, but I haven't seen him since."

"When did he leave?" Alyna asked, her stomach dropping like a stone.

Charles now looked worried as well. "Hilde came and got him and said you'd sent her to fetch him for you."

"Hilde?" Alyna and Enid asked in unison.

"Aye. She said the boy was to come with her, that you'd asked her to fetch him for you. He seemed a bit reluctant, but I thought it was because he didn't want to leave the horses." Charles's face had gone pale with worry. "I told him he had to go, that he could help me with the horses later."

"Oh, dear Lord," Alyna said as panic took hold. "I didn't speak with Hilde today, and I would never have had *her* come and get Nicholas."

"Is there some sort of problem with her?"

Alyna shared a look with Enid. Her maid shared her opinion of both women. "She and Lady Florence have been up to no good, but surely they wouldn't harm Nicholas. You two search the grounds, and I'll see what Florence has to say."

Alyna hurried across the bailey, back to the keep, where she passed through the hall, then into the kitchen, but no one had seen Nicholas. She made certain everyone knew she searched for him. She peeked in her own chamber and called out his name, hoping against hope to see him playing there.

Nothing.

Trying to contain her panic, she knocked on Florence's chamber door. "Lady Florence? 'Tis Alyna."

No sound emitted from within the chamber. Alyna was about to turn away when the door opened slowly.

"What is it?" Florence asked impatiently.

Alyna gritted her teeth. Could the woman never be civil? "Have you seen Hilde?"

"Why?"

"I need to speak with her."

"Why would I know the whereabouts of a servant?"

Alyna realized if she failed to gain Florence's cooperation, it would just take that much longer to find Hilde and Nicholas. Time was something she couldn't spare. "Nicholas is missing. Hilde spoke to him earlier today, and I'd like to know when she last saw him."

Florence scoffed. "She has nothing to do with that child. Why would she?"

"I don't know. That's what I'd like to ask her. Please, Florence. Do you know where Hilde might be?"

"I haven't seen her since earlier in the day. She was in the hall then."

Alyna's panic escalated. As she'd suspected, Florence was no help. Perhaps Charles and Enid had already found Nicholas. If not, she'd find Hilde. Without Florence's assistance.

"It's no wonder you can't find that boy. He wanders around as though he's the lord of this keep. You should watch him more closely."

The last thing Alyna needed was a lecture on Nicholas's care. Though sharp words came to mind, Alyna didn't voice them. She didn't have time to argue. Instead, she said, "Please let me know right away if you see either of them."

Florence didn't bother to respond, but shut the door in Alyna's face.

On her way outside, Alyna asked a servant to find her grandfather as quickly as possible. Although she might be overreacting, the situation didn't seem right. More importantly, it didn't feel right. For a fleeting moment, she longed for Royce. He would know what to do.

From the top of the steps of the keep, she scanned the bailey for Charles or Enid. She spotted Charles first, striding at a brisk pace toward her. From the grim look on his face, the news was not good. Tears filled her eyes, and she put her hand over her mouth to stop sobs from escaping. Now was not the time. She had to try to stay calm, to think of where Nicholas could be.

"Alyna?" Lord Blackwell joined her. "What's wrong?"

"Nicholas is missing." She looked at him, praying he'd tell her that her son was with him.

"Are you certain?" he asked as Charles hurried up the steps.

"There's no sign of him, my lady," Charles said, breathless from his brisk pace. "But the guards at the gate did not see him leave either. Nor have they seen Hilde."

"Hilde? The maid?" Lord Blackwell looked confused. "What does she have to do with this?"

Alyna explained what little they knew, relieved to have his assistance. He immediately organized a search of the grounds and sent several of the men-at-arms into the village to look for Nicholas. Enid returned empty-handed as well, so she and Alyna went back into the keep to search every nook and cranny.

"Where could he have gone, my lady?" Enid asked as they entered the hall, tears in her eyes, worry in her voice.

Alyna shook her head as she hooked her arm through Enid's to support them both. Terror filled her, numbing her mind. Somehow, something horrible had happened, just as Gunnell had predicted. Florence had to know more than she'd let on. "Enid, go look in the kitchens one more time. Ask anyone you come across to help search for him. I'm going to speak with Florence again."

"Aye," Enid agreed as she wiped her eyes and rushed off.

Alyna started up the stairs as a servant entered the keep.

"Lady Alyna?" he called to her.

"Aye?" Hope rose within her, and she hurried toward him. "Have you found Nicholas?"

"Nay, but I've a message for you." He handed her a rolled parchment sealed with wax.

"Where did this come from?" She looked at the seal on the message, but didn't recognize it.

"It was delivered to the front gate a short time ago. Don't you worry. We're all searching for young Nicholas." The man bowed his head and left the keep.

Alyna sat down on the steps with the parchment in hand. She did not want to open it, for somehow she knew it held bad news. With trembling fingers, she broke the seal and unrolled the paper.

'My Dearest Alyna,

You have what I want, and it seems I now have what you want. If you would like to see what I have alive, come to me. Come alone and tell no one. An escort awaits your presence at the postern gate. And then we will both have what we want.'

The missive was signed with a 'T'.

"Oh, dear God." She buried her face in her hands. Lord Tegmont had Nicholas. Her poor baby must be so frightened. She would follow Tegmont's instructions to the letter, and she would hurry. Surely he wouldn't hurt her son.

There would be no need, for she would do anything he wanted to keep Nicholas safe.

CHAPTER TWENTY-ONE

"Combine lemon balm, catnip, and chamomile
to relieve nervousness."
Lady Catherine's Herbal Journal

Royce and Hugh surveyed the encampment from just inside the forest edge. The budding trees and bushes provided them with excellent cover. The rest of the men remained farther back in the woods with the horses.

Thomas had led them right to the camp. The thieves had picked an excellent location from which to wreak havoc. A sheer rock face protected the back of the camp, and a small river guarded the front and one side. It would be a simple matter to cross the river but not without being seen. The only side that could be approached without difficulty would force them to leave the cover of the trees and cross an open meadow.

"Well?" Hugh asked, his voice down to a whisper. "What do you think?"

Royce shook his head. "I don't see any sign that a trap has been laid for us."

"True enough, but I don't trust Edward. Nor do we have any reason to trust Thomas."

"He led us here well enough but we know this is only one of their camps."

"I say we watch for a bit longer and see what we

can see."

Royce nodded. "No reason to rush things." He tamped down the urge to take the camp now. The sooner they could have words with the leader, the sooner they could return home. Blackwell hadn't returned before they left, so Royce had left a message for him. But there was one important conversation he was eager to have with Blackwell that had to be in person.

"I told Edgar to keep a close eye on Thomas and make certain he doesn't leave his sight even to piss."

Royce smiled. "We'll take the camp when darkness falls. By then, we'll have a better idea of how many men there are. I want the leader, Daniel, alive, to provide the proof I need to make certain Larkspur becomes mine."

"Thomas will need to identify him for us. I'll fetch him."

Royce continued to watch the camp. The men he counted numbered no more than twelve, unless some were sleeping.

One man tended a horse, five sat by a small fire, two others prepared a meal, and at least five milled elsewhere about the large camp. All seemed in the same dirty, bedraggled state as Thomas had been. Bedding lay on the ground and several rough shelters were clustered near the rock wall.

Royce and his men were outnumbered, by how many it was hard to say, but that didn't worry him. His men were well-trained soldiers, whereas the thieves had banded together for the sake of a paltry reward. Their skills had been honed from life on the run, not from formal training. Plus, Royce's men would have the element of surprise on their side.

Royce wanted to make certain Daniel was in camp. He needed the leader to identify Tegmont as the one who paid the thieves and gave them orders. With luck, the man would also confirm that Tegmont had ordered an ambush on Pimbroke. That move had been a foolish one on his part. He'd risked far too much and it would cost him.

Hugh returned with both Thomas and Edgar in tow. Thomas's gaze was riveted on the camp. Royce wondered if he missed his fellow thieves or if he was simply curious to see who remained there.

"Do you see the leader?" Royce asked. "We want him alive."

Thomas cast a wary glance at Royce.

Hugh leaned forward and whispered in his ear, "Don't forget who pays you now and puts food in your belly."

Thomas nodded. "Not likely to forget, am I?" He looked again at the camp. "I don't see Daniel."

Hugh elbowed him in the back. "Take another look. Your life depends on it."

The thief watched for several more minutes. "I don't see him." He glanced nervously at Hugh. "But that isn't unusual. He doesn't always stay in camp."

Royce looked closely at the thief. "Where does he go?"

Thomas shrugged. "He travels to get orders and the coins to pay us. Sometimes he's only gone a short while and other times he's gone for a day or two."

Frustrated, Royce pulled Hugh to the side so they could talk privately. "Surely he wouldn't protect this Daniel."

"I don't think so. What purpose would it serve? Let us give it a bit more time. Perhaps the leader rests inside one of the shelters."

Thomas gestured for them to come nearer. "That's his horse there." He pointed to a large black steed that one of the men tended. "He can't be far."

Royce breathed a sigh of relief. The idea of waiting a few days to make their move was unacceptable.

Time passed slowly as they watched the camp but gave Thomas the chance to tell them where the weapons were and what they consisted of. Some men were armed with short swords, but many appeared to have nothing more than a knife upon their person.

A tall lean man with dark hair emerged from one of the shelters and stretched. "That's him," Thomas said excitedly.

"Are you certain?" Hugh peered over Thomas's shoulder, and the thief stepped forward warily, as though uncomfortable being so close to Hugh.

"Aye. I'd know him anywhere."

Daniel walked through the camp with an air of authority. He stopped near the fire, nudged one of the men with his boot, and sent him off on some errand. The man didn't appear to appreciate having his conversation interrupted and scowled at Daniel's back.

Royce observed a few moments longer to make certain Daniel wasn't preparing to leave. Then he ordered Edgar to keep watch while Royce, Hugh, and Thomas went back to gather the men and finalize their plans.

Royce had great faith in the men he'd brought with him. He explained in detail how he wanted the attack to proceed. Each of them got a good look at Daniel and knew to leave him for Royce.

The men and their horses moved as close to the edge of the trees as they dared. The horses were restless, stomping and snorting in the cool night air as though they sensed a battle drew near. When darkness fell, all were ready.

Royce raised his hand high for a moment then dropped it down. His men burst forth from the trees and crossed the meadow, the creak of their saddles, the rattling of their weapons, and the pounding of the horses' hooves the only warning the thieves received.

As they neared the camp, they fanned out, screeching war cries while they infiltrated the camp. The startled thieves stumbled out of the shelters and lurched to their feet.

The ringing of metal striking metal filled the night air. Men grunted and swore, increasing the mayhem. The firelight cast eerie shadows and added to the confusion.

Royce kept his gaze on Daniel as he rode toward him. Surprise registered briefly on the leader's face as he realized he was Royce's target before he drew his sword. He stood, legs braced apart, his sword gripped in both hands, waiting for an opportunity to defend his camp.

As Royce rode toward him, Daniel called out, "What fight do you have with us?"

Before Royce could answer, Daniel spotted Thomas. Then his gaze flew back to Royce. "So the one we seek has become the seeker."

"Your tactics left me no choice." Royce jumped down from his horse, sword in hand. He would fight with honor against his opponent.

Daniel's smile gleamed in the firelight as he circled Royce, his sword held at the ready. "I thought this day might come."

"My fight is not with you, but with the one who pays you," Royce said.

"Then your fight is with me," he answered, the light of battle in his eyes.

"Your loyalty is so strong that you would die for him?"

"There is a high price on your head." Daniel's smile grew even broader. "I'll be a rich man when I kill you."

Royce smiled at the man's audacity, misplaced as it was. "You will not kill me, Daniel. I have much to live for." Power surged through him as he thought of Alyna.

At the use of his name, the leader of the thieves sent a lethal stare at Thomas. "What else has that worthless traitor told you?"

"Not everything. That is why I'm here."

"I'll share nothing with you," Daniel said as he lunged at Royce.

Royce blocked his thrust and shoved the man back. "Reconsider."

Their conversation came to an abrupt halt as Daniel attacked again, his moves proving him to be a skilled swordsman. On their battle went, even as the chaos around them died. Back and forth their thrusts and blocks came and went.

Royce kept the man dancing, giving him no rest, wearing him down little by little. Still the thief did not give up. Royce left him no opening to attack, but forced him to defend himself over and over.

The silence of the camp seemed to at last penetrate Daniel's attention, and he stole a glance around to see his men defeated. His distraction gave Royce the opportunity he needed to knock Daniel's sword from his hand and shove the man to the ground.

Royce held his sword at the man's throat. "What say you now? Have you changed your mind?"

"Perhaps we should talk."

❈ ❈ ❈

Alyna paused before the postern gate and drew a shaky breath. No matter how much she wished otherwise, she held little hope she'd return to the keep with Nicholas in her arms.

She'd told no one about the note or where she might be going. Charles and Enid, and even her grandfather would worry about her, but Nicholas needed her more than they did. Hopefully she could send word to them once she had Nicholas back.

With a quick glance over her shoulder to be certain no one watched, she opened the door to find several men-at-arms waiting, along with a woman. Hilde. Her smirk infuriated Alyna.

"Where is Nicholas?" Alyna demanded.

"Perfectly safe. You worry for no reason. But first you have unfinished business with my lord."

Alyna's stomach dropped. The idea of seeing Tegmont when she thought she'd escaped him made her ill. And now he had what was most precious to her. She swallowed hard to keep the contents of her stomach in place. "Why are you here?"

"To provide you with a proper chaperone. We can't have your reputation ruined by you traveling with all these men, now can we?"

Alyna's gaze caught on Hilde's hand which was red and raw looking. "You should be more careful when you burn tapestries with lye. What was the purpose?"

"We didn't want you to get too comfortable and cozy with Blackwell. Lady Florence was supposed to make sure of that, but her attempts failed to convince you to leave. So I had to find another way. We thought that once Lord Blackwell realized you'd destroyed one of his beloved wife's tapestries, he wouldn't want you there anymore."

Alyna didn't bother to reply. Her grandfather had been dismayed when he'd seen the tapestry, but he hadn't been angry with her. With luck, it could be repaired.

Hilde might think she had the upper hand, but

Alyna would find an opportunity to change that. She brushed her thigh to feel the small knife strapped there. Having it within reach gave her great comfort.

⚜ ⚜ ⚜

The next morning, Alyna arched her back to ease its stiffness. The long ride on the horse and a night spent on the cold hard ground were only partly to blame. The tension that had gripped her since Nicholas's disappearance continued. She couldn't eat, couldn't sleep. She might know where her son was, but that knowledge did little to ease her fears.

The image of Nicholas scared and alone, wondering where she was, brought tears to her eyes. Tegmont was not someone she would trust with a pet dog, let alone her child.

"We should arrive at Larkspur by midday," one of her escorts announced.

She scanned the horizon, hoping for a glimpse of the holding. She'd done her best to keep her composure as they traveled. Only during the quiet of the night had she let her tears fall. She knew Hilde would report everything she did to Tegmont, and she didn't want her emotions used against her.

Without Nicholas and Royce, she felt as though she'd been cast adrift with no anchor. But she couldn't let her devastation or anger show, though both took turns pouring through her. She planned on presenting a strong and composed front to Tegmont, regardless of how she truly felt.

She focused all of her energy on Nicholas, praying he could somehow sense her. *I'm coming. I'll be there soon.*

They topped another of the rolling forested hills that blanketed the countryside and at last, Larkspur came into view. The meadows flanking the gate held drifts of pink and lavender larkspur, softening the austere look of the holding and providing its namesake. Alyna had seen the castle from a distance before since it bordered her father's holding but never been inside. How odd to think of Royce spending part of his childhood here.

The death of his parents had occurred before she was born, and while she'd heard rumors of a tragedy that had taken the previous lord and his family, she'd never paid much attention to them.

Alyna tried to imagine a young Royce running through the colorful meadows and fields that surrounded the holding, perhaps playing in the woods nearby. It was hard to picture the strong, capable man she knew as a little boy. Could she blame him for pushing everything aside and focusing on vengeance? If her mother and father had been murdered and she'd been left for dead, would she seek revenge or would she be able to forgive? Tegmont seemed to have no remorse for his actions, and that made forgiveness nearly impossible.

The gatehouse was smaller than the one at Northe Castle and the surrounding stone wall not as high. It had but one watchtower. The keep was square and sat near the back of the grounds and must've been rebuilt since Royce had lived there. The curtain wall did not enclose the village leaving the villeins to survive on their own in the event of an attack.

It was obvious even from this distance that it was falling into disrepair. Parts of the outer wall were crumbling. As they neared, she could see one side of the watchtower was half gone. Royce would have much work ahead of him if he was successful in reclaiming the holding.

It was all she could do not to kick her horse into a

gallop and ride straight through the gate to search for Nicholas. She took a deep breath to steady herself. Soon, she would confront Tegmont, and she needed to keep her wits about her when she did.

One of the men-at-arms who accompanied her called out a greeting. The portcullis rose to let them enter, then slammed shut behind them, locking her in.

She swallowed hard, hoping with all her might that she would soon hold her son in her arms and they could both escape.

Royce passed through the gate of Northe Castle the following morning, tired but his mood high. Daniel had been rather disgruntled about his defeat. However, his mood had soon been sweetened by the fact that he'd been allowed to live in exchange for bearing witness before the king against Tegmont.

Royce basked in the moment. He was certain they had enough proof to have Tegmont stripped of Larkspur.

Lord Blackwell should have returned by now. Royce would introduce him to Daniel, then explain his plan to present the evidence to Pimbroke who could take Daniel to the king, leaving Royce to claim Larkspur. After the attack against him and the information Blackwell had presented, Pimbroke was already suspicious of Tegmont.

The next thing he intended to do was ask Blackwell for Alyna's hand in marriage. If he wasn't mistaken, the emotion swelling through him was happiness. An unfamiliar but welcome feeling. Royce allowed himself a smile of satisfaction. Life was good. All his plans were coming together perfectly.

"What has you looking so pleased?" Hugh asked in

a quiet voice as he rode up beside him. He held the reins of the horse that carried a bound Daniel.

"I was just thinking how well our plans are coming together."

Hugh grunted, his expression dour. "You know what that means. Bad luck will surely follow."

Royce shook his head, well used to his friend's less than optimistic attitude. He didn't bother to argue. Perhaps something to break their fast would improve Hugh's mood.

The outer bailey was filled with activity, more so than usual. Men saddled horses and readied weapons.

"Sir Royce!" one of the guards shouted. "You're needed in the hall at once."

An uneasy feeling settled over Royce. Hugh shared a look with him that said I told you so.

Royce gestured to Edgar to keep an eye on Thomas. Then he caught Daniel's attention. "You stay with us."

The thief held up his bound hands, as though telling Royce he had little choice in the matter.

He kicked his horse into a gallop with Hugh and Daniel right behind him. As he rode through the bailey, the hurried activity continued. If he didn't know better, he'd think they prepared for a battle. Voices hailed him as he passed by quickly, but every one of the faces was somber.

They dismounted at the foot of the steps to the keep and a squire ran forward to take their horses. Lord Blackwell came out the door as Royce bounded up the steps. The lord appeared to have aged a good ten years since Royce had last seen him. "My lord? What's happened?"

"'Tis Alyna. She's missing. Nicholas, too."

Royce's heart stopped. He was certain of it. Then it pounded so loudly, he could hear nothing else. Hugh's mouth moved, and Blackwell seemed to answer, but Royce heard nothing.

Hugh grabbed his shoulder. "Royce?"

The odd sensation released its grip. "When? How?"

Blackwell shook his head. "We don't know. Yesterday at mid-day, Alyna discovered Nicholas was missing. We started to search for him and Hilde."

"Hilde? The new servant?"

"Aye. Shortly after that, Alyna disappeared. My only guess is that whoever took Nicholas also has Alyna."

Royce's normal calm and clear thinking deserted him when he needed them most. His stomach churned, and his head throbbed. He knew his lord counted on him to form a plan, to take action. He had nothing. He couldn't think. He could only feel.

"Who is this?" Lord Blackwell asked as he looked at Daniel.

Royce didn't answer. Couldn't answer. Hugh glanced at him with concern and answered in his place. Their words swirled around Royce.

We have much to talk about, you and I. How well he remembered the words he'd last spoken to Alyna. Why hadn't he told her how he felt? Told her of his intentions?

Lord Blackwell narrowed his eyes as he glared at Daniel. "So you're the one causing so many problems. Threatening people's lives and stealing livestock."

Daniel gave him a cocky smile. "At your service, my lord."

Blackwell shook his head in disgust. "Let us go inside, and I'll tell you the few details I know."

Hugh walked beside Royce as they followed Blackwell into the keep. Daniel followed behind. "Royce, are you well?" Hugh asked.

Royce pulled himself together as best he could.

"We must find Alyna and Nicholas. Immediately."

"Aye, that we will." Hugh held his gaze and nodded, his voice more confident than his expression.

When they entered the hall, Matthew sat at one of the tables, fully dressed, but pale with the effort. The young knight obviously hadn't fully recovered.

"Matthew," Lord Blackwell said. "What are you doing up?"

"I want to help search for Lady Alyna and Nicholas."

Hugh put a hand on Matthew's good shoulder. "I'm pleased to see you up and about, but I'm not sure you're ready to ride."

"I'll be fine," Matthew replied, his grim determination unmistakable.

The men sat at the high table. Pitchers of ale were quickly set before them along with bread and cheese. Royce wanted to shove all that to the floor, to rant and yell, to demand Alyna and Nicholas be returned. Instead, he drew a deep breath to calm his rage as best he could, to think clearly and logically. "Tell me all you know," he requested.

Lord Blackwell complied, ending with their discovery that Alyna no longer searched for Nicholas, but was missing as well. "I'm not sure where she would've gone or who could've taken her. None of the guards saw either of them leave through the gate."

"What about the message, my lord?" Matthew asked. "Who was it from?"

"What message?"

Matthew looked puzzled. "I heard a man from my chamber. He called for Lady Alyna and told her he had a message for her that had been left at the front gate."

"Who gave it to her, Matthew?" Lord Blackwell asked.

"I think it may have been George," he answered, "though I'm not sure."

Daniel leaned forward. "This Hilde you mentioned. What does she look like?"

Matthew described the servant, but Royce already knew without a doubt who had sent the message. He knew exactly where Alyna and Nicholas were. "Tegmont." His gaze met Lord Blackwell's. "Hilde took Nicholas to Tegmont, and Tegmont used Nicholas to get Alyna to Larkspur. The bastard has them both."

"My lord? Sir Royce?" Gunnell hurried into the hall, her eyes wild, her hair escaping its braid. She was breathless, and it appeared as though she'd run all the way from her cottage. She kept her gaze on Royce. "You're right. Tegmont has them both. You'd best hurry, for someone is going to be hurt badly. It may already be too late."

CHAPTER TWENTY-TWO

*"Mix lemon balm and honey in steaming
water and sip to calm an upset stomach."*
Lady Catherine's Herbal Journal

Alyna hurried into the cold, dim hall of Larkspur, hoping to find Nicholas, but the room was empty. She spun to face Hilde. "I demand to see my son."

"You're in no position to demand anything." Hilde sank onto a nearby bench.

The great hall was so huge, even the sound of Alyna's breath echoed in its vastness. She scanned the area once more, wishing she'd find Nicholas tucked in a corner. One lone tapestry graced a wall, its scene a faded memory. Tables and benches lined the far side of the room. The massive hearth could have easily heated the entire hall, but no fire burned to welcome the arrivals.

Unwilling to wait, Alyna moved toward the stairs, intending to search for Nicholas, but one of the men who had escorted her blocked her path, his hand on the hilt of his sword.

"You'll have to wait for his lordship," he advised.

She eyed the man, trying to decide what her chances were against him.

"I don't want to hurt you."

Realizing she wouldn't be of any help to Nicholas

if she were injured, she moved to pace in front of the hearth, too anxious to sit.

When it seemed she could wait no more, she heard footsteps approaching. Lord Tegmont entered. Alone. She swallowed tears of disappointment. "Where is my son?"

"Alyna, my dear, I'm so glad you're here." Tegmont had a gracious smile on his arresting face. Handsome to some perhaps, but not to her. His dark hair held a sprinkle of gray at the temples, and a few wrinkles creased the corners of his dark eyes since she'd last seen him. Those lines weren't from smiling.

Alyna clenched her jaw in an effort to keep from screaming at him. Instead, she asked again, "Where is Nicholas?"

He lifted her hand in his. "I've waited far too long for your arrival. You can't imagine my...disappointment when I learned you intended to delay our wedding."

She tried to tug her hand free to no avail. Delay the wedding? Surely he knew she'd intended to avoid marrying him altogether. What kind of game was he playing? "I want to see Nicholas. Now."

Tegmont's lips tightened. "If you want to see the boy, then you'll have to comply with my wishes."

Fear curled in the pit of her stomach. Though she already knew the answer, she forced herself to ask, "What wishes?"

"To fulfill our agreement, of course."

The fear unfurled, leaving her knees weak. "I am *not* going to marry you."

He smiled, continuing to grip her hand. "Your father bound you to the terms of our betrothal. Your agreement isn't necessary. In fact, I find it rather appealing that you escaped me for a time. It shows your strength and spirit. You'll give me fine sons."

"We wouldn't suit," she argued, swallowing the bile in her throat at the idea of spending the rest of her life with him.

"Oh, but we will. I've watched you grow into a fine lady." He reached for her, narrowly missing her breast when she jerked back. "A fine lady indeed."

"I won't marry you," she insisted, despite the realization that he could force her to do so.

"You will if you want to see your son. He's most anxious to be reunited with you. He seems rather frightened by all this," he said with a smile as though Nicholas's fear amused him.

"Please. Return him to me," she begged. "We'll leave and cast this from our memories. No one need ever know you've taken us against our will."

Tegmont tipped his head back and roared with laughter. "That doesn't concern me in the least. I've done far worse. Believe me."

Alyna stared at him with mounting horror. How could she have forgotten for even a moment what he'd done to Royce and his family? Tegmont would have no remorse in killing Nicholas or her if he so desired.

"Thank you, Hilde, for accompanying my bride-to-be," Tegmont said as he turned to look at the maid with a broad smile. "I shall reward you soon."

"I look forward to it," the maid said with a slow wink. She'd loosened the hair around her thin face, no doubt in an effort to look more attractive.

Alyna closed her eyes in disgust. No wonder the woman didn't act like a servant.

Tegmont returned his attention to Alyna. "No need to be jealous, my dear." He drew a finger down the side of Alyna's cheek, his dark gaze holding hers. "I will make plenty of time for you. We have much to do before we marry."

"Of course." She forced a smile and willed herself

not to pull back from his touch. Her only hope was to delay him as long as possible, and pray that somehow, she and Nicholas could escape. "It would relieve my mind considerably if I could see Nicholas. I'd be better able to focus on our plans."

He chuckled, sending a chill down Alyna's spine. "Perhaps you could give me a token of your affection to show me your sincerity. After all, I've waited so long to have you here with me."

Alarmed, Alyna paused. She hadn't expected him to make such a request. But she would do anything to keep Nicholas safe.

Anything.

She pushed aside her fear and put a tentative hand on his chest. Though she looked closely, she could find little resemblance to his nephew, the man who held her heart. Perhaps she could pretend he was Royce for just a moment if she closed her eyes. But even with her eyes shut, Tegmont was all wrong. The wrong scent. The wrong height. The wrong man.

Memories of Royce sent a pang of longing through her so sharp, her breath became a sob.

Tegmont grabbed her arms and gave her a shake. "You stupid woman."

Alyna took a deep breath to collect herself. "My lord, please. It's just that I miss Nicholas dearly." She moved closer and rose on her toes to place a brief kiss on his cheek. Hopefully that would suffice for now.

She drew back to find him looking down at her, his expression watchful. Scared her performance hadn't fooled him, she smiled, holding on to her emotions by a fine thread.

Apparently appeased with her offering, he returned her smile and tucked her hand in the crook of his arm. "You must be exhausted from your journey here." He led her to the stairs. "I'll show you to your chamber, and later we'll arrange a reunion with the boy."

"I'd prefer to see him now."

"I'll have a bath sent up to you," he continued, as though she hadn't spoken. He held her arm tightly as they moved up the stairs in unison. Tegmont took the side near the wall, leaving Alyna to walk near the edge that towered high above the entrance to the keep. As they approached the third floor, he gave her a small push, sending her perilously close to the edge of the stone steps.

Alyna caught a dizzying glimpse of the stone floor far below and gasped, stumbling back into Tegmont's arms.

He laughed in delight. "Just a little jest, Alyna. Although I must say, my last wife didn't find it very funny. Or was it the one before that?" He paused as though trying to remember. "No matter."

The light in his eyes erased her doubt that he'd murdered his previous wives, perhaps even with the help of these terrible stairs. Though her knife remained strapped to her thigh, it would be of little use until she located Nicholas.

He pulled her closer, and they mounted the last two steps to reach the third floor. He led her through a sparsely furnished chamber and continued into another that held only a narrow bed and two small chests. "This is where you'll be staying for now."

It mattered naught to Alyna. She saw no sign of Nicholas. Did she dare ask Tegmont again or would that only anger him?

She pulled away from him and stepped forward as though to examine the room more closely. Anything to be free of his touch. She stood near one of the chests and heard a thump come from within it.

"What was that?" Tegmont asked as he turned in

the direction of the sound.

Alyna had the oddest feeling. She turned quickly and looked at the lord. "Only me. I stubbed my toe against this chest."

"Be more careful, my dear."

If he called her that one more time, Alyna swore she'd pull out her knife after all. "Of course."

"Your bath will be here shortly. After you've had a chance to rest, we'll discuss the details of our marriage."

Alyna nodded then watched as Tegmont shut the door behind him. The lock turned in the door. So she was to be a prisoner here. No less than she'd expected.

She waited several long moments until she heard the sound of Tegmont's footsteps fade. Then, she hurried to the chest that had made the odd sound. With care, she opened the lid and found exactly what she was looking for.

⚬⚬⚬

Royce lay on the cold, hard ground, the sky above him radiant with stars too numerous to count. So numerous that Royce was certain their brilliance was the reason he could not sleep.

Nay, in truth, a night as black as tar would not have suited him any better.

He'd tried to close his eyes and will himself to sleep. In the past, he'd easily been able to shut down his mind and gain a few hours of rest before a battle or a tournament. The rest his body and mind needed could be the difference between life and death.

But not this night.

Royce knew Blackwell was as anxious as he to get to Larkspur, but the lord had insisted on stopping for a few hours of rest. Both the men and the horses needed it. Still, the urge to ride on had nearly overwhelmed Royce. His normal patience had deserted him.

The news of Alyna and Nicholas missing had devastated him. He couldn't stand to think of them both in Tegmont's hands. Though reluctant to delve into his heart to understand why he felt this way, it was past time he did so.

Alyna's gift of her innocence was beyond measure. Her passion had surprised him, but he'd been even more surprised by the absolute need he'd had for her. Never before had he experienced such emotions, such completeness of his soul. He shifted uncomfortably at the thought, but the truth could not be denied.

Only one explanation could account for how he felt.

Love.

Warmth rushed through him at the realization. Aye, he loved her. His love burned as brightly as the stars above him. Their passion for each other would last forever. He was certain of it.

He wanted Alyna by his side. Always.

He should never have left her without explaining himself and his intentions. Did she know Tegmont was his uncle? Why had he never told her? The only excuse he had was that a lifetime of keeping secrets was not easily changed.

Royce reasoned she'd be safe in Tegmont's hands, at least for the moment. His uncle had nothing to gain by her death. Although Royce worried over Nicholas's safety, Tegmont was smart enough to use the boy to get Alyna to comply with his wishes. Royce could only pray–something he hadn't done in years–that his uncle hadn't forced Alyna to marry him already.

Daniel had told them that Tegmont had a servant named Hilde whose description matched that of the maid who'd recently come to Northe Castle. He'd also said Tegmont had mentioned a lady who supplied Tegmont with information as to Royce's whereabouts. Royce knew that had to be Lady Florence. Though they'd looked briefly for her before they left, she was nowhere to be found.

Royce knew his goal of vengeance must end. He could not have both revenge and guarantee Alyna's safety. His uncle had outsmarted him, and that knowledge stung, but he no longer cared. Even if he didn't regain his family's holding, he would still have Alyna and that was all that truly mattered.

He would set aside his vow for Alyna and Nicholas and make a new vow to protect them. On the morrow, he'd offer the evidence he'd gathered, including Daniel, to Tegmont in exchange for Alyna and Nicholas's freedom.

He closed his eyes and spoke the words that burned in the back of his throat: *Mother and Father, I am sorry that I failed you, but I hope you understand.*

From the depths of his worry and despair, a strange sense of peace came over him. He realized his parents would have applauded his choice, for he was choosing love over hatred, the living over the dead. Aye, they would definitely approve, for love always won the day.

❈─❈─❈

"So what do you intend?" Hugh's quiet voice broke through Royce's thoughts as they made their preparations to break camp the next morning.

"I intend to get Alyna and Nicholas back." Royce refused to think about anything past that. Or the fact that without Larkspur he had little to offer Alyna. How could he propose marriage? He had accumulated some wealth, but a landless knight was no match for a lady. Even if Lord Blackwell would approve of the match, the king would not.

But all of that mattered little. What did matter were Alyna and Nicholas. Tegmont could not have them.

"How? Are we announcing ourselves at the gate?" Hugh asked.

Royce turned his attention back to Hugh as Lord Blackwell joined them. "I know a way to get in. There's a secret passage that leads to the kitchen. If it's still open, I'll find Alyna and Nicholas and get them to safety. Then, I'll confront Tegmont and offer the evidence we've gathered, including Daniel's silence, in exchange for Alyna and Nicholas."

Hugh's brow wrinkled in confusion. "If you've already got them, why offer Tegmont all the information we have?"

"We need him to break off the betrothal to Alyna. It's not enough for us to have her. The king could easily demand we give her back to Tegmont to fulfill the terms of the betrothal. We can't risk that."

Hugh nodded in agreement, but Blackwell said nothing. The lord gazed at the horizon, deep in thought. He shook his head. "There has to be some other way. Tegmont can't be allowed to get away with his crimes. The king's safety may depend upon it."

"We'll have to rely on Pimbroke to advise the king of the danger he is in," Royce said. "Perhaps he can convince him of Tegmont's guilt."

Blackwell's amber gaze met Royce's. "You can't give up your future. You've spent a lifetime on your quest. Larkspur should be yours."

"Nothing matters now except Alyna and Nicholas. Nothing, including my wish for revenge."

"Are you certain?" Blackwell asked.

While he appreciated Blackwell's concern, Royce had already reconciled himself to what lay ahead. He only hoped Blackwell thought him worthy of Alyna. If he didn't, Royce would work harder to earn that honor, no matter how long it took.

Royce swallowed hard and told Blackwell what he'd held back for too long. "Aye, because I love her. I would spend the rest of my life protecting her and Nicholas if she will have me."

Blackwell grinned and placed his hand on Royce's shoulder. "Nothing would please me more."

"Tegmont will get his due, either in this lifetime or the next," Royce said.

"Preferably this one," added Blackwell.

"Offer Daniel, but don't keep your silence," Hugh suggested, unwilling to let it go.

Royce shook his head. "Tegmont is a clever man. There's little chance he'll agree to that. We need leverage to force him to call off the wedding. The word of a thief is not enough evidence to condemn him, and he knows that."

Blackwell looked away, obviously frustrated with the situation.

Royce touched Blackwell's arm. "My lord, all will be well. We'll have them both back with us soon. That is what truly matters. Let us finalize our plans and be off."

❈ ❈ ❈

"My lord asks that you wear this kirtle, my lady."

Alyna eyed the pretty garment with trepidation. The deep blue of the fine linen was faded and the delicate lace that trimmed the neckline had yellowed with age. Alyna looked at the nervous maid. "Why?"

The maid's gaze darted around the room. "My lord

feels it will look very nice on you."

Alyna smiled at the young woman, hoping to encourage her to loosen her tongue. "Can you tell me anything about it? It would ease my mind to know its history."

"I believe it is the very same one each of his wives has worn on the day of their wedding. 'Tis tradition, he said."

Alyna closed her eyes as dread coiled through her. She'd hoped to escape with Nicholas by now. But it seemed Tegmont was well aware of her goal, for he had her guarded every moment of the day and night.

The two days since she'd arrived had been spent either in Tegmont's company or locked in her chamber with a guard outside the door.

The only thing that kept her sane was Nicholas. The situation might have been comical had it not felt as though her life hung in the balance. Nicholas had escaped the chamber Tegmont had put him in and remained hidden with her since her arrival. Tegmont continued to put her off with flimsy excuses whenever she asked to see Nicholas. He obviously had no idea where her son was and from the little she'd overheard, the servants had torn the keep apart looking for him. A guard had even searched her chamber while Nicholas had hid under the back of her kirtle as she stood in the corner.

Nicholas enjoyed the game and for one so young, remained remarkably quiet whenever someone entered her chamber. Even now, he was tucked in the chest near her feet. She'd managed to find an extra blanket to cushion his hiding spot.

Alyna smiled again at the maid. "The garment must be very special to Lord Tegmont."

The maid returned her smile with a shy one of her own. She lowered her voice and leaned toward Alyna.

"Some say it's the very tunic his brother's wife wore the day she said her vows."

"What happened to her?" Alyna was curious to hear what the servants thought had happened to Royce's parents.

The maid peeked over her shoulder at the door, then stepped closer to Alyna. "The lord, the lady, and their young son all died in a terrible fire in the great hall. That was many years ago, of course, but there are still a few here who remember it well. Lord Tegmont forbids anyone to speak of it."

Her whispered words gave Alyna pause. Apparently Royce's survival of that night was unknown to most.

"I'm to ask you to try on the gown, so we have time to make alterations prior to you saying your wedding vows this evening."

Alyna worried her lower lip. There was so little time left. She had to make a move soon, but what? Perhaps if she gained this maid's friendship, she might help her. The chances of it were slim, though, for Tegmont sent a different maid and guard each time. Still she had to try. If she earned the maid's sympathy, she could convince her to return instead of another stranger.

"Your name is Margaret?"

"Aye, my lady."

"Well, Margaret." Alyna paused to look again at the gown. How could she possibly wear it when the four women before her who had were all dead? The very idea made her ill. She couldn't help but wonder if Tegmont had coveted his brother's wife. Why else would he keep one of her gowns? "Could you come back a bit later? I'm not feeling my best and would like to rest before I try it on."

"Oh, but Lord Tegmont was most insistent you try

it now."

Alyna touched her forehead. "I feel rather weak. Perhaps if you could bring me a bit of bread and something to drink, it would help."

The maid looked suitably concerned. "As you wish, my lady. I'll fetch some now." She looked at Alyna's long hair with a discerning eye. "I've got some fine ribbon to braid in your hair. Lord Tegmont said it would match your eyes." She frowned. "But your eyes aren't blue at all."

Alyna swallowed hard. Which of the ladies who'd worn the gown had blue eyes? She had a suspicion it had been Royce's mother. Now she truly didn't feel well.

The maid took her leave, promising to return with food, and Nicholas immediately popped out of the trunk. "Mama, I must go."

"Where?" she asked, frightened at the idea.

Nicholas seemed to think on her question for a moment. "Down the stairs."

"You can't go anywhere without me." Alyna lifted him out and into her arms. "It's far too dangerous. You have to stay hidden."

"Nay, Mama. I need to get help. Now."

Alyna looked into his blue eyes, so wise beyond his years. Was this merely the whim of a child or something more? "Do you know what will happen next? Can you see it?"

"I'm going to get Royce."

"He's here?" she asked, hope catching her breath.

Nicholas nodded, no doubt in his expression.

"Then let us wait for him. He'll find us." The idea of letting Nicholas out of her sight even for a moment terrified her.

He considered her suggestion, his head tilted to the side. "I have to go help him so he can come in. He needs me."

Alyna's heart sank. "What if Lord Tegmont or someone catches you?"

"They won't."

"Nicholas, I can't let you go. I'm too afraid something will happen to you."

He put his hand on her cheek and smiled. "It's all right. I promise."

Torn with uncertainty, she tried to weigh the risks. Time was running out. She had to do something soon, and if Royce was near, they had to help him get into the keep.

"All right," she agreed at last, her heart pounding at the thought of Nicholas leaving her. "Hide behind the door and if you get the chance, escape when they have their backs to you."

"Aye," Nicholas agreed, his blue eyes wise and solemn.

She blinked to clear the tears clouding her vision. "Please be careful."

"She's coming," he whispered.

Alyna moved as far away from the door as possible and lay on the floor, pretending she'd fainted.

"My lady?" Margaret asked as she opened the door. "Come quick!" she called to the guard.

Alyna watched through narrowed eyes as the guard hurried into the room. Nicholas scooted out the door, taking her heart with him.

❀－❀－❀

Royce moved with caution along the low, narrow tunnel. He'd waited until dusk to enter it to avoid being seen by the guards on the curtain wall above. The wait had been excruciating, but he and Blackwell agreed the tunnel would be the key to their success.

Announcing themselves at the portcullis of the castle would serve no purpose other than to give Tegmont time to prepare for battle.

By the looks of it, no one had passed through the tunnel in years, perhaps even since he'd last traversed it as a boy. He still remembered each curve to where it ended in a small door tucked in the pantry.

An odd feeling stole over him as he made his way in the darkness. For a brief moment, he viewed it through the eyes of a small boy. His heart ached at the memories, at the feeling of knowing his mother and father waited for him in the hall.

A deep breath of the musty air helped him gather his focus on the task before him. He extinguished his torch as he rounded the last curve of the tunnel.

Calmer now, he edged forward, one hand on the wall, the other stretched before him, searching for the door. A few more steps and he saw thin strips of light ahead.

He reached forward and felt the edges of the small wooden door, even narrower than he remembered. A latch was all that prevented his entrance into the keep.

But the damned thing wouldn't budge. He had no choice but to force the door open. He listened for several moments but heard only silence from the other side. He backed up and rammed the door with his shoulder but the wood didn't give way.

The latch rattled from the other side and Royce drew his sword as the narrow door swung open.

"Sir Royce?"

Incredulous, Royce peered into the dimness. "Nicholas?"

The boy grinned and ran towards him to grab his leg and hold on tight. "I knew you were coming."

Royce lifted the boy and hugged him, amazed

Nicholas had found him. "What a smart lad you are. How do you fare? Have you seen your mother?"

Nicholas drew back to look at him, still smiling. "We're good. I'll take you to Mama. Hurry."

"She's well?"

Nicholas nodded and the knot in Royce's chest eased.

Suddenly, the door to the pantry flew open. "Who goes there?"

Light flooded in, temporarily blinding Royce. He shielded his eyes and saw a man standing before them, knife drawn.

Recognition came slow as his eyes adjusted to the light, bringing a smile to Royce's lips. "Samuel?"

The old man paused, his eyes narrowed, his knife still at the ready. "How do you know my name? Who are you?"

"'Tis I, Royce. Surely you remember me?"

Surprise struck the old man silent, his disbelief obvious. A long moment passed before he said, "Do not try to fool an old man. Lord Royce died many years past."

"Nay, Samuel. I did not die in the fire, though it was a close thing. Henry pulled me to safety and kept me hidden away."

"Henry? He died that night, too. I don't believe you."

Frustration filled Royce as he struggled to remember something that would prove his claim.

Nicholas tugged on his leg. "Show him the rocks."

It took a moment for Royce to realize what the boy meant. He drew his sword and held it out toward the servant, pommel extended. "Do you remember my father's sword? Or my mother's necklace?" He pulled the small blue crystal he wore from underneath his tunic. The crystals winked in the light.

Samuel ran his hand over the rose crystal embedded in the hilt of the sword, then reached a hesitant finger forward to touch the stone Royce wore around his neck. Then he looked long and hard into Royce's eyes. "If you are Lord Royce, where have you been all this time? And why are you in here in the...the pantry?"

Royce grinned in relief as he patted the servant with affection on the shoulder. "It's a long story, but right now, I'm in need of your aid."

A range of emotions passed over the old man's face and moisture filled his eyes. "Well, hell's teeth, boy, why didn't you say so?"

Royce chuckled. "Have you met Nicholas?"

Samuel looked down at the boy as he put away his dagger. "Are you the one they've been searching for?"

Nicholas giggled and nodded. "I'm a good hider."

"Indeed you are." The old man smiled.

"I need to find his mother, Lady Alyna," Royce explained. "Do you know where she is? I've come to stop my uncle's marriage."

Concern filled Samuel's wrinkled face. "My lord, I fear you're too late. The wedding is to take place this very night. They've already gone to the chapel. The vows have most likely been said by now."

CHAPTER TWENTY-THREE

*"Larkspur is said to ward off lightning,
but take heed as it is poisonous."*
Lady Catherine's Herbal Journal

Alyna glared at Lord Tegmont, arms folded in a gesture of defiance while her stomach jittered in fear. "I will not say the words until you bring Nicholas here. Now."

She knew she dared much by refusing him, but what choice did she have? She had to delay the wedding to give Nicholas a chance to find Royce.

The priest stood nearby, his nervousness evident in his stuttering speech. "My lady, I-I d-daresay you will see the child d-directly after the wedding. Lord Tegmont has a-assured me of this." His gaze darted to Lord Tegmont and back to her again.

Alyna had hoped the priest's presence would somehow ensure her safety. Now she had serious doubts as to whether it would make any difference. The stammering man seemed to fear Tegmont more than she did.

The small chapel was tucked against the keep in the bailey. Torches lit the long, narrow room, and cast eerie shadows dancing along the walls. Wooden timbers arched across the low ceiling and continued down the wall. A painted panel graced the altar, depicting the Virgin Mary and baby Jesus, giving Alyna hope for herself and her son.

"Alyna," Lord Tegmont said, his tone conciliatory. "You quibble over nothing. Hilde will bring him soon."

She forced a pleased smile on her face and looked up at Tegmont. The man lied to her with such sincerity that she would've believed him if she hadn't known the truth.

Unless he'd somehow caught Nicholas. She forced herself to calm. She wouldn't believe that unless she saw it for herself. "Thank you, my lord. I knew you'd understand."

"Nay. I believe you are the one confused." His dark eyes glittered dangerously in the torchlight. "We shall begin the ceremony at once."

Alyna kept her smile, hiding her fear as best she could. "I'd prefer to wait for them." Panic made it difficult for her to think. What should she do? She'd never dreamed she'd be on the brink of marriage to Tegmont.

The time that had passed since Nicholas's departure had been nerve-wracking. But he'd been so certain he could find Royce that Alyna had to keep hope. That meant putting off Tegmont for as long as possible.

"Let us begin." Tegmont gestured impatiently for her to come to him. "The child will come shortly."

"I've yet to see him since my arrival two days past. I insist we wait for him." Every moment she delayed the wedding provided more time for Nicholas to get help.

Tegmont chuckled, but it was not a pleasant sound. "We will start the wedding now, my dear." He reached for her hand.

Alyna did not take it. She feared if she did, he'd never let her go. She had to think of another way to distract him. "You haven't commented on my attire, my lord."

"You look lovely. The color suits you." He touched the faded lace near the neckline. "Beautiful." His eyes took on the strangest look, as though he saw something else. "So beautiful."

"I didn't have a chance to thank you for it. 'Tis lovely." She smoothed the soft, faded linen that had been pretty at one time, her thoughts on the women who'd worn it before her.

"You'll soon thank me for much more, my dear." His gaze traveled down her body with an intensity that made her want to turn away.

Instead, she gritted her teeth and tried to think of another topic to delay him. "Don't we require a witness to our marriage vows?" She gestured to the empty chapel.

"The priest will suffice. I promise we'll host a huge feast to celebrate." He smoothed his hand over her sleeve, almost as though he caressed the fabric rather than her. "We'll invite the entire village, and all will toast us and our happiness."

Alyna's heart sank as hopelessness filled her. How was she ever going to escape? Tears misted her vision, and her heart lay heavy in her chest. She bowed her head so Tegmont couldn't see her despair. "Aye. A feast would be lovely."

Had it only been a few days since her heart had felt light with love for Royce? It seemed as though an eternity had passed since then. She longed to see him again, to be in his arms. Was he here even now?

She realized he'd given her no reason to doubt him. Florence's comments and the doubt in her own heart had made her question him, but she knew he would not have used her in his quest for vengeance.

"Come, Alyna. I want to know you're mine

forever."

She took a deep breath to gather her courage. Resolve straightened her spine. She would not go through with this. He'd never let her keep Nicholas. No more would she pretend. "That is not possible. It will never be."

Tegmont's gaze narrowed. "Whatever do you mean?"

"You do not have Nicholas. You do not know where he is, nor have you known since my arrival."

His silence condemned him. The priest looked from her to his lord, as though unable to grasp the situation.

At last, Tegmont answered, "I should have gotten rid of him immediately. I knew he'd be nothing but trouble."

"I will not marry you," she said with conviction. "I demand that you let Nicholas and I leave Larkspur." Alyna forced herself to say the words without a tremor in her voice.

Tegmont chuckled. Then he threw back his head and laughed. "You are a clever thing, aren't you?" He circled around her, as though she were an exotic creature on display. "That is why I want you for my wife. You have spirit. Sadly, that is something my other wives lacked."

Alyna raised her chin. His reminder of his past wives and their rumored fates bolstered her courage. "I am sorry for any promises my father made to you on my behalf, but I will not marry you." It felt good to say it again; somehow it made it more real.

He came up behind her, and she threw a wary glance over her shoulder. He reached out and touched the thin veil that covered her braided hair, held in place by a narrow silver circlet. "I waited a long time for this day, Alyna. You captured my interest at the feast we shared years ago. Your beauty has only grown." He moved to her side and drew his finger along her neck.

The urge to step away from him was great, but it would reveal her fear. She needed to hold her ground. If only she could find some way to turn his desire for her into disgust. "Surely, you can find another woman to wed."

He stepped closer. "I will not be denied what is mine because of your sudden nervousness." His fingers curved over her jaw. "You are mine in every sense of the word."

The priest cleared his throat. "Shall we begin then?"

Alyna pulled back from Tegmont and glared at the priest in disbelief.

"Aye," Tegmont agreed, his dark gaze locked on her face.

With sudden clarity, Alyna knew what she had to do. "I fear I have not been completely honest with you, my lord."

He raised a brow. "Is that so?"

Alyna cleared her throat, the knot in her stomach tightening. She realized she was taking a huge risk. Rather than gain her the freedom she desired, it might cause him to fly into a rage and harm her. That was something she couldn't allow. Nicholas needed her. "I must tell you my heart belongs to another."

Tegmont leaned down, his face only a hand's width from hers; his warm breath reeked of garlic. "Who might that be?"

She hesitated. How much should she dare to tell him?

The door to the chapel opened, but it did not reveal anyone Alyna wanted to see.

Lady Florence entered with Hilde directly behind

her.

"What are you doing here?" Tegmont demanded.

"Lord Tegmont." Florence greeted him as though he was a long-lost, dear friend. "I waited for a message from you telling me to come, but it never arrived."

Alyna could see the effort Tegmont made to hold his temper.

"I told you that I'd send for you when I needed you," he said.

Florence stopped in front of him, a desperate smile on her face. Her blue eyes seemed to plead with the lord for...for what? Alyna wondered.

"Matters at Northe Castle have changed and made it impossible for me to remain there." She glared at Alyna as she put her hand on Tegmont's sleeve. "I'm not certain what Alyna may have told you, but I have much to share with you."

"Your information is no longer of value to me." Tegmont removed her hand from his arm. "I have all I want from there now," he said, gesturing toward Alyna.

"Her? You wanted her?" Florence's gaze caught on Alyna's gown. "Where in the world did you find that old rag? I would think you'd spend more time on your appearance when you're in the presence of someone as important as Lord Tegmont."

Alyna merely smiled, certain of what Tegmont's reaction would be to her comment. Though Alyna didn't completely understand how Florence had come to be at Larkspur, she could venture a guess. Florence had been the one feeding information to the thieves. That meant the thieves were connected to Tegmont. And that had to mean Tegmont knew Royce lived. But why would Florence choose to help Tegmont? What had he promised her?

Tegmont rubbed the bridge of his nose as though

trying to find patience. "I'm afraid you've interrupted us at a very inopportune time, Lady Florence." He gestured toward the priest.

Florence at last realized what she'd interrupted. Anger distorted her features. "How dare you! You made promises to me! You said *I* would be your wife!"

"I'm afraid I cannot break my betrothal to Alyna." Tegmont took Alyna's hand and tucked it in the crook of his arm. "After all, it was made first. But, if you'd like, you can stand as a witness to our vows."

Florence sputtered in outrage. "After all I've done for you, this is how you repay me? I thought it was Royce you were after, not her. You promised me you'd set her aside. Does your word mean nothing?"

With a lopsided smile on his handsome face, Tegmont answered, "I meant what I said at the time. Now, if you'll excuse us—"

"I will not!" Florence glared at Alyna. "Why would you want her for a wife? Has she told you she's given herself to another man? To Royce? Did she tell you that?"

Alyna gasped. How could Florence possibly know?

A flush of rage filled Tegmont's face.

Florence's expression turned from anger to triumph. "You've been less than honest with Lord Tegmont, haven't you, Alyna?"

"I was just—"

"You know not of what you speak." Tegmont waved a hand in dismissal at Florence, not giving Alyna a chance to talk.

Alyna tried again. "Lord Tegmont, I told you I have not been honest with you."

"See?" Florence pointed at Alyna. "Listen to her."

"You just advised me not to believe what she says," Tegmont reminded Florence.

Alyna tugged her hand from Tegmont's arm,

wondering if there was a chance of escape while the two of them argued.

"Well, now she's trying to tell you the truth," Florence argued, her face flushed. "Can't you see for yourself? She gave herself to your nephew, the very man you're trying to kill." Hands on hips, Florence waited for his reaction. "How can you be sure she's not carrying his bastard?"

Alyna caught herself before she put a hand on her stomach. She'd nearly forgotten that possibility. Could it be true?

"Shut your mouth, Florence. You know nothing." Tegmont's face tightened with rage. He turned to Alyna. "That cannot be true."

"I told you I will not marry you. My heart belongs to Royce."

"Nay!" Tegmont yelled. "I will not have it! You will pay for your treachery." He shoved Florence back and raised his hand to strike Alyna.

❊–❊–❊

Royce paused as he, Samuel, and Nicholas entered the great hall. Memories of his parents swirled about him.

His mother smiled down at him, her vivid blue eyes full of laughter. His father shared a look with her, smiling in return, then ruffled Royce's hair, something he'd done frequently. Royce swore he felt his hair stir under the pressure of his father's hand.

"Royce?" Nicholas touched his hand. "Let's find Mama."

Royce looked up at the wooden beams overhead. No evidence remained of the fire that had destroyed his home and nearly taken his life.

"Lord Royce? Are you unwell?" Samuel studied

him with concern.

"Nay. I'm fine." Royce scrubbed a hand over his face. How odd to be called Lord Royce after all these years. "There are many memories here." He looked at Nicholas. "Let us find your mother."

Royce kept the boy's hand firmly in his and followed Samuel outside to the small chapel in the bailey.

He flung open the door to find Tegmont's hand poised above Alyna, preparing to strike. "Halt!"

Tegmont looked up and saw Royce. An incredulous expression came over his face. "Nay!"

Royce wondered if his uncle denied Royce's entrance or his existence.

Tegmont grabbed Alyna and held her before him. "How did you get in?"

"Let her go," Royce commanded. He gestured for Nicholas to remain beside Samuel then walked forward slowly.

"Stay back!"

"Let her go." Royce continued forward.

"Nay. She is mine. The betrothal agreement holds. She is mine."

Fear lit Alyna's eyes. She wore a faded blue gown that looked oddly familiar. The tightness in his chest eased for the first time since he'd learned of her disappearance. He hoped his presence brought her the same comfort.

Royce glanced around the room and was not surprised to see Florence with Hilde behind her. He did not bother with a greeting, for they would be dealt with soon enough. He briefly wondered what lure his uncle had used to gain Florence's loyalty.

"Your quarrel is with me," he told Tegmont. "Release Alyna."

Tegmont regained his composure. "Well, if you

insist, you can stay and witness our vows along with Lady Florence." He looked down at Alyna. "See, my dear, I told you the boy would be here."

Alyna tried to wrench free, but he held her firmly.

"Mama?" Nicholas seemed to sense the danger and remained behind Royce rather than going to his mother.

"Stay with Royce, Nicholas," Alyna said.

"There will be no wedding vows said here today." Royce glanced at Nicholas to make sure he stayed back, then took another step closer. "Alyna, come to me."

Alyna moved forward, only to be jerked back by Tegmont. He put his arm around her neck to keep her more firmly in place. "I just heard the strangest thing, Royce." Tegmont stroked a hand down Alyna's veil-covered hair. "I heard you forced yourself on my betrothed. I believe the law allows me to punish you for that."

Royce looked at Alyna. Had she told him of their afternoon together? Surely not. Did she understand how he felt? That he loved her? That he would give his life for her? He needed to make certain he had the chance to tell her all that and more.

"I suggest we make a trade," he offered Tegmont.

"What could you possibly have that I want?" Tegmont drew his hand slowly down the front of Alyna's body as he smiled at Royce.

Royce's hand found the hilt of his sword. It was all he could do not to stride forward and wrest Alyna from the man's arms. Apparently, some of his desire must've shown on his face, for Tegmont smiled and curled his arm tighter around Alyna's neck.

Royce tried to keep his focus on Tegmont. "I have someone I think you know well."

Caution filled Tegmont's eyes. "Who might that

be?"

"His name is Daniel. He has many colorful tales, all about you."

Tegmont scoffed. "I don't know anyone named Daniel."

His denial was a bluff, Royce was certain. "He has some interesting details about a band of thieves that have caused Lord Blackwell much distress."

Tegmont's eyes narrowed.

The nervous priest who stood behind Tegmont took several steps back toward the alter.

"Why are you bothering me with this?" Tegmont caressed Alyna again. Alyna flinched; disgust warred with fear on her face. "I have more important matters to attend to."

Royce clenched his teeth. Protesting Tegmont's actions would only give him more power, something that would not aid Alyna. "I think Lord Pimbroke would be interested in speaking with Daniel if you're not."

Tegmont's composure disappeared at the mention of Pimbroke. "You bastard!"

"Let Alyna go. Now."

"Let her go, my lord," Florence pleaded. "You and I can continue with our plans."

Tegmont shook his head. "You are of no value to me anymore. Be gone with you." He looked back to Royce as he withdrew a knife from his belt and held it at Alyna's throat. "She will die before I let her be yours."

"Is that why you killed my mother?" Royce eased closer. "Because she wouldn't agree to become yours?"

Tegmont's eyes went wide with alarm. "You know nothing of what you speak."

Royce took another step. "I think I do. I have had many years to consider what you did and why."

"I did nothing! They were killed in a terrible fire." The whine in Tegmont's voice disgusted Royce.

"A fire you set before you murdered them both. Have you forgotten I was there? A witness to your crime. Surely you remember, because you left me pinned under a burning beam to die." Royce held Tegmont's gaze as he moved closer still.

Tegmont's gaze darted around the room nervously. He jerked the knife against Alyna's throat, and she gasped in pain. "It was an accident. It was all an accident."

"Nay. It was all you."

"Your mother was a beautiful woman. She should've loved me, not my brother. He had everything. Why should he have had your mother, too? She was supposed to be mine. Our father was making the arrangements when my own brother stole her from me."

Royce gripped the hilt of his sword, wanting nothing more than to yank it free of its sheath and thrust it through Tegmont. "He did not steal her. She loved him."

"It all should've been mine—this keep, your mother, even you, Royce. You should've been my son." Tegmont cursed at his loss. "The deaths of your parents cursed me. I've had nothing but bad luck since. I haven't sired even one heir. I've tried to break the curse, but nothing works." He turned his attention to Alyna once again. "But this one. She will break it. I've known it since the moment I saw her. She'll give me fine sons."

"Dressing Alyna in my mother's garments will not break the curse." Royce was certain the kirtle had been his mother's. "What happened to your other wives? Did you kill them, just like you killed my mother?" Royce stole a glance at Alyna, trying to reassure her that she would soon be free.

Tegmont shook his head. "They were nothing. They didn't matter. When they failed to provide me with an heir, an accident befell each of them. Accidents aren't my fault."

"You are mad!" Florence exclaimed. Royce glanced at her and saw even Hilde looked horrified.

Royce felt the same way. His uncle was more of a monster than he'd realized. "Let Alyna go. I'll give you Daniel in her place."

Tegmont seemed to consider the trade for a moment. He sneered at Royce. "Never! Alyna is the key to my future. Soon a new king will be in power and I'll be richly rewarded." He shifted, bringing the blade against Alyna's throat. A trickle of blood emerged. "Leave us else I'll kill her."

CHAPTER TWENTY-FOUR

*"Use the juice of chicory blended with
oil to gain a wish more easily."*
Lady Catherine's Journal

Alyna's cry was nearly Royce's undoing. "Let her go!" he demanded again. "I will give you my silence about what you did to my mother and father. You can keep Larkspur."

Tegmont tightened his grip on her as he dragged her to the wall, his gaze on Royce. "You were supposed to die that night. You can't imagine my surprise when I heard the rumors of your survival." He glanced at the wall behind him, then quickly back at Royce. "I could not determine whether they were true. When you finally returned to England, I decided it didn't matter. I'd kill you anyway."

Tegmont reached the wall. Torchlight cast shifting shadows across his features. "Daniel and his band of thieves were supposed to draw you out, to make your death look like the result of a fight. Alas, he was unsuccessful."

His blade still at Alyna's throat, he reached up with his free hand and took a torch from the wall.

Royce froze, unable to believe his uncle would repeat the past.

Alyna tried to jerk free, but Tegmont used the

knife to hold her fast. He eyed the flame of the torch as though he looked into the face of a lover. "Do you remember the fire, Royce? Do you remember the feel of the heat? The roar of the flames? The power of it? Tonight, I'll remind you."

Alyna's eyes widened in horror as the flame neared her face. "Nay!"

"Quiet!" He dropped the torch near the foot of a timber. The pitch in the wood caught fire quickly and flames raced up the beam, crackling and snapping as they grew. He chuckled as he watched it spread.

Florence bolted past Samuel, screaming as she ran out the door with Hilde and the priest right behind her.

"Tegmont! Let her go." Royce called out. The fear in Alyna's face made his heart race, but he didn't dare make a move while Tegmont had the knife at her throat. He remembered only too well what Tegmont had done to his mother. Royce hadn't gotten this close to rescuing Alyna only to lose her.

"Mama?" Nicholas's voice held the same fear Royce felt.

"It's all right, Nicholas." Her voice quivered as she instructed her son. "Stay behind Royce."

Royce knew she had to feel the heat from the fire. He knew how it felt. Alyna's gaze moved from Nicholas to Royce.

He could see the determination in her face. She held his gaze, as though she wanted him to read her mind. He tensed in anticipation, trying to grasp her intention.

She glanced down and Royce saw a glint of metal in the firelight. She raised her fist and thrust a small knife into the arm wrapped around her neck.

Tegmont cried out in pain, releasing her.

It was all the opportunity Royce needed. He

yanked his sword free of its scabbard as Alyna ran behind him. She gathered Nicholas in her arms and held him tight, moving toward the door.

The fire spread to the ceiling of the chapel and smoke rolled through the room. Heat filled the small space quickly.

"Damn you!" Tegmont cursed Alyna. "Return to me!"

Royce backed up with Alyna and Nicholas behind him to where Samuel stood near the door. "Tegmont, we must get out."

Tegmont laughed in response. "Nay! We will all die in this fire. Samuel, shut the door!"

The old servant looked in confusion at Tegmont, then back at Royce as though unsure who to believe.

"Samuel, get out!" Royce told him. "We'll be right behind you."

"Shut the door. Lock it!" Tegmont ordered.

"We must leave now, Lord Royce!" Samuel called out, ignoring Tegmont's command.

Royce turned back to Tegmont. His uncle drew his sword and advanced toward Royce. "You are not going anywhere. You will die in this fire as you were meant to all those years ago."

"We're leaving, and if you have any sense you'll come with us," Royce answered. He backed slowly toward the door with Alyna and Nicholas, confident Samuel would not lock them in.

"Halt!" Tegmont lunged forward, his sword pointed at Royce's chest.

Royce blocked him, then struck Tegmont's sword, trying to dislodge the weapon from his uncle's hand.

But his uncle was quicker than Royce anticipated. He dodged the blow, then lunged at Royce again.

"Alyna, take Nicholas and leave," Royce ordered.

"Not without you," Alyna argued. She stepped

toward Samuel to give Royce more room but held her ground.

Royce turned his attention to Tegmont, determined to get them all out. His uncle's eyes held a hint of madness in them, much as they had that night so many years ago. Royce swore this night would end much differently.

The fire rumbled in his ears; the heat was suffocating. He moved back toward the door in the hope that Tegmont would follow, and they'd all get out alive. A fire was no place for anyone to die.

"Stay where you are!" Tegmont demanded as he shifted to Royce's side.

Determined not to allow Tegmont between him and Alyna, Royce lunged again, driving Tegmont back toward the flames. "Surrender and you can walk out of here alive."

"Never!"

Royce clenched his jaw in determination. "Then you leave me no choice."

Royce attacked but his uncle matched him stroke for stroke.

"Yield!" Royce demanded.

"Nay!" Tegmont's chest heaved and his sword arm lowered slightly, evidence of his exhaustion. The smoke was taking its toll on both of them.

Royce struck again, at last knocking the sword from Tegmont's hand. The weapon skidded across the floor out of reach.

Tegmont stared at Royce with a perplexed look upon his face. He touched his shoulder and drew his hand back covered in blood; sweat trickled down his face. "Finish it."

Royce raised his sword. It would be so easy. Visions of his mother and father flashed through his mind, but this time, he saw them as they'd lived and loved, not as they'd died. He felt Alyna's presence behind him, waiting for him.

He lowered his weapon. "Nay. I will not take your life, for that would make me no better than you." Royce picked up Tegmont's sword. "We are all leaving. Now."

Royce turned to look at Alyna.

Her face lit up with relief and joy.

Royce returned her smile. "Let us go. Hurry!" He bent to take Nicholas from her.

"Royce!" Alyna screamed.

He spun around as Tegmont came after him with the knife he'd had at Alyna's throat. The blade glanced off Royce's shoulder. He shoved Tegmont back and drew his sword just as Tegmont lunged forward to stab him again. Royce's sword sank deep into his uncle's chest.

"Oh!" Alyna cried out as she spun Nicholas away from the sight.

"Nay!" Tegmont screamed. "What have you done?"

Royce shook his head. "It's you. You made the choice."

Tegmont staggered back, the sword in his chest. He put his hands on the hilt and pulled it out. The sword clattered to the stone floor. Tegmont looked at Royce, then at Alyna. He opened his mouth to speak, but nothing came out except a trickle of blood. He collapsed onto the floor, eyes wide, blood seeping through his tunic.

Samuel touched Royce's sleeve. "Lord Royce? We must go."

"Aye," Royce agreed. He bent to pick up Tegmont's body.

"Nay, my lord. Let him be. 'Tis best this way." Samuel looked down at Tegmont, shaking his head. "If I hadn't seen it with my own eyes, I wouldn't have believed it." He retrieved Royce's sword, wiped it clean, then handed it to him.

They hurried out the chapel door and into the fresh air as Lord Blackwell and Hugh arrived with the men.

"Are you all right?" Hugh demanded.

"Indeed," Royce answered. "Let's get this fire put out."

Hugh stepped away to bark orders and men scrambled to comply.

"Thank God," Lord Blackwell said as he took Alyna in his arms and held her and Nicholas close for a long moment. At last he leaned back to look at her face, his gaze taking in the cut on her neck. "What of Tegmont?"

"Dead." Royce shook his head.

"And Alyna? How do you fare?" Blackwell asked.

She looked at Royce before she answered. "We are all fine." She hugged Nicholas tightly. "This little one is my hero."

Blackwell smiled down at Nicholas. "He is, is he?"

"He led me to Alyna," Royce added. "He is a hero."

The little boy beamed, his face lit with the praise.

"Tegmont refused to leave the chapel with us," Alyna said. "He started the fire himself. He intended for us all to die in there. Luckily, he failed, thanks to Royce."

"He would not give up," Royce said.

"Indeed, my lord, if your lady hadn't called out, you'd most likely be dead," Samuel added.

"I'm glad to find you in one piece." Hugh joined them, slapping Royce on the shoulder. He frowned at Royce's wince. "What's wrong with you?"

"Lord Tegmont stabbed him in the back," Samuel said. "I can hardly believe it, but I witnessed it myself. Lord Royce killed him in self defense."

"That solves many problems, does it not?" asked Blackwell.

"Justice won the day," Hugh said as he grinned at Royce. "You've fulfilled your vow of vengeance after all these years."

Royce considered the idea for a moment. Tegmont's death did not put to right all the terrible things the man had done. "In the end, I realized it was not about revenge. It was about love." He smiled at Alyna. The relief that filled him to know she was safe knew no bounds.

The bailey filled with villeins and men-at-arms, alarmed by the smoke. They joined the effort to extinguish the fire.

Blackwell looked from Royce to Alyna and back again. As though sensing the emotions between them, he smiled, then took Nicholas from Alyna's arms. "I think we'd best see if we can help, eh, Nicholas?"

Hugh grinned. "Indeed. I believe I'm also needed to assist with that fire."

"Let me look at your shoulder." Alyna started around to Royce's back.

"Nay." He pulled her to him and held her tight, breathing in her essence, needing to hold her just for a moment. "I must help with the fire first."

At last, Royce eased back to look into her tear-filled eyes. "Royce, you did the right thing. You could've killed him when you had the chance, but you didn't. You've honored your parents well this day."

Her words brought him a sense of peace, and he knew she was right. "Thank you."

"Let me look at your wound. It will only take a moment."

He shook his head. "I'll be back after we see to the fire and then you can care for it." He trailed his fingers along the softness of her jaw, his gaze holding hers. "As I said before, we have much to speak of, you and I, as soon as the fire is out."

~❦~❦~❦~

A rose hue washed the dawn sky as a tired Alyna sat on the steps of the keep at Larkspur, Nicholas cuddled on her lap. "Isn't the sky beautiful, Nicholas?"

Her little boy gave a small nod, then burrowed deeper in her arms, his exhaustion getting the better of him after all the excitement.

The fire had been extinguished at last before spreading far. Alyna had helped to treat the minor burns and other injuries incurred by the servants and men-at-arms who'd fought the flames. Smoke permeated the air. Even Nicholas's hair smelled of it. Alyna knew she did as well. They both sorely needed a bath.

She'd caught glimpses of Royce as he shouted orders and directions to the scrambling men. He was a natural leader, that was certain.

Now that the fire was out, her patience was nearly at end. Where was he? Enough, she wanted to shout. It's our turn.

"He's coming, Mama," said Nicholas in a sleepy voice without opening his eyes.

Startled, Alyna looked around, but did not see Royce's tall form anywhere.

"What have we here?" A familiar deep voice whispered from behind her.

Shivers ran down her spine and her stomach trembled in anticipation. She turned her head as Royce sat down on the step beside her. "I was wondering where you'd gone."

His warm gray eyes held hers with an intensity that took her breath away. "Only to you, my lady."

She tried to regain her balance and calm her sudden nerves. "Let me see to your shoulder."

"It's fine. Someone needs to lie down for a bit, I think," Royce said as he put his hand on Nicholas's back.

As though he'd been watching for the right moment, Hugh emerged from the shadows and mounted the steps. "Are there any strong young men here in need of rest?"

Nicholas held up his hand, and Royce and Alyna laughed.

"Come here, Sir Nicholas. I think you may have earned your spurs this day with your bravery. Let us discuss the possibility with Lord Blackwell." Hugh lifted the boy easily, then winked at Alyna. "We're off to find some food and then a bed. Right, Nicholas?"

The little boy nodded and yawned. "Good night, Mama and Royce."

The cool pre-dawn air chilled the warmth that Nicholas's form had provided, and Alyna rubbed her arms in response.

Royce pulled her close. "I think I mentioned earlier that I needed to speak with you." He nuzzled her neck and breathed softly in her ear.

Alyna's shivers returned. "You did indeed."

"That time has come at last." He paused, his mouth before hers, then touched his lips tenderly to hers. Once. Twice.

She sighed in response, desire soothing her nerves. Love warming her from the inside out.

"I'm not going to let another moment pass before I tell you what's in my heart," he murmured against her lips, then kissed her again, his passion heating her thoroughly, his desire for her undeniable.

He drew back, his gaze locking on hers. "Alyna, I should've told you how I felt the day we made love. I wanted to wait until I had everything planned. Until I had everything resolved."

Alyna bowed her head. "When you left, and my grandfather told me that Lord Tegmont was your uncle, I thought you had somehow used me to aid you in your revenge." She looked up at him, her amber eyes solemn. "I'm sorry to have doubted you."

"Nay. I should've told you he was my uncle from the start." Royce shook his head. "I've waited my entire life to fulfill my vow of vengeance. Yet when you were gone, I realized it no longer mattered. Only you. Only you matter, Alyna. I love you."

Her eyes filled with tears, her throat tight with emotion, and joy sang in her heart. "And I love you."

Royce placed a gentle hand on her cheek. "I will cherish you. I swear it." He rested his forehead against hers. "Please say you'll marry me. My life will only be complete with you by my side."

Alyna hesitated. "I, too, made a vow I intend to keep. I know you care for Nicholas, Royce, but I need to know if you care enough to raise him with me."

Royce answered without hesitation. "I love him as well, and I would be honored if he chose to call me father."

"Then my answer is yes." Deep joy speared through Alyna, and she threw her arms around Royce. Surely, she was the happiest woman in all of England.

He held her tight then kissed her passionately. Alyna swore she could feel all the love in his heart, flowing into hers.

"I vow here and now to love you always," he promised.

"Always and forever," she agreed and kissed him again.

THE END

Acknowledgements:

A special thanks to Mom and my sister, Linda for your edits and encouragement over the years.

To my entire family, who kept asking about my writing.

To Annie MacFarlane, Michelle Major, and Jodi Anderson, my critique partners and anchors in all things.

To Robin, Jessica, Heidi, who encouraged me in so many ways.

6414121R00200

Made in the USA
San Bernardino, CA
12 December 2013